PATRICIA WRIGHT

✝

I am England

AN EPIC NOVEL OF PASSION, HARDSHIP AND BRAVERY
THROUGH 1500 YEARS OF ENGLISH HISTORY

PATRICIA WRIGHT

✠

I am England

AN EPIC NOVEL OF PASSION, HARDSHIP AND BRAVERY
THROUGH 1500 YEARS OF ENGLISH HISTORY

MEREO
Cirencester

'Once upon a time there was a ridge...'

The author has taken a single village in the Sussex Weald and through rich and powerful storytelling has portrayed an excitingly different vision of England's past. Shy forest people came first to the ridge, then ironsmiths; the great god Tiw and Christian monks; land-hungry adventurers and a silver-tongued teller of tales. These are 'the generations which passed and vanished, leaving a landscape as their memorial...The feel of them is everywhere, their unspoken hopes and fears, whispered loves, snatched lusts.' In five linked episodes of high drama and human conflict these vanished generations come alive. The reader, too, becomes an inhabitant of the ridge and its village of Furnace Green; begins to recognise its landmarks, sees the settlements grow and change; endures the gruelling labour which created fields out of forest, forged cannon from earth and fire and water which one day helped defeat the Spanish Armada.

But, above all, there are the people. A pageant of men and women whose greeds and sacrifice, strange drives of passion and wry humour forged a restless, ambitious England out of black swamps and wolf-infested forest. After reading the book you, too, will feel them around you.

PATRICIA WRIGHT

✠

I am England

The English are very bold, courageous, ardent, and cruel in war, fiery in attack and having little fear of death. They are not vindictive, but very inconstant, rash and vainglorious; light and deceiving, and very suspicious, especially of foreigners, whom they despise.

Van Meteren, 16th - century Dutch historian

Romaunce Books

1A The Wool Market Dyer Street Cirencester Gloucestershire GL7 2PR
An imprint of Memoirs Publishing www.mereobooks.com

I Am England: 978-1-86151-551-3

First published in Great Britain by Bodley Head, an imprint of
The Random House Group Ltd.
Published in 2016 by Romaunce Books

The address for Memoirs Publishing Group Limited can be found at
www.memoirspublishing.com

The Memoirs Publishing Group Ltd Reg. No. 7834348

The Memoirs Publishing Group supports both The Forest Stewardship Council®
(FSC®) and the PEFC® leading international forest-certification organisations. Our
books carrying both the FSC label and the PEFC® and are printed on FSC®-certified
paper. FSC® is the only forest-certification scheme supported by the leading
environmental organisations including Greenpeace. Our paper procurement policy
can be found at www.memoirspublishing.com/environment

Typeset in 9/13pt Plantin
by Wiltshire Associates Publisher Services Ltd. Printed and bound in Great Britain
by Printondemand-Worldwide, Peterborough PE2 6XD

CONTENTS

...THE WITNESS:

Once upon a time . . . The only way to begin a tale which weaves the years together. Once upon a time there was a ridge of land. One side of the ridge was steep, the other less so.

Below the ridge was forest and on the ridge more forest, except there the trees drew back a little. And because the trees drew back, on the ridge there were glades and bracken and a pool, between which wandered a narrow unhurried path.

Boar and wolves and many deer lived in the forest, which was so dense that Mother Earth herself could not number the beasts or the trees. In its deep places black spirits moaned, swamps gathered, mighty trees feel and rotted into the soil; there, the sun seldom reached, playing instead among the leaves and green trunks far above.

After many centuries there came to this ridge, this forest, Dymar of the distant people; Edred the Saxon, his wife Roda and his grandfather Alaric. Tostig Half-Axe came also, and Theobald the priest and Edmer, who preferred to build his hut apart from the rest by a stream he liked. He became the first dweller on the ridge to live by skill at his craft, and, because he had chosen the site for his home wisely and began a tradition of good workmanship, the place he settled remained a manufactory rather than a farmstead. A thousand years have passed since Edmer earned his living by making carts and a hundred different kinds of household ware out of timber, and that same flat place by the stream is still called Edmer's home, or Edenham in modern speech. A thousand years during which Edenham remained a place where corn was ground, iron smelted and poured, great water wheels thudded, and, less creditably, smugglers' goods were handled and repacked. It pleases me that after some interval when a changing world seemed to make this tradition a relic of the past, I have made Edenham Millhouse a place of craft again, laborious and elderly writer that I am. There is also cool efficient Sandra, who comes to shuttle my words on a computer screen, which is surely another mighty skill to follow all the rest. I wonder what Edmer and Francis Wyse would make of zapped green words: they remain a mystery to me. I only understand the tale I tell.

Ralf and Robert came next to the ridge, and took it. Rico of the Silver Tongue set up his booth there, and generations of oxen called Cheerful tilled the fields whose shape has scarcely changed. Even now, the Weald of Sussex is not the kind of land where machines gulp hedgerows whole, and nettles are still inclined to sprout where John the Carver's body was never found.

How do I know what happened? I was seventy-nine last March although I find it hard to realize; even so, I am not quite as old as time.

How can I not know what happened?

The cart-tracks of the ridge are mostly hard-surfaced now, those that are not overgrown by grass. Yet, where these enter the village, even modern juggernauts are nearly lost to sight between steep banks, the very surfaces they travel worn down by countless years of coming and going. This alone would call back the generations which passed along them, and vanished, leaving a landscape as their memorial. The barns, byres and homes of the ridge carry the stamp of their previous owners: the feel of them is everywhere. Their unspoken hopes and fears, whispered love, snatched lusts. Life indestructible, created by the dead.

I sit beside the hearth Bess Wyse offered to the forest spirits, behind it her father's splendid fireback which only yesterday a scholar came to see; the iron men scampering across its surface are nowadays regarded as valuable evidence of early industrial processes. It ought to be in a museum, the scholar said severely. Francis Wyse was a well-known ironmaster, after all. And his finger rested on the Edenham mark of crossed foreman's hammer and bracken fronds, FW 1553.

This was the place for which he lived and died, I answered. So long as I live his fireback stays where it belongs, at Edenham.

Time plays strange tricks. When so much is lost, casually it will keep a name, a memory, alive. As a boy my imagination was seldom still, roaming in search of something, anything, to feed on and I gathered a strange collection from the ridge's past. This didn't amount to much: a carved scrap of stone, a great many garbled tales, a map glimpsed on the vicar's wall, some iron slag which then was easily found along the banks of Edenham's stream. Above all there was the land itself: the pool, the fallen oak, the warp of fields and weft of work.

Then one day, I found the arrow.

Soon after William of Normandy conquered England, which was after Edmer of Edenham died, a stranger called Robert picked up an arrowhead which, although he did not know it, had been made by Brac of the Hill People yet another thousand years before that time in which Robert lived. Robert cleaned and polished the arrow he'd found, then notched it on a freshly whittled shaft, but before he could use it he became ill. So his wife took it and went instead to shoot a hare for the pot, and missed her aim. Though she intended to return and dig the arrowhead out of green bark where it had lodged, she forgot, and in time the sapling grew into a tree with the arrowhead in its heart. It was this same oak which eventually caused a quarrel between the parson and the man who cut it down, since both considered it was theirs.

The quarrel flourished and perhaps contributed to a murder, but long before then the oak had been split into lengths, and one of the lengths adzed to form the arch over Edenham's new hearth. Within that beam the arrowhead lay hidden.

There I found it as a boy, idle fingers picking at age-blackened oak. And once I felt something there and had tediously pared out four hundred years of soot to loosen it, it came out quite easily. As if someone else had found it a long time before, and greased it before sliding it back for safety.

So I slid it back too, patted in new soot and goose fat to keep it sealed, told no one about this my greatest treasure. That was when I first began to dream about the ridge. To sense a laughing girl beside me sometimes, who knew about the arrow. To wonder about that other smith who made the arrow, whose mark still showed as scratchings on its fragile iron. An unimaginably older mark than FW1553; how much older I did not dare to ask. I feared that once I showed my arrow to outsiders they would think like the scholar yesterday, and say that treasures had no business to be hidden in our beam. After several sneaked looks, I decided the scratchings might, just might, represent a deer.

Once upon a time a smith named Brac used a deer sign as his mark, because they were the only creatures he considered as beautiful, as wild and strange, as his wife.

Once upon a time . . . How infuriating of me to create confusion where none exists.

I watch Sandra frown at her keyboard over my tottery writing, green letters flickering impatiently on her screen: perhaps I ought to keep her computer company, be thoroughly modern and declare that where art is concerned, chronology does not matter. The ridge is one in the same way a nation is one: Brac, Lulla, Bess and I part of the same earth. Yet, for the living, the problem of distance and time remains. It makes no difference that Brac solved it for us, a long time ago on the day he forged that particular arrow, flighted to transcend the centuries. No difference either that I solved it, briefly and very painfully, just over forty years ago. Though I wasn't thinking about the time-and-distance problem when it happened . . . No. I mustn't pretend that because I'm old, I can do exactly what I like; start at the end of my story because that is where I am, when everyone else would much prefer to begin at the beginning.

Which means you have to wait before discovering any more about the distance-time problem, but then no one can expect to read a story as long as this one without exercising a little patience.

The ridge is you as much as it is me. That is completely clear. The valley, coast or moor your ancestors settled as individual as mine, and yet the same. We are them and they are us. From these places we all came, these lives we lived and with our toil we made each hedge and field and building in the land, with tools we also made.

I am England now, let that be my life. The first Queen Elizabeth said that, and was loved by her people for her pride in Englishness. The rest of us, who made the look and feel of England, should also be remembered. We are England too.

So I shall begin far away from me, when my part of our land still waited for its people.

1

IN THE BEGINNING
AD 70 - 71

The she-wolf was old and lame. One of her pads was putrefying and the pack had turned on her when the stench confused hunting scents by night and made them ruthless by day. The old she-wolf, her belly heavy with litter soon to be born, had trailed the pack for two nights, trying to remain part of the only life she understood: then the urge to find a refuge came on her, the pain in her foreleg so bad she tore at it until pus slipped on her tongue.

Her litter was born in dry leaves beneath a fallen beech, two living cubs and one which never moved. The she-wolf's dugs were ragged from much impatient suckling over the years, her milk insufficient even for the two young nuzzling her, who mewed almost at once from hunger. So next day the urge to hunt returned, although if she had been with the pack she could have expected to be brought the food she needed. Now she must hunt alone; a rotting foot and sagging belly would kill her soon but the drive to save her cubs was as strong as when she bore her first litter, many seasons ago.

That first night she caught a single vole and nothing else at all. When she returned to her cubs they would not leave her alone, thrusting spitefully at her dugs, nourishing themselves with blood, and chilling close to death as night paled to a crisp, clear dawn.

Deep in her throat the she-wolf began to vibrate the howls she wanted to loose into the darkness. She understood that she must not die while her cubs depended on her, and instinct made her nose at them, pressing, licking. Rhythmically her tongue pulsed on wet and chilly fur, trying to preserve their lives; instinct also beginning to urge her into taking life instead, when a weak cub eaten might offer life to the stronger for a while. Lick, lick; revulsion still strong enough to keep her from eating what was hers to preserve. Lick, lick; the honing of desire for the snap and swallow which dominated the remainder of her senses.

The sky was high and pitiless, the oaks and beeches a light green-yellow with the rising sap of spring. Where the she-wolf lay the forest swept up to a ridge along which ran a foot-trail almost invisible under bracken. A small group of people was moving in single file along this trail, brushing aside the unfolding ferns. They seldom spoke, being a people who spoke only when it was necessary and at the moment there was no need for the cry which meant danger, the quick chatter which decided whether they turned this way or that.

They knew the ridge well and travelled this way regularly. Above the steepness where the she-wolf lay hidden were natural clearings in the forest where water gathered and animals came to drink at night; here the people of Gytha came in the spring, on their way to the Bare Hills. The steep sweep down to the west was dangerous, though. Wolves and boar lived there, and the roots tangled in swamp made it a place of dark spirits who waited to trap anyone venturing far from the ridge. The young men sometimes hunted in such places to prove their courage, but if they killed there then they poured the blood of their quarry on the earth, as an offering of respect.

Gytha's people felt safe on the ridge, though. Its glades were good places for the sling-shot and throwing stick, water not only abundant but sweet; deer, hare and badger were plentiful at all seasons of the year. And at the end of the ridge grew a hill, a place of marvel, where they always spent a night gaping at the strange habits of the people who lived there. They called it The Place Where Weapons May be found, because the hill –dwellers forged sharpness out of earth and air; Gytha's people often picked up scraps they valued there, even if the hill people regarded such fragments as waste.

Gytha's people had come this way each spring since before anyone now living could remember. Winter was spent among estuary marshes to the north, spring on this journey; summer on the Bare Hills several days' journey to the south, from where they could see the sea which framed the edges of the land. On the Bare Hills they worked a short while at harvest time and took grain in exchange for their labour, in the autumn they retraced their steps to the estuary. So it had always been, and so it would remain, though there were other days when they sniffed the wind and hunted instead of journeying; periods when they idled in hides and burrows without speaking of the reasons why they neither hunted nor marched until the omens should change. Only the brief season of labour on the Bare Hills was a discipline they must submit to if they wished to live a safer life than their ancestors, and carry home a reserve of grain for the winter: the estuary and forest alone could no longer sustain their slowly increasing numbers.

At all other times Gytha's people never stayed anywhere for long, but ebbed and flowed like wind through the trees, and like the wind they died if they ceased to move.

Gytha turned and smiled when he reached the ridge, and his people smiled back at him, strung out as they were up the winding ascent. They all loved this single morning's journey along the ridge, where a watch was scarcely necessary and they could see the forest flowing away into the distance. On the ridge they could forget days spent struggling through swamps, the days to come when they must toil through thickets to reach the Bare Hills. So each walked easily when the path flattened above where the she-wolf lay, and Gytha whistled as he walked.

Quite soon, he stopped whistling and frowned instead.

Ayi must stay here. They could not take her into The Place Where Weapons May Be Found because she had her fate on her, and already smelt unlucky.

Gytha had put off this decision yesterday, but today must be her last day with his people. He felt reluctant, because Ayi had struggled bravely through the swamp and not asked for help when he expected her to drown. Gytha also felt resentful that she had not drowned, and saved him having to tell her she must remain behind. But he was chief, and owed a duty to his people.

He must decide, and he had decided.

Gytha turned.

There were fifteen people following him. Six women and nine men, as well as a straggle of children who did not count until they were more use than hindrance. Gytha always experienced an itchy feeling in his spine if any of his people disappeared for more than a few instants, but seldom worried if one of the children vanished. The young were a burden and a wise man rejoiced when a burden was light, accepted what he must when it was heavy.

Ayi saw Gytha turn, step aside, stand waiting by the path, and her heart thumped painfully in her throat. Gytha led and did not wait. If he waited, then this time it must be for her. She had known he would, but when he did not wait before the swamp she began to hope that he had decided to allow his people to help her through the thickets. If only she could be granted just a little help, she would be able to reach the Bare Hills and another summer of life. But the old seldom received assistance. Children might be a burden and not count as people, yet they were helped because one day they would become the strength of Gytha's kindred. Adults offered whatever they could to their people; hunting skill, child-bearing, bone and muscle; once their offering lost its value, they were discarded before they consumed more than they could provide.

Keep moving, or be left to die.

Ayi supposed she was lucky to be left behind on the ridge, which she loved. The swamp would have been death by terror; here, her spirit would be at rest.

Yet she was not ready to die.

Once she'd rested she would feel well; her herb-learning was only partially passed on to her daughter, Dymar, because Ayi had believed that so long as such knowledge was hers alone, then she would not be left behind to die. Now it was too late. Children as yet unborn would have to relearn through suffering the herb-lore Ayi could have freely offered.

Ah well.

Ayi smiled at Gytha. He possessed a fine body she admired, although his uncle, Druic, had been far better even when past his prime.

Ah well.

Gytha thought Ayi almost beautiful when in spring sunlight she smiled back at him. But she was old and as soon as he looked closer, there was only a softness of eye to set beside the wrinkles. Whereas Dymar, her daughter . . . No. Dymar was a maid and Gytha wanted her, but she must be left for the time of the harvest moon. The low-hanging red moon of the Bare Hills which marked the time when maids were exchanged with other kindreds around blazing harvest fires.

Few words were needed when Ayi reached Gytha; her time was come, and she knew it. Words expressed what one did not know, signalled when a boar broke left or right or a man caught a scent the rest had missed.

Already Ayi had ceased to think about how the ridge would become the place where her spirit stayed. Instead she was remembering the warmth of Druic's thigh, how she had taught Gytha some love-skills younger women now enjoyed from him. She and Gytha looked at each other smiling and remembering, and also knowing each other's thoughts.

'The ridge' he said, and nodded.

'Aye, the ridge' she replied, and shook her head.

This is a good place to die, his tone meant. It is a pity to die in the sweetness of spring, while the blood remembered how it was to lie with a man, her shaken head answered, and accepted.

He raised his hand in salute, a lithely built hunting man dressed in untanned leather, then he turned and left her. Already he was estimating how far they still had to go before reaching The Place Where Weapons May Be Found.

Ayi watched his back until trees dappled it with shadow, then stretched and looked about her. It would be pleasant to sit in the sun and wait, after days of hauling her aching bones from one sodden tussock to the next. But how unimaginable also, just to sit and never leave this place.

She heard her daughter, Dymar, cry out from some-where ahead of Gytha and then the girl came running back, 'Mother! Not here, not yet! Four days through the thickets-'

Ayi spread her fingers. 'Five at least for me. Better to die here than there.'

'No' said Dymar. I stay, and tomorrow we go.' She held her mother's hand, meaning, we go together or not at all.

Gytha came striding back through the young bracken, shouldering everyone off the path, his face angry. 'Come.'

'No,' answered Dymar. 'She is my mother.' she rubbed her face on the hand she held because Ayi had been good to her, and twice nursed her through a fever. But she lacked the skill to express a loyalty rooted in defiance, and the need frightened and bewildered her.

'You are our harvest maid,' answered Gytha.

Dymar nodded, but rubbed her mother's hand again.

White clouds were beginning to tumble across the sky as Gytha stared at her, astonished. Insects hummed in the bracken and his people gathered around, shuffling their feet and marvelling at a girl who defied her kindred-chief. A girl moreover who had itched with longing all winter, begging for a man, and now stood as straight as thrown water, saying she wanted to die beside a worn-out mother.

The waiting must have addled her wits, they thought, and exchanged covert looks. It often happened. The custom of their people was for a maid to be exchanged at harvest time for one from another kindred: a habit dedicated to the gods of harvest but eagerly anticipated all the same, the single element of chance in their relationships. A small people like Gytha's often wearied of each other. A fresh and different maid, the bargaining, the estimating of comparative worths, gave an edge to speculation throughout the winter. Dymar was also the best offering they had brought to trade in years.

Last season, a sickly girl was the only untouched female they possessed and an idiot all they obtained in exchange; the year before their maid died in the thickets and they were forced to sit disconsolately through all of a season's chaffering.

But Dymar was strong. Dymar was quick and fool-hardy, with tantalizing eyes and a fleet, tough body. Useless, some men said. Not willing. Not submissive. But even so, they all agreed how painful it had been to keep away from her once she was chosen as their harvest maid, and she was particularly striking this fine spring day, with polished shells from the estuary around her neck and waist, a sprig of young leaves thrust into her hair. They were all a little crazed by not lying with her, and when Gytha jerked his head the men enjoyed the act of tearing her from Ayi's side.

Dymar screamed and fought, dramatizing her own excitement after a winter of sulking alone, surrounded by people passing the cold season in the comfort of each other's bodies. Deep down, she was angry too, and surprised by her anger. Her people were her people, and where they went, she went. What they did, she did. But today, on the ridge her own thoughts mattered more than theirs. She would be shamed if Ayi was left behind, as other old people about whom she had never thought were left, to die alone.

The struggle lasted as long as the men wanted it to last, then Gytha ordered her to be tied and she was led away. 'Ayi!' she shouted, head turned, a smear of blood on her face.

Ayi lifted both hands in a gesture of parting and of fortune on her life, stood watching until the children straggling behind Gytha's people vanished between the trees. She had not wept nor responded to Dymar's desire to stay, a desire so unexpected that Ayi's mind needed to fumble with a great many images in an attempt to understand it.

The drive for life was all that counted, and Dymar was . . . what? Fourteen summers old and newly into season.

Ayi shook her head, not understanding. Then looked about her as peace took the place of struggle and she felt at ease in spite of being left. Part of this peace was a consequence of Dymar wanting to stay behind; such wilfulness might be dangerous to a kindred, but at the end of life it was good to know that her daughter would have stayed to die with her.

Good, not good. Want, not want. Of Course, the girl had known she would not be allowed to stay, but still . . .

Ayi moved away from the path, looking about her; already the landscape seemed changed because she was set apart from it. The spring colours appeared more intense, a doe did not take fright when she came on it drinking from a pool. Ayi knelt to drink too, suddenly feeling all the weaknesses for which she had been left behind. How strange to find so large a pool of water high on the ridge. No matter how dry the weather, in all the years Ayi remembered travelling along the ridge, she had never seen this pool dry.

She sat beside the water's edge all day, dozing some-times.

She woke as the evening chilled, her belly whining hungrily. It did not occur to her that even alone she would probably be able to trap some animal in the dark; a solitary woman could seldom survive in the forest for long. By accepting death she eased this time of waiting and would give rest to her spirit when it returned into the earth.

But she did not want to die by the pool

Ayi thought about this and knew she was right. The pool gave life, she ought not to offer it her death.

When she dragged herself to her feet, her bones felt heavy as rock, her feet hesitating on the path as if even now she was tempted to use the last of her strength in trying to follow her people. Then she turned down the steep slope to the west.

Down where wolves and lynx and wild boar lived around the root-filled swamps, a darkness where black spirits howled. Halfway down the slope, Ayi tripped and fell. It took her a long time to stand again, but when she did she laughed, the sound echoing eerily with the call of owls. She had just realized it did not matter any longer if she failed to hide her weakness because she was already dead. Fear vanished once burdens were left behind. I am free, she thought, without understanding what it was she thought. There is nothing more for me to do, and I am free. I am alone, she also thought, and shivered.

She found a fallen beech and sat listening to the sounds of the night, a wet wind strengthening against her skin. Heard the distant cough of some hunting animal, the squeal of a mating boar; bent down to take a handful of forest soil in her hand and let it trickle through her fingers. This land, she thought, which was another instinct she could not frame, except she knew she loved this place where her life would end. She was part, and would be part of it for ever; she tilted her head to listen and caught the echo of Druic's voice from long ago, calling her name. Strange that though he had been dead many seasons he should be the one she remembered now.

Ayi lay back to sleep and as she slept she smiled.

Close by, the she-wolf crouched, one living cub beside her. Pain loosened her sinews, but this stupidly helpless creature roused instinct one last time. Dragging her useless leg, the she-wolf lurched from her lair, stood staring into shadow where the woman slept; normally she would have fled from any human, but, burdened by a cub, had been too weak to do so. Now the flesh she craved had come so close that a single effort might bring her a week of food, time for her leg to harden and the cub to gain some strength for itself.

The she-wolf crept on her belly closer to the shadow, no longer able to kill by strength or speed, only by patience and endurance. The moon slipped behind a bank of clouds and below the ridge darkness was complete, only the starving cub whimpered once and then was silent.

Dymar was tied by a sinew rope around her waist between two burly half-brothers. Her father had sired them on a female stray he found along the estuary one winter; no one else in the kindred had felt that so wild a creature would bring them fortune, so when the birthing was over they kept the children but turned the woman out to wander the marshes again. Dymar did not like her half-brothers and had been happy when she was chosen as the harvest maiden, so would never have to lie with them. Gytha, she coveted. The other men of the kindred would do well enough, but Gytha she desired constantly and today as she watched him the passionate air of spring rioted in her blood.

If the rope had been tied between herself and him, she would have accepted Ayi's death as soon as she was left behind, since this would be her doom too, one day, when her usefulness was ended. A cruel acceptance was bred in her just as in all the rest; she was still astonished by her own refusal to accept Ayi's end as she had that of so many others. Astonished, but unaware that her refusal marked a new departure in her life. And because the rope tied her to her half-brothers and not Gytha, she continued to stare at them in hate, spitting when they touched her. This hatred, as well as the ripeness which possessed her, caused recollection of Ayi to persist, until eventually it changed into sullen determination to honour a loyalty she did not understand. When they untie me, I will return she thought. She lifted her face proudly and looked at the tremendous trees all around her, conscious for the first time of separateness from the rest of humankind.

I, she thought exultantly. This thing I will do.

As the afternoon dulled they came to the place where the ridge dipped and then climbed sharply, breaking out of forest into a kind of upland heath, where a single hill curved upward. The hill was steep and on its crest a palisade stood out against the evening sky. Gytha's blood beat strongly as he gazed at that masterpiece of labour from men's hands; he came here twice a year but the magic remained, fresh as when he first saw it as a child.

The ridge path forked when it reached the shoulder of the hill. A faint track shied away to the left, allowing timorous folk to avoid the hill and plunge directly into the thicket country. A more deeply worn way climbed up the slope, and this was the one Gytha chose. It was worn because the people of the hill came down each day to work by the forest water, lighting their fires and hammering earth into metal, often bickering among themselves. Gytha thought this as strange as all the rest. In the forests, men seldom fought. They saw other kindreds only rarely and pitted their strength against cold and wet and hunger, against spirit-ridden swamps and animals lying in wait; they possessed little and had to replace any losses from the wilderness around them; fighting simply added un-necessary hazards to a completely hazardous life. The hill people were different. They owned huts and weapons and stockades full of herded animals which made them unpredictable to those who lived a more ancient life.

When Gytha's people reached the summit of the hill, the causeway through the settlement palisade was still unblocked. At nightfall it would be closed by hurdles threaded with gorse, so Gytha immediately led the way across; the hill dwellers allowed travelling strangers to sleep in their beast-pens, providing they kept their hands off other men's belongings.

Gytha's people found this latter prohibition very hard since they normally picked up anything useful they found, but after several generations of being beaten with gorse every time anything was missed they had learned their lesson. Now, they picked up discarded scraps and used great cunning over stealing articles of value.

They camped in mud among the swine, little huts like bushes all around them. The people of the hill never moved and their village stank, but they cut down trees with their edged tools and built fires which burned like the sun, as well as turning dug earth into metal. Such lives were spent in angering the spirits, Gytha's people said, awestruck by the foolhardiness of it all. They gathered in deliciously fearful groups, twittering reassurance among themselves, and watched everything as if they had never visited the hilltop in their lives before.

Dymar was untied and sent to fetch water since no one except her remembered Ayi any more and, anyway, by now the causeway would be closed for the night. As for Dymar, she remembered her pride of the afternoon without clearly recollecting why pride had been born. The camp on the hill filled all her reality now. She crept to look into one of the huts, tucked close to the shelter of the palisade. The interior was lit by flames from a hearth and a woman knelt to stir something savoury in a pot. The hut looked warm, and surely it must be easier to look after a fire sheltered by walls; only in winter did Gytha's people build flimsy burrows among such bushes as grew along the estuary, and they were always wet.

Someone spoke behind her, and Dymar jumped. A man, wearing woven cloth instead of skin stood close; he looked tall to her eyes and had the narrow face and sharper bones of a hill-dweller.

Dymar did not understand what he said and wanted at first to run. But almost immediately she remembered her pride and poked her nose in the air, studying him out of the corners of her eyes. He looked strong and more than willing; tonight, particularly, it seemed a long time to wait until campfire bargainings after harvest brought a new kindred who would bed her.

He laughed, and she understood that well enough. Smiled back, although she did not look directly at him, since a single unwary look could let in an evil spirit.

Then he said a great deal more, grunts and sucks which made Dymar want to giggle; why speak so much when each understood the other? She showed him the waterskin she carried, and as she hoped, he realized at once that this meant Gytha expected her back very soon. So he led her into the darkness between hut and palisade without more ado. Dymar did giggled then, from anticipation, because he was taller and stronger than any of her people.

'Your name?' she asked, forgetting he would not understand.

'I saw that you were tied' he answered in his own tongue, not comprehending anything except that she was bold and supple.

'Your name must be one of strength, like the great trees.' Dymar felt him dreamily, gestured at the trunks of beeches which made up the palisade.

The man watched the movements of her hands intently. 'You want chopped wood as your gift-price?' I enjoy chopping wood as a change from fires and iron.'

Dymar felt confused, as he continued to talk and did not take her immediately. Perhaps hill-dwellers coupled only with the spirits. She tried to edge away from his grasp. 'I go.'

'Or would you prefer a knife which has a chip in the blade and is of little use to me, instead of wood?'

Dymar touched his knife obligingly, realizing from his tone and pointed finger that she was being asked a question.

'That's a good choice. A knife brings good fortune.' He took it from his belt and offered it to her, since his people never lay with an unwed woman without offering a gift first. As soon as she took it there was no reason to waste more time, and he mounted her in a drift of wet leaves.

Dymar was worried by the knife, imagining it part of a ritual to cut his mark on her, and covertly threw it out of reach while he uncovered her body. Then she forgot mystification, also the knife as his body drove into hers.

She had expected him to be as fierce as the axes his people forged and was not disappointed; desired pain to mark her womanhood, and received it; wanted his doom to seize hers because this was her first time and she defied her people by not waiting until harvest. So she did not lie and accept but reached eagerly for him, then was astonished when the strength in him turned to a sorcery of the senses.

They both forgot that Gytha would be waiting for her.

The hill-dweller stood at last and left her, too soon for Dymar but too late for her to pretend that she had wasted so much time searching for water. Even then she did not hurry but lingered in her leaf-bed, staring at stars sprayed overhead. She smiled, shuffling her hands sensuously in moss and earth. Clear stars splintering light across her uncovered body was how it ought to be, on the night she first learned male enchantments.

She stood at last, and ran across the stinking spaces between the huts back to where her people camped. She felt too joyful not to run, and was too much a creature of the moment not to flaunt delight. Gytha jumped up as soon as he saw her in the flow of the fire, and stood with his nostrils flaring. The other men stood too, and the women stared. They saw a different Dymar, lips pouting red in the firelight, triumph gathered about her like leaves opening in the sun. They did not need to be told what had happened, and when Gytha struck her he smelt Hillman stench.

Snarling and crafty-eyed, Gytha's people gathered around as Dymar fell under the force of his blows. They had kept her virgin because she was their offering in the harvest-trade, now they circled close, watching for a way to slake their fury over yet another year in which they would be forced to stand aside from Bare Hills bargainings.

Dymar laughed at them from where she lay, and raised her foot to push at the first of them to come at her. She felt unafraid and glad, now she remembered it, to be revenged for Ayi's death.

'You,' said Gytha, bewildered. He could not describe what he saw in her flushed, triumphant face, but understood it very well. You Dymar. Not us, the kinsfolk of Gytha.

'I,' gloated Dymar, glorying in it. She came lightly to her feet, hands on her body. Her body, mine. His, the unknown hill-dweller's. Not Gytha's nor his people's any more. And she sent a great cry up at the stars, so Gytha and the rest drew back fearfully from the spell she must carry to act so strangely. Then, as if by a carefully argued decision, Gytha's kindred turned away and squatted back by the fire, beginning to eat. Her spirit was not at one with theirs any longer; she was finished, outcast, too dangerous to touch, and meanwhile food smelt good to empty bellies.

Dymar stood watching them, her eyes ugly with hate. She had been deeply satisfied by her own defiance, but rejection was cold and cruel and very strange. She hesitated, not knowing what to do, and watched them for a while, sitting a little apart with her knees drawn up to her chin. No one spoke or turned, and so her anger increased. Eventually, she slipped back to the bed of scuffed leaves below the palisade where she had lain with the hill man; she slept after a while, and smiled as she slept.

In the morning Dymar stood by the causeway to watch her people leave, filled by a kind of frightened rage. The hill women around her murmured when they realized she was to be left behind, and one of them shouted, wanting her to go.

'No,' said Dymar, 'I stay.'

I'll be hurt here! Was her thought, and she touched the birth-gift of estuary shells hanging at her neck. I cannot live on one hill for ever, but neither can I go with Gytha.

The woman shouted again, and another threw a handful of gathered muck, which made Gytha pause and return to the causeway. The morning sky was filled with blustering clouds and he looked oddly insignificant to Dymar's scornful eyes, when only yesterday desire for him had filled her senses. I hope you all die in the thickets, she thought.

Gytha caught her wish in the way a kindred could sense one another's thoughts, and turned away again, shouting at his people. At this ending of a lifetime's familiarity the tears boiled into Dymar's eyes, but when the voice of last night grunted behind her, she turned at once, nodding. Surely the hill-dweller must be asking whether she had left her people, or whether she would come to live with him, and to both the answer was a nod.

'Brac,' he said, and thumped his chest to show possession of his name.

'Dymar,' she whispered.

And so within a day, all of her doom was changed.

Dymar thought of her doom as a large black bird with its wings outstretched, but now it had coupled with the doom of Brac, a smith from the hill settlement, she knew it could be a bird no longer. His doom she saw as a strong-built fighting boar, which was good and at the same time, bad. Boar-meat tasted sweet but they were seldom trapped by forest people.

Brac waited while Dymar watched her kindred go, slipping like deer into shadow beneath the hill. Then he turned to lead his new woman to his hut, and for the first time in his life he thought how a woman could be as beautiful as well-crafted iron. Her lithe eagerness had snared him when a quick coupling was all he looked for – all he had ever looked for – and in daylight he remained bewitched by her mystery and grace, the shells at her neck and waist emphasizing her difference from settlement women, who wore iron adornments and were solidly build for work.

Dymar found her new life very hard, the early days of her time on the hill passing in a haze of fright and bewilderment. She learned the hill people's language quickly, since she possessed the memory of a kindred who needed to recall every marked tree and dry tussock from the estuary and she continued to enjoy Brac's body at night, but living in one hut oppressed her. Also, the other women were spitefully jealous. Until she came, Brac had lived with three women and everyone was satisfied. Now he wore himself out pleasing an insatiable forest harpy, and the rest bickered fretfully.

Dymar was also disconcerted to find that she was not allowed to lie with other men. Hill men kept their women each for himself and it was a cause for quarrelling if one slipped into a different hut. Dymar thought this restriction so unreasonable that as time passed she began to take pleasure in demanding even more from Brac, hoping – yet not truly hoping – that he would weary of her. She did not understand that even if he did, still she would not be free of him; but he did not weary, and when autumn came Gytha's people passed by the hill on their way back to the estuary. Dymar had been looking forward to their coming and felt miserable when they passed without spending their customary night in the settlement; she couldn't understand it, since she had long ago forgotten her own anger. Her restlessness grew after she watched them dwindle away into the distance. For her, every day was now the same. Except at full and new moon that is, when Brac's people sacrificed to their Earth Goddess. Otherwise, each dawning she must walk the same short distance to Brac's smelter's hearth by the stream below the hill; or gather nuts and fruit and scanty grain from around the settlement, whereas she longed to journey again, and wake not knowing what pattern of trees she would see next day. Brac stifled her discontents with his strength at night and even changed his maker's mark on iron to a deer, which he said reminded him of her, his creature from the forest, but none of this made up for the punishment of staying in one place. Dymar might remain fond of Brac, but she was not reliant on him in the way hill women were on their men, and fondness had nothing to do with loss.

Tedious lengths of time had to be passed in squatting on her haunches, rocking her weight from one hand to the other so that goatskin bellows blew air at the flames on Brac's hearth by the stream. Dymar had a child in her belly too, and the days of crouching pained her, especially when she had never before worked consistently at anything in her life, and one day late autumn, not long after Gytha's kindred had passed by the hill, she sat back on her heels. 'I want to walk along the ridge.'

Brac stopped hammering metal. 'Why?'

'My mother was left there when we passed.'

'Why? Brac was always asking why, another habit Dymar failed to understand. Things happened or they did not happen, that was all. But at least in a settlement there was no need to leave the old behind when they could not keep up on a journey.

'I want to go.' She repeated. 'My mother's spirit begs an offering of respect. It is custom of my people.'

Brac nodded, he accepted custom as a reason. 'Soon I take iron to sell and others will help to carry it. You may come.'

'When?' demanded Dymar, overjoyed.

He shrugged. 'When I finish'

'Where will you take it?'

He gestured to the east. 'Where a people called Roman live in great houses and come to buy.'

Dymar felt no interest in yet another kindred camped in settlements, but the promise of travelling to the east roused anticipation to fever pitch. Gytha's people journeyed to the Bare Hills away to the South, but seldom ventured west, where deep wet valleys prevented the passage of anyone except the foolhardy hunters, not east, where settled peoples treated light-fingered forest folk as if they were destructive boar, hunting them to death with spears and dogs.

As the evening air began to bite Brac packed up his tools and led the way back up the path towards the settlement. Holly berries flamed in a wintry sunset and frost lay unmelted in the shade, while above them the familiar hill-shape was hammered against the sky, its curve so smooth that the hill people called their palisade a nipple on Earth Mother's breast. They worshipped iron and also the female fruitfulness of their hill, purifying their dead in great funeral pyres before allowing their ashes to enter sacred earth. As an act of respect, all new-born babies were exposed during their second night of life, on a stone in the centre of the encampment. Only the tough survived but since those who died were suckled for ever by the goddess, they were not considered particularly unfortunate.

Dymar feared and hated the hill goddess, who appeared to her capriciously cruel compared to the spirits of marsh and trees and deer worshipped by her people. In truth everything about the hill angered her now, even the food, of which there was greater abundance than she had ever known. Insipid, she thought, it and she had also discovered that cooking in pots meant infinitely more work than roasting meat on sticks. That night, as usual, she poked at gruel and green stuff, wolfed the meat, then pulled a face. 'Why is meat cooked in water instead of ashes here?'

Brac signed. She asked the same question every night. 'Eat, and fill your belly.'

'Wallow with the swine where you belong, and cook your meat how you wish,' said Cledis, who was mother of three living sons by Brac and hated Dymar with bitter abiding hatred.

'I will.' Dymar spat a bone into the pot. 'Make sure you count your children when I light the fire.'

Cledis's face remained expressionless, but her mouth puckered as if to bite. She did not believe that the forest people ate children, but was prepared to imagine anything of Dymar. 'I would butcher you for the goddess while you still fumbled for a spark.'

Fright paled Dymar's skin. She might bluster, but knew she lived under bare tolerance in a place full of alien powers who might kill her any time they chose. Cledis had also touched another weakness, since Dymar could not learn how to kindle fire reliably. 'I am going away.' She said at length.

Cledis's lip curled. 'Good'

'With Brac, to the east when he goes to sell iron.'

Cledis burst out laughing. 'Good again.'

Dymar could not understand it: she had been certain Cledis would be jealous at being left out of the most exciting thing to happen on the hill all season. 'A journey will give my child strength to be born. The hearth-bellows cramp in my belly.'

Cledis shrugged. 'All work cramps forest dwellers.'

Every night was filled by similarly bitter wrangles, and Brac put his head in his hands to keep the clacking voices out. But the moment his hearing dulled, he again remembered Dymar's slender body and eager giving in the dark. How she moved always as if about to flee, each foot placed with a delicate wariness of which he never tired: he called her his deer, and so she remained – an elusive, untamed, turbulently graceful creature of the forest. Hill women were toughly built and diligent: never once had Brac experienced with one of them the frenzy and longing Dymar brought him by simply being there.

Two weeks later a line of figures trailed down the hill, bent under the weight of iron pieces for the Romans. Besides Brac, there were ten men carrying goatskin packs, and Dymar, seven months gone with child.

A good journey,' said Cledis, standing on the causeway to watch them go, feet planted wide, hands on her hips.

'Yes, oh yes,' said Dymar, so enchanted to be going that Cledis's spite passed her by. She was warmly dressed in a goatskin robe over woven cloth and carried the grain they needed for the journey. She darted from side to side of the path with sheer delight as soon as Cledis was out of site.

They crossed the stream where Brac usually worked and climbed up the valley beyond, through undergrowth that needed to be slashed before their line could pass.

'The ridge,' Dymar said, tugging at Brac's sleeve.

'On our way back. Then you and I will go there together. Until we have sold the iron it is best to travel directly to our market.'

'The ridge is easy walking.'

'But not the way to the Roman settlements.'

Dymar stared at his pack with loathing. 'Then leave your iron behind and walk like a man instead of a beast.'

Brac's jaw dropped. He could not believe she was serious. Leave a season's work behind and talk of walking like a man? He turned away impatiently yelling at the axemen to hurry.

Dymar felt the weight of her pack as the succession of hills and valleys lengthened. They were travelling across the grain of the land, which was a thing her people never did: they followed ridges and drier ways and did not care how short or long a distance they travelled in a day. This was not a journey as she understood it, but labour worse than that of the bellows.

During the second day, Dymar began to weep. Her sure-footedness had vanished, her shoulders and belly griped with pain. When Brac and his companions lit a fire that evening she crawled away into a bush, ashamed of tears which would not stop, and of herself for grovelling like a beetle through the forest, where men should walk like gods.

After a while, Brac hauled her back to the fire to eat, while the other men jeered at his concern. He held her tightly that night, lying apart from the rest so they could talk alone. 'Dymar, why did you cry today?' He spoke tentatively and very quietly, not wanting the men to laugh at him again, nor to rouse Dymar into scorn.

'Why?' screamed Dymar. 'Why?' two days bent like a beast which never sees the sky, and you ask me why?' Cledis sneered when she watched me go and I wondered why. I do not wonder now, nor at these others who mock each time they see me stumble.'

Brac heard his companions stir at her screeching, and winced. He ought not to let her make him look foolish, yet he would only cease to be the butt of jokes if he turned her away into the forest again, where she would perish, all alone. 'This is a hard journey until we have sold the iron, but profitable.'

Dymar's teeth fastened in his biceps and he exclaimed aloud, but partly in pleasure still. He forgot everything except his passions then: the curve of her belly like the curve of his fruitful hill, her breasts so puffed with milk that when he bit a nipple in sweet revenge, his body sang like hammered iron. For Dymar it was different and for the first time she felt no pleasure at all in Brac. An aching despair filled her senses and his teeth were painful on her swollen breasts. This man whose strength she had admired seemed clumsily huge, oppressively heavy, as if he would never be satisfied until he had ground her into the earth his goddess claimed, and so she began to dream of the lithe people of her estuary again.

Ayi, she thought suddenly and with a dreadful clarity. She must have cursed me in her death. That day on the ridge was the time my life began to canker.

If she had not fought against Gytha's decision to leave Ayi behind, then she wouldn't have been cut off from her people, with a child in her belly who must be exposed to a hateful and hating goddess on the second night after it was born. For her child would not live. Cledis made sure Dymar understood that. Children exposed in the depths of winter never lived, and the hill women saw to it that if they wanted to keep a child then they birthed it by harvest time at latest. Only an ignorant forest dweller conceived in early spring. This, of course, was why Brac had been willing to take her on this journey. If the child was born while they were out of the settlement, by the time they returned it would be past the second day. Then their child need not be exposed and so might have a slender change of life.

Suddenly Dymar drew up her legs and kicked out with her knees, heaved the drowsing Brac off her and stood. Before he could gather his scattered senses she had bolted into the bushes, burrowing into the undergrowth in wild and headlong flight.

When daylight came, Brac searched for her all along the valley, calling and trying to follow where she had gone. But he was an ironsmith, born of many generations of smiths, and his ancestors' tracking skills were blunted in him. Dymar watched him from where she lay snugly protected in a drift of pine needles, and thought only what a fool he was to waste so much of a day. In the end, his companions stopped laughing long enough to become impatient, so, eventually, he was forced to leave with them as the day dulled under a stormy sky.

Before he went, he stood on the stream bank and called in the voice which he used when he wanted to be heard above the beat of hammers. 'Dymar! You cannot live long in the forest, alone. When we are gone, you will see only to your own death and the death of your child.'

Dymar did not move. Brac was a good man, but hill people were weaklings, after all. The forest would not kill her.

'Dymar!' His voice echoed through the trees and with it the longing he could not speak. 'Dymar! Come!'

When still she did not answer, his chin was on his shoulder all the way as he climbed out of the valley, and he left something lying on a stone by the stream, wrapped in skin.

The sound of his voice remained in her ears as Dymar picked her way down to see what he had left; even with her new-found fluency with words she could not have described how she felt about Brac, but now he had gone she was sad.

He had left a small bag of grain and an arrowhead, and she picked up both, weighing them carefully in her hands. Enough grain for three days perhaps and the arrowhead bore the maker's mark he had changed to a deer for love of her, from   to   . Dymar looked at the scratchings thoughtfully. Brac's message was clear enough; grain meant life and forgiveness, the offering of his mark the gift of his spirit also. Even after this, Brac would receive her back if she chose to return; he might be outcast by derision as a consequence, yet he would take her if she asked.

Dymar kept the arrowhead but threw the grain into the stream, since obligation was another burden she did not want to carry and providence a virtue she had never learned. For what was left of the day she travelled eagerly and fast. Dancing in and out of the trees like a sprite, calling and running sometimes, lingering as the fancy took her. She felt neither tired nor cold, though the wind gusted winter rain in her face; nor lonely, though forest spread in billows to a grey horizon.

She slept in the kind of dry bank her people always found no matter what the weather, and ate the food they knew how to discover, especially at this season when earth had fruited but was not yet chilled into deadness. On the third evening after she left Brac, and by following her own instinct without conscious thought as to where it would lead her, Dymar reached the ridge.

Colour streaked the sky beyond the steep western slope she remembered; Dymar stood in winter-brown bracken and stared at the most magnificent sunset she had ever seen wanting to hold back the night so she could watch more closely. She sensed Ayi lingering somewhere very close, but could not yet tell whether her spirit was happy or unhappy, would bless or curse her when they touched. Slowly, light vanished from the sky and the distant valleys became dark, leaving Dymar aware that she was hungry. She had eaten roots and fungi, grasses, nuts and sapwood since she let Brac but neither grain nor meat, to which she had become accustomed during her months on the hill. The child kicked impatiently in her belly and instinctively she calmed it with her hands. 'Wait', she said aloud. 'It is too soon. Wait, and I will eat. Wait, and I will find Ayi. Then perhaps I can take you to my kindred, and when you are born you will see the estuary of Gytha's people.'

The child kicked again, and pain shot from her thighs to her swollen breasts. It is too soon, thought Dymar, panic-stricken. Stay in safety, little one. The ridge in winter is no place for even a forest child to be born. She turned aside into tangled bracken and after a while reached an open glade containing a deep pool she remembered. By this time the night was very dark, and so silent the fall of a late leaf could be heard. Only the starlight reflected from the cold surface of the pool showed her where it was. Dymar dropped to her knees and drank, willing herself not to feel any more birth-pains, and after she had rested for a while, they ended.

'I am alone,' she spoke aloud again. Alone, alone, alone. Never in her life had she been so completely alone. The words crackled through silence as if through trampled ice. She needed a fire and food, somewhere warm to sleep. Then the child would wait to be born and she could make peace with Ayi's spirit before leaving on the long journey back to her own people.

Dymar shivered, realizing just how far across swamps and tangled forest the estuary was from here. A distance she had never travelled alone, and which her kin never travelled in winter. 'I am alone,' she said again.

She came slowly to her feet and stood beside the pool, breathing carefully. Alone, she could live and travel until the snows came, but would lose a new born babe within a single icy, underfed night.

No more pains came even when she began pulling bracken out by its succulent roots, and Dymar relaxed. I am tired, she thought; I will sleep and tomorrow there will be food. Ayi is here. I am not alone while I feel her close. The night was becoming very cold and wind ruffled the surface of the pool; to sleep safely on such a night she knew she must find deeply drifted leaves, gather them to form a burrow, pile more above her.

She was so draggingly tired it seemed to take most of the night before she was warm and safe, then, when she was snugly comfortable at last, she discovered she was thirsty. Punishingly, pantingly thirsty, the child stirring again as if it was gulping her lifeblood, draining her dry.

Dymar moaned, curled in her leaves.

Moaned again as pain struck out of nowhere. Floundered in terror from her burrow and stumbled through bracken to the pool; when she had drunk she would feel better.

The pool was black and deep and crinkled by the wind. When Dymar lifted her head after drinking she saw a deer on the far bank, its head lifted as if she looked indeed at an image of herself. Its nostrils quivered but the wind was blowing towards her so it did not catch her scent; it was puzzled and uncertain though, and after a while retreated delicately into the undergrowth and was gone. Meat, Dymar thought, thrusting other meanings firmly on one side. I wonder how I could trap a deer tomorrow.

Back again under the leaves she felt more comfortable, and slept almost instantly curled like a hedgehog around her swollen belly. After a while she began to dream. Instead of a deer she saw a wolf; the wolf was not by the pool hunting, and when it turned to measure its leap Dymar saw that its teeth were iron blades and its face Ayi's face.

She stirred, whimpering a little, but did not wake.

The wolf was turning, intent on its prey, Ayi's face made terrible by blood dripping from those iron teeth. A deer came into sight, stupidly careless as it grazed across an open glade which Dymar recognized as the one which contained the pool. The wolf growled and went down on its belly, waiting to tear out the deer's throat and with a single spring. Dymar stood in sunshine, mouth gaping in a silent scream because this deer was surely her, and the wolf had Ayi's face. Shaded her eyes against the sun, not wanting to see what happened when she knew from a thousand kills what happened, the light on estuary water so brilliant that she had to turn her head away, only to see Ayi's oblivious face widen into terror as the wolf leaped and blood spurted, jaws closing with the sound of iron. Ayi's scream changed to a crunching sob, her eyes watching Dymar standing safely in the sun; Ayi's calm eyes instead of her own in the deer's tormented face, blood pouring over where Dymar lay.

Dymar woke trembling among the leaves, knowing she had touched Ayi's spirit, but the blood she had seen flowed warmly between her legs. Her muscles bit, driving pain into every part of her, slackened, bit again.

'Ayi!' shouted Dymar, alone in the dark, her child writhing half-born between her thighs.

'Ayi! Come!' Pain came instead and oozed more blood over leaves and her twisting body, over the thing she no longer thought of as her child. If Ayi had been there she would have helped it through this last fragment of its journey; if any of her people had been there, they would have known what she ought next to do. Dymar had seen births many times: the reaching hand, the twist and mewling cry which meant success. Alone, she did not think she could reach. Her fingers slithered on blood and slime and leaves, the next burst of agony seeming to tighten her thighs instead of loosening them, as if the child wanted to force its way back into the womb.

'You can't!' cried Dymar in terror, the night snapping and crackling around her.

As morning came the child was still only half born and Dymar understood that neither of them could live much longer.

Floundering like a drowning fawn, she bent and drove her arm deep where she knew she must felt the child kick again when it had been lying still, heard Ayi say quite clearly: 'Come, you are well again,' as she used to after Dymar took a fever. Saw her figure against the morning sky and felt her place a red and yelling creature in her arms.

Dymar lay stupefied for a long time after that, slowly losing blood but sleeping the worst of her pain away.

She woke when the child woke, and drowsily put it to her breast. Neither knew much about what they were doing and leaves were stickily plastered everywhere: Dymar felt a laugh start in the distance and come closer, glittering between the two of them. In the years ahead, surely they would often laugh together.

Just now, the child yelled angrily; it looked like Brac and once she held it firmly to her breast, was as well satisfied by her body as he. Not long ago Brac's teeth had been where his . . . Dymar felt the child experimentally and nodded to herself. His son. Brac's son, and still attached to his cord. Her fingers encountered the length of it and she used Brac's arrowhead to saw it through, the metal slipped in her fingers as she finished, fell unregarded into the nest of leaves. The struggle to knot the cord left her gasping; she needed food and again was fiercely thirsty.

Ayi, she thought, and smiled. Ayi, you were with me and today you are not with me, but from your bones a new life has grown. Then Dymar remembered the wolf of her dreams and held her son more tightly. The ridge was a place which took life as well as gave it, since Ayi's death had surely been a terrible one. Yet by coming here she had brought rest to her mother's spirit and so was freed from obligation.

But not free in a quite different way, Dymar looked at the child sleeping against her breast. There was milk on his mouth and his skin was wrinkling against the cold; he would not survive for long beneath a drift of leaves, but nor could she feed him through a winter journey back to the estuary, weakened as she had been by his birth. And how long had she been away from her people? A long time. A long, long time.

Not yet a year, Dymar realized. A lifetime.

From the ridge to the hill settlement was less than half a day's journey even for a weakened woman carrying a child: she could manage that tomorrow or the next day. By then Brac's son would be past the time when he must be exposed, and the stored grain of the settlement would save his life. Farewell, my people, Dymar thought. Iron and bellows-labour await me for the remainder of my life.

But my son will live. Brac will teach him to be a smith and I shall offer him the forest as a gift, since both are in his blood. I will sing about how he was born far from any settlement, and one day he will feel that this, too, is his inheritance. This ridge where Ayi died and he was born between deer and wolf.

This ridge which joins my people to his; this ridge where water, trees and bracken flare orange in the evening sun. But because Brac left me his forgiveness when I ran away, I will also tell him how his father's mark on iron was changed because of me.

Dymar slept again as the sun blazed out of a cold and polished sky, and below the ridge a wolf sniffed the air as it caught the reek of freshly spilled blood. As darkness came it began to howl with longing, but because this wolf had been born to an outcast mother with a putrid foot it had never been accepted into the pack. Alone, a wolf would not venture into the open spaces of the ridge, and so it howled but did not come to seek the creatures sheltering by the pool above.

. . . THE WITNESS:

When I was a child there was still a pool on the ridge which Dymar might have recognized, but within my lifetime it has vanished. Last week, in the twilight of a fine spring evening, I was walking close to where it used to be when a car drew up quite close.

'I wish I knew where the hell we are,' the boy behind the wheel said plaintively.

'Nowhere, really,' his girlfriend answered. 'Come on, there'll be a road sign further on and then we'll see how to reach the motorway.'

They kissed, young and in love enough to kiss most times they touched. They drove off again almost immediately and rejoined the traffic racing along the ridge, three minutes or less before they would have passed Brac's Hill.

Nowhere, really.

The ridge; its pool and church, the pub and single street of houses, its tens of generations: Could this indeed be nowhere, really?

I walked back to Edenham slowly, needing a stick these days, and when I reached it went at once to prise Brac's arrow out of the oak beam above the hearth. In all the years since I came back to live at Edenham I had left it safely in its hiding place, but that evening I needed to touch the past. Maybe I made too much of a casual overheard remark, which seemed to confirm an old man's forebodings. I like the modern young but their break-neck heedlessness appears to me more destructive than the conventional vices they inherit. Those youngsters had shaken me, driving their car from nowhere into nowhere.

After so long in the building, would England soon become no more than a place where motorways failed to meet.

2

A MOULD IS SET
AD 891 – 898

Eight hundred years passed, and very little changed on the ridge. The path still meandered the easiest way from one glade to the next, bracken grew head high in summer and the pool brimmed with water even in the driest years. But away to the south the hill settlement was long since deserted; called Tiw's Hill after an earth goddess whom people believed had built the mighty ditch and banks, it was worshipped from a respectful distance. Except at harvest time, when men from all the clearings in the forest danced there holding green branches, and afterwards became mightily drunk. For the rest of the year the only sounds on a hill where hammers once had clinked all day were those of wind and rain, the bray of rutting deer, and the call of the birds.

The Romans too had gone, leaving few signs that they had ever entered the Andredsweald, as the great forest was now called. In their place was a new people, Saxons from across the sea, but as yet only a few of them had penetrated the forest: in an underpopulated land the river valleys and open hills offered an easier living. But it was those few who began the task of taming the Andredsweald, as they did so they drove both the ancient forest people and the hill-settlers away from their few clearings, so that no one knew where eventually they went.

The first Saxons on the ridge settled close to the pool and within a single lifetime had felled enough timber for two yokes of oxen to be set to the plough; they also built a huddle of timber huts set back between the pool and their new-cleared land. By the time Alaric died, who had been the first to leave his kindred on the coast and search for a holding of his own in Andredsweald, the two families he established by the pool had become six.

Alaric had wandered for a long time in the forest before he came to the ridge, but when he saw its water, light soil and good drainage, he decided he had wandered far enough. He sent for a wife from his village, and when she came the family of Britnoth came too. So Alaric and Britnoth sat in council under a great oak near the pool, then hammered in stakes where they decided their huts and barns should be, where swine should be penned and oxen tethered. That winter Britnoth returned to the coast and his soft tongue persuaded more footloose wanderers to come into the forest where land was free for the taking. The ridge, he said, was open. And so it was, between the trees. Alaric and Britnoth laughed at the new arrivals' consternation when they saw the mighty work which awaited them before a plough could be put to the soil, and after a while the newcomers stopped cursing for long enough to laugh too, since the land indeed was free.

So they began digging sod shelters and burning and chopping at the trees with fluted, easily dulled axes. For several years, game was their main source of food, and ale became a wistful memory.

Time passed tranquilly and very little happened beyond the excitement of seeing scratched plots grow into ploughland, the anxiety that crops might be ruined by marauding deer, and the occasional murder at feasts held with other folk who like themselves were carving out homes in the wilderness. When Alaric died, an old man but still fit to chop down a tree on the morning of the day he fell frothing on the path home from his workplace, the settlement on the ridge contained twenty-seven people. All wore warm clothes and their split-log homes kept out the worst of the winter storms, so Alaric died a contented man and was buried with honour beneath the oak where he and Britnoth first held counsel together. Once word spread of a carouse to be held in memory of Alaric, kinsfolk and acquaintance came in great numbers to Ferenthe – which means the Place of the Fern – as Alaric's folk called their settlement on the ridge.

When all their guests had departed and peace returned, the six families agreed that the funeral had passed off better than anyone could have dared hope, and that Alaric had enjoyed a death which would long be remembered. No blood feuds had been started, and every settlement that anyone had heard of now owed them hospitality. Only Wynfyrtha, Alaric's daughter-in-law, had the ill-grace to remark that wolf-toothed guests had consumed practically all their reserves both wet and dry. But everyone else felt that Wynfyrtha's complaining came from habit, and Guthlac her husband shouted at her until she was silent. 'I know you spend your days in counting ears of grain,' he said, 'but game and small beer satisfy a man after good feasting, so long as harvest is not far off.'

Wynfyrtha scowled, but did not answer, contenting herself with kicking at dirty trenchers until the men were out of earshot.

'She has always been sour-tempered,' said Guthlac excusingly. He did not care to seem afraid of his wife, as was in fact the case.

'You should have beaten her every day for the first year of your marriage,' answered Britnoth, son of Britnoth, holding the ache in his head and squinting at the sun. 'Then perhaps she would have learned to hold her tongue. Today my head feels as though a sword had split it, and Wynfyrtha's carping has added a saw-edge to the iron,'

The rest laughed, feeling at peace with themselves and the forest after such good feasting. They worked very lightly that day, not yet being accustomed to the idea that Alaric's bellow was silenced for ever. Even in old age he had struck out at anyone he saw idling, and Guthlac was not feared as his father had been. When the sun became hot they stopped work altogether and settled to drowse their headaches away.

Edred, Guthlac's only surviving son and grandson to Alaric, saw them snoring like swine when he walked past at midday and despised them, but then Edred despised people very easily. Knobby limbed and big-handed, he possessed a distinctive face which the older men of Ferenthe said was like that of Alaric in his youth: a high brow above blue eyes, thick cheekbones and a jaw over which the skin was tightly stretched. Because he behaved like a man although still only fifteen or sixteen summers old, Wynfyrtha his mother often fretted that he would die young like her other sons. Edred for his part accepted the titbits Wynfyrtha's worrying brought him, but otherwise never gave her anxiety a thought; he was in truth exceptionally tough, and accepted his exclusion from adult gatherings only because he preferred his own way in everything.

Among the men of Ferenthe, Edred had truly respected only his grandfather. Consequently he alone was not surprised when after Alaric's death the settlement ceased to enjoy its previous good fortune. Thunderstorms ruined the harvest, which after such carousings was more urgently needed than usual, and this was followed by an uncommonly dry winter and spring. At first Ferenthe prospered during this drought, since no matter what shortages there might be elsewhere, the pool on the ridge never dried up. Then, one day, Wynfyrtha came in wide-eyed. 'The pool is losing water.'

'You are always complaining, woman, and now I know it is for the pleasure of listening to your own tongue whine. The pool of Ferenthe never dries,' answered Guthlac

'It is drying now,' Wynfyrtha insisted.

It had not been quite full yesterday, Edred remembered. He had noticed a rim of slime when he knelt to drink, but after so many months of drought this had not seemed surprising. When he went again to look for himself, the difference from the night before was dramatic. The edge of slime was now an arm's length wide, trampled already by the tracks of animals who also depended on the pool.

By the following day, the water level had sunk again and by the end of the week the pool had become a stinking morass with scarcely room in it to dip a pitcher. The animals bawled with thirst, women and children laboured backwards and forwards to springs far down the western scarp with yoked waterskins hanging from their shoulders, without satisfying the needs of stock or people on the ridge above. 'We ought to dig out the pool,' Edred said one night to Guthlac. 'Then perhaps we would find the crack through which our water is being lost, and be able to repair it with clay and wattle.'

'The Earth-Mother has sent us such a year of dryness as men have never known before. When it rains again the pool will fill,' replied Guthlac.

'It has taken more than dryness to empty a pool which has never so much as dropped its level before.'

'Nonsense!' roared Guthlac, who always shouted in an argument. 'What else could empty a pool of water?'

'It stayed filled through all the rest of the time we have been without rain.' Edred stared at his father out of contemptuous blue eyes. 'Then within three days lost half its water, and the remainder followed as quickly. Perhaps when it rains the pool will continue to leak. Ferenthe can never prosper if every drop of water must be fetched up a slope beset by animals which threaten even an armed man.' Two children had already vanished while carrying water, and no one knew whether they became lost in such tangled country or whether wolves had found them first.

'We go boar-hunting tonight.' Said Guthlac, cheering up at the thought. Game had deserted the ridge since the pool died. 'See that you are ready before the time set, it is an insult to your elders if you make them call for you.'

Edred did not answer, but he felt very much angered by the implication that he was afraid of hunting at night. He had argued against the project when it was first suggested but out of prudence, not fear. Night hunting was dangerous and usually unproductive; in the present crisis Ferenthe needed meat and uninjured men rather than windy boastings.

While Guthlac lovingly trimmed a new crosspiece for his boar spear, Edred went out of the hut and stood looking at young forest leaves which were all that was left of spring. There had never been such dryness. The sun rose every morning in a grey-blue sky, and set at night unhidden by mist or cloud. The days were hushed and filled with hot clear sunlight; grazing died in glades and clearings, the crops withered in the furrow. At first they had been delighted by warmth which dried out damp huts and gave more time for standing about and gossiping since there was little hay to cut; people felt on edge as apprehension grey, yet also friendlier because of their common peril. Now, when Edred left to walk across the ploughland, the fresh-turned soil whirled away underfoot. An axe swung loosely from a thong about his wrist and as he walked he looked about him, frowning. Already it was too late in the year to replant lost crops, and the previous autumn's seedlings were patched and yellow. If another harvest failed, then all Alaric had striven for would be lost within two seasons of his death.

On his way, Edred stopped once, to fondle Ferenthe's oxen. Patient, moist-muzzled, worried creatures, grazing off tussocks and coughing mighty dust-coughs. He spoke to them softly, running a hand over their staring bones. Oxen were better than men, any day. They always gave of their best, would plough and pull logs until they dropped in the yoke.

Edred chopped all morning at a tree the swine had part-uprooted, enjoying the swing of his axe, the sense of strength growing in his shoulders and the hot wind on his skin. None of the other men came near him, and he was content to have it so. If they were so feeble of judgement as to believe that lack of courage made Alaric's grandson call a night boar-hunt foolhardy, then he could only pity their witlessness.

When the other men rested at noon, he shouldered his axe and walked to the monks' hole, a place inhabited by followers of three monks who had come to Ferenthe when Edred was a child. They came without weapons which greatly astonished Alaric, who pointed out how lucky they were to be alive when he usually killed strangers who stole up to his thorn fence in the night.

'Ah, but I am wiser than you,' had replied the eldest monk, who looked too frail to be boldly demanding entry into fortified settlements. 'I am a follower of Christ, and able to call His strength to my aid, a strength which exceeds that of ten thousand maddened boar.'

Alaric was even more surprised by such a statement. 'If this Christ indeed has the power of more boar than I have ever seen, I would be foolish not to pledge myself to such a god.'

'No man deals with Christ as if He were a bargain in the market,' answered the monk sternly. 'You need first to repent of your sins and go down on your knees to thank God and His Son, Christ, for your deliverance.'

This, however, Alaric refused to do, saying that his good name would be mocked if he knelt before an unarmed priest, and without any guarantee that he would benefit as a result. 'If this Christ's strength failed to rescue me at a time of peril, it would be too late to go on my knees to ask a second time. Nor could I then return to a more warlike god since my cause would be already lost,' he pointed out reasonably. 'Either way, my blood would be on the ground, and my own strength wasted.'

The old monk thought about this problem in front of Alaric's fire, for it was winter and Alaric content to allow hearth room to a man whose oddities amused him so much. Both enjoyed passing such a dull time of year in argument, but try as he would, the monk never succeeded in converting Alaric to Christ. He did not give up hope, however, having taken a fancy to a man who enjoyed dispute, as he did, for the sheer pleasure of spark-struck words, even though his soul was not saved. And when spring came, instead of resuming their journey, the monks settled down in Ferenthe to dig their hole.

This was what Alaric called it, because the priests did not build a timber hut like other men, but lived in a sod-roofed dugout set at some distance from the village so they could pray undisturbed either by carousings or the women, who remained fascinated by a settlement of wifeless men. The cold and wet of the dugout kept the priests awake to pray constantly, which the priests counted as gain and Alaric considered proof that so much kneeling made a mockery of pride and sense.

But one by one over the following years, the inhabitants of Ferenthe accepted baptism when they were sick, or injured, or saw their interests otherwise served by acknowledging a god whom the priests maintained steadfastly would save them from any ill. Only Alaric remained obdurate. He never suffered a day's illness until the evening he died, so saw no need to change habits which served him well, but since he continued to relish the old priest's company he gave out that anyone who insulted the dugout people insulted Alaric himself. Consequently, the priests were treated with extreme circumspection, which eventually spawned rumours of divine protection over their interests. These whisperings brought occasional miracle-seekers to Ferenthe, in search of cures or to satisfy their curiosity, and some of these, too, succumbed to the old priest's eloquence and were baptized. Alaric only killed one of these strangers, who arrived so drunk he judged that the man made the priests look foolish, but when the old priest died of a trifling fever he was only confirmed in his belief that this new god was as powerless as the rest when outmanoeuvred by a resolute enemy.

Edred grew up among these arguments, but he too had never been baptized. This was partly out of respect for Alaric, but also because he was too set up in his own conceit to consider he might possess sins which ought to be mauled over by priests. Yet, recently, a newcomer had arrived in Ferenthe priest-hovel, and today Edred felt sufficiently isolated to desire very much to discuss his position with somebody he believed might offer censorious but unbiased judgement.

Brother Theobald was scarcely like a priest at all, since he was very easily angered and preferred chopping down trees to crouching underground on his knees. When Edred reached the clearing around the priest-hovel – a roofed excavation had grown from the original dugout – he found Brother Theobald with the skirts of his habit tied around his waist, digging energetically.

'Have you not enough holes already?' Demanded Edred, crouching so that his face was almost level with Theobald's nose.

Theobald wiped his face, smearing soil from eye to jaw. 'I am searching for a spring, so we may dig a well close to our church.'

'And did your god instruct you to dig on the very crest of a hill?' inquired Edred sarcastically.

'I used the sense He gave me, and followed the line from your pool to the spring yonder.'

Edred looked over his shoulder measuringly. 'Then perhaps you should next pray for water to fill your hole.'

Theobald was odd. He was angered over trifles but amused by insults: Edred could not make him out at all. This time he simply smiled and knelt.

'There is still no water,' said Edred softly.

'Did you expect there would be?'

'Not I, but you, Brother Priest.'

'No,' he answered, smiling still. 'This is God's dry season, when it is easy for me to dig a well which one day may serve a great priory. He will choose when His springs will flow, not I.'

'Yours is a fortunate god.' Said Edred sourly. 'Since men such as you will always find excuses for whatever he chooses to inflict on his followers.'

Theobald threw back his head and laughed. 'What else will make them happier or more filled with strength, than seeing good wherever they choose to look?'

Edred shrugged. 'Scrabble through your store of god-wisdom then, and tell me what good you see in hunting boar by night, when a clean strike is impossible.'

'The men are hunting boar tonight?'

Edred nodded.

'Why?'

Because we are all tired of half-empty bellies, no strong beer to drink nor crops to tend. We need boar meat now the deer have vanished from the ridge, and the excitement of a night hunt will keep men from each other's throats a little longer.'

'So, a dead boar-hunter is perhaps the price which must be paid to prevent a blood feud from breeding out of idleness.'

'If Alaric was alive he would neither allow quarrelling among ourselves, nor need to prove his courage in such a foolish way'.

'Alaric is dead, and was capable of doing anything in his anger, if the doing of it took his fancy.'

Edred smiled, proud that such a man had been his grandfather. 'I do not wish Ferenthe, which was of his making, to perish. One day I should like to point out to my son the oak where the great Alaric was buried, and see my oxen plough more soil than a man can walk over in a day.'

'And when you possess a son, and oxen, and much land, will you wonder then whether this and nothing else was your existence?'

Edred often thought about what he wished, or meant, to do. He had never felt the least wonder towards himself. Until Brother Theobald said those words, standing by a dry well-shaft with his unremarkable figure smeared in dirt, it hadn't entered his head that there was anything out of the ordinary in the fact that he existed. Even then he did not reflect upon it, but an unease settled on him, as if the earth had moved.

He shook his head, annoyed with himself for coming to the priest-hovel at all. A priory, Brother Theobald called it. Edred looked at earth dugouts roofed with sod, and his lip curled in derision.

'As for a night boar-hunt, I could wish that men did not risk themselves foolishly, but this is a matter for them not God,' added Theobald. 'From what I hear, we are likely to see Danish raiding parties in the Andredsweald before long and will need all the spears we have to defend ourselves.

'This land is too poor to attract Vikings.' answered Edred.

They are everywhere. Two monasteries of our order were burned last year, and the kingdoms of Mercia and Northumbria are lost. Only King Aelfred's Wessex resists, but Vikings hunt and move like wolves; in their ships today and across ten valleys tomorrow.

Edred left Theobald to his diggings then, since his counsel was so bad. Everyone knew that no matter what rumours of disaster were brought by wayfarers, marauding armies would not plunge into the Andredsweald. Why should they, when there was nothing for them to find but forest and a few settlements struggling for existence?

Meanwhile, there was the boar-hunt, and foul water, and Wynfyrtha's cooking which was the worst in the village. She just threw things in a pot and let it boil; Alaric had grumbled through every meal since his daughter-in-law took over at the hearth.

By dusk, everything was ready for the hunt. Men came eagerly from their huts, weighing hunting spears in their hands; the last repairs were made and torches bound ready for lighting. The sun set late since it was already nearly midsummer, but when true darkness came at last the men called cheerfully to each other as they began the steep downward climb off the ridge. The women stood silently, watching them go. A strong man killed – or worse still, crippled – meant disaster for his kin, but women could only wait, and then count who came back safely in the dawn.

Edred walked behind Britnoth the Younger, carrying the spare torches. Only a grown man could handle a boar spear, which needed to be exceptionally heavy and sharp; a cross-bar was bound across the shaft to prevent it, once driven in, from sinking so deep that the holder was brought within range of the boar's charge. Boar were powerful and brave, their tushes capable of splitting a man from crotch to throat, and could only be cleanly killed by a strike between the shoulders or into an eye.

Below the ridge untouched forest was so dense that the men needed to fight every step of the way. Insects stung and bit, roots tripped, snakes abounded in places such as this. For a while, no one complained, they knew what the forest swamps were like, and had come seeking a chance to prove their courage. But after a while, when they had neither seen nor scented boar – for boar reeked and never troubled to hide their coming – they became discontented. A night spent in danger of drowning, or attack by wolves or snakes was not the stuff of hearthside boastings, and the women would make their lives miserable if they returned without meat.

Guthlac attempted to calm their grumbles with cheering words, since he loved hunting better than anything else and became eloquent whenever he thought of boar. 'No one can provide against ill-fortune,' he said. 'And a true Saxon is not dispirited by a few setbacks. If we reach the great swamp which lies in the blackest part of the forest, then assuredly we shall find boar,'

'The edge of a swamp is not a good place to face a charging boar,' objected Britnoth the Elder.

Guthlac spat on his spear. 'I will withstand the first charge wherever it is offered.

So they went on again, the ground every moment more densely packed with roots, branches and whip-edged bushes. The glitter of eyes occasionally revealed where wildcats watched malevolently from the safety of a tree. Slowly, a greyish light began to illuminate the topmost branches and, realising they were about to be robbed of the test offered by a night-hunt and might as well wait for full daylight and better circumstances, the hunters were about to turn back when Guthlac stiffened. 'I scent boar,'

Then they all smelt it, thick on the dawn air. Guthlac swept his hand at them and stepped aside into the undergrowth, while the boys shinned up any tree with branches low enough to reach. Edred found an oak overhanging the black waters of the swamp they had been skirting, and once he was safely lying along a massive branch, he turned his head methodically, trying to penetrate the darkness which engulfed everything except the leaves high above his head.

Then, above the singing birds of dawn, Edred heard the crashing of bulk being forced through tangled growth, and saw red eyes reflected in light from swamp water. Let Guthlac have enough sense to wait awhile, thought Edred. This treacherous dawn murk is the worst of all. He must wait now until there is more light.

But Guthlac had come for sport and forgot everything except the boar as soon as he saw those red eyes, did not want daylight to spoil his chances of achieving a famous feat. He stepped from behind his tree and shouted, calling defiance at the boar. The eyes blinked and disappeared, as if the creature was looking around, uncertain what was expected of it. So far into the forest, this boar might never have seen a man before.

Then Britnoth the Younger shouted, knee deep in swamp water and several paces to the right of Guthlac.

The boar lifted its head, and charged. A thunder of sound as without any warning at all the creature hurled itself at Britnoth, though he had intended simply to confuse and enrage it, since boar were said to dislike water. He screamed and lost his footing on slippery swamp bottom as he tried to dodge, leathery haunches sweeping over the place where he had been, the water frothing in the uncertain light.

Guthlac did not hesitate; he came from his cover and shouted to draw off the boar, thus enabling others to rescue Britnoth if they could. The creature scuffed water, stirring leaves and slime as if determined to leave nothing of its enemy behind, but did not move.

Edred watched from his branch, his anger at men's foolishness changing to dread as he realized that Ferenthe would lose more than Britnoth's life to this boar, for it behaved like no other he had seen. One of the boys began throwing stones and shouting from his tree, since boys had a duty to rouse and deflect a cornered boar, but still it did not move. Britnoth was certainly dead by now.

'Hnaef,' called Guthlac. 'Throw your spear and then climb quickly up a tree.'

Hnaef was pleased at being chosen for his straight arm in a throw; also, when dealing with such an unpredictable beast an honourable scramble up a tree was not unwelcome. He advanced to the edge of the swamp, climbing from root to root to get close to the boar, secure in the knowledge that such treacherous footing protected him from a spindle-legged adversary.

With this boar, calculation was proved wrong.

As Hnaef poised himself to throw his spear, it came at him fast, slewed once on trapping roots, then dipped its head and sent him screaming into the water with blood pouring from his legs. The boar followed him, and there was sufficient light for them all to see how uncannily it used its weight to stamp and smother; then it sidled, stopped, as Hnaef's struggles faded. And this time did not wait, but charged directly where Guthlac stood slack-jawed on the bank.

Only a hunter's reflexes saved Guthlac from that charge, since he had been so much appalled by the swiftness with which both Hnaef and Britnoth had been killed that for once he had forgotten the spear in his hand. He leaped aside as the boar grazed his thigh, tossing its head high and snapping its grinders on leather instead of flesh; then instinct struck on the flint of his skill again, he pivoted on one leg and planted his spear squarely into the creature's side.

He lived another instant as the boar skidded to a stop and stood blinking at the spear embedded in its hide, before it turned and charged again. Disarmed, Guthlac sidestepped once more but this time blood spouted as the boar's tushes gashed his thigh, and he fell as it thundered past. Even then, he managed to put his hands on the spear shaft as the creature came back to finish what it had begun. Wrenched, jerked the point clear, then feebly tried, but failed to drive it into exposed belly as the boar trampled him into mud.

The boar stood where the early rays of the sun struck through the trees, its hide slashed and with Guthlac's blood on its muzzle, but its power almost untouched. From up trees and behind bushes the men of Ferenthe watched it, struck motionless by so great a disaster occurring in such a short time. They recovered quickly, however, since disaster was something men became used to and they now owed blood vengeance for Guthlac, Britnoth and Hnaef. Two of them began to work their way cautiously behind the boar, while Rheged and Elfgar offered themselves to its charge. Edred shouted at the boys to start spreading their nets to entangle the animal when it moved, everything except the need to kill forgotten. If this boar escaped them now, they would be accursed.

With the low moaning grunt of its kind, the boar charged once more, but slower; Guthlac had certainly hurt it. Elfgar was brave and stood motionless to place his spear, his body curved as he drove it deep into muscled ribs. Too deep, and too far back. The point slid over bone allowing the boar to reach Elfgar with the remaining force of its charge and they all heard his spine snap. But the boar was dizzy now, and tiring, so when Rheged stepped into Elfgar's place he was able to choose his moment and sink his spear driven with the full strength of a man who chopped trees every day of his life, into the socket of one eye. The beast shrieked, and fell dead on the ground.

Guthlac would have been angry, Edred thought. He had considered Rheged clumsy with a spear, and would have grudged him a kill so spirited.

Four men out of eleven died on the night boar-hunt, and two boys disappeared during the journey home. No one missed them until the rest were trudging up the scarp towards the ridge, but by then everyone was so weary it was impossible to go back. They carried the bodies of Guthlac and Elfgar,the sodden shreds of Britnoth and Hnaef, and such hunks of boar as they could manage in addition. The boys had been equally burdened and must have reeled into some morass unseeingly; anyway, they were gone.

The women were wailing before the men reached the ridge, and rushed up calling and weeping, trying to see who remained alive. Even Wynfyrtha wept, but chiefly with relief, touching Edred tenderly as he leaned dizzily against a tree. 'You are alive, my son.'

'Guthlac is dead.'

'On a boar-hunt as he would have wished,' she answered, scarcely looking at his slashed body, so that even Edred felt that Guthlac deserved some greater acknowledgement of his courage for standing against the boar.

How strange were the ways of women. While Guthlac was alive, Wynfyrtha had defended his right to do whatever he pleased, whether it was beating his son or starting a blood feud, yet now he was dead it was clear that she did not cherish even a trifling affection for him. Edred's thoughts blurred, as he tripped and fell into fern beside the path, asleep before he struck the ground.

All the way back from the swamp one thought had hammered at his brain: with four out of its eleven grown men dead, with the beasts growing scrawny from poor keep and their fields blowing into dust, surely the village of Alaric could not survive much longer.

It survived less than another day.

While the men who had returned from the hunt slept off their exhaustion and the women washed their dead, a Viking raiding part was approaching from the south.

The twenty men who followed Tostig Half -Axe into the Andredsweald did so because raiding had become less easy of late. The King of Wessex was an active, courageous and unpredictable adversary, to the point that it was no longer possible to loot England at leisure. The fastest-moving marauder couldn't be sure of outpacing pursuit, and pursuit had become a commonplace hazard facing anyone raiding England's southern coasts. Which was all very well for large armies, since a worthy opponent made a warrior's life more rewarding, but upsetting for a single Viking crew seeing their fortune by scavenging on the wreckage of great events.

So when Tostig's followers found defended settlements along the coast, they decided to conceal their boat and try their luck inland. This had not proved an entirely happy choice. The King of Wessex's arm was strong even in distant Kent, and they found the peasants alert and threatening, braying alarm-horns from one village to the next in the most aggravating way. So they took advantage of the cover offered by the great forest which skirted the Kentish settlements, until eventually they became lost in its vastness.

After three days of floundering under trees, where a seaman's sense of direction easily faltered, they were glad to see a trodden path which suggested a settlement must be close.

'These will be soft people who have never suffered a raid,' said Tostig Half-Axe. 'We will approach their village quietly, but raise a great shout when we charge. Then will the men's sinews loosen and the women shriek, making our task easy.'

His followers accepted this good counsel. They had come for loot rather than glory, and were tired and hungry besides. The ridge offered easy travel and as soon as ploughland came into view they scattered among the trees.

At first sight the village appeared almost deserted and Tostig felt disappointed that they should have come to so poor a place. Still, there must be other settlements close by, and a prisoner would be able to tell them where to look; so Tostig shook his half-bladed axe in the sunlight and burst howling from the trees without more ado.

A man stumbled out of one of the huts, heavy with sleep although it was midday, and Tostig clove his head from his shoulders with one stroke, feeling that an undignified end served him right for being a sluggard. Two other men appeared with boar spears in their hands, and both attacked Tostig, probably because they realized he was the leader. Tostig thought even more poorly of villagers who attempted to defend themselves with boar spears against fully armed Vikings, but for a moment was hard put to it to defend himself against so unexpected a weapon. The other Vikings ran past him in their haste to make sure no fugitives were able to escape, so Tostig despatched his enemies with the first method that occurred to him: by throwing his shield in the face of one so the spike entered his eye, and disarming the second by snapping the shaft of his spear with a single stroke of his axe.

After that, it was all finished. The villagers seemed half asleep and as easy to skewer as rats in a cooking pot, although later the Vikings discovered some bodies and pieces of boar and decided they must have been out hunting in the night, which made the raiders feel that perhaps the ridge people had not been so cowardly as they at first supposed. At the time, however, they were much disgusted, and confirmed in their belief that farming made a people soft. When they could find no living men left, and Knut and Noseless had returned in high good humour with an account of how he had speared some priests, squealing, in a hole, Tostig held his bloodied axe high before his face and declared the village open for pillage.

'Make haste,' he added. 'We will take the younger women with us until we need to march swiftly again, so do not waste time on them now. Gather food and drink and weapons, then discover whether the priests have precious metals hidden. When I blow my horn we will leave, and the women can disclose to us where the next settlement is hidden in this accursed forest.'

This admirable plan was carried through, but set adrift at the last. The Vikings became so much enraged when they discovered how little the village contained, how ugly and terrified the women appeared and how emaciated the stock, that they began to destroy for the love of it. Some embers from a hearth were kicked aside and with everything shrivelled from drought, flames driven by the wind swiftly consumed the huts, leaped over the dry place where the pool had been and began to rage in the forest also, so that oxen, geese and goats roasted alive or escaped out of reach.

Long and bitterly did Tostig curse such carelessness, knowing that neighbouring settlements would see the smoke and send to find out what had happened. The few women kept alive wailed and screeched even after Grinulf used the flat of his sword on them, and the worse of their dread was amply fulfilled during the following days, as the Vikings withdrew in some disorder to try their fortune in another part of the Andredsweald.

By the time Edred recovered his senses it was dark again, though when he opened his eyes there seemed an odd hot glow in what was certainly a night sky. He felt sick and dazed after such a long sleep on an empty belly, following a night filled by great fears and exhausting labour. For a while he lay staring at that strange sky and thought only of how his belly flapped with hunger. Then his senses steadied and he smelt the odour of roasting meat; a better cook than Wynfyrtha must be in charge of the boar-feast.

But when he sat up everything he saw seemed completely strange, although he distinctly remembered reaching the ridge and telling Wynfyrtha that Guthlac was dead. He looked out from the gulley where he had reeled into sleep, over a considerable open space where steam coiled against blackness, which almost convinced him he was still dreaming. Nevertheless, it was odd he should feel so hungry and yet lack his other senses. Then his eyes lighted on a fragment of hut still charring in the wind and he recognized the bare space where the pool had been, measured the bole of a great tree whose branches were like bones stripped of flesh, and he knew he looked on Alaric's oak and what he saw was the ruin of Ferenthe.

He wiped his face with trembling hands, and looked again.

Nothing moved. No beast or human, only smoke and steam blowing upward in the bright moonlight. Further away towards the cleared fields a wall of fire still burned, nearby there was nothing left to burn. Where he stood the bracken had shrivelled in the heat and he would have roasted as he slept except the wind had driven the flames in the opposite direction.

As he stumbled from one charred hut to another, from cindered bodies to shattered corn pits, Edred at first believed he looked at the results of unforgivable carelessness. Fire had been the settlement's great fear since the drought began, and several times the alarm had brought everyone running with pitchers and beaters. But when he reached the place where the priest-hovel had been and looked down into Brother Theobald's well, he knew he had deceived himself. The huddle of black-habited bodies was only intermittently visible because of steam rising from the damp shaft, but they had escaped burning and Edred could see enough to observe a Viking axe left upright in the topmost back, and in the hovel itself he found another dead Brother, stripped naked and contorted by torment before he died.

Edred wandered in the gutted remnants of the village for what was left of the night, neither considering the need for caution nor seeking to exercise it, since it was clear the pirates had gone. By dawn he had made a reckoning and knew there was nothing and no one left besides himself. The oxen were mostly cinder but the flesh nearest the earth remained just edible, so Edred ate. He needed strength and was not squeamish, although he regretted the oxen. For the rest, there was Rheged's sword which had fallen under a collapsing wall and was preserved except for the wood grips; some fowl which eyed him warily from the remaining trees, a little grain below a charred upper layer in Guthlac's corn pit.

There were also twenty-one bodies to be treated with honour. Edred stoked up some embers, piled on as many incompletely consumed timbers as he could find, and heaved his dead kinsfolk on the blaze with very little ceremony. He would avenge them, but until he did them ceremony would not help their spirits to rest. He left the dead priests down their well, considering that they might be offended if he offered them to Mother Earth, and when he had gathered everything which might help him on his journey, he set off to follow the Vikings' trail.

As he struck northwards off the ridge, he did not look back to where Ferenthe still glowed redly beneath a smear of smoke, but kept up a steady pace through the remainder of the day. He carried some roast ox and grain in his jerkin and held Rheged's sword in his hand, his mind closed to all thoughts except revenge. He had consigned twenty-one bodies to the flames, a number which, from an estimate of their sizes, included children. This meant that most of the women must have been taken, probably including Hlaffa, Rheged's daughter, on whom Edred's fancy had fastened some time previously. He had liked her shy tenderness, being himself of decided opinions and not drawn to women who might set themselves against his will. Rheged, too, had been a hard-working man who might have been expected to give his daughter valuable gifts on her marriage.

By the following day Edred was forced to admit that the tracks he followed might no longer be those of the raiders he sought. He slept a little, but woke up sweating long before he was rested, glad to forget nightmares by stumbling on his way again. The path he followed continued westward for most of a day and then vanished in a swamp. If the tracks were indeed those of the pirates then clearly they were as thoroughly lost as he. The air was becoming ever more oppressive, and the next night a mighty thunderstorm ended the long drought. The god Thunor threw his thunderbolts across the sky, the dry streams swelled and within a short time of the storm beginning, lakes had formed on the iron-hard ground. Edred was forced to race for safety, wading thigh deep in a cataract swirling through trees where there had been only bracken a short time before. Any tracks the Vikings might have left were washed out, any hopes of overtaking them finally lost.

As the storm roared and flashed about him, Edred held Rheged's sword before his eyes and saw the blade lit by unearthly fire. Then he filled his throat with air and wetness, and shouted above the thunder about how he would not rest until his oath of vengeance was fulfilled. 'I will kill two Vikings for each kinsman of Ferenthe. Five for Hlaffa, who might have been my wife.' Then he thought of Wynfyrtha and Brother Theobald who, in spite of their failings, he remembered with affection, and added 'Five for them, and a Viking chief for Ferenthe itself, which my grandfather Alaric made his own.'

Edred had been feeling oppressed by his failure to avenge himself immediately on the raiders, but the storm lifted his spirits and made his oath seem doubly splendid. Amid crashes of thunder like split rock, he stood upright in white glare, an enormous shadow thrown against the earth from his upraised sword. Trees snapped and streams cascaded earth past his small safe place. The great number of Vikings he was committed to kill (he must notch a stick to be sure he reckoned his oath correctly) matched the magnificence of the moment. When at last the storm passed overhead and rumbled away into the distance, Edred at once set himself to climb out of the wasteland where he had followed the raiders, and to seek a track which would take him to the west. The time was past for fruitless pursuit, and he had already decided what he would do next: he would offer his sword to the King of Wessex, apparently the only man willing to fight and slaughter Vikings.

Edred walked steadily westward through the next five days, keeping to high ground and stepping aside from the track if he heard anyone approach. He met few travellers and spoke to fewer, taking cover at the first sound he heard. There was an occasional craftsman travelling the country with his tools stuck in his belt, some glimpses of cleared ground and huts where peasants laboured peacefully, once a man passed him on horseback, going fast.

'Likely he's a king's messenger,' observed a travelling cloth-finisher whom Edred stopped to ask the way. 'No matter where he is, the king hears at once if his realm's defences should be breached.'

Edred reflected sourly that no one had warned Ferenthe. 'What is the good for him to hear, if help always comes too late?'

'He comes when he can. Sometimes before the pirates expect, more often close behind their march, since Vikings move like a river in spate. But after the years of easy pickings, of one thing these accursed Danes may now be sure: soon or late, Aelfred of Wessex will exact retribution for maraudings.'

'But – here?' demanded Edred. 'We aren't in Wessex here.'

'Where else are we then?' jeered the cloth-finisher, spitting chewed seeds from between blackened teeth. 'Since Aelfred swears he will defend any Englishman who offers him his allegiance, no one is too particular about remembering how they were not Wessex once. Even proud Mercia calls him king today. The English are one people, Aelfred says. So, against the Dane, one people we are most thankful to become.'

'You are from Wessex?'

'Aye. Where else?'

'So far as I know, anywhere spewed out by Mother Earth,' retorted Edred, angered by the man's insolence.

The other grinned. 'You will need to change your oaths before the king, He is a Christian and might hot for piety.'

Edred swore aloud, by Mother Earth and mighty Tiw, before striding away from the cloth-finisher's laughter. What ill-fortune to discover that the one man who might lead him successfully against the Danes was Christian! Since the Christian god had preserved his monks no better than the other inhabitants of Ferenthe, Edred felt as disinclined as ever to kneel before him.

He had now left Andredsweald behind him and fields and slow-flowing rivers replaced forest. There were many trees as well, of course, but divided into woods and copses, the spread of ploughland and grazing cattle astonishing to anyone brought up in a single forest clearing. The drought did not look to have been so severe here, either. The harvest was ripe and full, the stock grazed adequate pasturage. Occasionally Edred came on a burned homestead or a swathe of country going back to scrub which told of past raids, but mostly he was entering a richer land than any he could have imagined.

When Edred first set out to look for the King of Wessex, everyone pointed west in answer to questions about where he might be found; now, he encountered great difficulties as he reached the chalk hills which formed Wessex's heartland, since no one seemed certain where the king's warband was campaigning. A raiding-party of Danes had passed up the Thames the month before and Aelfred had taken some followers in pursuit: for several days Edred was cast back and forth by rumour. If he had not been so intent on blooding his sword without delay, he would have taken harvest work to keep himself until winter when all the warbands returned to their own hearths; in Aelfred's case, to Winchester.

Then a surprising thing happened.

One day, when Edred learned he was close to where Aelfred had camped only a week before, people began to look at him strangely. If he asked where the king's warband was, and explained how he intended to join it, men muttered to themselves and the women glanced at him out of speculative eyes, refusing to answer. At first Edred thought they took him for a spy, but soon rejected the idea. They would have cut his throat the instant suspicion entered their minds. The looks he encountered were rather those of astonishment and conjecture.

He became uncomfortable under so concentrated an examination, and eventually, exasperated, began to avoid settlements when he could. The track he followed ran through flat country and was enclosed by high banks, the kind of place where a traveller might easily be surprised. Normally Edred would have been alert to every sound; that day, however, he was puzzling over the strangeness of the people among whom he found himself, and turned a corner with his eyes fixed on the ground. Too late, he saw strangers ahead and turned to leap out of sight. There was a shout and the sound of running feet, a stunning blow between the shoulders and he was flat on his nose in the dust.

He was hauled to his feet in front of a man who stood straddle-legged with his hands on a sword which must have been twice the weight of Edred's. 'Why did you run from us, churl?'

'Why make a habit of knocking any chance-met stranger into the dirt?' snapped Edred, furious at being caught off-guard.

The man had been probing with his eyes along the banks lining the lane as if he feared an ambush, now his gaze came back to Edred and set instantly. 'At least you aren't likely to be a Viking.' He answered after a short silence. 'Let him go, Godric.'

'I am searching for King Aelfred's warband.' The moment he was released, Edred grabbed instinctively for his sword.

The other grinned. 'Which might prove amusing to King Aelfred's followers who have somewhat starved of laughter these past weeks. Sit by the roadside then, and wait. The king passes this way today.'

'With his warband.'

'What is that to you?'

Edred swore loud and long by Mother Earth, not caring in the least that this man might be a Christian but the other scarcely waited for him to finish before falling into a fit of silent laughter, so Edred felt more bewildered than before. At that moment some spearmen came in sight. Four men on ponies jogged loose-reined behind them, and halted when they reached the group beside the road. As soon as he saw the centre rider of the four, Edred did not need to be told that he faced the King of Wessex. Though he was dusty, tired and badly mounted, no one encountering this one man among the rest could have doubted he faced a king, though he might remain at a loss to explain his certainty. Aelfred was not tall, nor made self-important by great matters, yet his face was distinctive: bright blue eyes, strong cheekbones and jaw, over which the skin was tightly stretched. Lines of strain and perhaps ill health ran from eye to mouth; his wide warrior's shoulders disproportionate to the rest of his slight frame. Neither face nor figure marked him out, but the ease with which he carried power: even in that first instant, Edred grasped that he might spend his life in discovering the nature of this man and still fail to understand the whole. Then, all else was forgotten because his stare became an ill-mannered gape: stripped of age and authority the features he looked at were strikingly similar to his own. People had stared and whispered because Edred son of Guthlac was a smudged image of King Aelfred before the years bitter striving wore him down.

For a dozen breaths king and forest dweller stared at each other, then Edred bowed. 'I come to offer you my sword, lord king.'

'A willing follower is always welcome,' answered Aelfred, his fingers playing absently with the scuffed harness of his pony. From whence you have come?'

'From Andredsweald, where the Danes destroyed my village. I am Edred, son of Guthlac, son of Alaric,' he added, so there could be no mistaking it. This likeness might be a sign of fortune on his vow, but could not come from linked blood. From this day on, if anyone looked at him aslant, the risk was his.

'Most men would regard it as an honour and not a burden to resemble the king in looks,' remarked Aelfred drily, but by speaking easily of it he banished awkwardness from the encounter. 'A man's sword, his loyalty, mercy and judgement mark him out, and by these will you be valued in our company. Aneirin here will bring you to Winchester.'

'Disappointing, when there was reason to hope for better.' Remarked Aneirin, Edred's captor. 'But then I never yet caught King Aelfred at a loss and Christ send I never shall.'

Edred rubbed his fingers over the bristles of his face. Now the king had gone it seemed a dream that Aelfred of Wessex could have looked like enough to be a kinsman. It had to be a sign. With so many Danes to kill, as well as a chieftain for Ferenthe, he would need a king's luck strengthening his doom.

When Edred reached Winchester, he stared at the town's stockade walls and busy streets, its market place and stone minster, staggered to find so much piled in one place. The noise stunned him and the colours made him blink; he felt suffocated by people jostling him all the time. He gawked uselessly by day, and slept as though pole-axed at night. But once Aneirin left him to fend for himself, saying that after the Christmas feast the king would decide whether he was fit to be accepted, not just into the warband where any fit man was welcome, but as a housecarl, he settled to his task with grim intensity.

A few days later he realized the king had gone again; Aelfred seldom stayed anywhere for long and had left for Wareham almost immediately after his return to Winchester. Even so, his courtyards continued to overflow with men, animals, priests and pedlars, though these too were constantly on the move. After a summer's journeying and fighting the most bloodthirsty warrior was anxious to reckon up his crops, beget new children and discover what disasters had struck his homestead while he had been away. Indeed, the king was hard-pressed to find an escort to ride with him to Wareham.

'The king's close followers will return for the Christmas feasting, which this year is to be kept in Winchester,' said Aneirin, who was a steward of the king's household and seemed to have no other life of his own. Since Edred had none either, the two encountered each other more often that might have been expected, considering the difference in their rank.

'And the Danes, where will they keep carouse?' demanded Edred, fingering his blade. Rheged's sword had been much coveted in Ferenthe; in Winchester, Edred soon discovered how poor a weapon it was. But beyond binding on a grip and honing the edge again and again, he lacked the means to improve it.

Aneirin shrugged. 'Away to the east in the Danelaw lands they have already conquered, I suppose. There was a time when they burst over us in winter as well as summer, but now the king has fortified all the country he rules and keeps our storehouses behind defences. So only in summer do we still scamper like pups in a rat-nest after pirates, which is a life more filled with effort than blood nowadays, but keeps most of our peoples safe. For how long Vikings will be content with such petty gains I cannot tell; while easier pickings may be found elsewhere, perhaps. Then, one day when they have swept all Frankland bare, they will break over us with a great army again.'

'Soon.' Said Edred, his eyes blue stones and his mind like the new sword he craved. 'By spring I shall be ready to kill any Viking who breathes.'

Winter came early that year, and the earth died. Crusted ice lay like rock in the streets of Winchester and in the countryside men chopped wood, fathered children and trapped game; there was little else to do and for weeks most lives were spent in chilled half-hibernation. Only the king's enclosures at Winchester were different, because there life and zest continued to flow mightily, as monks prayed and scratched quills, and men who had defended Wessex year after weary year came to keep Christmas feast together.

Edred felt very much alone as greetings roared across hall and enclosure, and though he would not admit it, confused by the sheer numbers of people everywhere, above all strange faces, when a single unknown figure coming down the track had spread alarm throughout Ferenthe. So he continued to exercise doggedly with blunted practice swords, willing his spirit into the kind of isolation he understood. He challenged anyone willing to try a bout against him, and lost his temper if they said that Christ's carouse was a time to forget fighting for a while.

He was not liked.

People came to Winchester in winter to enjoy themselves, to drink and shout applause at well-told tales; they came because Aelfred was there, and at this season judged every man's grievance. They also came because the king's winter feast had become a time which everyone recognized, however dimly, as the beginning of a new and different world. Here, in comradeship and counsel, something they could not reckon was being built.

So they argued and squabbled and occasionally risked the king's wrath by killing each other, but did not come thirsting to draw blood. Most had survived more campaigns than they could remember and saw more waiting to be fought than anyone could imagine; a season of feasting as the Christian followers of a pious king suited their temper very well.

On the tenth day after Christ's mass, Edred was studying some captured Danish axes in one of the yards behind the king's hall, when Edward, Aelfred's son, entered with some friends. He was not drunk, but nor was he entirely sober. And suddenly Edred, who still had not ventured into the crowds infesting the king's hall, saw a way opening before him which might assist in the fulfilment of his vow. He had begun to fancy his skill with a sword but understood that he would be killed in his first skirmish if the only weapon he possessed was Rheged's soft blade; nor would he ever be accepted as one of Aelfred's housecarls whilst so dismally armed. He also yearned to gain repute as a warrior, so his fellows might cease sniggering over some chance likeness to the king.

He stepped forward, a Viking axe held loosely in his hand. 'Lord Edward, may I ask whether you would try with this axe to break my head? I have been a long time practising and need to discover how well I may expect to fare in the Wessex battle line this coming season.' Bright stare and naked challenge in his face; no one could fail to understand that this would be more than a practice bout, regardless of his words.

Edward looked at him meditatively, the smile shrivelling from his eyes. He was much the same age as Edred, but dark and lithe, so that Edred looked more the king's son than he, except that Edward was already used to command. 'If you wish,' he answered after a pause. 'Edred from the Andredsweald, are you not?'

So the Atheling Edward, too, must have studied that unlikely likeness, wondering perhaps whether it offered him any danger.

'Of Ferenthe, Lord Edward. A village burned by the Danes.' Strange the pang it gave him to name his birthplace, when in recent weeks he had thought of it only as a spur to revenge.

Edward nodded. 'Come then, let us begin.'

He slipped out of his jerkin and stood bare-chested in bitter wind, aware that he needed quickly to recover his wits out of ale-fumes.

'Are you willing to offer a stake?' Edred felt stifled instead of triumphant, but it was too late for second thoughts.

'If you can match it, Edred of Ferenthe.'

Blood blackened Edred's sight; he had nothing to offer except his life and Edward knew it. 'I desire a good Danish sword so I may fight worthily this summer. If a forest farmer can best the Atheling of Wessex, then by my reckoning I shall have earned the one you carry in your belt.'

Edward's eyes dropped to the sword in Edred's belt, then back to his face again. He did not look drunk any more. Without answering, he took the axe and flicked it at his followers. 'Give us room. To the mastery, then.'

'Bid him to strip as you have, lord,' called a voice.

'Let him fight as he wishes,' answered Edward briefly.

No way out, though it was madness to fight a West Saxon prince when Vikings were his sworn quarry. Edred balanced his body as he had been taught, sword point raised, elbow high, watching for the slightest movement of Edward's axe hand. No Saxon was truly at ease with an axe, and even a poor sword gave Edred a considerable advantage of reach. He had to win a good blade somehow and if he failed today, then his life was as well expended here as in a battle.

Metal touched metal and slid away. 'Vikings fight with knife as well as axe.' Edward's voice was cold. 'If I was truly a pirate armed for battle, you would be already dead.'

Edred did not answer, but felt Edward's free hand touch his belly derisively as his companions laughed to see their chief make the swineherd from Andredsweald look foolish. Edward the Atheling was not loved as his father was, but for the younger man respect came before affection and Edward was respected.

Edred's temper burst hissing into flame as that laughter struck at him. His sword arm gained a life of its own and he forgot how he must not kill the king's son. When Edward drew upright for his next stroke, Edred jumped aside and drove his sword straight at his opponent's unprotected armpit. It was a killing blow and everyone in the yard cried out at once, thinking of Wessex without a grown Atheling to succeed his father. But Edward twisted like a broken-backed snake, drove his axe sideways to deflect the blow, and Edred's point merely grazed his upper arm, blood smearing bare skin and scattering across the frosted ruts.

Edred's lips parted in triumph: he had drawn first blood. To the mastery, the Atheling had said, and he had nearly won it.

The axe swept down, winter sun gleaming on the blade. Edred was late in parrying, but reached, just. An axe was an unhandy weapon away from the battle line, the upward stroke not covered by a comrade striking down. Even so, Edred's arm shook from the weight of that blow and it took an instant to force fighting sense back into the place where panic spurted.

'Never wait to see the result of one stroke before driving in the next.' Edward's taunting voice spoke again, clearly, without any sign of roughened breathing.

Whereas Edred could feel his own chest heave, and in desperation he loosed a flurry of blows against the axe which – surely – could not cover all of a man at close quarters. Edward gave way a pace at a time, frowning, the blood on his arm another disadvantage. Chips flew off the haft of his axe as he was forced to use that, too, to block Edred's strokes.

One more attack, thought Edred exultantly, and I will have him at my mercy. He no longer thought of Saxon, Dane or Atheling, only of an enemy to be killed. Sweat ran into his eyes despite the cold; thighs and braced feet aching, rage molten as he failed to shorten his aim fast enough when Edward unexpectedly changed retreat into attack.

And suddenly Edred was down, without knowing quite how Edward could have reached to hook his feet from under him. As he was forced to give ground, first knee then hip struck iron-hand ruts: Edward stood over him with poised axe while Edred took hold of the ground and waited for the gush of blood into his mouth. Ferenthe, he thought, remembering how it was before the Vikings came. Mother Earth, O Tiw, what am I doing sprawled in a Saxon yard, an axe edge at my throat?

To the mastery, we agreed,' Edward said and threw aside the axe. Edred of Ferenthe, you forgot you fought a companion of the English battle line, and not a Viking.'

Edred stood, his bones feeling lose beneath his flesh. 'I beg a return bout, Lord Edward.'

'You have had and lost your bout. Any warrior who fights berserker is untrustworthy in battle; in a practice contest at Christmas feast his madness also defies the king, whose peace protects all men in his halls. And when ungoverned rage looks from a countenance which might once have been my father's, it sickens me, for he has spent his life in ridding England of berserkers. Keep from my sight until next summer, then will I put you in my battle line, since killing crazed Danes must be where your talent lies.'

'That is all I ask,' answered Edred softly. 'The chance to kill fifty-one crazed Danes and a chieftain, for the burning of Ferenthe.'

Edward pulled on his jerkin, indifferent to blood on his arm and chest, his attention caught again. This savage from the Andredsweald was treacherously dangerous as a follower, but one day might be useful. In consequence, after he had reflected a little, Edward the Atheling sent Edred a captured Danish sword as a Twelfth Night gift, a gesture which set tongues wagging afresh over the likeness between Edred and the king.

Twelfth Night was a great occasion at Winchester. It ended the Christmas season and the following day men would begin drifting home. The king also intended to leave with the dawn, riding first to Exeter and then further west to confer with the Cornwelsh. And because it marked the end of one season and the beginning of the next, Twelfth Night possessed an atmosphere all its own. Goblins and bogles rode the wind, vows were made and debts discharged, the feast more splendid than all the rest. The leading companions of the king sprawled below the raised bench where he sat, while the women settled like starlings close to the fire: among them the king's wife, a pale woman who looked close to death, and his daughter Aethelflaed, reputed to be as brave and wise as any Atheling. Later, the men would become drunk and quarrelsome, but while the king's women stayed at the feast, his stewards stood hand on sword around the walls, ready to heave troublemakers into the nearest trough.

Twelfth Night was when Edred finally ventured into the king's hall. He ached with curiosity after hearing so many tales of savoury food and drinking bouts, of rhymed songs about brave deeds and how the king sat in judgement on his bench, but even so, it was an effort to enter with the rest. His clothes looked dingy among a throng which delighted in wearing the brightest colours each could find. He was also alone among a great company of men, most of whom had long been familiar with each other. Above all, the size of the hall remained oppressive for anyone bred in huts, the crush so great he felt like a wildcat treed by baiting dogs.

He found himself wedged among boys and grooms, though he had intended to sit among the warriors; by the time he realized his mistake, it was too late. Slaves sprinted between the benches with platters and jugs of ale; every space was taken, even under the boards of the table. Soon he was dazed by light from smoking torches, half stifled by fumes which lay in swathes above his head, but at least he saw the king clearly for the first time since their meeting in the lane. Why, he is old, Edred thought, startled by thin grey hair and rutted face which surely held no likeness to him at all. After twenty years of ruling, Aelfred showed the burden of a lifetime spent pelting hither and thither trying to cobble together the tears ripped in his realm by ruinous attacks.

A serving wench edged past him holding an ale pitcher and on impulse, because he was feeling very much alone, Edred grasped her round the waste. 'You must have filled a great many horns by now. Sit with me before pouring more.'

She considered him coolly. 'If you wish, since I am tired.'

She had a clear deliberate voice which scarcely fitted sharp features and pale skin.

'Have you served long in King Aelfred's hall?' Edred pulled her to the floor between his knees, his hands groping for her breasts. He wasn't interested in her answer and only spoke from habit.

She looked up, surprised, but also passive under his hands. 'I work in a tavern by the towngate. The king has servers of his own, but the citizens of Winchester give him this feast and so my master brought me as a helper.'

'Your name?' His grip tightened cruelly as he discovered her breasts were wizened by privation.

'Roda.' She spoke as clearly as before, only her stiffness against his knee betraying pain.

'I am Edred of Ferenthe.' She had not asked. 'I have come to train as a warrior, and will join the warband in the spring.'

She nodded. Most men here would join the warband in the spring. 'I am Danish.'

Edred recoiled. 'What!'

'Danish captives are sold if they are worth a price, the rest have their necks broken on the battlefield. Our camp was over-run and I taken in the flight. We believed Wessex was vanquished and were coming here to settle.' She sounded mocking rather than regretful, and did not notice the horror on Edred's face.

He moved abruptly, swept her sprawling like offal off a platter. 'Then get back to your ale-pourings. If this was not the king's own hall I would kill you, and have but fifty Danes instead of fifty-one to slaughter for an oath I swore.' *Tomorrow, by the towngate, I will kill her*, Edred thought.

She picked herself up. 'If the king seats a Dane in honour at his feet, why not you? As for myself, I scarcely remember my own kin, except I was not beaten then.'

'The king . . . which Dane?'

Seated below him is Stykkar, son of Hasta. He was taken as a pledge when his father swore to raid no more in England.

Edred stared across the hall, blue eyes blazing, to where the king laughed at something the blond boy at his feet was saying. Stykkar looked about fifteen, an age when any Viking might be expected to stick his knife into unguarded bellies. As Edred watched in contempt, Aelfred looked up and their gaze crossed.

Although Edred had not again encountered the king since their first meeting, the halls at Winchester had buzzed with the tale of his fight with the Atheling Edward. Not because Edred nearly won – in fact, he wondered afterwards whether Edward might not have lured him into error from the start – but because the story added fresh seasoning to speculation about Edred's likeness to the king. Certainly Aelfred would have heard it, and after that involuntary flash of recognition Edred was not surprised when a royal falconer fought his way through the throng to summon him to the royal dais.

The king's table was up two steps and swept clear of the stale bread used to mop up juices, but even so Edred nearly forgot to bow because the sight of Stykkar contentedly picking his teeth made him so angry.

'Lord king,' he said, and bowed so slightly the falconer behind him hissed between his lips.

'I have been enquiring from the monks and find that twenty of my followers here in Winchester have not yet been baptized, of whom you are one.' Aelfred spoke quietly, although he knew the meaning of short bows and insolent looks better than any man. 'If you wish to serve me, then you must accept the Christian faith.'

Edred was completely astonished, having expected fury; would have welcomed fury from this Dane-loving king. 'If it is necessary, then I will accept this sprinkling,' he answered after a pause. 'I have not done so before out of respect for my grandfather, but he would not have jeered at monk-mumblings if the death of his settlement was more easily avenged as a consequence.'

Aelfred shifted in his chair, perhaps from pain but more likely because blood-anger was not as far removed from him as he would like. 'Then let me tell you a story, as a gleeman would. Some years ago there were two armies in this land. One of them ravaged far and wide, overcame those warriors who attempted to stand in its way and slaughtered the defenceless in their huts. Hope was at an end. Then, one day, that army was defeated. So what would you do as a victor on the morrow of such deliverance?'

'Kill,' answered Edred unhesitatingly. 'Kill every Viking in reach of my sword, since I understand the Lord Aelfred speaks of the Viking Great Army.'

'I let them go.'

Edred drew a furious breath. 'And so my village was burned, while these same Vikings still laughed at the king's – '

'Take care,' said Aelfred softly. 'Some things no man may say to me, and live. They received my mercy not my weakness. Guthrum the Viking was baptized and became my godson, he offered an oath of peace and I accepted it, knowing there would be times it was not kept. We cannot kill all the Vikings now settled in England, must find peace wherever we may. The second of the two armies I spoke of had already taken land on which to settle, where they will one day be regarded as Englishman. It is God's grace and also common sense which makes me turn my back on blood whenever the chance arises. Baptism offers you this grace, God grant it grows in you. Perhaps common sense may follow,' he added.

Edred bit on his tongue. If Baptism so weakened a man that

afterwards even Guthrum the Viking thought twice about raiding, then he wanted none of it; yet alone he would never slaughter the fifty-one pirates of his oath. 'I will be baptized,' he said through his teeth.

Aelfred nodded, not deceived into thinking he looked on anything except deep aversion. But if his priests always awaited a genuine heart-longing for Christ, then with most men they would wait a long time. As a Christian king, he had a duty to see his followers were baptized, exhorted and encouraged, the rest he must leave to God. Like Edred, Aelfred believed that only by taking great risks would great ends be achieved.

Edred's thoughts wandered during the long service in a cold Winchester god-house. He could not make sense of a priest gobbling Latin and disliked thinking about an unpredictable Christian god settling like a parasite into his life. Mother Earth and Ferenthe's special patron, Tiw, he understood: you offered them respect and took gifts on procession days, in return they ripened the crops in due season. If you cheated on gifts or respect then they avenged themselves until the matter was rectified. Alaric had said that in his young days the elders cut the throat of anyone adjudged guilty of incurring such vengeance, and Edred had several times wondered whether the lack of cut throats during his lifetime had caused Tiw to destroy Ferenthe.

'In the name of the Father, Son and Holy Ghost,' intoned the priest.

'In the name of the Father, Son and this ghost of theirs,' responded Edred glibly.

'The Holy Ghost,' snapped the priest, tilting his candle so it spilt hot grease on Edred's hand.

He yelped and jumped up from his knees, only to be thrust back on the floor by a brawny deacon. 'The Holy Ghost,' he mumbled resentfully, and shivered as water was shaken over him.

Once the priestly dronings finished, Edred wrung wetness from his hair and went out into the sun again: Roda had said she was enslaved in a tavern near the towngate and without quite knowing why, he had decided to drink his Christianity into oblivion there. Mercy to the Danes who live in peace, King Aelfred said.

Well, mercy then. He would not kill Roda the scrawny Dane girl, but revenge his pride on her flesh instead.

The tavern was a clay-brick hove, a withered bush hung on the pole outside to show how long the ale had been brewed, and, as Edred expected from those crackle-dry leaves, the liquid tasted sour. Roda came in carrying the pitcher he ordered with her bare legs purple from the cold, only to be cuffed aside by the tavern wife as soon as she nodded to Edred in distant recognition. 'Men bargain with me, not you.'

'How much?' Edred touched the copper pieces the king gave to his followers on the day of their baptism.

The woman cackled. 'For a mating?'

The ale is not worth paying for. Two pieces for the girl.'

'Three.'

'Two.' He tossed the fragments on the floor, and ducked out of the entry. 'Roda!'

She came, hoping for a short time of warmth and the reward of food, her long hair tangled and her breasts showing through torn cloth. Edred felt a tremor of distaste then, which was both more and less than hate, since anything he did to Roda could not be worse than her life in the towngate tavern.

The tavern-wife screeched when she realized this was not to be a quick coupling on the floor, but in Winchester there was nowhere for a runaway slave to hide and the countryside was ironbound by frost, so her curses were more for show than fear of being robbed. The girl would be back tomorrow.

Edred slowed his pace, wrestling with an unexpected problem: where to find shelter for them both. He could not lie with Roda in the street and would not in that old hag's tavern, yet now she had followed when he called he immediately wanted her too badly for long hesitation. Around him the iced-mud streets were filled with horses, men and oxen floundering against flimsy wattle walls, everyone's pace adjusted to the slowest. The square in front of the church was filled by cries and colour, people packed together with scarcely room to bargain: clay-daubed house walls, stone and chalk town ramparts stained by the weather, timber halls and churches. Monks, housecarls, market women, a glimpse of the king returning from one of his journeys, head turned as he listened to some complaint.

'You can't come into the king's courtyard where I sleep.' Edred spoke his thoughts aloud, turning in irritation when Roda failed to reply. She was struggling to pass some pedlars, and when she reached him he saw just how sick she looked. He almost decided to leave her then, now, at once, so she would die in the frost that night. She was too feeble to be worthy of a warrior's revenge.

He rubbed his nose; wanting, not wanting to leave her. 'Can you walk?'

'I am walking.' No hesitation and her words accompanied by a look which nailed him to the ground.

'I shall have to hide you in the king's stable for the night.' If they could pass the guard, there would be grain to chew and warmth there to revive her. He had meant to leave her, all the same.

The outer yard of the king's hall was easy to pass now that many of Aelfred's followers were leaving Winchester, but the stables lay beyond a guarded gate. 'I will pick a quarrel with the guard.' Edred added, this being the most natural diversion to occur to one of his temperament. 'Take some firewood from the stack and go past bent under the load while their attention is elsewhere. There is a climbing pole to the stable loft.'

Roda nodded, lips tightly gripped on weakness.

The guard was huddled round a fire when Edred sauntered near, one of them looked up, then grinned. 'The king's devil, fresh baptized and ready to answer for his sins.'

'What do you mean?' Demanded Edred.

The man shook frost from his beard. 'Why, everyone knows that an Andredsweald savage will never make a Christian. Yet you resemble the king, so I expect the priests will never tire of reminding us how good and evil lie in a man's spirit instead of in his looks.

But Edred was weary of sneers and besides, had come to quarrel. He would have quarrelled anyway, but gnawed his lips in unfeigned fury and threw himself at the guard, so all five of them went down in a heap together. Edred received a blow which made him spit out a tooth, but was back on his feet at once. The man who had sneered stood too, and immediately they began pummelling each other while the rest of the guards yelled encouragement, rushing head on so their skulls crunched together, kicking and biting with their faces distorted by rage and bruises. The only trouble was that neither knew how to end matters cleanly, and they only fell apart when their breath ran out.

'At least you know how to battle like a Christian.' Conceded Edred's opponent as soon as he could speak.

'And you like an Atheling.' Answered Edred, squeezing his nose in an attempt to stop the flow of blood.

They all laughed, since everyone knew the Andredswealder had been worsted by Edward and they liked a man who did not bear a grudge once a fight was finished.

So they sat down to drink together and in this strange manner Edred made his first true friends in the Wessex warband. Wulfric had been his opponent and he and the other four all came from villages close to Winchester. They had served Aelfred for several years, some of their battles fought as far away as Kent, which was now dependent on Wessex. 'The king says that unless we stand together the Danes will chew us up separately,' said Wulfric. 'And Kent men fight well, although I never served with anyone from your forest before. Like you, I suppose they could learn how to fight in a battle line if only they had the sense to come.

Edred forgot about Roda for a long time because it was so pleasant to be accepted as equal around a fire, but then the guard changed he remembered her, and climbed to the stable loft. He found her curled up where warmth from the horses could just be felt between whistling draughts but she was in a pitiful state her body so chilled she seemed on the edge of death. He lay beside her, hearing her breathing falter as cold tightened its grip and laid rime across her eyes, even he had to blink to stop his sight from clouding. Several times the sounds hesitated, stopped, wearily began again: Edred looked at her in the light of slashed-ice moonbeams cutting through the reed roof and saw she was smiling slightly as if glad to die. He reached out and touched her cheek, drew back his hand, touched her again. Strange how she continued to live when nearly as cold as death itself, she still seemed ugly to him, but emaciation made her lips look enticingly enormous in her pinched face, her cheeks seem as smooth as bone.

Edred drew up his knees and rolled over, his face sweating into straw. He was heated by lust yet chilled by Roda's bloodlessness, clumsily began piling straw on her body before crawling back under the heap to use his body to bring her such heat as he could.

He was pleased when he woke to find her still alive. He had not expected to feel pleased and preferred not to think too closely about why he did. Instead, he slid down to milk one of the mares and after Roda had drunk a little of the warm liquid her breathing seemed to strengthen. He remembered how the moon had brought invitation to her lips and wondered whether it would take long for her to put some flesh on her bones, his taste being for women with round breasts and bellies which fitted into his hand.

When dawn came he crawled out of the straw and considered more dispassionately what he could see of Roda. Her hair was coppery, a colour considered unlucky in the Andredsweald but not unbecoming in a Dane; the only other quality he could find to praise in her – and why should he search to praise? – was pride, which was lost while she lay sick.

While she still slept, he went himself to eat in the Great Hall, where any of Aelfred's followers could share bread and dip it in the savoury messes kept bubbling on the hearth. Even at so early an hour, Aelfred was holding counsel with some priests and eldermen while men woke and shook out their cloaks around him, but then many matters went on at the same time there.

Edward the Atheling was standing by the door, choosing men to ride with him on some errand to the Thames, when his eye fell on Edred. 'Can you ride a distance, Edred of Ferenthe?'

'Of course' answered Edred, although he had only ridden oxen.

Edward stared at him, hands on his hips, eyes narrowed, 'I think not, unless swineherds live better in Andredsweald than Wessex. Go with the king instead, it is time you cooled your cravings in a fight. He is taking a small warband west, where pirates are raiding the coast of Devon. We will see how you enjoy a Wessex fast march in winter, when wise men stay by their hearths.'

'I shall endure anything, so long as there is blood at the end of it.'

'Good. You will learn most things better from my father than from me.'

Edred thought this a very strange and feeble thing to say, since Edward was infinitely stronger than the king. 'You taught me how to fight a Viking axeman.'

'Aye, perhaps. The king leaves Winchester when the bells sound Terce. Carry a spear as well as your sword, and bread for three days.

Edred was wildly excited at being included in a warband at last, and ran all the way to the outer enclosure where his few possessions lay: pouch, spare cloth, an old pelt given by Aneirin when he saw him shivering one night. He drew a spear from the smith and bread from the bakery, its warmth reminding him of Roda so he scampered for the stables, knowing Terce must be close.

She was drowsy but awake, sat up when he gabbled at her about marching west with the king. 'A safe journey, then,' she said when he had finished. 'What shall I do while you are gone?'

'I have brought bread, and by tomorrow you will be strong enough to find food for yourself.' Women always harked back to their own affairs, he thought impatiently. As if they mattered when set beside the Wessex warband.

Roda looked at him with eyes he now saw were grey, and somehow he found that look hard to face. 'I do not want to return to the tavern, but if I live, I will wait there for your return.' But because she wanted to hide her terror being left alone again in Winchester, he saw only haughtiness and went feeling glad to be rid of her.

The fifty men Aelfred was taking west travelled in a tight cluster, a few scouts out on the flanks and the king riding ahead with half a dozen close companions, so he could visit thanes and fortifications on the way.

The journey was harder than anything Edred could have anticipated. He thought of himself as strong and had toughened further with his training during the winter, but he had never attempted to travel any distance at high speed. The men trotted while one of them counted paces in a high drone, at the call of three times one hundred they paused briefly, then moved off at a fast walk until the next stretch of unbroken ground was reached – which might be half a day or only a single hill away – then came the dreaded trot again.

'We could not move at this speed in summer when the fyrd is with us,' said Wulfric at the third breath-halt of the day. 'Peasants with sickles would soon seize any excuse to drop behind, and disappear back to their clearings.'

They camped at dusk, which came mercifully early in dirty winter weather, and King Aelfred rode in soon after, though how he knew which tumbledown barn they occupied Edred could not guess. The food was meagre, dried meat off the housecarls' saddlebows and some of the bread each man carried, but there was little complaint. Everyone was exhausted and all they wanted was to rest. Only the group around the king continued to talk amongst themselves, a priest with a high thin voice reading from parchment during the pauses. As if parchment mattered, thought Edred, annoyed to discover that Aelfred, whom he regarded as old, could still talk when he himself could scarcely find strength to chew. But of course the king had ridden and not run a full day's journey.

'We must be close to the raiders now,' Wulfric said, when they camped the third night in a cattle pen.

'Will these raiders be Danish?' demanded Edred eagerly.

'What's the difference? A pirate is a pirate whatever land he hails from. I've forgotten how many seasons I've fought through burned-out villages and marched past gutted creatures rotting in the mud, but finding I'm tiring of it at last. My own hut in unravaged country is what I crave now.'

'Why stay then.'

Wulfric gave a sharp bark of laughter. 'So where is that unravaged country free of heathen? King Aelfred has fought twenty years and his brother and father before him, yet still we are not rid of them. He is mortal weary of it too, but my hut and his Latin must wait for our sons' sons to enjoy.'

Edred did not sleep immediately that night. He had sharpened his sword and lay holding it to his body as if it was a woman, thinking of the Danes. How very far from Andredsweald he had come to kill them, and it seemed that tomorrow his tally might begin. As usual, voices were still murmuring around the king. Edred began to listen through the snores of his companions, and was astonished to discover they talked about laws instead of tactics for the morrow.

'Aye, but a settled Dane must be reckoned equal to an Englishman,' observed the king, as if this was commonplace rather than outrageous. 'Forty silver pennies is fair in this matter, and it makes no difference the defaulter was a Dane.'

'The case is hard.' Objected an elderman in the harsh accents of the east. 'In London most merchants are Mercian. They acknowledge you as overlord, but –'

'Since they lost their kingdom to the Danes and had to seek protection from Wessex.' Interjected someone amid laughter.

'The law is sworn and scribed.' Repeated Aelfred. 'Mercia and Wessex are English lands with no distinction between them in wergild or service. If the settled Danes accept our laws and begin to think as Englishmen, then we gain good subjects. Forty silver pennies is my judgement in this case, against the Londoners. See that their elderman is informed.'

'Aye, my lord.' Answered a clerk. 'There is also the dispute between the ferrymen of Hamtun on the Solent which must be settled.'

'You are thane of those parts, Ailuned.' Aelfred turned to an elderly warrior with a dyed and plaited beard. 'I heard it was a case of merchants rather than ferrymen.'

Ailuned slapped his thigh. 'That's about it, my lord. The charges in the Solent have trebled since last year, but only newcomers are milked of the charge and by my reckoning the ferrymen divide their gains with the merchants of the town.'

'Ingenious, but against what is right,' commented Aelfred.

'Sinful,' interrupted a priest frowning.

'Aye, which is for the priests of Hamtun to correct. My laws are for me to enforce. And since in the matter of ferrymen's charges I

71

cannot recall a precise fine to fit my purpose, I will order an inquiry into the taxes paid by Hamtun merchants. A new assessment may change their minds quicker than fear of my judgement seat in Winchester.'

There was general laughter, and after the flurry died down the chiefs settled to sleep, leaving Aelfred and a priest poring over some writings. They spoke a language Edred could not understand so instead he studied the king through slitted lids, puzzling over why so unlikely a man could command a respect which went before him like banners in the wind. Why, even the Lord Edward, who was past the age when warriors began to challenge their sires for mastery, apparently failed to cherish such a natural ambition. As for Aelfred himself, he must be under a curse that he should waste good sleeping time gabbling strange tongues on the night before a battle. He looked worn out but at the same time alert and interested, chin on hand, answering the priest sometimes but listening mostly, as if it was a relief to listen when at other times he must always take the lead.

Edred slept with the drone of Latin still in his ears, and woke to find everything in a bustle, the king questioning a peasant blubbering in the doorway.

'The pirates are ashore half a day's journey down the estuary.' Said Wulfric in Edred's ear. The thane of these people gathered some Devonsaetas to oppose them, and was defeated. He thought he faced a single ship's crew and discovered that several had sailed in company. Now most of the men from ten villages are dead.'

'How many heathen to a ship?' Edred slid his sword through his fingers lovingly.

'Fifty, perhaps. It depends how great a reputation is held by the pirate chief. Those famed for their luck find it easy to stuff any craft full of men.'

'So many?' exclaimed Edred. 'Must we then wait long for more Devonsaetas to join us?'

'We shall not wait,' answered Wulfric indignantly. 'Fifty housecarls can rout twice one hundred pirates, who are interested only in loot.'

Dawn was breaking as they moved off and this time Aelfred

marched with them instead of riding far and wide, since only an imprudent man came mounted to battle. Horses were easily startled and the warrior who must wrestle with reins in the middle of a fight was likely to have his leg chopped by an axe.

They passed a blackened village without seeing any sign of life, though the trees around it were too wet to burn. Then scattered farmsteads, also burned and deserted. A child lay beside the path, bubbling bloody froth, and one of the men cut its throat as he passed. 'Poor mite,' said Wulfric. A night all alone while drowning in its blood. The priests say we may only kill in battle but have learned to look elsewhere when we follow a Viking trail.'

They marched on, steadily now instead of fast, watchers ahead and on either flank.

Edred saw the gleam of water through some trees, and blinked. He had heard travellers tell how pirates sailed across water as though they used an open trail, but he had never imagined so great an expanse of wetness. Rain slanted across it in gleaming shafts of light and waves snapped angrily; the Vikings instantly became more filled with menace because they could easily pass so great a barrier.

Suddenly, there was a flurry ahead. Shouts and crashing in the undergrowth as one of the watchers came pelting back. Aelfred called something, the bellow of it utterly unlike the priestly whisperings around last night's hearth, and Wulfric's hand fastened on Edred's arm, urging him to follow some men peeling off to the left.

'We're going away from the battle!' Edred cried agonized.

'We make sure there is one,' grunted Wulfric, crashing, leaping, forcing his way through tangled scrub.

Running now, led by a thane called Ethelred. Scramble up a bank, race through some woodland; Edred only wished he knew what was happening. Then everyone stopped, bumping and barging into each other, the word passed back for silence.

Move forward again, Edred aware of soaking clothes and red heat in his lungs. A ripple of movement as swords were drawn, knives loosened in belts. A whispered command to lie and crawl the last stretch forward. They had reached a bluff above the shore, an unsacked village lying just beneath, the figures of pirates running to form a battle line as the men who had remained with Aelfred emerged from trees beyond the village. They looked very few, the king's rank clearly exposed by his richer cloak and decorated shield. The companions around him had shields too, the peasants who had joined them during the morning only scythes, pikes and knives bound on poles. The pirates yelled when they realized they outnumbered the Saxons, and how great a chief they would slaughter when they won. Certainly they would not expect the king himself so far west in winter, but when they stripped his body the news would flash from shore to shore: the scourge of Danes is dead and England delivered up for easy plucking.

Edred was inflamed with fury that he might miss such a feast of killing, and but for Wulfric would have charged alone down the bluff. 'Patience, savage,' said Wulfric, grinning. 'Only the unskilful amongst us will tally less than five Vikings once the word is given.'

The pirates' very first charge bulged Aelfred's warband ominously inward, and several warriors fell. But Aelfred had chosen to fight at the wood's edge because the ground made outflanking more difficult: each housecarl had to fight ten enemies, but in succession rather than simultaneously.

There was a swirl, a chaotic welter, as the Vikings realized this and began to change the direction of their thrust, and this was the moment Thane Ethelred rose to his feet and chipped his hand in the air. 'Now!'

Only twenty men had followed his encircling movement to the bluff, but they drove into the struggle like a bolt out of the stormy sky. Edred felt wildly excited yet perfectly cool, partly because it never occurred to him that he would do other than kill a great many Danes. A huge pirate turned to face him, axe raised to strike and with spittle flecking his beard, but Edred had no difficulty at all in sinking his sword into the man's soft throat before the axe could descend.

One.

'Keep your sword low!' yelled Wulfric, sweeping his as if he was a woodsman clearing nettles. And as he struggled to clear his blade from bones and pipes, Edred understood the dangers of stabbing strokes in battle.

A tremor ran through the pirate line as each Viking struggled to turn and face this new attack. Time flashed past in blood and swordstroke, was briefly enlarged by terror before flashing past again. While he was fresh Ered's sword flicked lightning swift, every part of him stronger, more agile than ever in his life. But once the Vikings realized they were trapped and began to fight with all the fury of their kind, he soon felt himself begin to tire. It became more difficult to dodge those deadly two-handed swipes and he could no longer remember whether three or four Vikings had already fallen to his blade.

Suddenly, and not a moment too soon, it ended. Edred realized that the man he was about to strike was a Saxon grinning behind his shield: the two lines of Aelfred's warband had met and the pirates were wreckage beneath their feet. A few tenacious knots of them were still fighting but would be easily speared now their fellows were routed.

'Were they Danes?' was Edred's first thought when his breath returned.

Wulfric wiped his sword clean on a pirate beard. 'From their clothes, yes. We shall not know for certain until we find and burn their boats, for Danish skill in timber is unmistakable, but I would chance a wager on it.'

This was all that remained to make Edred's first battle perfect: if the pirates had been Frankish, he would have enjoyed his blooding but found little satisfaction in it. As it was, he joined three others in butchering the wounded, which put his score at twenty-two on this first day of his vengeance for Ferenthe, although he felt somewhat shamefaced at tallying these throat-cuttings with his battle dead.

Aelfred stayed the rest of the winter in the west, receiving the thanks of the Devonsaetas, parleying with the Cornwelsh and chasing off marauders who withdrew too fast to be caught. In all this time Edred failed to set eyes on another pirate, and he was glad when Aelfred led his warband back to Wessex for the new campaigning season about to open in the east.

Then, only a day's march short of Winchester, a messenger brought news that Irish berserkers were raiding up the Severn. So, weary, chafed and hungry, they were forced into the trotting, hill –consuming pace again at the very time when they had been looking forward to Easter ease, only to find that the raiders had ridden for the Thames, carrying their loot with them. And when at last they turned back for Winchester again, another appeal for help sent them scampering all over Berkshire for a week.

Wulfric seemed well satisfied by such hard labour, since, as he pointed out, the heathen had each time been thrown out of Wessex without being able to feel that their peril had been worthwhile, but Edred had never considered that service in Aelfred's warband would entail such privation for so little fighting. 'I came so I might kill Danes in vengeance for Ferenthe,' he said, when at last they were headed back again for Winchester. 'I did not come in order to be sent running from one hill to the next and never see an enemy at the end of it.'

Wulfric stroked his beard and looked thoughtful. 'We fight so that at the end of it we may never see a Dane again.'

'But we don't fight, do we?' shouted Edred, exasperated. 'In Winchester I will ask to join the Atheling Edward's warband for the summer, since the King of Wessex is too old to thirst after blood as a true warrior should.'

'The King of the English,' snapped Wulfric. 'That is what men begin to call him now and with reason, nor will he cease to fight until the whole of his realm is safe.'

'He will, because he will soon die.' Retorted Edred, and thought: the sooner he dies the better.

At this reply Wulfric became very angry and would not answer, beyond cursings for which any priest who heard them would have enforced a penance.

Winchester, at last. When the burgh came in sight Edred felt almost as if he was coming home, until the men around him began speaking about wives and newborn sons awaiting their return. Then Edred hated this stockade full of churches and halls, the rich ploughlands curving treeless from the river. Others might speak fine phrases about England and the English but if he survived the fulfilment of his oath, then he would return to the forest he understood. Meanwhile, the only welcome he could expect was from Roda, an ale-house whore as uninviting as a goat.

'Come to my hearth if you wish.' Said Wulfric after they had been paid the bronze pieces which were their due. 'It is less than a day's journey and you are a comrade after my own heart, although a barbarian in all matters except fighting.'

But Edred refused saying that he had journeyed far enough.

He spent the next two days idling about Winchester's streets, telling himself that he need not visit the stable loft. He wanted a woman badly, having had no time for such matters since the warband left Exeter, but Roda would have returned to her tavern, or starved, long ago. Besides she was Danish.

Each time his thoughts reached this word he was filled by a strange and amorous hatred, and his head rang with the refrains of loathing: Roda the toad-faced, Danish wolf-whelp, spawn of blood-drinkers. Yet the longer desire fed on itself, the more it tormented him. He had scarcely thought of her during the months he had been away and would not think of her again once he left Winchester with the warbands; but for these few days he could think of no one else. The blood beat in his veins and he became like a wild bull blundering about the town, roaring to himself about how he must not go in search of her. When he passed the king's stable for what must have been the hundredth time, his head cleared; he would look if she was there, why not?

But she wasn't there, and any memory that for a single night he had felt softly towards her immediately vanished.

Next day was Holy Friday, and Edred spent the time which was expected of him on his knees, his wonder reserved for the many candles burning in the church. In such matters Christ was a god who allowed no trifling, and that pleased Edred since he did not respect half-heartedness. St Peter, he thought, and fixed his eyes on the nearest statue, instinctively selecting a chief companion to receive his petition: I have many Danes and a chief still to kill. Put me this summer in a warband which will do more than march, for I do not see why I should waste a season simply to keep Wessex safe. Tentatively, he touched the figure's feet before he left, and vowed, I shall never pray to you again unless you give me Danes. He also touched his sword-hilt, since he had little confidence in saints, the name of one particular Dane still sticking annoyingly in his mind.

He saw her almost at once.

He was pushing past some men hammering timber booths for the Easter market when he glimpsed the turn of her head, and thin shoulders under a yoked burden.

'Roda!' he shouted, and ran to spin her round to face him. 'I looked in the stable and you were gone.'

She regarded him coolly, the same level stare he remembered. 'I would have been devoured by rats if I'd stayed there any longer.'

Edred shrugged and tightened his lips. Against his will he would have said something pleasant, now he felt repelled again. 'You said you would wait for me, if you lived.'

'Did I? I must have wandered in my mind. In truth I remember little from the time of my fever.'

She infuriated him beyond measure; one moment soft and the next as unrelenting as raiders on the prowl. 'I remembered.'

'And I live easier without remembering.' She certainly knew that once away from Winchester he never gave her plight another thought.

May her tongue rot in her throat, he thought furiously, wanting her so badly he could scarcely prevent himself from pinning her to a wall. 'Will you come with me?'

'Now?'

'Of course, now. I can't break Holy Friday vigil once the king's gates are closed.'

She laughed, a sunblaze of delight so she was no longer ugly. 'You mean that a vigil only suits those who enjoy Christian piety.'

'I mean that outside the gate neither your tavern-woman nor my king knows what we do.'

She stared at his thick –muscled figure, those disturbing blue eyes above. Understood better than he how rancorous a relationship theirs was likely to be. Yet when he turned and led the way towards the gate, she followed. Life had been so hard for her that she craved, just once, a man who stayed all night and woke remembering who she was. Surely it was very little to desire, and more than she had expected to receive.

There were turf bothies scattered around the burgh-fields outside Winchester, where husbandmen slept at seed and harvest time. Because the floor of the one Edred chose was wet, Roda insisted on carrying in some bracken before allowing him to take her: strange how the instinct to please a man survived so many barren years. 'Anyway I'm the one who will lie most in wetness,' she pointed out. If he would only smile then perhaps she might begin to hope.

But he stared at earth as if he neither understood nor cared for anything she said, and threw her down before the bracken was properly spread. Whatever hope she had harboured for this coupling flickered out; it was simply a task like any other. He was urgent and she half-starved; she had been foolish to consider hope.

Roda woke early, and since she possessed – survived because she forced herself to possess – a nature which looked for the best in everything, she lay and enjoyed the quietness. Outside the bothy the birds were rousing into dawn-song, and the softness of spring was in the air. She eased her body away from Edred, treasuring peace and not wanting him to wake, but, too soon, he reached for her. His hand moving drowsily from her breast to her hair, twisting the strands around thick knuckles. Half-asleep, instinct did not warn him she was Danish and Roda understood that Edred too was lonely; half-tamed, un-christian and, like herself, only valued for his muscle.

If she could only make him want her for other reasons than revenge, perhaps he would take her with him when he left. Roda feared neither Edred nor any other man, but loathed the day of her slavery more than the one before. So, when he reached for her she moved close, and touched him softly. 'My Lord, it is cold, lying alone in the dawn.'

He grunted and, still far from wakefulness, moved his head to ease the way for her caresses. Roda laughed, feeling in him a surprise she put down to astonishment that a Dane could please him, but which in fact was deeper rooted. Edred had never before considered that women might be tender, only lustful, frightened or necessary: in their hut in Ferenthe, Guthlac and Wynfyrtha had quarrelled constantly and struggled together in the night-straw like hounds fighting over a carcass.

Then wakefulness could no longer be held away, as he remembered all that Roda briefly made him forget. He sighed and stood, tumbling her aside like an importunate bitch. 'Tie some bracken into a bundle and I will pass you through the gate as a woman bringing bedding for the king's horses.'

'What if I should wait here until dark and then set out to seek my Danish kinsmen settled in the east?' Roda stared up at him, bitterly disappointed.

'You are a slave,' he answered, astonished. 'I would cut your throat before I allowed you to cheat a Saxon master.'

Roda had often considered fleeing Winchester, but the world was harsh to women lacking kin and no matter where she went, she would be enslaved again. A hearth and kindred of her own was the only sure escape; as she stood, she looked at Edred speculatively again. She did not like him and he hated her, but he represented the best chance so far to cross her path.

They heard the raucous sounds of Winchester before they crossed the outer ditch. The Easter fair lured merchants from far and wide, tempted warriors to come early for the spring muster, but there was more to this sound than crowds filling narrow lanes with the bargainings of good fellowship. Edred lengthened his stride as he grasped the meaning of what he heard, for these were the sounds of war. Deep baying horns and the clash of armourers' mallets, the pound of feet and voices bawling for order.

'What can have happened?' panted Roda. She was too poorly nourished to match his pace and had already dropped her burden of bracken.

'How can I know?' Edred spied Wulfric in the throng. 'Wulfric! What news?'

Wulfric kicked his way over, his face split by a grin of greeting. 'A Great Army is loose in England again. Word came in the night; Hasta has brought many hundreds of Vikings with him from Frankland, made alliance with those already settled here, and together they ravage far and wide.'

'Hasta? Hasta the sire of Stykkar, the whelp King Aelfred keeps as pledge for his kindred's oath to observe the peace?'

Wulfric nodded. 'His throat will be cut before nightfall.'

Which was some satisfaction, Edred supposed. He clapped Wulfric on the shoulder. 'How fortunate you came to celebrate Easter Feast in Winchester. If you had waited in your village, you would have missed the battle.'

But Wulfric pulled a face and confessed that he had married a wife, and had only come to enjoy the fair. 'A summer of skirmishing is all very well, but this is a Great Army again, which will only be defeated after several seasons of slaughter.

At this, the woman at his side set up a great wail and began hammering her forehead with her fists, so Edred felt disgusted just to look at her. 'You will never turn your back on the warband now!' he demanded.

Wulfric shook his head. 'I have served King Aelfred too long to desert just when his realm is split apart again.' Then he added to his wife, 'Go to my village, little one, and I will return there at the end of the season if I live. What of your woman, Edred? She could travel with Frifwith and wait with her; although it is not far, the journey would be safer for two women than for one alone.'

But Edred shook his head. 'She is Danish and another man's slave besides. Wulfric let us go at once to the king's hall; Christ's blood, surely he cannot be so pious as to waste two more days in East masses before marching east.'

Wulfric touched his woman's belly, the parting warrior's gesture towards the hope of a child to remember him if he died, and followed on Edred's heels. Soon, he became more cheerful. A woman out of sight was a woman forgotten, when all around them the king's courtyards were choked with warriors eagerly sharpening swords and burnishing linked mail. Others stood with their heads together, talking.

'Look at them,' said Edred, grinding his teeth in fury. 'If I were king I would have the warband out of here by nightfall, on the edge of my sword if necessary.'

Wulfric did not answer, as the crowd about them began to surge and split, bearing them with it to the king's hall. Aelfred stood at one end conferring with the elders gathered about him. He was bareheaded and wore a Lenten tunic of sackcloth, although at other times King Aelfred shared his people's love of bright colours.

The king turned and a single war-horn sounded, demanding silence, and immediately the shouting died away, everyone knew already that this was no trifling crisis but a threat to the realm itself. Then Aelfred moved to the edge of the dais; his face was calm and freshly shaved, his hands relaxed on the plain leather of his belt, blue eyes level: crisis was there to be defeated. This is a man who sees a lifetime's work in ruins and is undaunted, thought Edred grudgingly. Perhaps I, too, could follow him without counting the cost.

The horn brayed again, and Aelfred spoke. 'Two days ago a Danish Great Army returned to England after ten years of peace.' He smiled, eyes pausing here and there as smiles leaped in response to his. 'Such peace as was left by raiders we harried from barn and cornfield. Now we face a Great Army again, an army which has scraped all Frankland bare and must come here before they starve amid the ruin they have made. This army has allies among the Danes long settled under our peace in East Anglia and Northumbria. Half of this Great Army landed on the South Saxon shore –'

Ferenthe, thought Edred. May they spew on its ashes as they pass.

' – the other in North Kent, where they await their East Anglian kinsmen.' His glance moved from face to face as if he called each by name.' 'There lies our chance. We shall place ourselves between these parts of Hasta's army and defeat them, part by part. We march at once, and by God's grace shall reach our post before Hasta knows we're there.'

One of the priests flapped his arms in protest, a protest Aelfred answered so all could hear, and accept his judgement. 'We will keep Easter mass as good Christians should, but not in Winchester, God is no better served here than beneath His sky. We march at once.'

The protester squawked some further dissent, the other priests stared mournfully at the rafters. Aelfred merely nodded to his horn-blower, the sound dismissing a hurtling mob from hall to courtyard where each must find his weapons, shield and food in a press so great it threatened to flatten the stockade walls.

'You said the king wouldn't leave before tomorrow's mass,' yelled Wulfric over a dozen heads.

'You feared it too,' Edred shouted back, but to himself decided that in the hands of a chief who knew his trade, less of this Christianity was left to chance and priests than he had thought. And from that day onward he accepted with better grace some of its more disagreeable disciplines.

Fewer than six hundred men followed Aelfred out of Winchester, there were the great thanes and their followers, the housecarls and landless warriors like Edred who slept in the king's courtyard, and also a company of Winchester burghers, who regarded Aelfred as one of their own and understood that he needed men, any men, and quickly, to face two Danish armies.

On their headlong march eastwards, others came. By messenger and word of mouth rumour spread like a flash-fire across the south country: all that we have won is nearly lost and England likely to fall to the Danes at last. But England was the word they used, not the South Ridge people, the kin of Raeda or the Mercian Folk, and after twenty years of fierce endeavour, of generosity and cool judgings, it meant enough for men everywhere to abandon unsown fields and hasten to join their king.

When Aelfred halted his followers to take Easter mass, they had been travelling with only marching rests through a day and a night. A tough-looking bishop who had kept up with them spoke the mass, lingering on the prayers and fastening those who shuffled on weary knees with a knife-point gaze. Edred stared across to where Aelfred knelt, quite still, although he must be as weary as his followers. His face closed in devotion, his shoulders bowed. A king must kneel and a priest must prate, the king will do while the priest still prates. Edred grinned at his fancy, caught the bishop's scowl on him and hastily closed his eyes.

Throughout the following night Edred sensed Andredsweald coming closer. He could not see it since the night was black but it was there, and when the sun came up he looked down on trees as far as he could see. By nightfall they were close enough to Kent for Aelfred to be satisfied he had reached a good muster point, and even as his men flung themselves on the ground to rest, messengers brought the latest news: the Danes were ravaging along the South Saxon and Kentish shores but as yet showed no urgency to join the two parts of their army.

In two and a half days of gut-wrenching effort, although they were still very few, King Aelfred's warband had placed itself between its enemies.

They rested a day and then moved south, towards what was said to be the smaller force of the two. By then Aelfred had taken off his Lenten sackcloth and arrayed himself in a colourful tunic with cross-strapped belt and garterings of dyed leather. A king fought where men could see him, though his realm was ruined if he died: Edward the Atheling had already moved north to watch Hasta's army, leaving with the king perhaps seven or eight hundred warriors of all qualities, because as more men joined him others faltered with the punishing pace. Within a week their strength would greatly increase, but to wait now would sacrifice all the advantages of surprise.

They moved off at dusk, led by natives from the southern swamps of Andredsweald whom Aelfred knew from his past journeyings. No part of his realm had been left unvisited for long, and out of his arduous travellings were woven loyalties which now withstood the test of terror. Moving by night was another of Aelfred's tricks. Christ vanquished darkness, or so he said; let heathen Danes carouse while they wait for the day, we will use the night to hide how few we are.

Edred relished every moment of that march. No one crept more stealthily or muffled his sword more thoroughly than he, nor felt more filled with anticipation, and before dawn the warband was in a position to overlook the Danish encampment. Edred could see little to suggest alert guards, heard shouts and revelling from around fires crumbling palely in the dawn: he was incapable of counting numbers but reckoned there must be more men here than inhabited the whole burgh of Winchester. Away to his right came a buzzard's call and the warband drew swords, then began to trot, leaping tufts and bushes. They came very close before some hounds gave tongue and a guard yelled in alarm, immediately Aelfred's war-horns brayed in response and the first volley of arrows swept overhead.

Whooping, the Saxons surged into the invaders, who split like a kicked bee-swarm to furious defence. But surprise had been complete and many of the Danes were so drink-stupid that in places the killing was easy. Edred speared a naked man snoring sprawled across a girl, and leaped their bodies to knock another warrior flying even as he shook his axe in defiance. A swipe with his sword severed neck from shoulders before the man recovered his balance, then Edred joined the wild hunt after fugitives through the camp. As he overhauled one, a black-browed Viking rushed at him bellowing; Edred's sword bounced off the pirate's unlaced mail and he was very quickly fighting for his life, until, quite unexpectedly, his enemy sank on his knees spitting blood. Wulfric shouted then about how he had broken his sword driving it under such well-protected ribs. 'This is the best night's sport I have enjoyed in years,' he added. 'There is nothing to beat a well-sprung ambush, after all.' And he rushed off, leaving Edred to reflect that at least Wulfric had learned a cure for the gloom induced by marrying a wife.

Afterwards everyone agreed that it was indeed the best fight they could remember, and one which would long be rhymed among the great deeds of their people. Many Danes escaped in the confusion but more had been killed, and this part of the Great Army would henceforth behave as raiders always behaved, destructively, but not as a single force.

Only twenty of Aelfred's men had been killed or wounded and after resting a day on the battlefield, the survivors piled the dead into a pyre and set fire to it. 'The Kentish Great Army will hear of our victory here,' Aelfred said, after he had praised his followers' courage. 'We may outwit them if we are skilful, but shall not take them unaware again. So let their watchers see this beacon of our coming, and know what fear is.'

Next day they turned north again, and Edred looked about him eagerly, trying to see some landmark he recognized. But one tree-covered ridge was much like another, only Ferenthe so different that he could never mistake it.

'You are silent,' said Wulfric after most of the day had passed and they still marched, almost asleep on their feet.

'This is my country,' answered Edred.

'A plough and a woman, a fire in winter and children to tell of your deeds after your death. In his own country there are few men who do not think about such things,' agreed Wulfric.

'Yet men are happiest of all in battle. Last night we agreed that never in our lives would we be so well content again.'

'A measure to everything,' answered Wulfric, laughing. Like all the warband he was taut and eager now, a bowstring in King Aelfred's hand. 'We all yearn for a change of pleasures.'

'Next year when we have cleared the pirates into the sea, you can return home with honour and weave ballads behind the plough.'

But Wulfric pointed out that Edred had been fortunate so far in seeing Vikings only when they were surprised. 'It will take half a dozen seasons at least to clear out a Great Army. If I am alive at the end of it, then will I be happy never to lift a sword again. But whatever some men say, if the king had killed Stykkar the time would not have been shortened.'

'He has not yet killed Hasta's son, who was his hostage?' demanded Edred, aghast. 'The Danish whelp still lives?'

The king sent him under guard to Wareham before we left Winchester, to protect his life from murder, so he said.'

Edred could not speak, he felt so bitterly betrayed. 'A chief who spares a forsworn life is not worthy,' he said at last, and after a few more paces, stood still. He could not follow such a poor-spirited leader any further, must tread his own path even if it meant throwing himself berserker at the Danes.

When he explained this, Wulfric took him by the shoulders, exclaiming that the warband needed every sword and what the king did in such matters was his own affair. They stood by the path with their swords half drawn and quarrelling fiercely while the rest of the warband tramped past. Warriors quarrelled easily and the dispute was no affair of theirs.

It was Aneirin, the king's steward bringing up the rear who kicked them apart. 'Haven't you enough enemies to fight, when there are five thousand Danes waiting a short march north?' he demanded. 'Get back on the path and remember the king has ordered silence.'

'I shall not follow Aelfred any further,' answered Edred fiercely.

Aneirin's fist cracked against his beard, so he spat out blood. 'The likeness you bear to the king does not make you his kin, who alone dare to speak his name untitled.'

'The likeness is chance alone, and I am glad it is so. I would not spare a forsworn hostage as this false king has done, and bring ill fortune on all who followed me.'

Iron fingers fastened on Edred's throat and Aneirin's knee slammed into his belly. Some long time later Edred recovered his breath, he discovered his hands were tied and two of Aneirin's spearmen were bustling him through the warband. Had they not been holding him so tightly he would several times have fallen; when at last they hurled him sprawling on the ground, he grasped through his echoing senses that Aneirin was recounting his defiance to the king. He will not hang or hamstring me, Edred thought scornfully. Aelfred will judge softly and expect mercy to dampen rage. In fact, Edred's mood was such that he would have been easier appeased by retribution than mercy.

Some word must have been spoken because he was hauled upright and then flung down again, this time at the king's feet.

'Stand up.' Said Aelfred. 'Explain the words you spoke to Aneirin.'

After some difficulty with his tied hands Edred stood, not in respect but because he disliked grovelling at any man's feet. The figures around him were hidden by darkness but he could feel there were many of them; the king alone showed clearly in moonlight striking through the trees, his figure silvered and his face a harsh patched mask.

'Let me kill him while treachery still sticks to his lips,' said Aneirin, close by.

'Wait,' answered Aelfred, and they stood staring at each other; exhausted ruler who must face decisive battle on the morrow and a man who could have been taken for his son, brave and spitting hate. 'I am the king,' Aelfred added at last. 'I carry the fortune of my people and answer to God for His curse or blessing on them. Victory in this battle will be Christ's sign affirming that in matters of mercy I carry out His will.'

'And if you lose?' Edred's lip curled like that of a hound on a strange scent.

'I shall not lose.'

And, against his will, Edred could not prevent the stir of reawakened respect. Self-confident himself, he admired certainty in others, especially on the eve of unequal battle. 'Then I beg for myself the mercy of death in the forefront of your warband. I swear on my sword I will not be unfaithful.'

Aelfred nodded. 'Kneel in respect, and swear.'

Kings possess higher tempers than most men and for the first time Edred saw how Aelfred grudged each word he spoke, mercy no easy path but the hardest choice of all.

Edred knelt amid a mumble of protest from the men standing close. Aelfred silenced them at once, gesturing that Edred should be given back his sword. 'Swear.'

Edred's fingers fastened greedily on the iron grip. 'I swear by Dane-Eater, my sword, that I shall stand and fight until death. If I should live after the battle, then will I accept judgement at the king's hand.'

'A Christian swears by Christ,' snapped a monk.

Aelfred turned away. 'Sometimes it is simpler to fight one battle at a time, Brother Thomas.'

Now what could he have meant by that? Wondered Edred as he picked his way between sprawled men, looking for Wulfric. He possessed too simple a mind to wonder often about other men's motives, but he was not stupid. He and Aelfred shared some similarity of feature but little else, and as he began to consider this fact afresh he found it disconcerting. Two men, one face. One face, two natures; and it was the painfully shaped differences in the other which men loved.

This he must acknowledge, if Aelfred won tomorrow.

'He cannot win,' Edred said to Wulfric as they joined Atheling Edward's force and moved forward together in the dawn, to see the Danish Great Army standing in mist on a slope divided from them by a boggy lake. 'They are too many and this time they cannot be surprised.'

'He will not lose,' answered Wulfric curtly. 'He *will* not, don't you understand? Even if disaster should come in battle he is not a man to lose. Ever. A battle went against him once before, as this one may; battles are chancy affairs, after all. He was a fugitive then, flying for his life with less than thirty followers at his back, but after a season in the marshes he came out, and won. Because we knew even then that the Lord Aelfred refused to lose, and joined him when he called.' Wulfric had not forgiven Edred's disrespect, and this was the first time he had broken a long and sulky silence.

The mist cleared slowly and as it did so the size of the Great Army was revealed. The Danes were drawn up along a chalk scarp with the River Thames in the distance behind them, their front continuous but also grouped around their chiefs, who were marked out by horse-heads set on green-garlanded poles. King Hasta himself was in the centre of his line, beneath raven banners and three horse-heads, surrounded by berserkers who bit their spears and shook the ground with frenzy.

This awesome sight was what men meant when they spoke of a Great Army: a force many times larger than Aelfred's and every man in it a warrior, whereas the peasants and Winchester burghers filling their own rear ranks had only ever defended themselves against occasional raiding bands.

'When the berserkers charge, step aside and if it is possible, stab them in the back.' Said Wulfric. 'They are not men, but possessed. There is no dishonour in such a course,'

Aelfred was some twenty paces to the right of where they stood, and as he glanced towards the king Edred saw him gesture with his sword. Forward.

'Slowly,' yelled the thane leading Edred's group. 'No war-cries. Let the heathen sweat.'

A ripple of laughter, and they tramped forward. The men around Edred had fought with Aelfred before and knew how silence unnerved the heathens. The walked like ploughmen in the furrow, the dragon standard of Wessex fluttering above their heads and followed by priests carrying crucifixes. Eyes down, picking the easiest way, breathing steadily because the day would be long. No sound at all except feet in wet grass, which was so weird that one by one the Danes fell silent too, some touching the rings on their arms for reassurance.

When they reached within bowshot, the arrows began flying overhead and Edred felt his heart beat thickly as they spread out to climb up to the Danish line. This battle would be one of the greatest the land had seen. There was a flurry among the Danes just ahead, because on Aelfred's orders all the Saxon arrows had been directed at a single horse-head, instead of evenly across the slope. Many men fell around this standard, while on either side of it others struggled to fill the gap or to recoil from such obvious danger. The whole section was wavering and King Hasta, seeing what was happening, released his berserkers to win time for his jarls to regain control.

But the Saxon silence and the arrow-trap had betrayed Hasta into releasing them too early. Berserkers charge like sling-shot, cleaving the air as they came and were most deadly while their breath frothed easily in their beards. As it was, they had too much ground to cover and their charge was jaggedly delivered: Edred easily sidestepped the naked, stinking creature who flung himself at his shield, and killed him as Wulfric had advised, by a sword-point driven into his hairy back.

The Saxon line paused, shook itself free of the dead and resumed its advance. Each thane swore continuously at the men behind him, threatening death on anyone who shouted, but each man could see for himself that the pirates were unnerved by such strange behaviour. Unexpectedly, Edred found he wanted to laugh. He glanced sideways at Wulfric and saw a huge grin splitting his beard too, and more beyond him: between them they were twisting the hairy tails which everyone new Vikings kept inside their breeches.

Thirty paces from the pirate line. Twenty.

The Wessex war-horns sounded at last, the remaining ground covered at the charge. Edred was fighting almost where the arrow-storm had fallen, the number of dead and injured Vikings underfoot an additional hazard. Aelfred had sent his housecarls running at the last moment to this same spot, so that just here the English strength was unexpectedly trebled. Elsewhere it was weakened, since there were no reserves.

Edred felt himself borne forward by the weight of numbers, sensed the Danes give ground because they had already lost their leaders here and were still scrambling back into rank. He gathered his strength and leaped over bodies, caring nothing for his life, which was forfeit anyway; landed anyhow inside the Danish line. A warrior rushed at him with a raised axe, yelling. Edred ducked and then sprang upright, sinking his sword in the Viking's unguarded throat. 'Dane-Eater.' He shouted exultantly.

He killed two more Vikings in quick succession, then would have died himself except that a wounded Saxon on the ground cut upwards into his attacker's thigh.

The battle quivered, gave way, set solid again. Vikings were only ever with great difficulty killed. Exhilaration faded under the impact of brutal, endless hacking against superior odds. The thane in front of Edred fell, nailed through the belly by a spear. Yet this was the place where they must break the Danish shield-wall during the short time while Aelfred could hold together the remainder of his warband and continue to feed men into this breach so nearly made.

As soon as the thane died, Edred saw who had killed him: a Danish jarl wearing a gold band above his elbow and flanked by a pair of brawny giants holding horse-head standards. For Ferenthe and the great dark forest other men thought savage, here almost within his grasp was the chief he had bound himself to kill.

The jarl held an iron-bossed shield and was encouraging his followers by waving a double-edge axe as if it weighed nothing. He bellowed like a bull when Edred ran at him, since not many men attacked a fully-armed jarl when only protected by a leather jerkin. Edred's shield split under the first blow from the jarl's great axe but he drove the jagged edge with all his strength at his enemy's feet, which made him leap with pain and roar still more loudly. Then Edred drew back, holding Dane-Eater like a spear. In the Andredsweald men learned spear-craft young or died on the tushes of a boar. He whipped his whole body taut as if strung to a bow, and flung his sword singing through the air to transfix the jarl's throat, drowning his bellow in blood. Whooping Saxons immediately swept the bearers of his horse-head standards off their feet, splintering the poles and bursting through the Danish line behind. Edred was thrust forward in the turmoil,

Dane-Eater trampled underfoot together with the jarl. He carried a knife in his belt but a knife is no protection against axes, and the Danes quickly regained some order in their retreat. They had not terrorized all Frankland without learning how to preserve themselves from rout.

Nor had they mustered a Great Army with the idea of being slaughtered in a battle; they had come to enjoy themselves and grow rich. When King Hasta saw that his force was split in two, he ordered his war-horns to sound the retreat and within a short time many of the pirates managed to disengage from the fight and run in a very dishonourable way for a wooded knoll some distance away. Those who could not win free were killed, but the rest still formed an army which hovered on the horizon like a storm. The English followed as fast as they were able, whopping after stragglers until they themselves dropped on the turf for lack of breath. Then their own war-horns began to roar, commanding them into safety before the Vikings regained their courage.

In fact the pirates had never lost courage in the first place, merely behaved like prudent men. They drank some muddy Thames water, slept for a night and then wheeled westward, where the rest of England lay open to plunder.

Edred knew nothing of this. As the English assault split the Danish line he avoided an axe stroke only to run into the path of another, which caught him above the elbow. His leather sleeve turned its edge, but so great was the pain that at first he thought his arm was severed. Then pain faded and joyful English cries changed in his ears to a buzzing like summer flies.

He woke feeling sick and only loosely jointed to his carcass; when he moved, his bones moved too and he cried aloud. There were many men, both Danish and English, crying in pain around him and only when the English were called back to the Dragon banner did some of them begin to look for friends among the fallen. Dimly Edred felt his arm strapped tight; better still, he was hauled close to a fire and the heat of it probably saved his life.

Wulfric found him there next morning, and squatted down to commiserate with his injuries. 'It was like this with me for five whole seasons. I could scarcely draw my sword without coming to some harm. But then my luck turned and since my baptism no Dane has touched me.'

'I too have been baptized,' answered Edred sulkily, thinking that it would have been better if Wulfric sympathized with his hurts rather than prated of his own immunity.

'Oh, baptized men are often injured,' said Wulfric airily. 'But to me, it has brought good fortune.' He prodded Edred's injured elbow. 'The bone has been well set, but an injury is always serious for a warrior.'

Had any strength at all remained to him, Edred would have crammed Wulfric's smirk down his throat. However, he was determined not to be left behind for plunderers to find, so he dragged himself upright that same evening and with Wulfric's help wavered to the stewpot. The men around it were carousing on Danish ale and though he vomited more than he drank, Edred soon felt more cheerful in such company. His memory of the battle was confused but everyone seemed to know he had killed a great jarl and, better still, Dane-Eater had been found unbroken and was returned to him.

The English warband straggled off the estuary hills two days later, following the pirate track and urged on by Aelfred. He knew well enough that the Vikings had gone to ravage and loot but his men still believed they had won a lasting victory. Some were injured and others remembered their half-planted crops: within days Aelfred's meagre force halved in size, but at least those remaining were mostly experienced in the kind of warfare now required.

Edred recovered his strength rapidly although it would be many months before his elbow hardened sufficiently for battle. Meanwhile he practised left-handed swordstrokes.

Messengers reached Aelfred constantly, bringing news which was mostly bad: the Danes had circled London, picked up reinforcements from East Anglia and vanished into the Thames valley, leaving destruction in their wake.

Edred was dumbfounded by London. In an attempt to outmarch the Danes, who could not easily take this Mercian fortress and so were forced into a detour to avoid it, Aelfred crossed the Thames by an ancient bridge and led his men through the city: though London had belonged to the Mercian crown, its citizens had long ago accepted Aelfred as their overlord and turned out in their hundreds to cheer his veterans through the streets. Edred knew he was gaping at this welcome like a swineherd at a two-headed pig, but could not help himself. Winchester had frightened and confused him, but at least it was full of things he recognized: London was different not only because of its larger size and great river, but because it had been built by a race of extinct giants. There were bronze-strapped gates on rotting hinges, and walls so thick that three strides would not measure them. Squared paving underfoot, stone bowls full of rubbish, columns driving upward like rotted teeth biting into the sky: Edred twisted his neck from one direction to the next, marvelling, yet remained unable to understand why a people should have laboured to pile up such quantities of rubble, when reed and timber offered all the comfort a man could want. Huts did indeed huddle into every corner of flaking monumental walls, but Edred paused by one design. Never had he set eyes on such frank-fleshed prancings. Women, too. He licked his lips in horrified delight, tracing the colours with his fingers as if expecting to touch warmth.

Aelfred's warband halted while the Londoner's, who seemed hospitable, plied them with ale and food, and Edred seized the chance offered by this halt to present himself to Aelfred, as he was pledged to do. He was conscious of having fought bravely in the battle and hoped not only for mercy but to be included among the royal housecarls once his arm was healed. He could see Aelfred standing on some chipped stone steps, talking to a gaggle of merchants: the Londoners wore more colours than a meadow of spring flowers, and since no king wanted to be outdone by mere stallholders in such matters as gold belts and rainbow cloth, today Aelfred looked particularly fine. No matter that he had fought a great battle four days before and was still breathing carefully because of a cut across the ribs; men everywhere must remember greatness when they saw their king.

Edred butted his way through the crowds, taking care only of his arm. The Londoners he jostled swore at him and jostled back; their headman standing beside Aelfred would have struck him for treading on his crimson boots except that Aneirin turned at the commotion, and laughed. 'The Andredswealer again! Dane-killer and burden for all our backs. How many days do you expect to pass in the normal course of things without provoking a quarrel?'

Edred stared at him out of flaring eyes. 'I killed a jarl!'

'Aye, and a good stroke it was by all accounts.' Under that blue glare Aneirin left the rest of his jokes unspoken. Men of Edred's stamp made good killers but bad companions; you couldn't be too careful what you said to them between one fight and the next.

Aelfred finished with the London men at last, and glancing around as he always did to make sure he missed nothing of importance, saw Edred glowering between Aneirin and a thane. He sighed, but since he needed every man in his lands to believe his duty lay with the House of Wessex, he made time to deal with a brittle-tempered tribesman even in the midst of pursuing Vikings and dickering with purse-tight London.

When the king beckoned, Edred went forward but did not kneel. By his reckoning he had earned mercy if it was offered and would take it, or not, as it suited him best. 'You ordered me to return after the battle, if I survived.'

'And you did survive?'

'As you see,' answered Edred, astonished.

'But as a warrior, disciplined for use, or a heathen rejected by God and men?'

'As a housecarl, so I hope.' Edred stared boldly at the king.

'No. Never.'

'I killed a jarl! Who else except perhaps a thane did likewise?'

'Three other jarls died in the battle. One was killed by Thane Eilured, one by a housecarl and one by me.' Precise information offered without any inflection of voice.

Edred stared at him, baffled. Only four jarls killed and one of them was his, why should he not become a housecarl? 'My arm will heal,' he said at last.

'May God grant it. But what of your memory, Edred of Andredsweald?'

Then Edred understood that a ritual humiliation was required. 'My memory is good, Lord Aelfred. You won the battle, so I acknowledge that your judgement must have found favour with this Christ, where mine would not.'

Aelfred burst out laughing, then stopped, holding his ribs. 'What if Stykkar the Dane was standing beside me know?'

'I would plan how best to kill him.'

'Yet you have just acknowledged mercy as a virtue, proven by trial before God in battle.'

'Your mercy, Lord Aelfred, not mine. I kill Danes when I see them and do not trouble to crack words over it.'

Aneirin grunted. He too preferred simply killing Danes.

Aelfred turned to the most splendidly attired of Londoners. 'Well, Sigurd, what think you?'

'God deliver me from Edred of Andredsweald,' answered Sigurd promptly. He had a long droll face and clever eyes. 'For my life's sake, take him with you when you leave, my lord.'

'Sigurd is the son of a Viking whose life I spared after the battle of Edington fifteen seasons past, who has become a valiant defender of this city's walls. London is a place of many bloods, and so is England. The sword alone will never win battles nor afterwards keep the peace. Think therefore, and know why you can never be a housecarl of mine, who must be held on the leash of my will, to kill or not to kill as I bid him.' He paused, and then added more gently, 'Your skill is sorely needed in the warband.'

Edred held the shaft of his knife until his knuckles cracked. 'For Ferenthe I will stay with you until my tally of Danes is fulfilled, then I will go.' His eyes slid to Sigurd. 'A life in the king's service is too hard for me.'

The warband marched out of London the following morning; reinforced, well fed and where necessary re-armed. Thus began a spring and summer in which King Aelfred and Atheling Edward tried every trick they knew to bring the Danish army to battle again, to drive it away from settled richness and into the Midland forests to starve. A dozen skirmishes resulted, as well as unnumbered ambushes and forced marches while slowly the raiders were worn down. They lost more than a hundred men on an island in the Thames when Edward stormed their camp; fifty outside Chester; a whole raiding party in the Severn valley. King Hasta himself had to scamper for safety when he tried his luck in Wessex. As winter approached, there was scarcely a man in Aelfred's exhausted, foot-weary warband who had not marched five hundred miles and fought a fistful of engagements, nor any who did not long for an early winter which would free them for a few snatched weeks beside their own hearths.

Then, unexpectedly, word spread that what remained of the Danish Great Army had offered to treat for terms.

'Christ's blood,' said Wulfric, and spat into their camp-fire flames. 'About time too. Let them crawl off to spend the winter with their East Anglian kin, there to think about easier pickings back in Frankland.'

'What if their kin refuse to take so many in? What then would King Aelfred do?' Edred hunched his torn cloak against bleak November wind and wriggled his feet deeper into leaves. He had killed only two more Danes in all of the time following the battle, and those had been hurt by others first. His right arm ached in the damp, while his left remained infuriatingly unskilful.

Wulfric shrugged. It was not his business to know what a king should do. 'I stayed so long only because Aelfred is as wet and belly-sick as I, yet refuses to let the invader rest.'

'So did I.' after he watched Sigurd the Viking snigger by the king's side in London, Edred had thought he was finished with a chief he could not understand. Yet, somehow, loyalty to Aelfred of Wessex refused to die. 'I am useless now to the warband, but did not wish others to think I could endure less than they. I shall not follow the Dragon banner when the muster is called next spring.' He rubbed his face on his drawn-up knees: his oath to Ferenthe was dead. During these past accursed moths slowly he had realized that man to man he would never kill another Dane.

'What happens to the men of Andredsweald when they are forsworn?' Wulfric asked in simple curiosity. Warriors fulfilled their oaths, or died.

Edred shook his head. He did not know and none of his kin remained alive to ask. Probably he was accursed.

When King Aelfred finally settled the terms of his truce with Hasta, Edred and Wulfric went with some other men to take their leave of the king. Aelfred looked much the same as when Edred first saw him more than a year before; for him, after all, this season had been only a little worse than the other twenty of his reign. His beard and hair were grey, his face exhausted, fine clothes long since ruined in one scuffle or another. He remained restless, sharp on a detail and unsparing of his time; though very much loved, King Aelfred was a tiring man to serve.

'I hope to welcome all of you at next year's muster,' he said, smiling now. 'Hasta will find it easier to remember his peace-oaths if we are in the field before him.'

They shuffled their feet at the thought of another spring muster but most of them also nodded. Once their fields were sown and a new year's sons conceived, many would be back if the king called them.

They knelt together in pelting rain while a priest blessed their service and the coming holy season. When this finished, Edred moved forward. 'Lord Aelfred, I shall not be returning to the warband. Although I have practised hard, I cannot defend myself left-handed and my right arm has not healed straight.

'Edred of Ferenthe,' said Aelfred slowly, his memory for names another of his strengths, 'I thank you for staying so long when you might have left with honour.'

'I stayed hoping to kill more Vikings. As the king has said, in such matters the leash of his will does not easily fit my neck.'

'Perhaps. Perhaps not. A season with the warband is not easily forgotten. Nor a baptism.

'Since I was sprinkled, Christ had guarded me better than Tiw.' agreed Edred cautiously. 'Although not without some harm I should prefer to be without.'

The severe line of Aelfred's mouth relaxed. 'May you remember His blessing then. Will you return to Andredsweald?'

Edred did not reply, since this was a matter he had not resolved. How could he return to a leaking pool and scrub encroaching on

Alaric's clearing, with only the full use of one arm? Yet the thought of Ferenthe filled him with desire: his place, where each clod of earth was familiar.

Aelfred snapped his fingers at a clerk. He had no more time to waste, but any warrior disabled in his service had a right to consideration. 'Make out a grant in freehold to this man, and pay him six bronze pieces and one of silver.' He turned back to Edred. Andredsweald is as much my realm as Wessex. Tell your fellows there to send word to me if they need help.'

Then he was gone. Edred never saw him again, although six years of his reign remained.

'A grant of land in Andredsweald, the Lord Aelfred said?' A priest-clerk wrestled with wet vellum under the relentless rain. 'That makes matters easier, such swamps and forest being unsettled land. Is it this Ferenthe you want, or somewhere else? Whichever way, definition will be difficult.' He shook his head over forest which defied clerkly scribblings. 'A holding in Wessex would be better where jurors may swear a title.

Edred thought of the rich lands of Wessex, where he would find neighbours to help if his arm fumbled a task; Wessex was full of warriors' kin who respected injuries taken in battle.

'Ferenthe,' he said, doubts vanishing with the word.

It was late in the season for Edred to return immediately to a ruined settlement in Andredsweald, and Wulfric invited him to spend the winter in his village, which invitation Edred gladly accepted. His arm was too painful for him to begin immediately on the arduous work of clearing scrub, digging smoke-pits and splitting logs; also he found himself strangely loath to leave the atmosphere of great events. All around Winchester lived men who had fought at Edington and Newbury, London's walls or along the coasts of Kent; scribes, priests and bishops rode past, thanes and ealdormen paused to exchange greetings with veterans they recognized. Andredsweald was where he belonged, but he did not yet crave its isolation.

So when Edred and Wulfric walked down White Pasture Hill to Byksbourn, Wulfric's village, they felt more comradely than while on campaign. Wulfric was in a joyful humour and Edred not much less so, the king's grant of land folded under his jerkin and a winter's idling in prospect during which the ache in his arm would surely settle.

'There is no place in England so fair and rich as this.' Wulfric's head was flung back and breath sang in his throat.

'It is rich,' agreed Edred, since he could not pretend that Ferenthe was as fertile as these curving hills.

'Seven months we have been away or is it eight? Perhaps I have a son by now.' Wulfric set such a fast pace down the hill that Edred was left behind: anyway, a returning warrior deserved a welcome to himself. So he sauntered on alone until he reached a cluster of stockade huts, conscious of speculative glances from some girls herding geese. He knew he looked the part of a battle-worn warrior and swaggered a little, feeling it as well.

Wulfric had already disappeared and there was a great fluttering of women, dogs and fowl. An elderly man came over while Edred looked around him. 'My son, I am Cerdic. I fought at Edington, and any man who follows the Lord Aelfred into battle is welcome here.'

Edred nodded, wondering whether this greeting carried with it an offer of a hut and warmth for the whole of a winter. He opened his mouth to phrase his thanks in such a way as to discover this, when he stiffened, his eyes fixed on a woman by the pond. 'That woman. Who is she?'

Cerdic looked offended, as well he might, since not even his greeting had been returned. 'An ex-slave called Roda, brought here by Frifwith, Wulfric's wife.'

'She is no ex-slave, but still bound,' said Edred between his teeth. 'Don't you know you could be flogged for harbouring a runaway Dane in your village?'

'God's blood, of course I know! As a young man I killed Danes, and would do so again if they came raiding here, but what we need now is hands to help while our sons serve in the warband. It is not Danes who stick in my gullet, for I never met one who was not a valiant fighter, but Danes who ravage and burn. She is not ravaging or burning.'

Edred opened his mouth to say something which would have caused him to be thrown in the midden ditch of Byksbourn, but changed his mind and allowed Cerdic to lead him to a hut the village kept for travellers. He was left there with little ceremony: Cerdic had joined the many men who did not like Edred of Ferenthe. This, Edred understood and regretted, since he had become accustomed to others finding only faults in him whereas he felt himself to be full of fine qualities.

The hut was empty except for a sow with her litter. She, too, rolled a hostile eye at him and squealed angrily when he kicked up a bracken bed for himself. Feeling unwanted, Edred went outside again. Early winter dusk was falling and there was no sign of Wulfric. It must be pleasant to return to a wife who expected a coupling the moment her man came through the entry, Edred thought enviously. Which brought him back to Roda, and after a brief search he found her grinding corn. Her fingers danced, clicking husk from the ground meal, her face flushed with exertion. She was laughing at something another woman said, and looked different from how he recalled her.

He said so, and only afterwards remembered he had not wished to compliment her.

Roda considered, the smile still on her lips. 'I am not half-starved now.'

'Why are you here?'

'Wulfric's wife asked me to accompany her and I accepted. There was great confusion in Winchester on the day the warband left, and no one stopped me. I have lived here ever since, and been happy.' Happy for the first time since she ceased to be Ragnar the Tall's daughter on her way to settle conquered Wessex, she might have added.

'I killed a jarl.' Edred said. 'We fought and won two battles, and spent the rest of the season harrying your king through the land.'

She shrugged and began grinding corn again. 'Why should I care? All lands are full of men dying in their blood, and women weeping for them.'

He stared at her, baffled, and soon left her to her grinding.

He could not forget her, though. Byksbourn was small: a huddle of huts, a stockade for the beasts and a pond, no more. A woman like Roda could not be missed in such a confined space. She had a way of turning her hip on him when his eye rested on her, of carrying pails or a bundle of fodder so that what he saw was not the burden, but her healthy body underneath. Roda was making up for the years she had existed on scrapings and ate hugely at every meal, so that her appetite had become a joke rather than grounds for rebuke. Soft, the Wessex folk, Edred thought.

So Roda's cheeks were as rounded as autumn apples, her hair sprang into long tresses when she teased out the tangles on Sunday, her lips were full and red, and she watched Edred without seeming to, from the corners of her eyes.

'Take her with you when you return to Andredsweald,' said Wulfric carelessly one day; to him that winter all men should be wedded like himself. 'She cannot marry here because a priest would require her parentage to be declared, and we are too close to Winchester for falsehood to endure. Then would she be taken and flogged as a runaway slave. One day it will happen if she stays here, when some traveller recognizes her from the time she spent at the tavern.'

Edred was silent. Insidiously, this thought had come to him, too, during the long cold winter nights. In Wulfric's village: a man married or went elsewhere to slake his lust: even a woman without kin like Roda could not be forced against her will, so Cerdic said. In the lands around Winchester King Aelfred's piety wore sharp claws, as did his justice. Nevertheless, most of the young men tried their fortune with Roda, including Edred, but she was annoyingly careful where she went. 'She is a slave,' he said aloud. 'I do not want Ferenthe bred from a slave who is a Dane.'

'She works hard and is healthy,' answered Wulfric practically. 'You also need to spend the bronze and silver King Aelfred gave you on oxen, not squander them on a wife who must be purchased from her kin.'

This was unanswerable, especially as Edred had come to realize that his right arm would remain a hindrance for ever. And, as well as being a slave who might be set to work in harness like an ox, Roda was a chief's daughter who ought to breed courageous sons. Edred kicked irritably at frozen clay, so it skidded in clods across the icy village pond, disliking the snare in which he found himself. Yet, each time Roda walked where he could watch, his judgement clouded with desire. To change the subject, he said, 'The winter has been dry since we reached here, but your pond is as full as when we arrived. How is it in the summer?'

'Full,' answered Wulfric. 'There is a spring which feeds it, and the pond itself was tramped in my grandsire's time, so it does not leak.'

'Tramped?'

'Aye. Is it so wet in Andredsweald that you do not need to use any skills with water?'

'No,' said Edred slowly, staring at Byksbourn's brimming pond. 'Not always. During the drought before the Vikings came, our pond dried into mud.'

'It needs treading,' said Wulfric confidently.

When the cold weather broke and a cold wind blew from the west, Wulfric took him to a village half a day's journey away, where a pond had been trodden. 'You cannot do it in frost, nor yet in downpour,' he explained. 'And any skimping of the work risks calling down a curse. First the springs must be captured and the pond dug out, far deeper than before. Then there must be clay and chalk and straw, layered and trodden firm-.'

'But what if it rains?' Edred asked. 'Often it rains hard enough to fill any hole faster than men can dig.'

'Then the women bale and the children use fleeces to soak up the dregs, before the men begin to dig again.'

Edred saw that exactly this great labour was going on when they reached the village whose pond was being trodden. A shower had left a hand's depth of water in the pond's dug bed, and a dozen women were slithering on clay while they ladled it out with pots and stirring-spoons. Children yelled and plastered each other with glutinous mud, loving every moment of their task, although the women complained continually.

A dwarf capered among them, kicking those who shirked and pointing out hollows where water still lay. 'He is named Luel,' said

Wulfric. 'He is one of the Little People who lived here before we Saxons came. They alone understand this work and their spirits bless a finished pond.'

Edred did not find this odd, since it was only natural that the spirits who lived in pools must be entreated after so much disturbance of their dwelling. It was a nuisance all the same, for where in Andredsweald would he find spirits prepared to adapt themselves to Luel's craft?

He watched all day and through the next day too, while Luel shrieked at his gangs of villagers, flying at them in fury if they brought the wrong mix of clay or too much straw. 'I must stay longer,' he said when Wulfric became bored. 'There will be no Luel in Ferenthe.'

So Wulfric went off to try out a new spear he had whittled, leaving Edred to follow every move Luel made. He even splattered barefoot in straw-mixed clay, and rammed chalk until his elbow flared like a brazier in the wind. He lay nursing the pain all night, cursing Danes and wondering how much scrub already grew on Ferenthe's ploughland, which he must clear before beginning on luxuries like a proofed pond or a weathertight hut.

Before he left, he went to Luel and addressed him very civilly, inquiring what manner of prayers the spirits of trodden ponds expected, if a new pool was to endure.

Luel was spry and tiny, his face all corners: three-cornered mouth, pointing ears, cheekbones as sharp as stone. 'Spirits curse easier than they bless.'

'You know the right prayers and propitious times.' answered Edred patiently. All men say that Luel's pools never leak.'

The little man closed one eye and laughed. 'Ah, but I belong to the pool spirits and they to me.'

'And I? What must I do, besides dig and layer and tramp, if I wish to make a pool very far from here?'

'Fear death,' answered Luel promptly. 'Only the Little People may entreat the spirits of a pool.'

Edred felt a chill of premonition, and shivered. 'Nevertheless, I must do it. So tell me, what must I say?'

Luel peered up into his face, until Edred felt those malevolent green eyes grasp at his spirit. But his mind was made up; Ferenthe must have its pool, and if he was cursed as a consequence, why, a true chief must be willing to offer what was demanded of him.

'I see you are determined on this course.' Luel was hopping from one foot to another with impatience. 'Therefore, when the work is finished you must offer blood to the water as it fills.'

Edred seized the creature and shook him. 'What blood? Of boar, or eagle? Which?'

Luel hung from his hand and though his nose turned blue, he was still grinning, because he knew Edred dared not injure him. He poked a finger at Edred's chest, and cackled. From your own nipples, like a woman. Then watch each day to see which part of you rots first.'

He whirled on his toes and rushed back to the villagers treading muck in their pond, raining blows on them and kicking at their shins. Men must suffer before they received any good, lest they hold the giver cheap.

Edred watched through narrowed eyes, wondering. Tiw was a mighty, ancient god who would not kill at the bidding of such petty spirits as Luel served: nevertheless, as he walked back to Byksbourn considering all that he had seen and how he might offer the place he loved a pool which would last for ever, Edred had already accepted that his life might be the price this gift demanded from him.

Next day he went to Roda and asked her without preamble whether she would accompany him when he journeyed to Ferenthe. Alone, he could accomplish nothing. She tipped back on her heels and looked up at him as she had on the day he came to Byksbourn. 'As your slave?'

'There are few unwilling slaves in Andredsweald, the forest is too great for any man to keep another captive long.'

She nodded, such an answer made more sense than pledges. 'I would have a place by your hearth so long as I lived, though I might be sick or barren?'

She had better not be sick or barren. 'If either of us sickens there, we shall both die. Ferenthe isn't like Byksbourn, with food to spare and kindred to help in hard times.'

Roda recognized this as the only guarantee she would get, and her only chance of a place which would be hers by right. She stood up. 'Yes, I will come with you to Andredsweald.'

So simply was the bargain struck, which might in other circumstances have taken a winter of haggling between members of each kindred. So too was Ferenthe's future woven, the pattern of its fields, the customs of people who would live there long after Edred and Roda were dead, the names of some of its places, the superstitions which would endure for a thousand years to come.

As dusk fell Roda came into Edred's hut and began calmly to build a cooking fire in one corner. She did not speak and Edred sat silent too, watching deft movements as she threw grated roots or chopped herbage in the pot. The smell was good. As the savoury aroma grew and her shadow danced before his eyes, his senses stirred and when she came over with a trencher of food, he found himself liking the way she moved and comfort crept closer, unrecognized. It was the first time he had eaten in his own hut since Ferenthe was destroyed. Roda was also a better cook than Wynfyrtha and the stew hotter than when he dipped it from a common pot.

He spat a mouthful of bones on the floor. 'Eat now yourself, before it cools.'

Roda smiled, seeing that he wanted her to share his pleasure. They had begun better than before. She scooped the pot clean and sat cross-legged at his side. 'When will we leave here?'

'As soon as the land dries sufficiently for us to be able to travel easily in the forest. Andredweald hills are steep, which makes each valley into a swamp.'

Roda shivered; she could not imagine spending the rest of her life confined by trees, but she had chosen her path and did not intend to change course now.

When Edred had finished eating she went quietly about the business of banking up the fire and spreading bracken in a corner of the hut away from the sow, then lay down as if she and Edred had inhabited the same bed together for a long time already. This seemed right to both of them, since there were no old crones to calculate auspicious days, nor men of Edred's blood to hurl ale on the floor and shout when he dropped on the bed beside her. This marriage was as it was, and they must make the best of it.

A cold night breeze blew through the hut opening, setting a single flame dancing from the banked fire. I will cut deerskin to cover the opening to my own hut in Ferenthe, thought Roda, before she turned both mind and body towards pleasing Edred.

He was surprised by how well pleased he was, and each time his eye rested on Roda while they stayed at Byksbourn, he remembered that they might already have made the first of many sons between them. Now, he could not wait to begin his journey back to the ridge and the great labour which waited for them there, and within a week they bundled together the pot and skinning knives and loom-weights given them by the people of Byksbourn, and left.

Their way took them along the hills skirting Winchester, and Roda watched with satisfaction as its reed-thatched roofs vanished into mist. No tavern-keeper would reclaim her now, nor priest demand marriage ceremonies which neither she nor Edred understood. Instead they were bound together by the strongest of all ties: each knowing that alone they perished.

The third day after leaving Byksbourn they began to skirt the forest, and two days after that they left the South Ridge and plunged into darkness. This was how Andredsweald seemed to Roda. Edred looked about him eagerly and often called for her to look at one thing or another: how the light fell on leaves or a squirrel hurtled from branch to branch. He never seemed to tire even though he was forced to cast back and forth, searching out trails which took them across the grain of the land. The forest was like the belly of a swine, Roda thought. Dark, dirty and full of bristles.

'Look there!' Edred cried, at last. 'The hill of Tiw.'

They were standing in a small clear space looking out over the forest. 'That one?' asked Roda. All hills covered with trees looked the same to her.

He nodded. 'Ferenthe lies along the ridge to the north of it, so our cleared lands must have been-' he broke off, afraid she might notice the tremble in his voice.

Edred refused to stop that night, plunging on through thickets, twisting and panting like a maddened hound after the paths he wanted. A dozen times Roda nearly lost him; she called but he did not seem to hear. Somehow she clung to his trail, but when dawn came she was exhausted, her spine chafed raw from the bundle on her back. Sunlight slanted in shafts to the forest floor, gnarled beech roots writhed across sheer banks, which were also covered by brambles. All through the night she had heard wolves howling close by and other heavier creatures crashing in the undergrowth.

Edred stood part-way up a steeper slope than ever, his beard out-thrust against an eggshell sky. 'Ferenthe is on the ridge above.'

Roda smiled, the effort so great it seemed to take the last of her strength. This dark accursed place was Ferenthe! She ground her palms into her eyes to stop the tears from flowing, her first surrender to weakness in all the years of her captivity. She had chanced so much on a place she had seen through Edred's eyes, a fierce man whose only weakness was love for a wilderness he called his own, now this was what she found. After a while she began to climb from root to root up that steep ascent, undergrowth reaching like claws to hold her back. She scarcely realized when she reached the top, but lay in bracken with blackness behind her eyes.

When her sight cleared, she seemed to be alone. Wind blew through grasses and swallows swooped against distant blue. After a while she levered herself upright and saw a large space free of trees, the forest flowing away below and on every side until it met the curving sky.

'Why, it is like the sea!' she exclaimed joyfully.

Edred turned. 'Fields which took two generations to clear have gone back to scrub and bush again.'

'As you told me they would'

He shook his head. Until he saw thickets where huts and fields had been, he had not truly believed that Ferenthe could look so desolate. 'Tomorrow I must start searching for someone who has oxen to sell.

Swine too; their rootling clears trees fast as any axe, and more profitably.'

Roda breathed deeply, eyes closed. She could live on this high and windy ridge without ever hankering for the sand promontories of her childhood. So soon after her moment of despair Ferenthe was better, far better than she had dared to hope. 'It is beautiful. If you can buy the beasts we need, then within two seasons we shall have it cleared again.'

He nodded, feeling very much softened towards her because she, too, found this ridge beautiful, although he knew the forest filled her with dread. Ah, Mother Earth, he thought, strengthen my weakened arm so I may make this place fruitful again before I die. Then he led Roda through the tall bracken and showed her where Ferenthe's huts had been; together they stood staring at the blackened trunks of trees which had burned in the great fire following the Viking raid. 'Before the fire our two fields ended where the ground begins to fall again to the east, now-' he estimated the distance cleared by the flames '- if we can plough again before the saplings root, there must be double the quantity of open land.'

Roda hesitated, searching through careful words. Edred felt so deeply about this place she wasn't sure how best to phrase her thought. 'When you find someone willing to sell you oxen, you should also ask their drover to come back with you.'

'Aye, perhaps. There has always been more land than people here.'

She did not answer but left a seed planted in his mind: certainly there was more land on Ferenthe Ridge than they could ever till. That night they slept wrapped in their cloaks by the pool, and in the morning Edred began splitting branches for Roda to weave into hut walls. Even in spring the ridge was cold, exposed as it was to every wind. At dusk a splay-legged fawn trotted into bowshot so they had meat to add to roots and tender shoots in Roda's pot, but the pool water tasted sour even after long simmerings.

'Oxen first so we may plant some grain this season, 'Edred said that night. 'Then the pool. The water here used to be sweet but this filth makes me retch.'

It also made their bellies gripe. After the village burned, the animals on the ridge had again become used to drinking at Ferenthe's pool, and now the water stayed shallow they turned it into sludge. So much so that Roda found it difficult not to believe that Edred's memory must have betrayed him when he spoke of how clear it once had been.

Two days after they arrived at Ferenthe, Edred left again, to search for a yoke of oxen. If he had not possessed the bronze and silver clippings Aelfred had ordered to be paid to him, then he and Roda would have harnessed themselves in turn to a fire-hardened digging stick, but with oxen the task would be faster and infinitely better done. Roda stood to watch him out of sight, and when he had gone she set out to float over her new domain. There was a great deal to do before Edred came back; pits must be dug, snares set and bracken pulled, a start made on hand-clearing the nearer plots: the tally was endless. But first she wanted to look and wander, completely alone for the first time in her life.

The sun was burning haze off the ridge while it stayed like a white sea all around, so Roda could believe she looked down on an enchanted land. Above, the sky glowed blue and for once there was little wind. A hare bounded through the bracken and a flicker in the shadows showed where deer grazed new sapling shoots. Roda laughed aloud, and ran across to the pool. She stripped off her stiff and grimy clothes and washed in the murky water, scrubbing her body dry on scented bracken and tossing wet hair in the sun. The water was so cold her teeth rattled in her head, but when she had bathed she danced, quite slowly and with her arms stretched upward to the sky.

Roda remembered almost nothing of her childhood gods, and Christianity belonged to her captors, which meant that so far she had rejected its beliefs. But this new place needed a blessing on it, and so, obeying some instinct lost beyond the mists of memory, unheeding, unthinking and alone, she danced naked to the sun. She dozed lightly afterwards, in a curved dell which lay some distance beyond the pool. Vetch and bluebells grew on its sheltered slopes so that from where she sprawled at ease their blue rioted into the blue of the sky, the air filled with fragrance each time she stirred. Children of her blood would love this place, would flourish and wither here for reasons she would never know, but no one would ever again see it as she had today: untouched and waiting under the sky.

She was roused by cold and ran all the way back to her clothes by the pool, her skin dappled like a fawn's by light and shade.

A man was sitting beside the water, his chin on his drawn-up knees. Roda skidded to a stop, limbs flailing with the shock of it, and bolted back to the nearest stand of bracken, while he stood laughing, and called after her: 'I wondered how far you had wandered, leaving your clothes behind. I'll come back later.'

Astonished, she watched him stride off across the clearing and vanish into the trees which edged it. He wore skirts like a priest but his hair was unshorn, his words slurred so she scarcely understood him. But he said he would come back. She darted out from the bracken the moment he disappeared, solitude so suddenly and crudely disembowelled that her only thought was of escape; scrambled into her clothes, began to race round gathering their few possessions into a heap. She must hide them and herself, exist somehow out of sight until Edred should come back.

But the stranger had not gone. When she returned from hiding their cooking pot, he was waiting for her beside the pool.

Edred was away a full three weeks, oxen being difficult to find in Andredsweald and harder still to drive. A small boy called Toki returned with him, the sole survivor of a family stricken by a sickness. The men of the settlement where Edred bought his beasts were pleased to add the child as part of the bargain, since they could then share his inheritance. Too young to know he had been cheated, Toki darted about the oxen, shouting, or sat on their withers hammering with hard brown heels to make them quicken pace. He never succeeded. Oxen trudged until they dropped, but changed gait only to suit themselves. Edred had always liked oxen and his heart burned with pride in these his own possessions; besides his sword, a few bronze pieces and a woman, these were the first things truly to be his. He walked behind them admiring the way they placed their short thick legs on treacherous slopes, stamping down firmly through leaves as if they already ploughed his fields. He took no more notice of Toki than the oxen did, swatted him away if he came too close and as a consequence, the child eventually became discouraged. By the time they reached Ferenthe he trudged head down like the oxen and did not caper or shout anymore.

Edred expected Roda to be looking out for him and was disappointed when there was no sign of her on the path which led from Tiw's Hill along the spine of the ridge. Quite soon, he became angry. She ought to have been looking out for him, no matter now busy she might be. He halted by the pool and the beasts waded in gratefully, nuzzling water. Toki too, dropped on his knees and drank, but soon pulled a face. 'Nasty.'

'You can go down the slope to a spring if you don't like it, but watch out for wolves on the way,' snapped Edred, any criticism of Ferenthe a mortal insult to his ownership.

The hut he had built was still trim, flowers woven into a garland above the entry. Trust a Dane to waste time weaving garlands, Edred thought sourly, shouting so loudly for Roda that the birds flew out of the trees. This time he heard her answer, a long way away or so it seemed to him; he reached halfway across the old settlement clearing before she came running towards him.

'Where have you been?' he demanded.

Her smile faded. 'I was cutting gorse. Around Winchester they tie it on a drag-line and use it to uproot the weeds.'

He looked around him, to estimate how hard she had worked since he left. 'I've brought two oxen.'

'Good.'

The journey from where I bargained for them has been very hard.'

She shrugged. 'Journeying through the forest is not unpleasant at this season.'

He shook her savagely. 'Not many men could find good oxen in the forest and also be able to pay for them.'

'Not many men would return to a woman left a long time alone, without a word of greeting.' She answered sadly. 'Where are the oxen?'

'By the pool.'

She twisted out of his grasp and led the way back to their hut; these weeks alone had changed her in ways Edred did not like or understand. Roda exclaimed when she saw Toki and called to him merrily, so that a child who only a short time before had been plunged in misery at once smiled back and began to chatter about the oxen. 'You must be quick footed to climb up and then not fall off each time Edred drove them down a slope!' she exclaimed. When he explained how he had goaded them along. 'You will have to show me how to manage such great beasts, or I shall be weeding and planting while you ride at ease.'

'I will,' promised Toki. 'I whisper in their ears and they do whatever I wish.'

It was only later, after Edred had eaten, that Roda told him they were not alone on the ridge. 'There is a hermit tending his plot not far to the north. You go through the scrub there, and a thicket of rowans. He has a hut and a crucifix and a great sword-cut across his face, which makes his words difficult to understand.'

'Ferenthe is mine! I will show him my deed from the king and bid him leave at once.' Edred leapt to his feet.

'He says he has lived here longer then any man now alive, and will die here.'

'That's a lie! A hermit, eh? Fugitive Viking, more like, fleeing from Aelfred's vengeance. I wondered why you seemed so cool towards me.' He stalked across to where he had left his sword, raced panting over moonlit earth until prudence made him watch where he put his feet. If Danes there were, one of them would be on watch. He thought again of Roda and ground his teeth, picturing her in the bracken with a pirate while his back was turned.

He looked around him and recognized the place he had reached; the priest-hovel had been dug near here and the open space reclaimed by their pastured swine. The moonlight was bright but deceptive, huge shadows thrown by every change in the ground.

'Greetings, my son. I ought to have know that if anyone survived it would be you.' Edred started violently, skin roaching up along his spine as a shadow detached itself from an oak-stump and stood where he could see. 'Edred? If you no longer recognize me, then perhaps I should show you how my well fills at all seasons with a span of water.'

'Theobald? Theobald!' Edred shouted, and flung himself across the clearing. 'You died! I saw you lying in your well after the Vikings left!'

'I lay speared in my blood under Brother Berteold, where his body and the wet shaft saved me while fire burned overhead. A miracle of God.' Theobald gripped Edred, smiling. 'Welcome back to your place, Edred grandson of Alaric.'

Edred wiped shaming wetness from his eyes. 'That's why I returned.'

'Aye. Through the help of Christ it will take more than Vikings to destroy our ridge.' Theobald picked up a drinking horn. 'See I have even brewed a kind of ale again.'

Edred drank deeply and wiped froth from his upper lip. Ale steadied him and he thumped Theobald on the back. 'Two men, two oxen, a boy and a woman. Christ's blood, we shall have Ferenthe rebuilt within five seasons.'

'Not if you blaspheme. Roda told me you had fought in Aelfred's warband; I thought they would have taught you better manners there.'

'Oh, piety.' Edred pulled a face. 'Tiw and Mother Earth brought fruitfulness to Ferenthe.'

'And looked the other way while it burned. I see that disaster, revenge, and now a safe return have taught you nothing.'

'I am very much changed!' Edred exclaimed indignantly.

Theobald fingered the raw red slash which split his face from eyebrow to mouth. 'Then I propose a bargain, since only bargains interest you. My strength in your yoke to help reclaim your fields; yours in my chapel this winter, because alone I cannot shape the roof.'

Edred saw that where the priest-hovel had been, four timber walls now stood, the space above them laced over with branches to form a ramshackle roof. 'The space is too great for branches to keep out the rain.'

'Twelve paces long and seven wide,' agreed Theobald. 'By the time you have re-established a kindred in Ferenthe, there will be a chapel large enough for them to worship Christ beneath a beamed roof.' He was smiling, his brawny arms showing through tears in his cloth. 'Tiw dies with you, my son.'

'Sons learn from their father.'

'And daughters from their mother. Sons too, or so I think. I baptized Roda while you were buying oxen.'

Edred stared at the earth between his feet, and Theobald's words seemed to make it move. Roda had been charmed from her past while he was away. Roda lightly yielding something – quite what he did not know – which rightfully belonged to him. 'So that's why she is changed,' he said dully. 'You need never expect to see me in your chapel, beamed roof or not.'

'I offered you a bargain.' Said Theobald sternly. 'Take it and be thankful. My roof in exchange for labour in your fields. As the years pass, we will see then whether you alone of all your kin refuse to ask Christ for his blessing.'

Edred nodded, since he had no choice but to accept so favourable an offer, but his rancour against both Theobald and Roda was not appeased.

For four years the strangely assorted inhabitants of Ferenthe knew little else besides labour. In summer, flies and gnats whirled in clouds around them; in autumn, dust coated their skin as they flailed sparse crops of grain. They were never far from starvation, since the soil was not naturally rich and game became harder to trap as activity on the ridge increased, but by the end of that time, Theobald's chapel squatted under a hewn-beamed roof and Ferenth's ploughlands sprouted grain instead of scrub. A tiny window above the altar was filled with pieces of horn which Theobald spent a winter scraping thin: looking through it was like staring at a great storm boiling out of mud brown clouds. Toki had sprouted like a sapling, and hatched a cough which brought blood to his lips; he worked like a demon, loved Roda and mourned because he would never love her as he wished.

Two more men and a woman they shared between them had also settled on the ridge. They climbed the slope one day carrying their belongings with them, helped cut the hay in exchange for food, and never left. A child had been born to them, and they lived in a hut on the far side of the pool.

Edred was skilful with the oxen and in trapping game but no matter how painfully he endured, the kind of labour Ferenthe most needed was beyond him: the stiffness in his right arm so shortening his stroke with an axe that he could not split timber cleanly. Yet timber was the basis of everything they did: ploughs, harrows, huts, sleds and fences, all came from the forest, and unless they kept on clearing land two bad seasons would kill them all. As a consequence, Edred's temper shortened almost daily and no one guessed how hard he fought to keep it muzzled. The slightest thing irritated him and when he saw the bond which existed between Roda and Theobald he could not help imagining them pleasuring each other behind his back and calling it Christian rights.

Roda too often found her life very hard. Sometimes she felt as if she, too, was earth under the plough. At others she moulded moist brown soil lovingly in her palms because she again possessed an inheritance, her babes no longer nameless foetuses thrown on a Winchester midden. In this, at least, Edred could make no complaint of her. Each winter she conceived and each autumn after harvest she bore a healthy child – three boys and two girls in under five years. What a life, she sometimes thought. But, what a life! She sometimes also thought, when skylarks sang in spring and four-year-old Alaric came bounding towards her over new-sown furrows. What a joyous life when all her children were healthy, along with six swine, three oxen and five geese which lived with them on a ridge they could call their own.

Each week she knelt in Theobald's chapel, saying, Jesus this is me, Roda, do You remember? I was once a Dane and am now your baptized follower. Protect my children, please, and give us a harvest. Also a deer for the pot would help.

She never prayed for herself.

'Why not?' asked Theobald. 'Christ cares for all, although not to be thought of as a wizard brewing spells.'

But Roda shook her head and refused to answer.

During the fifth winter after Edred returned to Ferenthe the season was dry and cold, so he determined not to put off remaking the pool any longer. He could have found time before but always there was some reason to hang back: the weather was too wet, there was more urgent work to be done, or insufficient help to finish the treading to his satisfaction. But these were excuses. Edred had not forgotten that Luel's spirit might claim his life once he tampered in their affairs, and he desired to accomplish as much as possible before accepting the burden of such a risk. But the shortage of good water on the ridge was now hindering the growth of Ferenthe, so when the fifth winter began Edred gathered everyone together and explained his intention. Then he took Toki with him and drove their oxen to Tiw's hill, where a seam of clay had been used for making pots since before memory began, and the great work on the pool was started.

First of all they dug out the bottom and banks to give a greater size than before the pool began to dry, the newcomers Ostric and Aelle using timber spades they had whittled and then hardened with fire: a skill they brought with them from the Mercian village where they were born. Edred despised wooden spades and traded corn with the forest smiths for one made of metal; because he never troubled to hide his scorn for inferior work a great rivalry developed between him and the other two men over this matter of spades. At first, Edred spent his time showing Toki which clay to dig and how to dry it for the ox-sled, but as soon as Toki developed an eye for the best seams, Roda led the oxen and Edred was able to join Ostric, Aelle and Theobald in digging. Spades swing and glittered in the winter air, the men like monsters in their pelts of foul-smelling mud, their diggings hiding them from sight as the pool-bed deepened.

'Hela!' exclaimed Ostric on the eighth day after they began to dig. 'Anyone can see that a timber spade is lighter and quicker than iron.'

'Quicker, lighter and sharper,' nodded Aelle, who agreed with Ostric in everything.

'Let Ostric begin spreading the spoil on the fields, and you then may dig in contest with me,' shouted Edred. In this he was cunning, for Aelle was less powerful and also lazier than Ostric.

Ostric considered, wiping mud from his face. He was tired of digging in icy slop and would enjoy sledging earth to the fields for a change. 'What is the pledge?'

The three men stared at each other, nonplussed. They none of them possessed anything they could afford to lose.

'A night with the loser's woman?' suggested Aelle.

Ostric nodded, grinning, for even after five children and years of toil, Roda was more comely than their woman, who answered to the name of Ik –or, very roughly, Hey You.

'I agree,' said Edred proudly knowing, as always, that he would win. Afraid – terrified – that he might lose as the day wore on. Roda came back with Toki twice during that time and stood at the edge of the pool begging him not to kill himself by working at such a pace. But Ostric and Aelle laughed so immoderately at her concern that she felt uncomfortable and when Edred did not so much as look up from his labours, she went away again. And, secretly, each time Edred cursed her for going, because while she stayed Aelle eyed her so greedily that he scarcely dug at all.

The iron spade was both clumsy and heavy; it moved greater quantities of pool-bottom than Aelle's wooden one, but also demanded more endurance from the man who used it. Edred would never normally have attempted to dig throughout an entire day, but now that he did, the sky turned grey and spiked shafts stuck into his chest and elbow. If he could not be sure of out-digging Aelle, then, somehow, he must outlast him.

And so, in the end, he did.

'It is clear that a wooden spade is best, since at the end of a day's digging I am still strong. Only, I do not wish to kill myself for a woman,' said Aelle sulkily, and threw his spade down at last.

Then Edred sank to his knees on the pool bottom and retched exhaustion into the mud, before rolling over and staring at stars in a silver sky. 'Bring Ik to me here.'

Aelle and Ostric brought her over, a thick-shanked woman with cunning eyes and dull wits. When she had learned of her place in this contest of strength between men, she felt significant for the only time in her life, and now walked gladly to where Edred lay. Around him the water trickled and froze and soaked through the dug earth, murmuring its secrets. Ik smiled when she saw him watching her, starlight reflected from his eyes. Then she waded out from the bank and dropped on him, giggling, impatient for so uncommon a mating.

With a quick slither, Edred shifted weight and Ik's scream changed to a gurgle as mud poured into her throat, for she and not he was underneath. Aelle and Ostric watched silently from the pool edge as Edred took her even while she drowned. From the moment he had demanded Ik be brought to him in the pool itself, they had known she would die. A life for a life. A new kind of pool was being born, and sacrifice to a new being was as old as time itself. They were astounded when the flailing in mud ceased almost at once and Edred hauled Ik out with a sucking plop, staggered to the edge of the pool and threw her where she could retch up slime in safety.

Edred slept just as he was beside the hearth in his hut, and woke remembering how he had intended to offer Ik's life in place of his own. Only in the instant when his body entered hers had he understood that this was cheating; he alone must appease Luel's spirits and if his courage failed then the strength of Ferenthe's pool might not outlast him. He sat up, creakingly stiff, and saw Roda. 'You should be sledging clay.'

'I waited to heat water for you.' She answered calmly.

Mud crackled on his skin as he moved, and his belly rumbled with hunger. 'Water from the pool?'

She nodded. 'While you slept we baled out all that had gathered in the bottom. You can see quite clearly how it fills from the springs.'

He could not wait to see, and bounded out of the hut to stand watching three rivulets run down the steeply dug sides of the pool. Theobald stood bare-legged in icy water, while Ostric and Aelle puddled clay. Ik smirked and looked at her feet when Edred appeared: she bore him no malice and remembered only that he had dug like a berserker all day to win her.

Edred did not even see Ik, but eagerly studied the water gathering and freezing where Theobald stood. 'See how clear and fresh it flows!'

Theobald nodded. 'No great quantity, but enough for men and beasts so long as the bottom does not leak.'

'After we finish it will never leak again,' he answered confidently.

In some strange way the pool made the settlers at Ferenthe part of one another, as they never had been before. It was the great event of their lives. Edred had fought in King Aelfred's warband; Ostric and Aelle were outlawed for some crime; Roda had been a slave and Toki orphaned, Theobald was a man who spoke directly to his god. But for all of them the pool became the work of their hands which would outlast them, where beasts would drink and the sky be reflected long after they were tumbled bones.

They argued passionately over each detail, wasted days solving the problem of tapping the springs their diggings uncovered, lost an ox which broke its leg when a sled carrying clay overturned down a slope. This last was a devastating loss, but not unexpected. If men ventured to meddle with spirits, inevitably some of their battles would be lost.

Twenty-seven loads of clay were brought from Tiw's Hill to the pool, tipped into its excavated depths and tramped down to form a watertight bed. Straw saved stalk by stalk from their harvest was layered on top, then more clay, since Ferenthe lacked the chalk Edred had seen Luel use. The frosty spell held throughout all this time, so their hands cracked and their feet turned blue as they worked, but the cold made it easier to keep the pool bed dry. As the last sled of clay was tipped, clouds blew over the western horizon, the trees roared around them, rain hammered on bent shoulders as they raced to finish the final smoothings and caulkings of the bottom.

Theobald crossed himself. 'It is a sign that God has blessed our labour.'

Edred grinned, rain streaming off his face. 'I think your god has not been well remembered while we laboured here.'

'I will bless the pool in His name as it fills.' Edred's words stung because Theobald knew they contained much truth. While the pool was being made he had thought more of clay and springs than of Christ.

'See whose god is strongest by throwing them both in and watching who floats,' suggested Ostric. And they were all so filled with the joy of a great enterprise finished, that at once Aelle, Toki and Ik joined Ostric in tipping first Theobald and then Edred down the bank so they rolled into the rising water with a splash.

Spitting, choking and yelling, the two men floundered in water which was already above their waists. Edred shook wetness from his eyes, laughing and swallowing; he had never been so happy in his life. 'With water such as this, we shall brew the best ale in the forest!'

'If I swallow much more, there won't be any left for brewing.' Theobald punched Edred in the ribs so they both lost balance and swallowed a great deal more. Then little Alaric ran in to join them while Roda ran distractedly on the bank, stopping the smaller children from following him.

'Anyone can see that one day he will become a great warrior, since he does not know the meaning of fear,' said Edred proudly, swinging the child up on his shoulders out of danger.

What a day! What a night too, as the last of their summer brewings were drunk, although before they began their carouse Theobald drove them out into the rain again and cuffed them all to their knees, even Edred, who was in a compliant mood, while he blessed the water.

Before the sky lightened next morning, Edred disentangled himself from drunken arms and legs and crept outside. The rain had stopped but the air was wet and raw. He stretched, shaking his head to clear it, and then walked over to the pool. As he expected after such a night of rain, it was over half full and the level still rising: in his heart he knew that what they had done was good, and all that remained was to offer himself to Luel's spirits

He took a knife out of his belt and knelt, seeing the clouds which raced across the sky reflected in the water; Luel lived where those clouds had come from, which he hoped was an omen. Then he pulled his jerkin open and, feeling carefully for his nipples cut with a knife. Left, then right. Perhaps it should be right, then left? He should have asked, and he worried about it for a moment. He mustn't blight Ferenthe's pool by blundering now.

The blade stung and he leaned out over the water until he saw ripples wrinkle in its black surface to show that blood and water mingled. A willing gift, he thought. This price is better worth paying than most.

'My son,' said Theobald behind him. Do you remember what I said to you before the burning of Ferenthe? When one day you have oxen, and children, and land under your plough-.'

'Will I then wonder whether this and nothing else is my existence? I remember.' Edred did not turn.

'Now I ask you again. Is a pool to be worshipped in place of God? Life offered for Ferenthe instead of for your soul?' When Edred did not answer Theobald added, 'I am going to ask something of you I have never asked before, although it has been many times in my mind. Come and kneel in my chapel while I pray.'

'Yes, of course.'

Theobald laughed, taken by surprise. 'I would have asked before if I had thought it would be easy. Why, of course?'

Edred turned then, smiling too. 'I think this is the last day of my life.'

Even in the dimness he could see how Theobald's scar swelled with rage until it gleamed across his face. 'No-one dies save in God's time.'

'I do not want to die,' answered Edred sharply. 'Come then, I have much to do today.'

All the same, they did not walk directly to the chapel. Feeling his doom rub at his cut nipples, Edred wanted first to look at Ferenthe as he used to in his youth. To caress it with his thoughts, and touch in love its trees and fern and soil. He paused by Alaric's oak, a stark burned trunk since the Viking raid. 'Will you see that young Alaric plants an acorn here and tends the tree which grows from it? Any village worth its name should have a Meeting Oak, and old Alaric's bones will shake a warning from the earth if a question is wrongly decided where he can hear.'

Theobald stopped. 'Edred, I beg of you. Ask Christ to heal your pride. If you would only ask, then faith will come.'

'No' said Edred sombrely, untying his jerkin so Theobald could see his bloodied chest. 'I am sold elsewhere, and come to kneel in your chapel because it is yours, not this Christ's.'

Theobald exclaimed aloud and crossed himself when he saw what Edred had done; grasped him by the shoulders and swore at him, good Saxon oaths from the forest. 'A slashed chest heals within days! If you will only believe then it has no power over you! Spill your accursed pride before Christ instead of your blood to demons, and I pledge you your life.'

Edred flipped a piece of bark. 'Aye, if you like. As Ostric said, throw us both in and we'll see whose convictions float.'

So they knelt together in the tiny earth-floored chapel, its shutters open to the winter air. Theobald prayed, while Edred stared at the horn-filled window over the altar and felt comforted by sonorous words. He could not imagine uttering them himself, but he liked them all the same.

Theobald understood then that he had failed and while they still knelt together, said quietly, 'You have a good wife and five children who are still too young to labour for themselves.'

'They will not starve. Roda has sufficient work left in her to keep them fed until they are strong enough to manage their own lives.'

'And who will defend and comfort her while she labours?'

'Ostric and Aelle share a woman, they will be pleased to offer Roda a place by their hearth if she requires it.' Edred frowned, disliking the thought of Roda by Ostric's swine-pen hearth. 'I do not want to die, you understand.'

'If you would have faith in Christ, you will die only in His good time and then to rise again.'

Edred stood and looked down at Theobald, smiling crookedly. 'Tomorrow I will believe in your god. If I am alive.'

He decided to go next to Tiw's Hill, since it was only courteous to bid farewell to a place which had watched over the ridge since before Alaric, his grandfather, came. He took his axe as if he intended to fell timber but stuck it in his belt as soon as he was beyond the sight of those who would ask why he idled in working time; then walked quite slowly along the ridge until, about midday, he came to the lower slopes of Tiw's Hill. It is like a woman's breast, he thought unaware that generations had worshipped it as such. As he climbed higher he was able to look out over trees rising and falling above unseen valleys further than the eye could see. Beyond the forest lay Wessex and Winchester; London too; north of here, he supposed.

Edred gazed at winter-brown tree crests, remembering his time with Aelfred. Even in Ferenthe they would hear when King Aelfred died, so he was still carrying the burden of his realm until it sucked him dry of life: a Christian king who understood as Edred did that a true chief died for his people.

A pool or a kingdom, men built where they could and Edred was well pleased by his building. He laughed, caught by the absurdity of it. Here I am, he thought, staring out over Andredsweald but thinking of Winchester. Of England, too, perhaps. King Aelfred said a season with his warband wasn't easily out-lived: he should be well pleased with his building, too.

After a while Edred pulled the axe from his belt and went to chop some hazel withies from which he could plait a garland to offer Tiw: at this season there was nothing else green to offer.

His arm was very awkward. The day of furious digging when he won Ik had further damaged it and he grunted with annoyance, striking harder. The blade turned on green wood and flew out of his weakened grip, driving into his leg. He stumbled back, clutching at blood-soaked leather. The wound was deep and he could feel blood spurting from his leg with every heart-beat. Frantically he tore at his clothes to find a loose end of leather, acceptance of death forgotten. Somehow he staunched the flow sufficiently to begin struggling downwards to the path. If this had happened a week before, Toki would still have been digging clay close by.

But it had happened now, as he had known it would. Not at all as he had known it would, how he had never dreamed it would, chopping for hazel for a garland. Terror struck at him; he did not want to die.

He dragged himself down the hill a step at a time, blood marking the trail he took. Night came early at this time of year, and the air was colder than he expected. The trees turned grey while he looked at them, and icy air swept into his mind.

A packman found Edred's body and lit a fire beside it to keep the wolves away, so that when Toki fetched him back to Ferenthe on the ox-sled next morning Edred might almost have been sleeping. No one could imagine what he had been doing on Tiw's Hill with an axe, and

Theobald, who might have guessed, said nothing.

Edred was buried near Old Alaric under the burned oak, and the only ceremony came from Roda, who poured a pitcher of pool water over the earth where he lay.

Two days later Theobald came and sat beside her hearth. He looked a different man haggard and pithless. 'Edred left a dying wish.'

Roda's eyes widened. 'You were there?'

'No. Before he went out that morning, he came to the chapel and knelt with me. He said that if he died he wanted young Alaric to tend an acorn near the place where the great oak trunk still stands.'

Roda knitted her brows. 'He expected to die?'

Theobald hesitated. 'He did not intend to kill himself. The axe was how he died, and Tiw's Hill where. The why, I tried to save him from, and failed.'

Roda thought for a long time, chin on her knees. 'He only spoke of the oak? He left no word for me?'

'No' he answered gently, and stared at the child Alaric sleeping, fist in his mouth. He could have been mine, Theobald thought. Those three weeks while Edred was away and I found Roda after I'd lived two years alone on Ferenthe Ridge. If she hadn't been already breeding that would have been my son.

'Why couldn't you reach him?' asked Roda softly.

Theobald looked up. 'You know why. I did not love him. Because of you I hated him in my heart, and when the time came for me to try and save him, he was sealed in behind a wall I could not scale.'

'I wanted to love him, once. But I, too, could never scale his wall. He built where he wanted to build, and destroyed what he wanted to destroy. Except for the Danes he failed to kill,' she added bitterly.

Theobald stood. 'I'll talk to young Alaric tomorrow.

Roda looked up at him, her eyes bright. 'I will survive.'

'With care,' he answered, smiling. 'Ask for my help when you need it and if necessary I shall yoke myself alongside your ox.'

'I have decided what to do. I cannot live beside the pool alone, with Ostric and Aelle thickness of timber away. I want to go to the dell by the edge of the fields where – 'She stopped. Where she and Theobald had lain together in spring madness while Edred was away. 'To me, it is a place of good fortune rather than sin,' she added softly.

Theobald did not answer. Chastity was a penance and not necessarily an everyday estate of the flesh, but now Edred's soul had slipped past his prayers he felt a deep aversion from bedding his woman. Though, God knew, he had knelt through enough nights, feverishly trying to avoid bedding her in his dreams.

In the years which followed, as Edred had said, sufficient work remained in Roda for her to support her children until they could fend for themselves. One died from fever, the other four grew to full age. Theobald cut timbers to build her a hut and barn in the dell, where a tiny spring gave a trickle of clear water: if she wanted more then it had to be carried across the fields from the pool. Roda never rested. In winter she spun and cured and stitched by rushlight; at other seasons she was in the fields from before dawn until after dark. She thatched roofs, dug ditches, tended swine, geese and their remaining ox, on whom survival depended. When young Alaric was ten years old, he went on his first boar-hunt, and proved himself both courageous and impetuous. At eleven, Peffa, beloved daughter whose hair was as blonde as that of her grandfather Ragnar the Tall, was spoken for by the son of a new settler and went to live in his kindred's hut to be trained in their ways. Roda wept bitterly but the boy was besotted and the family hard-working: child-marriage was better than abduction by a passing packman.

Roda herself was protected from Ostric and Aelle by Theobald's threats of damnation if they took her against her will, and through unremitting care her little steading prospered.

'Remember,' said Roda to Alaric, her son. 'The vellum your father was given by King Alfred shows that the whole of this clearing belongs to us, and each Christ's mass the others here must acknowledge our ownership. When I die they will ty to make you forget to claim your due.'

'I will remember,' answered Alaric, and clutched his dagger, looking fierce. He possessed the same blue eyes as Edred which leaped into rage without warning. Into laughter sometimes, too, which his father's had seldom done. 'And when I go to follow King Edward, I will send each year to make sure they pay.'

Roda sighed. Alaric took it for granted that one day he would leave Ferenthe to fight the Danes, and hung on rumour-mongers' tales, fingering his father's sword. She put King Aelfred's deed, which she could not read, back in the pot where it was kept sealed against the damp. 'Promise you will never let go of the land.'

'I promise,' he said. 'It is ours, Edredsland, and two more of us after me to hold it.'

Two more of her sons, he meant. Not dear little Peffa, already sick from breeding at thirteen years old. Ah Christ, how hard is this life. In all the time since Edred died, Theobald had never once come to share her bed.

Ah Christ, how hard. Yet one thing gave her much pleasure: the settlers in this part of Andredsweald seldom spoke of Edredsland, though it was their holding's proper name, but of the Danish Woman's steading: Danesdell for simplicity. Danes were a rarity in the forest, and women who held a dead husband's land alone, and survived, were rarer still. So this was not a name spoken with derision, instead it marked achievement and would preserve the memory of her endurance in a land she had learned to love.

But she was old, old, old! How old she did not know, thirty-four or – five perhaps, which meant she must fight hard not to sicken before her youngest son could manage for himself. As she walked across her cleared land one damp winter day some years after Edred died, Roda gazed around her, remembering how the ridge had looked on that one enchanted day when she had danced naked to the sun. And how she had spent the following night in Theobald's arms where now her hut was built, lapped in such fire and grace that ever afterwards when she prayed to the god he served, she had never dared ask anything for herself.

A single day of idleness, a few nights when she had given herself joyfully to a man capable of softness: it was not much to reap from her life.

She smiled, and eased the yoked pitchers on her shoulders. A warm hearth and strong sons standing free on their own land. A ridge, a pool, a dell sheltered from the seasons; these were a goodly harvest, after all.

... THE WITNESS:

Danesdell stands just across the green from where those youngsters peered at their map, searching for the motorway. The house seems Georgian, although behind the façade lie older Tudor beams and higgledy-piggledy farm backquarters, including a large snug kitchen. Modernized now, of course.

But should you dig straight down below the eye-level microwave, you would come first to Victorian flagstones, then to Georgian brick and, below again, to a beaten earth floor. But dig again and reach four flat stones. These Roda used as a hearth, and because she chose to cook exactly there in her dell, every family from then to now has cooked in the same place.

Is this so extraordinary as to be almost beyond belief, or only natural once you really think about it.

By the time Roda died, not only Danesdell hearth but the map of Ferenthe itself was already set. The common ground around the pool is common still, most jealously guarded against encroachment. The green we call it, and play cricket there. The village street follows the same line as the foot trail which grew from the pool to Theobald's chapel; our church stands where Alaric's monks first dug their hole and the fact that Vikings slaughtered them there made no difference. A couple of miles away along the ridge, thirty-ton trucks still have to negotiate a nasty curve where, out of respect, travellers used to shy away from the lower slopes of Tiw's Hill.

And Alaric's oak?

Well, the oak Young Alaric planted in memory of his father lived and died, and was followed by a successor whose gaunt skeleton I remember as a boy.

It must be twenty years since I planted a new Meeting Oak on the green. Poor fellow, poor old sod, the village thought. See here, Mr Smith, don't you go planting oaks too near the wicket. Over by the swings? That's fine, but why not make it a flowering cherry? We'll all be dead before an oak's worth looking at. Ah, but there's glory in an oak, I said. Four hundred years to grow, a hundred in its prime, two hundred more to die. Three oaks take us back to Brac.

So they shrugged and let me be. Poor fellow, poor old sod. But the oak is healthy and by my reckoning has six hundred and eighty years of life ahead, give or take a few. Providing we allow it to enjoy them.

Young Alaric's oak was approaching its prime when Edmer came to settle the place which bears his name: I pause and look up from my writing, to gaze out of Edenham's window at the slope whose history he has moulded . . . while Edmer was still alive the Normans conquered England, raiders whose forebears Aelfred and his kin defeated. The oak survived, though a corpse hung in its branches; this time it was a people who faced destruction.

3

THE HORSEMEN
1068 – 1072

Everyone knew that Hwita was not beautiful. A good worker, her father, Edmer, said. As dull as rainwater Leofric's pretty sister Lulla said: Leofric, surely you could marry a woman who wasn't quite so joyless?

Of course he could since he had inherited a deed which said that most of the ploughland of Ferenthe owed him rent; the inducement was that Edmer offered an enclosure as his daughter's dower which Leofric's kin had long desired. And what was a plain countenance, after all? Hwita was strong and young enough to learn whatever Leofric wished to teach her. All the same, it rankled that he would never be envied because his wife was pretty.

On his wedding day Leofric lay abed a few moments longer than usual, thinking of the new enclosure he would own before another evening came, then leaped up and went outside, stretching. A soft wind promised rain, a good omen when the soil had stayed baked hard since harvest. A good omen in other ways too, perhaps. Rain and sun, woman and man; this was the pulsebeat of life. Leofric had wanted a woman very badly ever since a vomiting sickness had killed the rest of their family, leaving him and his sister, Lulla, alone together at Danesdell. Lulla, who promised more than any maid Leofric had ever seen: Lulla a torment to any man who lived in the same hut with her, though he was her brother and the sin of desiring so great it terrified him. Such sinners were accursed, and Leofric, now the last male of a bloodline which stretched back father-to-son all the way to Old Alaric, did not intend to try his chances with the Devil.

He stretched again and decided after all to go to the pool himself as other young men did on their marriage day. This practice was rooted in ancient Ferenthe lore which said that long ago the pool was born when a warrior-god coupled there with the spirit of the ridge. But nowadays, though the waters of Ferenthe never failed, successive priests condemned the practice of entreating fertility by ritual bathing a marriage-dawn and the rest of the village jeered if they caught you. Then did the same themselves, shamefaced, when their time came.

If he was quick, no one would see. Leofric ran from his hut at Danesdell across dry stubble to the pool, his blood beating warmly against his skin.

The pool lay still and pale beneath a lightening sky as Leofric stripped off his clothes and waded in. He grunted at the cold shock of it, then held his nose and ducked beneath the surface, once, twice, three times. Muscles clenched against the cold, feet braced on the slippery bottom, not shivering, concentrating hard.

'Wherever have you been? cried Lulla when he returned to Danesdell, before breaking into a peal of laughter. 'Leofric! You went to the pool before anyone was up to see you!'

'I have work to do before spending the rest of the day carousing,' he answered, annoyed.

'Ah, nonsense! You didn't want anyone to see Leofric the Great in the pond, with his teeth chattering like a goose-girl's.'

'Well, they didn't chatter,' said Leofric proudly, 'I thought they would, but they didn't. Which ought to mean a good foretelling for us.'

Lulla pulled down her lips, at her most enchanting when she tried to be serious. 'Indeed, I hope so. You need all the foretellings you can sweep together if Hwita is ever to be more than a beast of burden. Oh, Leofric, I wish you had not chosen her! Why not Gilgifu or Byrtha?

His face tightened. 'Neither of them is ready for marriage until next year. Besides –'

'Besides, besides,' she said impatiently. 'Why not wait then, rather than wed a dough-faced booby?'

Leofric stared at her, bitterly hurt, yet Lulla's pointed face was so lovely he could not be angry. Ah, if only he could wed her! No one else in the village possessed such delicate features as Lulla's, nor her dark grace either; Leofric had sometimes wondered how she could be of his father's getting. But of that there could be no doubt, since she and Leofric shared the same high-bridged nose, slanted eyebrows and dimpled chin, and if these sat oddly on a man, they became a woman uncommonly well.

'Hwita is mine,' he said, after a pause. 'You must never speak of her thus to me again.'

Lulla shrugged and turned away. 'After today will be too late. I wanted to change your mind while there is still time.'

Leofric ate nothing before his wedding feast, as was the custom.

Instead, to fill the time, he yoked his oxen and delivered some grain to the ironsmiths who lived scattered through the forest below Tiwshill. And as always, the forest soothed him. He also liked the ironsmiths, whom most men feared to look in the eye; they lived almost unseen, and if anyone tried to find them by the sound of their hammers, then he discovered only hot hearths and heaps of dirt. But when Leofric whistled, often they would come and chatter in their singing voices, though today he lacked heart for such niceties, offloaded his graIn and immediately turned back for Ferenthe.

He glanced at the sun and shouted at his oxen, realizing he had been unwise to come so far. Edmer would be very much offended if he should be late for the procession.

'Heh, what a tardy bridegroom!' yelled Swein from beside the pool. He went down on all fours and howled like a dog while the other men laughed and stamped their feet. They were already cheerful from deep drinking and agreed that only Leofric would have thought to spend his wedding morning hauling grain. Well, they would see what jokes they could play on him before the day was out: a sober groom might please the priest but meant resentful friends.

'I promised both rye and wheat to the blackened people,' explained Leofric when teased about his morning's work; his supporters' drunkenness made him feel humiliated and conspicuous.

'Throw him in the pool' suggested Eglaf, slyly. 'Any bride would forgive a wet husband so long as he brought the pool-spirits' blessing to her bed.'

Leofric put his hand to his belt. 'The pool is for women and beasts. I knife the first man to touch me.'

At that, they gathered round him, hooting. 'For women, is it?' demanded Wulfstan. 'I saw you scuttling back across the fields as day dawned, your breeches dripping as you went.'

Leofric ground his teeth in fury; so much for good fortune. 'My warning stands. Touch me and you will drop blood instead of ale. Now, do I have to go alone to fetch my woman?'

They shouted a great deal more at that, but when Leofric set out a great crowd followed, thirsting to sample Edmer's hospitality. There were perhaps sixty men, women and children living on the ridge by then, and a wedding always attracted families from the neighbouring settlement of Reredfelle, half a day's journey through the forest.

The procession of men wound round the village, from pool to Meeting Oak to Leofric's own holding at Danesdell, before striking out across the ploughland to Edmer's clearing in the forest to the east. No one knew why marriage processions visited each of these places before setting out, nor remembered that in oak and dell and pool lay Ferenthe's beginnings, but so it was and so it would be for a long time yet.

Some of the men tapped little hand drums and others plucked two-stringed lutes, a few blew down whittled stems. All leapt and capered, jostling each other as they went. Leofric walked steadily, eyes on his feet. He wished fervently that today was over, but as the procession left the village he looked across towards the enclosure Hwita would add to his holding. Its earth was rich and neatly shut in by hurdles, as many furrows there as an ox might take two days to plough. Each year it grew the best crops in the settlement and because the land rose in a gentle curve, it was called Corndown in consequence. Today this became his, and joy of possession helped Leofric to shout and leap with the rest when they reached the forest.

Their voices echoed under the mighty trees, mingling with the first soft hiss of falling rain. Drums fell out of beat as the men began to hurry to reach Edmer's clearing. When it appeared through the trees, Leofric thought again how Edmer's three roomed hut made Ferenthe's other dwellings look mean, which had but a single space for all the business of living. Edmer chose to earn his bread by making carts with woven wattle sides, whose wheels were cut from a single round of timber; he hunted game and used his axe like a magician. No one could rival him for economy or grace of stroke. So he prospered and did not regret giving Corndown to Leofric, since it meant that Hwita was off his hands. He thought the boy greedy over land but likely to be kind to a willing wife. As for Edmer himself, he could afford to buy such grain as he needed and he detested tramping behind oxen through the mud.

Edmer stood at the entrance to his hut and saw how Leofric's eyes flickered from side to side, noting his squared split-log walls and roof, the fine little stream purling past the door. All Ferenthe envied Edmer his stream, but only now did Leofric realize how snug a man could be on the profits of labour unconnected with the plough, which made him calculate afresh how he might rebuild tumbledown Danesdell. Once he and Hwita were wed Edmer might work on his daughter's home for little more than bread and ale, and this immediately made him feel more cheerful. All Edmer saw of these thoughts was Leofric's glance of envy at his hut, which made him puff out his chest with pride: land is not everything, he thought.

'Welcome to you all,' Edmer said. 'Enter and drink, my friends.'

By the time Edmer brought Hwita out from the inner room, not many of his guests could see straight enough to snigger behind their fingers at her height, which was like a man's, or at her lack-brained face. Leofric saw both clearly enough, although Edmer's ale heaved in his empty belly, and the remaining dregs of his anticipation soured. During the marriage negotiations he had thought of land and a woman who would breed strong sons, while at the same time easing his mind of desire for Lulla. Now he realized he had quite simply been a fool.

Too late; Edmer's sharp eyes saw Leofric begin gulping ale, and he ran about like an ox-boy, goading men back into a procession, thrusting Leofric towards the bridegroom's place, screeching at them all to hurry or the night's feast would spoil. He had two other daughters and three young sons, all as lively as grasshoppers; once dull Hwita was cared for, Edmer could see no major problems remaining in his life – and not many men were able to say that.

The procession wound back through the forest to the chapel, much less raucously than it had come as those left on their feet concentrated on staying upright. The chapel stood in its own clearing, the women and children waiting by the door while ancient Brother Athelstan stood doddering by his rough-carved alter; a saintly man but older than anyone had the right to be. Ferenthe people were resigned to his masses taking three times longer than they should; they bowed and knelt in most of the right places but also whiled the time away by chattering like starlings, or slept off ale to make room for more. Leofric knelt beside Hwita, thinking of land again. What else could he think of which would offer comfort, as he knelt on the wet earth floor repeating his vows to Hwita?

At Westminster, forty miles away to the north, a very different marriage feast was being celebrated, although the bridegroom there, too, had thoughts of land firmly in his head. No paltry double-ox ploughland this time, but splendid manors held as fiefdom of the king, and today, also a wife pert enough for lust to settle like oil even over such joyful thoughts as these.

Christ's bones, but he was a lucky fellow! Ralf d'Escoville looked around him, revelling in more good fortune than any man could hope for in a single life. He even looked lucky, he thought, squinting at his image in a silver cup. His hair gleamed black and was cut away from his forehead in the Norman style; his cheeks were ruddy, his body agreeably muscled.

He had been poor, and now was rich.

Rich, rich, rich; a great lord in a land sliced up by its conqueror for his faithful and greedy followers. Ralf d'Escoville had been born the youngest son of a poor Norman knight, and one night he had lain in ambush to rob a careless merchant of his pack. This he had sold and used the proceeds to buy himself a horse. Not a good horse because the pack was disappointingly thin, but a beast with four stout legs which he spent a winter training. In the spring he rode far enough away from his family manor to feel safe and then waylaid two knights who came singing along the road which led from Falaise to Lisieux. They were two and he was one, so he felt he deserved the spoils he won: two swords, a shield, and a helmet, although he regretted that one of the knights he left sprawled in the dust seemed to be dead. Thus equipped, he had ridden to join Duke William of Normandy on campaign, and discovered that the duke planned to invade England as soon as he had gathered sufficient ships. If only he should succeed! What spoils might be reaped from such an enterprise!

When the ships set sail at last, Ralf was seasick all the way to England, so very sick indeed that he lacked strength even to curse when a great gale drove the ships back to Normandy again. And while most of his companions looked over their shoulders at manors and farms and kin left behind in Normandy, landless and seasick Ralf d'Escoville swore never to cross the sea again. Whatever the result of Duke Williams's invasion, his future lay in England.

As it happened, events worked very much in his favour.

In the battle where the English king was killed, Ralf made sure he caught Duke William's eye. He was neither braver nor cleverer than other men, only completely clear in what he wanted. Where most of the Norman army fought because fighting was their trade – from which plunder naturally flowed providing one survived – Ralf fought to win as much as possible for himself and in that cause was prepared to be courageous, although he preferred to gain his ends by cunning.

Duke Williams's knights mocked Ralf's old round pot of a helmet, his thick-shanked horse and patched shield, but as a consequence he was not easily overlooked in combat. At the critical moment of the battle, when the English broke ranks to pursue a defeated Norman charge, Ralf scooped up a dozen riderless horses and drove them like a juggler tossing balls at the flank of Harold's housecarls. One man and twelve panicked horses carved a swathe through the confusion which reigned on either side, and a section of English prudently retreated before they realized Ralf's wedge of horseflesh was just that and nothing more. When they saw what had happened, the Normans sucked breath into their vomiting lungs, and laughed.

So Ralf d'Escoville's fortune was made.

He was knighted and chosen to feast at the duke's own table when the battle was won. He held William's jerkin while he was crowned at Westminster as king of conquered England. He learned more quickly than greater lords, who despised such mundane accomplishments, how to swear in Saxon and deal to advantage in English courts: Norman law might now rule the land but any sensible man could see that fat bribes could be harvested by cracking open English rights. London traders quickly grasped that it was desirable to pay Ralf d'Escoville to keep out of their affairs, and as his pouch filled with coins he bought good arms and horses and recruited as large a following as he could afford to pay, about a dozen men. Most of these were past their prime and therefore cheap, but looked impressive at a distance. Above all, Ralf placed his skills at the king's service and made sure William knew that the Sieur d'Escoville lacked a power-hungry kindred at his back. William had already spent a lifetime remembering who was connected to whom so that no family grew too great; a loyal and crafty knight who owned no land in Normandy to add to his gains in England soon became a useful tool.

Two years passed. The English were quiet but sullen, the greater Normans scuttling back and forth between England and Normandy: sometimes they felt quite dizzy with the sheer quantity of land they must now defend against their enemies. Late in September 1068, Ralf was summoned to the king's presence in Westminster Hall. He found him seated on a bench surrounded by priests – the writing rather than the praying kind, which was always hopeful – and, being of a naturally optimistic temperament, Ralf's expectations soared.

William looked up, his heavy-jowled face jutting like a bailey wall. 'Ralf. Have you ever ridden into Sussex?'

'Yes, my lord. To Pevensey, escorting supplies.' This was not true, since he had peeled off half a dozen men from the escort and led them to the more lucrative task of punishing a disaffected village in Kent, leaving the supplies to be delivered by his sergeant, but Ralf never admitted ignorance if he might safely pretend to knowledge.

'Then you will understand how swamps and forests make it some of the hardest country for travellers in this realm. Yet travel it we must, to reach between our English and Norman Lands.'

'When I hear lords tell how their oxen founder and their wives in labour die there, I am more content than ever that I never need to return to Normandy.' Answered Ralf, who never passed a good opportunity of thrusting his unrewarded landlessness under the king's nose.

William snapped his fingers at a clerk. 'I have decided to grant you five knight's fees in Sussex, which includes licence to fortify a castle and an obligation to secure that part of the route between London and Pevensey which passes through your lands. Found churches and stuff them full of priests who may be trusted to preach submission, build bridges, what you will. When next I ride for Normandy I expect to pass through your manors as swiftly as I would from Caen to Bayeux.

'My lord.' Said Ralf, delighted. Manors totalling five knight's fees was not bad as a start, although better still if they had not been in a wilderness. But he'd see to it that each time the king passed by, as pass he must on his way to Normandy, he would observe fresh reasons for trusting Ralf d'Escoville with wider and richer lands. So Ralf placed his hands in William's and swore fealty for the manors of Belsyewe, Catstrete, Verrigge, Reredfelle and Ferenthe, promising also to keep them (and himself) loyal and quiet.

'One thing more' said William as Ralf stood. Whether as king or duke, he conducted business fast and went hunting in the time he saved. 'I expect you to live on these Sussex manors for whatever time it takes to pacify and fortify them. I leave for York tomorrow and would see you wed before I go.'

Ralf blinked. 'My lord –'

'You will need a woman to keep you warm in the wilderness, and the queen has a wench she wishes to place before the court leaves for Normandy. The daughter of Walter de Nonant.'

Ralf shut his mouth and swallowed. 'Aye, my lord.'

I will dower her, of course.' Said William briskly. 'And attend your marriage feast. Speak to a priest and see he fits his masses to my steward's convenience.'

'Aye, my lord,' repeated Ralf, for once bereft of words. He did not place much reliance on Williams's promise to dower Walter de Nonant's daughter, but refusal to wed her was clearly out of the question. In one way or another, everything had its price.

At his nuptial feast next day, Ralf discovered that the price was less onerous than he feared. Walter de Nonant had been caught the year before with his hand in the royal coffers, but died of a seizure before the king returned to judge him, leaving an unbetrothed daughter seventeen years old. Beggared by the fines on her menfolk, his widow retired to nurse her shame in a convent, so the girl was swept up with other hangers-on into the court of Queen Matilda, where she played much the same game as Ralf d'Escoville had played with the king, hoping for reward. It was probably only just that they should end up together, and pleasant to find that on this occasion justice showed so agreeable a countenance.

During the short time the king remained at Ralf's wedding feast the guests stayed docile, but once William clattered out, taking his lords with him, those smaller fry left behind began to shout and spill wine, while the women loosened their bodices and lolled against them. Joint after joint, vintage after vintage, the banquet kept its course. Ralf drank deeply too, his blood singing in his ears and for once not grudging expenditure, while his new wife, Isabelle, sat primly beside him, hands folded across her girdle. She did not often behave well but on this occasion avoided Ralf's hot stares, rejoicing in her modesty. Let him grope without response, she thought with relish. Like that, I'll have him dancing to my tune even before we leave our wedding-board.

Isabelle de Nonant possessed all the fragile-seeming delicacy of the very strong; long limbs, well-swung hips, fine skin. Her eyes were too bold, her mouth too wide, her hands too square; but at her marriage feast men saw only her lowered lids as they shouted to tell Ralf what a lucky dog he was, which put him in an even better humour.

At last Queen Matilda's attendants came to escort Isabelle away. A stall in the stables had been set aside where they could be alone for the night, thereafter they would seldom sleep with more than a thickness of cloth between them and their household. As soon as Isabelle left, Ralf began to imagine how her attendants would undress his wife, the whisperings and slaps which would drive her pretending unwillingness into his straw. For she was willing; even half stupefied as he was, Ralf had seen past Isabelle's modesty to unashamed desire.

He stood, trying not to let anyone see his trembling, since no man of sense showed care for his wife, who was bought for breeding and to rule his house. Men jostled around him as he walked across a narrow court behind Westminster Hall, crowing like cocks and yelling more advice than a prime stallion could follow in one night.

Isabelle was waiting for him, dressed in a shift and sitting upright under a rich cloth spread on straw. Despite herself, she lifted her downcast eyes when Ralf ducked through the entry, the tips of her pointed teeth showing against full red lips. A great many people milled about while Ralf self-consciously sat under the coverlet beside her, the stench of sweat and wine overpowering in so small a space. Out of sight, Ralf's fingers touched Isabell's leg beneath the cloth but both stared steadfastly at the wall and crossed themselves when a priest came in to bless their bed.

'Remember boldness is best in love,' shouted Gaucelm de Launay, 'A fair lady despises caution.'

Ralf bit on the retort he longed to make, the sooner entertainment palled the sooner they would go.

'Try not to look too much like dead mutton on a platter,' added another voice. Most of Ralf's acquaintance were landless younger sons and jealous of the knights' fees he had gained. They had hoped the bride foisted on him would be ugly.

Eventually, as he had calculated, they grew tired of unanswered jibes and went to finish the wine. Some new married beddings ended in bloodshed when the groom's temper broke, but Ralf had no wish to provoke King William on this auspicious day by brawling in his courtyard.

Once they were alone together, neither Ralf nor Isabelle could think how to break the silence. Horses stamped the other side of a partition and flares crackled in the yard outside, but in their tiny retreat silence and blackness were complete. Then Ralf lay back with a sigh. 'God's mercy, what a time they took to go.'

'I wish they had not taken all the flambeaux with them,' answered Isabelle pettishly.

'And I, since then I could see whether your eyes are truly black or only brown, a question which has troubled me all day.'

'Oh?' she was uncertain whether he was laughing at her.

'Of course I could run outside in my shirt and beg for a tallow-dip,' he added musingly. Isabelle felt straw shift as he stretched out more comfortably.

'No!' she said sharply. 'We were lucky as it was that no one set light to the straw.'

He laughed and rolled over. 'I agree. Definitely no. We've wasted enough of the night with drunken swine.'

'You're drunk too.'

'Not much. Enough. Has no one in the queens court ever told you that it is better to lie than sit in your wedding bed?'

'Yes, and a great deal more besides. As the Sieur de Launay also gave you advice, my lord.'

Ralf bit back annoyance, wondering whether he would do best to beat the insolence out of his high-starched wife before it set a tidemark on everything they did. He was, however, scheming rather than rash by inclination and also preferred his women willing. 'Gaucelm de Launay's boldness is best suited to seduction in a ditch, lady. You are my wife, so I take the time God gives us to become acquainted.'

'Oh, this darkness!' exclaimed Isabelle, and lay down beside him. 'I cannot see whether you laugh at me or not.'

Ralf immediately kissed her, his face rougher than she expected: Isabelle's boldness as well as the ill-reputation of her family meant that the queen's ladies had ruled her harshly, so she imagined a great many things but knew almost nothing about male lusts.

'Come here,' Ralf said, and his face scraped hers again. Scraped and stayed this time, as his hands stayed under her shift.

'You're strong,' she answered, pleased to find him strong.

Gradually his lips moved from her cheek, to her lips, to her breast. Ralf believed in taking trouble to soften a woman, and merely laughed when her shift and his breeches became entangled as they wriggled free of them in the straw. He enjoyed his passions and wanted his wife to enjoy them too; a little indulgence now should pay for itself with future ease. But Isabelle had been plotting her way out of Queen Matilda's restrictions for so long that she felt triumphant on her wedding night, she despised indulgence and wanted a man for wanting's sake. An inclination which, after some initial surprise, also pleased her husband, that most adaptable of men.

No one bothered them in the morning. Some grooms fetched straw for the horse, but a wedding was unremarkable once the feasting finished and they scarcely glanced at the couple in the corner. Ralf and

Isabelle even had to help each other dress, the Queen's quarters being far removed from the stable yard.

'I shall wish you helped me to dress each day,' Ralf said. 'My lady, I never saw such white skin before.'

'Even the queen's attendants thought my bosom good,' answered Isabelle eagerly. After a night which had proved both satisfying and unexpectedly strenuous, she felt calm and soft towards him, her usual tartness forgotten.

Ralf gave a shout of laughter, and went out calling for his sergeant. They had a long way to ride that day.

The sergeant was a wiry Breton called Robert the Falconer, because as a boy he'd trained to handle hunting birds. He was still skilled with every kind of beast and like all good sergeants kept his men well fed and mounted without caring too much about the method. He was, however, old, but served Ralf with stolid loyalty because he had picked him out of a Westminster gutter after he was left to die of a fever.

That morning, it took even Robert some time to rouse Ralf's followers out of the wine-sodden sleep and kick them up on horseback, but by noon they had left London behind and were riding south, Ralf singing as he went:

'Lallay, a knight went riding out,
Lallay, his fortune all to find.'

He sang, twisting the words of a ballad popular among William's followers to suit his joy. Joy, joy to be alive, a young man in a conquered land, a willing woman riding at his back and a fiefdom in his belt.

In Ferenthe, most of the villagers were out on their ploughlands when a woman drawing water from the pool looked up to see horses between the trees. She left her pitcher and ran for cover before the intruders saw her, then bolted for the fields. Two years before, when King Harold of England lost his battle with the Norman invaders away to the south of Ferenthe, the village had been plagued by his routed followers, some wounded, others brutally unscrupulous in their desperation to be away from the pursuing Normans. A few of Duke William's men halted by the pool to drink soon after, and more as time passed. The Normans never seemed to stop travelling, but providing they were offered bread and ale, they caused little trouble. Soon, except for shamed fury which ran too deep to be spoken of, it was possible to forget that, after centuries of struggle, England had finally fallen to the bastard sons of Viking pirates.

Now the conquerors had come in force and, by the time the villagers came in from their fields, already looked set to stay longer than it took to drink and breathe their horses. Lances were laid criss-cross, point outward, to form a fence; the men kept together and still wore their laced war-jerkins.

Isabelle d'Escoville looked around her curiously. Until they reached the forest England looked much like Normandy to her, but this God-forsaken clearing filled her with alarm. She could rot a lifetime here and have nothing to show for it in the end. 'Christ's gullet, what a place,' she said and crossed herself.

'It's mine,' answered Ralf cheerfully. 'Hey, Robert! Drive those villeins over here so I may read King William's deed to them.' He pulled vellum from his belt and beat out the creases, relishing every moment.

Isabelle looked at the large clear pool and meagre fields enclosed by forest and wattle hurdles. 'How long will it take to build a keep?'

'I shall have something finished before the winter, but the king's clerk said the best site might be at Reredfelle, five miles to the west.' Though Ferenthe consisted of no more than a dozen wattle huts roofed by reeds, Ralf looked at it without disparagement. This place was now his and henceforth suffused by a glow of ownership.

As soon as he ordered the peasants to be herded closer, his men wheeled their horses to reach behind them. 'Take it slowly there,' yelled Robert warningly.

But almost immediately panic spread. Women seized their children and men turned to shove their way to where their weapons hung. 'Stand,' said Robert quietly, but in a voice which froze each of Ralf's men to his saddle. 'They're unarmed, so let's keep it that way, eh?' Villeins were valuable in an underpopulated land. He pulled his horse out of line and sheathed his sword, making sweeping motions with his hand. He spoke only a little English, but had dealt with thickskulls all his life.

The line of villagers wavered, looking up at the mailed soldiers fearfully, who stared back at them from under beaked nosepieces.

Ralf waited tranquilly; he did not expect trouble from people who spent their days grubbing in the soil, and, caught between his confidence and Robert's persuasions, the villagers paused, the whites of their eyes showing beneath shaggy hair.

'I am Ralf d'Escoville, your lord,' said Ralf pleasantly as soon as they were still. He had no quarrel with these people and prided himself on his command of English. 'Oderic, your English thane, was killed in the great battle as you know, and in his place King William has granted the manor of Fernet-le-Forêt to me.' He held William's sealed deed where all could see it. 'This was delivered before witnesses at Westminster and from today this land is mine, and you also. Let no man challenge my rights.'

The peasants eyed each other uncertainly; Ralf's grasp of the English tongue was less complete than he believed, and the people of Andredsweald spoke a dialect of their own. Then a wide-shouldered man of rather less than Ralf's age and as fair as he was dark, stepped forward. 'We are not beasts to be herded from one hand to another. Ferenthe is a free village and belongs to us. Thane Oderic never ruled here.'

The same pause followed while Ralf struggled, as had the villagers, with unfamiliar words. Then his face reddened. 'The king grants land, not you. See, here is his seal, which gives me the power to judge and rule you.

'By what right, since Ferenthe is ours?' the other answered coolly.

'By right of conquest,' snapped Ralf. 'Oderic was killed opposing the man now crowned your king.'

'And you have lordship of Ferenthe because this king granted you Thane Oderic's lands.'

'Why not listen the first time?' said Ralf sarcastically, aware that by trying to speak English he risked looking foolish. 'All possessions of

Thane Oderic, killed by William, King of England, are now mine, including the manor of Ferenthe, henceforth called Fernet-le-Forêt.'

The Englishman grinned, light eyes above thick bones. 'You did not say it clearly before. I understand you hold not by right of conquest but because the new king declares Oderic a rebel, although he served King Harold, as was his duty. You hold by the law. A new king's unjust law, but still the law. Call a folkmoot and I will bring jurors from far and wide to swear that Ferenthe never belonged to Oderic, although Reredfelle was his. My kindred have held this place since long before my grandsire's time, by grant from a better king than your William.'

Ralf stared at him, flabbergasted. Never had he heard one man say so many treasonable and insolent things in a single breath before; he had long considered the English system of folkmoots a great mistake, and now was sure of it. 'Stand aside or hang from your own oak. If you are headman here, then I hold you responsible for bringing the young men of Fernet-le-Forêt to work on my castle, Robert will tell you where. Your name, villein?'

'Leofric. Of Ferenthe,' he added mockingly. 'And you may not build your castle within my lands, which stretch along the ridge to the ploughland yonder.'

Ralf nodded to Robert. 'String him up.'

A sound like water over stones swept through the listening villagers, most of whom understood less than one word in three, but Ralf's meaning was not difficult to interpret. From behind Ralf's back, Isabelle watched gnarled and dirt-seamed faces pucker up in hate; she was not afraid of villeins, only of monotony, and waited with excitement for the killing to begin.

'My lord, we are fourteen men and a woman facing thirty,' said Robert. 'But I will hang him if you wish it.'

Ralf's eyes flickered from Leofric to his men; mounted and mailed though his Normans were, at close quarters peasant knives could hamstring more horses than he could afford to lose, and in the tumult irreplaceable villeins would be killed. He turned his back to Leofric. 'If you have writings to prove this place is yours, show them to me.'

Leofric shook his head, smiling. 'Do Normans think all Saxons are fools? Name a day and I will bring jurors to the Hundred Court.'

Ralf heard Isabelle suck breath between her teeth; she spoke no English but a child could follow the gist of this dispute. Had he been alone he would have stepped back from a barren contest, waited, and then seized Fernet-le-Forêt at a better time, making sure Leofric alone was killed. But with Isabelle watching, he could not draw back and remain undiminished in her sight: after only three days of marriage he had a shrewd estimate of her scorn for weakness.

He drew his sword, cursing the over-confidence which had left his mail unlaced. 'Hang him from his oak and then fire the huts.' If there were writings here which pretended to give these oafs title to Ralf d'Escoville's land, then he wanted them destroyed.

But Robert was either unwilling, or, for once, unprepared. While he still fingered his sword, Leofric ducked under his horse's belly, which brought him face to face with Isabelle.

Isabelle opened her mouth to scream, but Leofric swerved. A woman was no use to him. He needed the lord, a capture which just might give him time to rub Norman noses in King Aelfred's writings. Killing was no answer either, although he yearned to kill, since he would simply join Oderic as a dispossessed rebel. The air filled with yells and children's screams as the Normans rode into peasants who had no room to flee. Swords struck at random and cries changed to wails. Frightened horses plunged and stamped, trampling anyone who fell; the villagers struck back with knives and tools brought from the fields, a horse galloped wildly off with its entrails trailing. Then a mother screeched so dreadfully as her child was trampled that everyone paused in midstroke, and Robert seized this instant of uncertainty to start flailing his men off with the flat of his sword. Hurling obscenities at those adrift in bloodlust. When he had them in hand at last, he turned to find Ralf wiping his sword clear of blood and brains, Leofric face down on the grass at his feet.

Robert blew out his cheeks with relief. He thought he had seen his duty clear, but a fine fool he would have looked, saving villeins at the cost of his seigneur's life. 'My lord, we have lost three horses and Gullaume is wounded in the shoulder. I am cut across the leg.'

Ralf scowled; calamity had struck so fast it was hard to believe that only this morning he had been singing as he rode through the forest. 'Keep the churls guarded while you fire their huts.'

The villagers howled like wolves when sparks flew and roofs exploded into flame, and Robert, too, winced at the sound. He had been driven by robbers from his own small plot in Brittany many years before, his wife and newborn son dead of cold the following winter; the sounds of burning always recalled the horror of it to his memory.

One of the women left the huddle of peasants and walked over to him, as a dream-walker would, eyes open but seeing nothing.

Robert cleared his throat 'Get back with the rest.'

She simply walked past him and knelt in the man Leofric's blood, her hair drawn over her face in grief.

'I'll fetch her back,' said one of the men-at-arms eagerly.

'You move before I say and we'll repair our harness with your guts.' Robert kept his eyes on the muttering howling English; this idiocy could still end in a massacre.

But after that, everyone gradually calmed down.

The woman continued to kneel beside the dead man, her husband Robert supposed, as he kicked off any of his men bold enough to try and molest her. Ralf and his lady put their heads together and chattered like crows before eventually deciding to pass the night in a tumbledown chapel they had seen on their way into the village; the villeins slid into the shadows as the fireglow from their huts dimmed. Since Ralf had not ordered Robert to stop them, he let them pass one at a time, then dismounted his men to drink at the pool. They were in boisterous spirits after such excitement, shouting and throwing water at each other like brats at play; in such a mêlée they had been lucky to escape with only one man hurt besides himself. His legging had stuck to the slash in his leg, preventing more bleeding, but he worried about it in such a place as this. Cuts from saw-edged peasant knives had a habit of puffing like bladders in the sun, and men died raving from them three days later.

Eventually Ralf came over to where Robert stood. 'Get that woman on her feet, I want to talk to her.'

Robert stirred her with his foot. 'The Sieur d'Escoville would speak with you.'

She shivered and looked up, her lips bloody where she had kissed the dead man.

Robert jerked his head. 'Up.'

Christ in heaven, but she was a sight to melt any man: all tragic eyes and ripeness ready for picking.

Ralf d'Escoville did not think so, and stared at Lulla out of eyes as hard as horn. 'Tell your people that tomorrow they must come with their oxen and dig where they are told. If they do not, I will garrison this place and see that not one of you harvests a crop. Those who work willingly may live in peace, paying only half their yield to me in food-rent, and in return I shall defend them from their enemies.'

'You killed my brother, Leofric,' the woman answered, as if she grasped nothing else.

'He nearly killed me and my lady,' answered Ralf shortly. 'Say, quickly, which is it to be?'

She shrugged. 'Yes, we will dig rather than starve. No, Ferenthe is not yours, ever.'

Robert shook his head in admiration as she stalked off into the dark. 'His sister, now that is strange. I believed her to be his wife.'

'String up this carrion from the oak and then we'll leave them a night to think about my words.' Ralf swung back in the saddle. 'There's nothing to be gained by half-measures now.'

This certainly was true, so Robert did as he was told before the Normans withdrew to the chapel, also to spend a night in thought.

Lulla wept again as soon as her back was turned on those beaked, contemptuous helmets, but when she saw how they had hanged Leofric's corpse from Young Alaric's oak, she spat on the ground, set her foot on the spittle and swore to be avenged.

Hwita stood at her side, her speechless gaze on Leofric. Married and widowed within four days, she showed no more emotion than she had when Lulla crept out to leave her alone with Leofric on her marriage night. 'I will dig the grave if you will help me to cut him down.' She said, as if she discussed the best way to broil meat.

Lulla slapped her face. 'You haven't even wept for him!'

'What would be the good? He is dead and never felt softly towards me, nor ever could he have.' This time her voice held a kind of helpless wistfulness, as if a future without a hut or husband was no worse than a past with both.

Lulla was silenced. Hwita was so stupid she found it hard to take her seriously, but a deeper tragedy than one day's killing shaped those words. 'I will climb the tree and cut him down if you will take his weight,' she said at last. In the forest it was considered unlucky for anyone except blood kin to inter the dead. The rest of the village only gathered round when they had cut Leofric's grave into earth between the oak roots, not far from where his ancestors Alaric and Edred lay. Then they scattered again to run from one task to the next while moonlight lasted. Oxen lowed where they had been abandoned under the yoke when the Normans came, and there was a good deal to be saved from huts which in some cases had only smouldered in the damp.

Left alone again under the oak, Lulla and Hwita stood side by side, Lulla wriggling her toes absently in fresh turned soil, still scarcely believing that the sweetness of her life had been lost with such deadly speed. When she had seen horsemen emerging from the forest so short a time before, all she had thought of was how fine a sight they made.

Hwita stirred. 'We will go to Edmer, my father. His hut is far enough into the forest to be safe.'

'You go if you wish. The Normans did not see Danesdell in its hollow so it remains unburnt; they will have to kill me too before I leave my own place.' Lulla thought for a moment. 'Hwita, will you swear something on Leofric's grave?'

'If it is something I can do.'

'I shouldn't ask you, if it wasn't!' snapped Lulla, exasperated. 'The writings King Aelfred gave our forebears lies in a pot at Danesdell. If I tell you where I shall hide it, will you swear never to tell anyone else, so long as I live?'

Hwita's brow furrowed. 'I can't promise that.'

'Why not? If you don't swear then I shan't tell you.'

'I slept four nights with Leofric. If I bear his son, the writings belong to him.'

The wrangle, petty though it was, helped ease the moment when Lulla must turn aside from Leofric's grave. And then there was a pack of things to do. Most important of all she must hide King Aelfred's deed, because tomorrow the Normans might easily return to discover how much was left unburned.

But as soon as she left the oak to return to Danesdell, anxious soot-smeared people broke off from their labour to demand that she should save them with her writings. 'Leofric tried, and died because of it.' She answered, quickening her pace. 'Is that what you want from me?'

'Leofric knew his time to pay had come.' Answered Ylifa, a snag-toothed crone who had whined each year when Leofric demanded acknowledgement of his title. 'A true lord dies for his people when he must, and you are the last of your kindred's blood.'

'Leofric died, but Ferenthe has not yet been saved.'

'He did not have his writings.' Answered Ylifa. 'Fetch them to show the Norman, or have you tricked us all these years?'

'Show the Norman your writings!' shouted all those close enough to hear. 'Go to him now, and then he will ride away to Thane Oderic's manor at Reredfelle and leave us in peace.'

Lulla stopped where the path from the pool dipped towards the slope where Danesdell lay. 'Listen, fools. What if I show this Norman my writings and he throws them in the fire?'

They muttered a great deal at that, many of the men being in favour of burning down the chapel while the Normans slept inside.

Lulla let them argue it a dozen ways among themselves without coming to agreement, and only when they fell silent did she speak again. 'Do you want to live always as outlaws in the forest?'

No, certainly they did not want that, when more generations than anyone could remember had laboured to hack their fields from wilderness.

'Then we cannot burn Normans to death in a chapel, when everyone would know we had done it.'

'There will never be a better chance for us to be rid of them,' muttered a voice in darkness.

Lulla shook her head. Enough Normans had ridden their great

arrogant horses through Ferenthe these past two years for anyone of sense to know who ruled England now. They might rid themselves of these particular raiders, and the dark spirits of the forest knew how much she wanted to burn them alive, but other and bloodier ones would come in their place. Of all the people left in Ferenthe, only Lulla had grown up beside a hearth whose men attended folkmoots held under the King's Peace as a matter of right; she knew that a good standing before the law was a weapon like any other and not lightly to be thrown away. 'We must go with our oxen to dig as the Norman ordered,' she said at last. 'Why he should desire this I do not know, but if digging will satisfy him, so be it. He has a right to Reredfelle if he has been put in Oderic's place, and soon he will go there. What robber does not secure the easiest prize first? Then, before he returns to Ferenthe, we must find a priest who is able to read King Aelfred's writings and jurors to swear my right.'

The villagers drifted resentfully back to work again after that, and when dawn came they harnessed the team of eight oxen which between them they possessed, and trudged across the ploughland and through the thicket to the chapel.

Ralf, too, scarcely slept during the night. When Isabelle tried to fondle him he thrust her off angrily; if she spoke he told her to hold her tongue.

He must decide immediately what to do, when this day's work had come close to ruining him. Whether as king or duke, William had cancelled grants and charters by the hundred but always on some pretext of law: he would not forgive even a favoured follower (and Ralf was not especially favoured) who killed one of his subjects to pleading an established right.

Ralf left the tiny chapel and paced a long time under the stars. Somehow he had to prevent the tale of this day's doings from reaching the king's ears. Yet that was impossible. His own followers would talk. The churls would talk, since he could not massacre all of them without leaving some tale behind.

So what could he do?

Get hold of the woman's written title, if it existed.

Build defences as though his rights were unquestioned, and make sure that William's instructions to keep his forest lands at peace were carried out to the letter. Among his own followers, Ralf thought that only Robert understood enough English to realise that Leofric had claimed Ferenthe as his by right of a previous royal grant. So Robert, too, would have to be silenced. Back and forth Ralf paced, between chapel door and the well Theobald had begun to dig before other raiders came. Paused at last in his pacing and stretched until his sinews crackled, in mocking acknowledgement to the moon, mother of invention. There were more ways of silencing a man than killing him.

When the Ferenthe villagers came next morning to the chapel, they were astonished to be told they must start digging a ditch between the chapel and the well.

'It is a foolish place to dig,' grumbled Wiglaf, who complained whatever he did. 'There is no need for drainage, and God will be offended to find mud piles on his doorstep.'

But Robert showed then, with many gestures, where the dug earth was to be piled and at first the villagers dug willingly enough, the circumstances so strange that this alone gave some interest to the work. But when the Normans shouted each time a man rested or a woman fed her child, they became exasperated. Most had come expecting to perform some ritual task which would speed the intruders on their way, not to waste the whole day of good ploughing weather. Towards midday, the first man left; Edward-of-the-bees as he was called, for his skills in tracking down bee-swarms in the forest and taking their honey; a man more than half wild, who stifled labouring in a crowd. He simply cast down his mattock and walked away, perhaps scenting bees in the way he sometimes did.

'Hey! Get back to work!' the nearest Norman yelled, running to jab him in the buttock with his sword.

Edward fled screeching but before he could reach the thicket's cover, he tripped and fell, an arrow protruding from his back. Like the events of the previous day, it all happened so quickly no one else had time to move. Only when the Normans began shouting among themselves, obviously congratulating one of their number on his marksmanship, did the villagers exchange stupefied glances, their first instinctive, half-ashamed thought: how shall we ever find honey in the forest now?

'Work!' shouted Ralf. He waved his arms, annoyed by this wastage of a man. 'You work until you are told to stop.'

'These Normans are bewitched,' said Ylifa, with conviction. 'I never heard of a man being killed for a ditch before, and this is a ditch to nowhere.'

But as the ditch deepened and lengthened, they saw that it enclosed a space around the well some fifty paces square, the mound of spoil tamped solid to give a defensive rampart the height of a man. It still made little sense to them, nor to Isabelle either, who watched from the chapel step until she tired of glowering looks. 'They will kill us the moment we turn our backs, and a pitiful moat like that won't stop them,' she observed when Ralf came by.

'Then we must never allow them to get behind us.' He had woken fresh from very short sleep and had no patience with misgivings. Isabelle would spend the rest of her life ruling Sussex oafs and the sooner she realized it, the better. 'Tomorrow we ride to Reredfelle, which even these pigs agree was Thane Oderic's manor,' he added.

'Leaving an empty site as the only evidence of your claim?' she flicked a disdainful finger at the ditch and its enclosure. They will flatten it within a day and use the palisade stakes to repair their huts.'

'It won't be empty.'

Isabelle stared at the complacent expression beneath the nose-piece of Ralf's helmet. 'We are too few for leaving garrisons scattered through the forest. My lord, we need a mound four times the height of this one for even a makeshift stronghold, and a tower to top it; Nonant was often raided in my childhood, and I know that nothing less will do.'

'Aye, and we will build both tower and bailey, but not here. God's blood, do you think I would site my stronghold where there is so little water and any Norman riding out would risk an arrow in the back? I want to hunt when I wish and ride where I will, not turn monk behind walls I dare not pass.'

Isabelle laughed; just for a moment she had been afraid that Ralf intended to leave her behind to hold this accursed wallow in the forest. 'I cannot see you as a monk, my lord. What is your purpose then with this stockade?'

'Wait,' answered Ralf. 'I have learned other things in England besides how to build a bailey.'

And though Isabelle begged him to tell, he primmed his lips as if wanting to laugh, and refused.

Thirty men, their women and their children can dig a fair ditch in a day, when driven hard. By nightfall the enclosure Robert had pegged out lay inside a fence of pointed stakes, broken only by a split-birch gate hung on leather straps. Within, there was a small mound flattened to take a hut, the well and space sufficient to hold twenty men and their horses for a night.

When the last stake was driven, Ralf bade his men light torches and called everyone over to listen to what he had to say. Even Isabelle came out from the chapel, where she had been sheltering since a fine rain began to fall, all agog to hear what was to happen next. The flaring torches made Ralf's face glow as red as the devil's among his men-at-arms. They knew something was afoot and the Sieur d'Escoville enjoyed an enviable reputation for resource among his men.

'Inhabitants of Fernet-le-Forêt, I thank you for your labour,' he began. 'You will find me a generous master of those who serve me well.'

The villagers muttered a good deal at that but were too tired to do more: no amount of saying it made any man their master.

'I ride tomorrow for Reredfelle,' Ralf resumed, 'where I expect to build a stronghold which will keep safe the roads and protect you from harm. I am glad to see this pleases you,' he added sarcastically, for all his listeners cheered up at these words. The men-at-arms because to them the ridge seemed like a trap, and the English because tomorrow these intruders would be gone.

'It pleases us very much!' yelled an English voice out of the darkness, and everywhere surliness split into grins.

Ralf tugged at his swordbelt angrily, but realized he could not punish a man for agreeing with him. 'I shall be back. I am your lord and my sons after me. My lands in Sussex are valued by the king at five knights' fees, so you must pay in food or goods to keep these knights equipped.'

On the edge of the crowd Lulla felt hands begin to push her forward, although she tried to stay in the shadows. She was too tired to fight the Normans now, and, besmeared by mud, at too much of a disadvantage. In the end, it was Wiglaf who fairly hurled her at the Norman's feet.

'Well?' said Ralf, smiling. 'Get up, woman, but be still.'

Lulla scrambled to her feet, furious that he spoke to her as if to a goat. 'The inhabitants of Ferenthe bid me swear as Leofric did yesterday, that they are free and always have been.'

'Ah,' said Ralf, smiling still, although his face tightened. Your brother tied to kill me.'

'He tried to tell you that Ferenthe was his.'

'And because he believed this idiocy, you believe it too?'

Lulla nodded.

'Why? Even in England it must be unusual for sisters to inherit.'

Lulla hesitated. It was dangerous, surely, to admit that she and Leofric were the last of their line, except for a child whom Hwita might, or might not, carry.

Ralf nodded, well satisfied. The wench would be pretty if she was clean; she was also too simple to deceive him, who had cheated bishops in his time. Whatever the reason, she and these people believed that the claim to this land was now hers alone. 'Robert,' he called. 'Come here, and Walter – hold this woman.'

One of the men-at-arms held her greedily while Robert limped forward. 'My lord?'

'Robert the Falconer, you have served me faithfully and time for reward has come. It is in my mind to grant you my manor of Fernet-le-Forêt, for which you will pay the rent due on a knight, or come yourself in service when I ask.'

Robert wiped his face, slowly, first with one sleeve then the other. Him, a freeholder! Close to the age when being on the road every day became a burden, and he was offered a gift straight from paradise! 'My lord,' he said, and stopped: My lord, for such a prize I would try to furnish two knights if you asked.'

Ralf jerked his head at the stockade behind his back. 'Behold, your strong place. Swear your oath to me, and when we ride out tomorrow, you stay here. If you can rule this settlement and the woman, both are yours.'

Behind Ralf's back Isabelle laughed aloud, such ingenuity appealed to her. Robert was old and his leg might easily purify if he rode with them on the morrow; Ralf lost nothing by leaving him behind. In fact, because he planned to marry Robert to this Saxon woman who claimed Ferenthe, Ralf would gain whether his former sergeant lived of died.

'My lord, she may be a wife already.' Said Robert blankly.

'She is not. I asked the priest. Which reminds me, fetch the good Brother here, one of you.'

Norman and Englishman stood side by side, while the priest was fetched. He was frail and somewhat fuddled in his head, although a holy man.

'Come, Brother, begin your paternosters,' shouted Ralf as soon as he appeared. We have a brave man here who is willing to wed a slut.'

The priest peered at Lulla. 'She is no slut.'

'A slut who took her brother into her bed,' answered Ralf firmly, and watched the English, who had become restless, grow very still. 'She is lucky to be given a fine husband when only yesterday her shame was clear for all to see. Come gabble your mass before my good Robert changes his mind.'

The priest hesitated. He often felt confused, but knew this brew was of the devil's making. 'There are no rings, and neither of them has confessed.'

'Marry them without more chatter and I will find you rings!' Ralf's good humour was now so intense that he gasped his words like a man close to frenzy while those around him greeted each sally with a shout. 'My lady, give me rings from off your pretty fingers.'

Isabelle came over, eyes snapping with excitement, and dragged off the two plainest rings Ralf's friends had offered at her nuptial feast. How dull her days had been before she wed Ralf d'Escoville!

Robert choked on his own spittle. 'My lord –'

'Swear your oath for the knight's fee of Fernet-le-Forêt, and all here will be your witness.' Commanded Ralf.

When Robert had stumbled to the end of his oath, Ralf turned again to Lulla. 'Kneel beside him, you. How little did we guess what fortunes would be made in England, eh, Robert.'

'I will not marry a man who yesterday took my brother's blood,' said Lulla flatly.

'His blood was on my sword, not his,' answered Ralf, as if he recognized this reasonable objection if sustained. He nodded to the man who held her, and he tumbled her down beside Robert. Then he turned to the priest and under that compelling stare Brother Athelstan began his mass. Incest. The girl had not denied the Norman's charge, so finding her a husband might be God's work after all.

Robert stayed as still as Lulla, who could not move in Walter's grip, and allowed himself to be married without protest. Nor, when Lulla might hold writings which gave her a claim to land which now was his, did he want to protest.

The moment the benediction was finished, Ralf ordered the new-wed pair inside their ditch. 'Call it your keep,' he said, laughing harder than ever. 'What rare good fortune to spend a bridal night between your own walls!'

Robert grabbed Lulla's hand and dragged her through the birch-branch gate, while loud-mouthed jesting beat on his ears; this the first time anyone had laughed at him and kept their pelt intact since he became a sergeant. Lulla was trembling so much her teeth chattered, but when the gate thumped shut behind them she immediately pushed Robert away. 'Leave me alone. It wasn't a true marriage. Brother Athelstan was enchanted by that devil of a Norman.'

Robert struggled to understand her meaning. 'It was a marriage, and a guard will be put on the gate to see we stay together.'

'I could climb that fence, were it twice as high,' answered Lulla contemptuously, and he heard her squelch over to the wall.

Robert rubbed his leg, wincing. He certainly could not climb staked walls or chase a reluctant woman tonight. 'Wait. Think about what has happened before you go.

'There is nothing to think about.'

'Before witnesses, you are my wife.'

'False witnesses.'

Christ's throat, why did the English speak so vile a tongue? 'They are witness to what they saw.'

'Your lord wished to torment me. Tomorrow he will think of a different jest and unmarry us.'

'But this suits him very well, don't you see? If you climb that wall you are my runaway property, to be seized and flogged by whoever catches you. You would be discredited before ever you tried to plead before jurors over writings you say you hold. Which now are mine. And if you ran a second time from your husband, in Normandy the punishment is death. Here . . . I suppose the law is much the same.' Her silence suggested he was right, and Robert plunged on while she was listening. 'If you stay, we live as freemen on our own land, owing knight service only to my seigneur.'

'God curse all Normans.' Lulla's hoarse voice came out of darkness. 'God curse you, and the Holy Virgin too.'

'You cannot curse the Virgin.' Robert crossed himself.

'Why not? Brother Athelstan prays all day then dared not tell your baron to look to his soul for the evil he did to me.'

Robert stayed silent, relieved that she seemed to have given up the idea of climbing the palisade. They were standing just inside the gate, and nowhere was there any cover from the rain. What a nuptial, he thought. A wife who hated him, and a mud enclosure which lacked even a bush to huddle under.

He limped round the walls to find the most sheltered corner. 'The wind is less between the mound and the fence, but even there we'll freeze alone.'

Lulla answered, but he could not disentangle the English. Her meaning was clear, however.

'Be sensible, woman. We are here and must make the best of it.' Robert thrust her towards such shelter as he had found; in truth, no shelter at all, except the edge was off the wind. They had not even twigs to sit on and the ground was sodden. ''Everything can only be better once this night is endured, but you will die unless you share my cloak,' he added.

Lulla sighed. 'Death would be welcome.'

'You will have no cause to complain of me. I will keep our pot filled and I have enough coins to buy seed for sowing in the spring.'

'No-one will sell to you, Norman. You do not belong here. I do not belong to you.'

'I belong here now.' And you will belong to me, he thought. Not tonight like swine in a wallow, but soon. He jerked her closer to the wall, then wrapped his heavy frieze cloak about them both; he never had been a man for arguing. He did what needed doing and that was all there was to it. When she tried to struggle he beat her soundly, not enjoying it as some men might, but knowing he must keep her beside him if she was to survive the night.

But afterwards he did lie with her in the mud, because he could not help himself.

They even slept a little afterwards, instinctively coiling together under the cloak. Lulla woke first, her back icy from the ooze beneath her. Water occasionally drained across the floor at Danesdell, but she never remembered such discomfort as this. Nor the weight of a man pegging her to the earth. She stared in revulsion at the face which was close enough for her to sink her teeth in it if she wished; by the law of God and of man, this bandy-legged goblin of a man was hers for the remaining years of her life. Beyond the palisade she heard the sound of hoofs as the other Normans left, and Robert stirred. His eyes were green; somehow Lulla expected them to be dirt brown, like the rest of him. 'My true wife,' he said, and touched her face. 'I did not want our first bedding to be in the mud.'

'But it was.'

He rolled off her, and stood. 'The Sieur d'Escoville will have fed before he left. Come, we will go and find his fire.'

Lulla was too absorbed in her wretchedness to argue. She watched while Robert grubbed for dry sticks from beneath bushes and blew the abandoned campfire into flame, drank and ate what he gave her, shivered each time he touched her. In daylight he looked the alien conqueror he was, sword at his side, chain-mail laced across his chest. He kept looking around him too, as if he expected an ambush.

Brother Athelstan peered out of his chapel at them as they ate, crossed himself and disappeared again.

'I am fouled the same as you, now.' Said Lulla bitterly. 'A stranger in my own place.'

Robert glanced at her, wanting to demand whether she had indeed lain with her brother. The priest had shied from Ralf's words as if there might be truth in them, might even have defied the Normans but for that. 'I must start building a shelter if it is to be finished by nightfall. You will not want another such night in the rain.'

'No, I don't want another such night,' answered Lulla.

Robert shrugged. He had not meant to take her in the mud, but could not feel sorry about it. Christ's blood, he was not so old that he did not know how to please a woman! Meanwhile, she was best left to get over her sulks.

Lulla had expected him to insist she stayed in his sight as a kind of prisoner but he went off, whistling, to chop the withies he wanted for his shelter and left her to fetch her belongings from Danesdell,. She walked quite slowly by the path through the thicket and across ploughland feeling filled with grief, dry and gritty to the taste. How could life change so completely, and the sun rise as if everything was the same? She met Edwige, Wiglaf's wife, on her way and stopped; if she could only talk about what had happened perhaps it would settle in her mind. But the woman looked away when Lulla called, and refused to answer.

Then there was Raedmer. He was driving a team of oxen and Lulla stopped to watch; after a life in which very little happened, the past two days had had been so filled with abominable happenings that every familiarity seemed doubly precious. She raised her hand as Raedmer passed, but he kept working, head down. Well, a man needed two hands to hold a plough.

On the bank above Danesdell, Lulla paused. Here the ground formed a tussocky bank before sloping to where their homestead stood. She looked down at her ancestral huts and byres, craving past contentment, then yelled and started running down the slope. Wiglaf was there, sitting on a stone and watching his swine gobble their way around the dell, trampling grain, hay and drying herbs underfoot.

Lulla grabbed a stick as she ran, belabouring the swine aside to reach Wiglaf. 'Get them out of here! What do you think you are doing?'

'There is good feed here.' Wiglaf swiped lazily at a fly.

'Get them out! Do you want us to eat pig-shit through the winter?' Lulla began thrashing the nearest animal towards the slope, but Wiglaf dug his goad into its side so it bolted in the opposite direction, panicking those in its way. A basket tipped over and the grain poured into a puddle.

'What are you doing? Lulla stood there, utterly bewildered. No one ever behaved as Wiglaf was doing. Then in a spurt of fury she brought her stick down on his head. 'Get out! Get out, do you hear me? How dare you find an easy day's pasturage here?'

Wiglaf leapt up with a yell and drove his fist at her face. 'Bitch! My swine have a better right here than you.'

Lulla rolled blood on her tongue and spat it on the ground. Her eyes watered and she was so angry she could have killed Wiglaf. She pushed past him to the hut, where Leofric's sword hung on the wall. A piglet was rootling by the hearth and Wiglaf roared with laughter when she drove it out with a bedcloth caught across its rump.

She held the sword ready to strike. 'I will slash as many pigs as I can reach if they are still here when the next cloud crosses the sun.'

'It didn't take you long to learn Norman habits,' he answered spitefully, before unhurriedly beginning to herd his swine up the bank. 'We're lucky the runt they gave you as husband is too old for breeding strong sons.'

When he disappeared beyond the bank at last, Lulla sat limply and surveyed the mess. Wiglaf must have been there some time, and perhaps half their winter stocks were fouled or eaten. She had scarcely begun picking grain out of the mire when Hwita came down the bank. 'Hwita! Do you see what Wiglaf has done? He must have been possessed by a devil! He brought his swine here and watched while they ate even the gruel in our pot.'

Hwita stared about her. I will find a broom.'

'Is that all you can say! I tell you, he came here with his swine as if Danesdell was the forest.'

'He will come again if you stay.'

Lulla paled, opened her mouth to answer and closed it again, remembering how Raedmer had failed to return her greeting. 'They cannot think I wanted to marry a Norman.'

'But you are wed and took Ferenthe as brideprice to a Norman bed. Wiglaf said you should have thrown yourself on their swords as Leofric did, rather than allow us to be sold.'

'How could I? And if I had died, there would be no one left of our blood to hold Ferenthe. So the Normans would take it anyway.'

'It is what they say you should have done,' answered Hwita indifferently. 'And also that once you were alone with him last night, you could have knifed the Norman if you wished.'

'Both of which are sins to terrify the soul.'

'Much you care about sin if it suited you.' Sometimes Hwita came out with a devastating truth, apparently without realizing it.

Lulla choked then giggled. 'But I didn't do either, and now I don't suppose I could.' She thought of Robert going whistling to cut withies, and also of the first taste of mating-pleasures he had given her in the night, however much against her will. 'Oh, Hwita, what shall I do?' she cried.

But Hwita did not know. 'I have been to visit my father and he says I may live at Edmersham again, but I see now that I must stay here or there will be no inheritance left for my son.'

'You probably aren't breeding and if you are it will very likely be a girl,' answered Lulla crossly. 'Besides, you can't raise Danesdell's crops alone. Everyone knows Edmer, your father, hates working with the soil.'

'Once I am known to carry Leofric's son, many men will wish to marry me for a share in his inheritance,' Hwita said complacently.

In the short time since Hwita came as a bride to Danesdell, Lulla had become used to choking back exasperation and she did so again now. The Norman baron had taken an easy way to hold Ferenthe because after a killing he did not want to risk wranglings in a court over title, but he would never listen to an oaf like Hwita begging on behalf of an unborn brat. But there was no point arguing, all Lulla could do was gather what she could carry on her back and go.

As Lulla walked along the foot-trail which led to the pool, desolation filled her heart. Danesdell was bred in her, she could not give it up. How could she have spoken of Robert to Hwita as if staying with him was even possible? She hated Robert, a cur left mockingly by his master to run wild amongst them. A different thought struck her and she stood still to consider it; Hwita knew where yesterday (only yesterday!) she had hidden King Aelfred's writings. Hwita, who would dispossess her if she could, without more ado Lulla left the basket she was carrying and ran to the forest edge, tearing her legs on brambles in her haste.

She was panting by the time she heaved the heavy basket on her shoulder again and she hesitated, tempted to go straight back to Robert, her enemy. All the world an enemy now, when only two days before she had lived in peace among good neighbours. But Danesdell was so close to the pool that already people there could see her, and so she trudged to meet them. Once she explained what Robert had told her, perhaps they would understand that unless she fled unimaginably far away, she could not escape a witnessed marriage. And whether she fled or not now, Robert held both Norman and Saxon titles to Ferenthe. What was the good of leaving the only place she knew, when as a wanderer she would become all men's prey? Ylifa was not a dolt like Hwita, she would know that Lulla had no choice except to stay with Robert, Norman though he was.

There were several women around the pool, which was the place where they always gathered to wash clothes and talk, and today there was more than enough to talk about. Lulla slid the basket from her shoulders and greeted them in the usual way: the women stared at her and did not answer. 'I came to ask advice on what I should do,' Lulla added, unaware that she had just decided to stay with Robert.

'I couldn't say, I'm sure,' answered Ylifa, slapping cloth.

'Nor I,' echoed Edwige, Raedmer's wife, although she would have liked to ask whether Normans really did have tails tied down one leg of their breeches, as Ylifa said.

'Brother Athelstan married me to Robert so there is little to be done about that,' said Lulla doggedly. 'But –'

Ylifa flung up her hands. 'One Norman with a slashed leg! Sweet Jesus in heaven, and she says there is nothing to be done.'

'Tell me what you would do,' screamed Lulla.

But they were not willing to say, merely crossing their fingers as if against a spell each time Lulla looked at them. She was the one kicked into a Norman bed, let her decide what to do. All they understood was that, through her, their homes had fallen to a conqueror.

Lulla stood staring at them, her toes curled into poolside grass, brown legs uncovered nearly to the knees. Her hair glinted as it always did, reminding men of autumn leaves and women of jealousy for her beauty, but today it was tangled and her lips swollen from Wiglaf's blow. And as she stood there, she heard someone laugh and say, 'Trust a Norman to split lips when he takes a woman.' Tears blinded her then, this grief sharper than any she had felt for Leofric. He had died as a man should, because he preferred death to being enslaved on his own land; she had nothing left worth dying for.

She turned to leave the pool, but something stung her leg and another her hand. She whipped round, and caught Edwige in the act of flinging an oak-nut. Edwige, who had always stopped at Danesdell for a gossip on her way home from the fields. For an instant she looked ashamed, then she sniggered. 'Hurry inside your Norman ditch for surely as Tiw is on his hill, you'll need all the protection you can find.'

'And so will you,' said Lulla furiously. 'Norman you call me, so Norman I shall be. They've won, and I'll be a winner too.'

She could hear Robert chopping wood from some distance away, and found him by the mound inside their palisade, weaving branches around driven stakes. He sprang on guard at the sound of her approach, hand reaching for his sword. Lulla nodded approvingly: he was right to fear attack. 'Shall I cut bracken for the floor?'

Robert saw her bruised face but decided to leave well alone. 'When I have finished we will be warm except when the wind is in the south. And as soon as I have killed a deer we will hang its skin across the entry.'

'I brought Leofric's axe, a cooking pot and some grain. That's all.'

'I've fed a troop of men with less.' He turned back to his weaving.

Lulla sighed, but after all, she might have done a great deal worse than a brown nut of a man who would see she did not starve.

They both worked steadily for what was left of the day. Haste meant botched work and chatter wasted time they might regret once night fell. Anyway, they had little to talk about until they became used to each other. Robert snared a squirrel and put aside such edible plants as he discovered while chopping branches, which, when cooked with a handful of grain, made an agreeably savoury meal. There were even woven stools to sit on by a fire lit in the hut entry, and a frame to lift their bedding off the ground. Lulla had never seen weaving used for so many purposes before and Robert told her that such skills were often used by soldiers who never stayed long in one place. He also tried to hide his pleasure at her praise, but Lulla was not deceived. She was somewhat cheered when she saw how easily he was softened by her words: Normans were not as different from other men as she had supposed.

The wind of the night before had dropped and their fire glowed warmly; an owl hooted close by and then was silent. They might have been the only humans on the ridge. 'It is better than last night,' said Lulla carefully, at last,

'And better again tomorrow, what happened when you returned to your hearth?'

'What happened?'

'I have seen enough foraging parties return with their tails between their legs to read the signs. I wondered if I should go with you, but thought you might do better alone.'

'We would certainly have done worse together.' Lulla then told him exactly what had happened, sorting it in her mind as she spoke. 'I don't think that while your king is so much feared they will dare to kill us, but all our work will have to be done alone,' she added. This last was serious, since the toil of clearing a new holding usually required more muscle than could be mustered by a single household.

'King William will remain feared, and his son after him.' Robert studied Lulla out of the corners of his eyes.

'You are wondering whether they urged me to kill you. Yes, they did. And no, you need not fear I shall put a skinning knife into your back one night.'

Alarm and pleasure warred in Robert's mind, the English words he needed scuttering on his tongue. No matter what perils he must face while holding his new-granted land, God had given him a woman whom many richer men than he would covet. A woman who faced him as a soldier might, directly and with courage. Also she was young and strong; younger and stronger and more beautiful than a battered old sergeant deserved.

Lulla knew him too slightly to guess how he felt. 'Would you like me to bathe your leg?'

He nodded, and when she brought water from the well, lay patiently while she soaked leather free from torn flesh. A puffed and angry cut emerged, stretching from buttock to knee. 'God's bones, I shall be lucky if this heals cleanly.' He said.

'The well here is thought to be holy,' offered Lulla.

'Once, long ago, when wicked men came to kill and torture,' tis said that a priest sat beneath the water for a whole day and night while they searched for him, and when they had gone he climbed out breathing as softly as you or I. My father said that his sister jumped in and tried to do the same, she being much given to visions and frenzies, but God cannot have liked her much because she drowned.'

Robert flexed his leg gingerly. 'If the water is holy only to the sinless, then I cannot expect a cure. Do what you can and bind it up again.'

Lulla tried to remember the herbs which were said to be best for poisons, but in Ferenthe everyone ran for Ylifa if there was an injury in their household, and she never shared her secrets.

So began the most extraordinary year in Lulla's life. Brother Athelstan needed to use the well which was now enclosed within Robert's palisade, and was too mild a man not to bless them when he did so; otherwise no one spoke to them, there were no commonplace barterings of wool for skins, or venison for nuts. Always in Ferenthe there had been gossip and assignations by the pool, ale drinkings for deaths or births, the special days everyone joined together in some great task with a feasting to look forward to when it was finished. This had been the framework of Lulla's life, and it was gone.

As soon as his leg was part-healed, Robert walked to Reredfelle, where Ralf d'Escoville was raising a timber castle on a mound, surrounded by a bailey many times the size of their palisade. 'The horse I rode was mine,' Robert had told Lulla several times. 'When the Sieur granted me this fee he had no right to take my horse with him when he left.'

'I doubt whether a baron who kills so easily cares what is right or wrong,' answered Lulla but was proved wrong. Ralf did not cheat his own followers and gave Robert an ox to replace his horse, as well as five silver pieces to buy goods in the market. Robert returned to Ferenthe two days later, and as soon as Lulla saw him driving a laden ox she ran down the slope to greet him, breathless with excitement,

Any excitement, please God, to break the monotony of days made up of silent labour, anything which helped break through the hatred surrounding them, although hatred seemed the only emotion left which wasn't as drab as clay.

'I'll call him Cheerful,' said Lulla, stroking the ox's muzzle.

'As you wish,' answered Robert, who thought it an odd name for an ox. 'An ox and five pieces of silver! I never thought the Sieur would give so much.'

'I do not call it giving when he stole your horse.'

'He'd lost horses in the fight by the pool and now had paid three times its value. You should see his castle, set on a mound as high as a talk oak and the keep entered only by a ladder to make it safe!'

'Pray for the villagers of Reredfelle who have to labour on such works, and ever afterwards endure your baron as a neighbour.'

'If they accept the Sieur d'Escoville with good grace they'll very likely prosper as a consequence. They say his lady is already breeding.'

'So am I.'

Robert stood still. She said it as if the matter lacked meaning, but to him – he could not express what it meant to him, twenty years after he had buried his wife and son in Breton soil. He lifted the bundle of wood she had been carrying to meet him and said thickly, 'You lead Cheerful then he is docile and you should not be carrying burdens.'

Lulla laughed, but gladly took the tether he handed her. 'I don't need coddling like a Norman baron's brood mare.'

Robert's leg swelled again after his journey to Reredfelle. It had never completely healed and now the flesh became dark edged with white, red streaks running from knee to groin. Lulla stared at it, dismayed. She had seen putrefaction start in a wound before and knew how easily it killed.

'Heat water and fetch a stick.' Robert lay wearily on bracken in their hut. 'Hurry, while I have my senses and can tell you what to do. You need freshly-broken stick the thickness of my finger, with bark which may be peeled.'

Lulla ran to find it, prayer and curses jumbled together on her lips. If Robert died, how could she and her child survive? She was immediately ashamed of so selfish a thought, and broke the stick in the sign of a cross, for contrition.

Robert's eyes had closed, but flicked open when she knelt beside him. 'Strip the bark. All of the twig must be fresh if it is to gather the evil humours. Use it to tear off the scab and rake out the wound.'

'Tear off. . . merciful Christ,' whispered Lulla.

Robert lay back, his eyes closed again. 'Quickly.'

So she did it quickly, while he writhed and swore beneath her hands. Once the scab was off a stream of pus oozed out, then more blood and pus each time she raked. Shen all was finished she poured cold water over it, unable to bear the idea of heat on that bloody rawness, and covered it with moss.

By then Robert had ceased to moan and was lying as still as a corpse. He muttered a little but said nothing sensible and his skin became baking hot as the night wore on Lulla was so weary she dozed from time to time, waking in a sweat of fear and terror. Worst of all was her helplessness. There were herbs which sometimes exorcized demons from the blood, but only Ylifa knew them; also spells, although Lulla was doubtful whether even Ylifa possessed a sorcerer's powers.

In the end, she couldn't bear her helplessness any longer. Surely Ylifa would not refuse advice in such extremity, and if she did then a silver coin might change her mind. Dawn was close when Lulla reached the huddle of huts by the pool. A dog leapt out snarling as she passed but when she spoke it licked her hand, recognizing a voice which until recently had come here often. Dogs had more sense than men, Lulla thought. Ylifa was snoring on warm ashes outside her hut, and woke at a touch. Midwife, herb-woman and bonesetter of Ferenthe, she was well used to night-time wakenings.

She peered up at Lulla's face. 'The Norman whore. You are not welcome here.'

Whore is one thing you cannot call me, when I was wed before your eyes. Ylifa, in the name of Christ, come with me to tend Robert, who is grievously sick from demons devouring his leg.'

Ylifa yawned. 'Sick from a good English knife-stroke, more like. Would that his baron sickened too.'

'We have settled where no one has ploughed before, and Robert will deal fairly with you over rents, bear his share of charges from his baron. What more can you ask of a man than that?'

'That he should go away, and take all Norman robbers with him. You should be glad he is sick and not come begging for help to revive him.' She closed her eyes, and neither slaps nor curses would open them again. The noise started the dogs barking and men began to tumble out of their huts, sleepily holding weapons.

'She wants help for her Norman!' called Ylifa from her ashes. 'I ask you, brothers. Help for those who pillage us.'

'I can pay, if you will only come,' whispered Lulla, for Ylifa's ears only.

'Let me see.'

Lulla held a coin so it glinted.

'Let me test its trueness for myself, then I might think about coming.'

'Not think, come. And give the same advice you would to any neighbour.

Ylifa shrugged. If she was lucky she handled silver once a year at harvest. 'Very well.'

'These men are witnesses,' said Lulla, and gave her the coin she did not trust Ylifa, but no one broke a word sworn in front of neighbours.

Ylifa tucked it in her belt and lay down again. 'Go tend your man yourself. At least I now have one coin saved from all that these

Normans take from us.'

When Lulla cried out and snatched at Ylifa's belt the men hauled her off, although they avoided her eyes as she pushed past them, running now for Danesdell. She was past pride or even rage for the moment, and thought only of how long Robert had been left alone. Yet she could not bear to return, bringing only her own helplessness to aid him. Hwita was dull-witted but she had lived in the forest and might know more than those who dwelt on cleared land.

Hwita came to the door holding an iron-tipped goad.

'Who is it?'

'Lulla. Tell me, are you skilled in herbs?'

'What if I am?'

Lulla let out a gasp of relief. Hwita's tone suggested that she might know more than which roots were useful as purges. Hastily, she gabbled out about Robert and how his leg had worsened after walking to Reredfelle.

Hwita placed her goad upright by the door. 'Ask Ylifa. My knowledge is nothing beside hers.'

'She won't come.'

'Then if I went, Ylifa and the others would put the evil eye on me. None of us forget, as you do, that your Norman murdered Leofric, my son's father.'

Lulla saw that Hwita was indeed breeding, as she'd said she would. 'Robert did not kill Leofric. That was his lord, the Sieur d'Escoville.'

'Ha! See how easily the names of robbers drip off your tongue. God's curse on all of them, say I, when one alone could have done nothing.'

Lulla bit her lip; she often felt troubled because she could not hate Robert. Tonight she even came close to loving him, because she was so terrified he would die and leave her alone, surrounded by hate. 'In the name of Christ and the Virgin, tell me how to save a life. I too am breeding and if Robert dies -.'

'You'll starve, and your brat with you. Good riddance. Do you think we want Norman whelps infesting Ferenthe?'

'You fool,' said Lulla slowly. 'Ferenthe will be left alone only so long as Robert lives. His lord was afraid when he heard that our family held writings signed by a king, because Robert says conqueror kings must especially guard the powers they usurp. But if Robert dies without a grown up son to discharge his knight service, then Ferenthe reverts to his lords. That is Norman law. While Robert is alive he will collect Norman tax from you, but he also stands between you and his greedy lord. Let him die, and that greed will be put in his place.'

'Well now,' said Hwita blankly. Argument meant nothing if it collided with matters she accepted as established truth.

Lulla moistened her lips. 'I will give your son King Aelfred's writings, if you cure Robert.

'They are his by right already.'

'By my life, if you refuse this mercy, then I will burn them rather than see any son of yours inherit.'

'Wiglaf would kill me if I came.'

'Wiglaf? What has he to say to anything? You can't mean to put that ox-turd in Leofric's place? You can't! He has a wife.'

'She died in childbirth a week ago and Wiglaf is willing to wed me at the next full moon.'

'One last time. Do you come with me, or not?'

'I can't. Wiglaf would kill me if I did, Hwita repeated.

'Not he! You are worth more to him alive while Leofric's inheritance is in your belly,' answered Lulla viciously. She ran back across the fields, scarcely slackening pace when she reached the thickets which divided the chapel and palisade from the ploughland of Ferenthe. She had thought to leave Robert only for a short time alone and it seemed as if a lifetime had passed in futile beggings for help.

But when she reached their hut, Brother Athelstan stood beside their sleeping place. 'You ought not to leave a man who is so ill.'

'Is he still alive?'

'Only prayer can save him. On your knees, my daughter, where you should have been before.'

Lulla knelt obediently but soon Robert's fever reached across to her and she scrambled to her feet again; surely spring water would help cool such a great heat? He did indeed seem easier once she had wiped off his sweats and trickled a little water between his dry lips, and fell gradually into an uneasy doze. As soon as he lay still, she uncovered his leg and saw that another scab had formed.

'Do you think I should prise off the crust again?'

Athelstan's eyes stayed closed. 'Pray, my daughter, and wait on God's good time.'

Lulla stared at Robert's leg in a panic of indecision. Surely the evil humours were more gathered than before? Why had they gathered? Were they more dangerous if let loose, or safer as Robert said? Christ and the spirit Tiw have mercy, tell me which it is. Christ forgive me for speaking of Tiw. Tiw, remember how at harvest time we still leave grain for you. Her mind reeled among the things she must not do, the spells and cures which might or might not help. Once, Robert spoke, and it was her name on his lips. She caught his hand in hers and held it tightly, hoping he would now know she was there; aware also of Athelstan's condemnation. Steadfastness in prayer was the only cure he knew.

I can't just kneel and watch Robert die, Lulla thought. I can't. I am not so made that I can only watch and pray.

She came to her feet again, stiff with weariness, and went outside to find the straightest, best-omened twig anyone could imagine. The well was holy, men said. Holding her twig in a pitcher of freshly drawn water, she entreated she knew not which spirits, then broke it cleanly and made the sign of the cross. When she went back into the hut Robert was tossing and mumbling again but without waking, Athelstan still on his knees.

Hastily she turned back Robert's covers, while her resolution lasted; scraped at the crusted scab, then took a deep breath and drove into the dark swelling beneath. Pus squirted everywhere: over her skirts, into bracken and across Athelstan's praying hands. Robert growled like an animal deep in his throat but seemed too weak to struggle, so Lulla continued to squeeze and scrape until only blood welled from the wound. Then she packed it with moss again and sat back on her heels, feeling utterly worn out. All she could do now was wait.

Athelstan waited too, for which she was grateful; afraid as never before of being left to face death alone.

They waited a long time. Robert tossed and moaned as before, and when Lulla set her ear to his chest she could hear his heart scampering in search of blood. Only his strength, which after twenty years of soldiering was like that of seasoned oak, still resisted the assault of so many demons at one time, and in the end outlasted them. The next time Lulla scraped his leg she allowed the cleansing blood to flow longer before binding it up again, and when she finished his eyes were open.

'The ox will make your work lighter,' he whispered.

Lulla snuffled on unwanted tears. 'Don't try to talk.'

His eyes closed again. 'Not bound for hell this time.'

Soon he drifted into his first healthy sleep since returning from Reredfelle, fever flush fading and his breathing easy. Lulla yawned, thankfulness spinning out of reach as exhaustion tumbled her, too, into almost instant sleep.

She woke suddenly, knowing some strange sound had roused her. Athelstan had gone and Robert was lying on his back, snoring peacefully. Then the sound came again and Lulla breathed out in relief. It was their ox, unwatered and unfed since its arrival, lowing and stamping at the hitching post outside. Still half asleep, Lulla ran to the well and then on to their corn-pit; on to the wood-pile, back to the well and into the forest to dig roots before visiting Robert's snores again. He, as well as the ox, must have food soon. While rekindling their fire in the entry to their hut she paused, eyeing Robert's hunting bow. As fortune would have it, their snares were empty, and if she was to prepare the kind of food he needed then she must look for it herself. As a child she'd often hunted small game with Leofric. God send she hadn't lost the quickness of eye that he'd praised then.

There were hares in plenty on the slope, beyond the chapel, their white scuts flickering in the dusk, and Lulla stalked them with the enjoyment of relief, tongue between her teeth in concentration. Notch, like so, aim right and above, remember to hold a spare arrow between her lips. Something startled the fat buck she had her eye on, and it bobbed behind a sapling oak.

Lulla waited, feeling fresh and joyous, as if she was a girl again and Leofric alive. A squirrel ran along the branch above her head, throwing acorns on the ground: an eagle swung high in the sky and tree-shadows stretched towards her across bracken fronds. In the peace of a still afternoon cleared from worry Lulla savoured every moment while she waited, only moving to kiss her arrow tip for luck. As she did so she saw it was made from an iron fragment she remembered Robert picking up and honing for re-use. She had not noticed before, but the metal was obviously very old and a faint design still showed; idly, Lulla ran her fingers over it, wondering. She often wondered about things others accepted without remark. The design was strange and her skin tingled when she touched it: a deer she thought, this the head and that the antler. She stared at the marked arrow and found herself wondering more strangely still, this time about those who had lived on the ridge before her. . . And suddenly one of them seemed to stand beside her. She couldn't see him, but felt his presence as if he reached out to touch the iron she held and said, I remember setting my mark there.

Lulla turned, wanting to discover whether he was tall or short, content or not with how he'd lived his life, but as she did so, he vanished.

Of course, she was very tired, half-dreaming on her feet.

The hare hopped unexpectedly from behind its tree and Lulla released the deer-marked arrow without the care she'd intended. It flew high, and buried itself in bark. She fumbled her spare one too, and the hare cocked its nose scornfully in the air before scampering swiftly away.

Lulla laughed. More hares would come out with the dusk and she did not mind if she missed. She went over to prise her arrow out of the bark, thinking she would like to wear it as a talisman around her neck, but the iron stuck fast in sapwood and in the end Lulla had to leave it there. She would ask Robert to come one day and gouge it out with his knife.

Soon afterwards, she killed a dog fox cleanly, with an arrow through the throat.

Robert lay for three days regaining his strength, talking little and eating everything Lulla brought him. On the fourth day, when she drove Cheerful the ox back from the ground they were clearing she found him balanced on one leg, splitting twigs for kindling, and on the fifth he roused when she did at first light.

'I will feed the ox today,' he said.

Lulla kissed him in relief. 'You won't make your leg worse again by using it before it is healed?'

'Thanks to you it is nearly healed,' he answered, and went off without waiting for more argument. He still limped like a broken-kneed horse, but his mind was made up. In a new holding like theirs, next year's survival depended on breaking enough ground to sow before the frosts set hard.

Each day thereafter, they rose before dawn and ate whatever scraps were left from the night before. Then, as soon as it was light enough to see, Robert yoked the ox and they went to the rowan thicket, where they chopped and hauled out scrub and bracken roots all day.

That was all there was to it, really.

The endurance to slash and tug and burn without pause from dawn to dusk. This was how a livelihood was created where only deer and hares had been before. At dusk, Robert went to set his traps and collect whatever was caught there, while Lulla trudged home on trembling legs to blow up embers, chop roots or smoke deer; otherwise they worked even-paced and too hard for chatter. Even so, they spoke more often than before; to the ox who pulled up bushes by the roots, to encourage each other when they began to tire and in companionship by the fire at night; since Robert's illness they were no longer ashamed to show affection.

Affection. Sometimes when Lulla was too tired to sleep she lay beside her uncomplaining work-ox of a husband, and became a prey to wonderings of a different kind to those which, when she handled an ancient arrow-point, had made her sense its maker standing by her side. She had married a good man, except that he was a Norman. A cunning provider who knew how to please a woman. And yet, O God have mercy, there was nothing about him which made her heart feel lighter.

It was hard to accept that this was all there was; a life without lightness and made up of toil.

It was during one of those wondering nights that Lulla decided not to ask Robert to gouge out the deer-marked arrow tip. Let it lie in the heart of a great oak as it grew through more years than she could imagine, a secret she shared with the man who's stood beside her and touched the iron he made.

When Lulla's breeding-pains began she fled to the shed which Robert had built for Cheerful, and crouched in straw. She would die rather than beg for Ylifa's help, and had long ago prepared the shed by leaving a pitcher and piece of sinew for tying there; now all she had to do was bury her face in Cheerful's flank and wait. Ylifa attended only unnatural birthings, and Lulla had seen many women drive their men outside while they crouched to deliver their child into a bowl. She knew what to do, but would have liked another woman's encouragement while she did it.

'Your time has come?' asked Robert from the door.

'Get out! Christ have mercy, leave me! Don't you know that a man at a birthing brings the evil eye?'

He hesitated. 'I shall not be far if you want me.'

Lulla moaned but did not answer. Everyone knew that males at a birthing were ill-omened. Perhaps being a soldier cut a man off from common sense. Cheerful was male, but she couldn't help that now. Cheerful. Why had she called him that when he, too, was born to toil under a yoke? But when he came up to the ridge with Robert, cheerfulness had seemed to Lulla the most necessary of all virtues, now she could only think about how she would drag a full belly around with her every year until a birthing would kill her, or her womb shrivelled.

Lulla came out of the ox-shed holding her child half a day later, and found Robert sitting on a stone close by.

'See how beautiful he is,' she said proudly.

Robert leaped to his feet. 'He is alive?'

'Alive and very well,' she answered, and kissed the babe's soft skull. Wretchedness had vanished the moment she lifted her son out of the pitcher between her thighs, and she was again the radiant Lulla whom

Leofric had so sinfully desired. Robert paused to look at her; she never looked like that for him and jealousy struck like a thunderbolt out of heaven. Ah well, he had received all the fortune any man could expect; a holding, a wife he loved and a son within a single year.

Lulla understood none of this, only saw him hesitate as he came to kiss her. Norman habits, she called such behaviour to herself. In Ferenthe if a man wished to fondle his wife then he did so in privacy of their bedstraw; all the same she was pleased by his kiss and smiled at him with such a happy and tender look that jealousy seemed pitiful. So he smiled too, and took her hand and led her back to their hut, where he had kept a good fire burning.

She drowsed soon after, holding the child in her arms, although she looked less weary than after a day's work in the rowan thickets. She was young, perhaps not yet eighteen seasons old, and a child something to show for a day's labour, after all.

When Lulla woke she found Robert regarding her very steadily, and blurred out a question she'd wanted to ask before. 'You must have fathered children in a dozen villages. Did you ever see one as fair as this before?'

'I had a son who was no bastard once. I loved him and he died.'

Colour flooded Lulla's cheeks; she had never considered how cruel joy could sometimes be. 'Forgive me.'

Should I not always forgive her, no matter how she hurt me? He thought painfully. Fool that I am. 'Did you know that one of my earliest pleasures with you was watching how you faced me like a soldier? No excuses, but apology or defiance, whichever was due, eye to eye as a warrior might.'

'But you have discovered other pleasures since?' she asked teasingly.

'Aye. Many others.'

Lulla waited expectantly: how altogether young and renewed she felt tonight.

Robert spat out the root he was chewing, the name of Leofric on his tongue. If he asked, tonight she would tell him whether she had ever lain with her brother. Then he shook his head; the risk of asking was too great.

'My skin has not yet roughened,' offered Lulla hopefully.

'No,' he agreed. She was his heart and blood, yet he did not know how to speak on such matters.

Lulla was disappointed but not unduly cast down when he stayed silent. She knew he loved her, but did not herself care very deeply what else he thought.

She had other matters on her mind.

They'd already decided to call the baby Garin. Lulla thought this the best of Robert's suggestions and, for reasons of her own, was happy for her son to be given a Norman name. So after she had suckled him that night, she grew thoughtful, twisting her fingers as she sometimes did when preoccupied. 'I want to tell you a secret,' she said eventually.

'About the writings which gave Fernet-le-Forêt to your kin.

'I wish you wouldn't call it that! How did you know?'

'I was wed to you in order that I might gain them,' he said drily.

'Aye, for your grasping Baron Ralf. But he did us less evil than he thought, didn't he?' Tonight Lulla could laugh and cry and laugh again, all in a single breath. She was also ripe for scheming.

'Very much less. But I have watched you plot a dozen times and then not tell me what you planned. Tonight you have decided not to wait any longer.'

Lulla clicked her lips in mock annoyance. 'I've a good mind to make you wait again, because you see too much.' She took a deep breath. 'You remember how Hwita came last month, accusing me of taking my writings from where they had been hidden?'

Robert nodded. He had needed to draw his sword before Hwita and Wiglaf could be forced to leave.

'I told her an animal must have broken open the seal on the pot and eaten the deed inside. That wasn't true.'

'I never believed it was.'

'She did, but then she's stupider than a sheep.'

'Did she? I'm not sure. Wiglaf has taken to pasturing his swine in the thicket recently, which suits us since they help to clear the ground. It is a toilsome place for a swineherd to keep his stock, though. I think he is watching where we go.'

Lulla broke into laughter. 'May his backside freeze in the snow we've had. I took the writings and hid them in the chapel a long time ago. They're behind the altar.'

Robert crossed himself. 'You went into Christ's own sanctuary.'

Lulla shrugged. Sometimes the trappings of Christianity seemed mere wood and cloth to her, at others so filled with power she wanted to howl on her knees before them. Once she had decided to hide her writings behind the altar, she simply begged all the spirits she could think of for protection while she did it, and so far was safe from harm. 'It was a safe place.' She said at last.

Robert scratched his head. 'Safe for what?'

'To wait for the right time to make Ferenthe a freeholding from your king.'

'I hold it freely, but from the Sieur d'Escoville.'

'My kindred held directly from the king, and so shall Garin.'

'Hwita believes her son has the right of inheritance, because he was fathered by your brother Loefric.'

Lulla scowled. 'I swore an oath after she refused to help you, that I would keep it from her. In cases of dispute the folkmoot decides who is worthiest to succeed.

'This will not go to a folkmoot, but before a Norman king.'

'But don't you see? The folkmoot would not decide for us, because you are a Norman.'

And Robert did see. If Lulla's writings contained what she thought they contained, then Norman justice would prefer a Norman to inherit. Him. He, Robert the Falconer would then become a freeholder directly under the king, subordinate to no other man, and his son after him. He leaned forward, trembling with excitement. 'How could we do it.'

'We wait until your king comes,' she answered calmly.

Robert sat for a long time by warm embers, thinking about what Lulla had said. Ralf d'Escoville had been sent to clear and secure this part of the route between London and Normandy, a route already heavily used. Few weeks went by without a messenger pausing by Ferenthe pool to water his horse, and already two great households had spent the night within Robert's palisade: a chaos of ox-carts, impudent squires and barons carrying hooded hawks on their wrists.

They only had to wait and eventually William would come this way too, his life being filled by strenuous journeyings. Probably he would stay at Ralf d'Escoville's new castle, but at Ferenthe they would certainly hear if the king came as close as Reredfelle. And when he did, they would petition him to judge whether Lulla's writings nullified Ralf d'Escoville's title to the manor of Fernet-le-Forêt. If only he would decide in their favour, then Hwita would have no chance against the ruling of the king.

In the event, Ralf himself came first to visit them. He was hunting with a falcon on his wrist, a sport best followed along the more open spaces of the ridge, and rode with his lady to see how Robert was making out on his holding. Lulla was the first to see bright colours among the trees, and she sighed, thinking of a night spent slaving over cauldrons for arrogant Norman travellers, then she stiffened. 'It is your murderous lord.'

Robert propped his axe against a tree, worried because Lulla had not learned to hide her hatred of all Normans except himself. Sometimes he thought the silence they lived in made her grow a little strange; she more than he needed the chatter of neighbours around the pool. 'Keep your eyes downcast and say nothing unless you must. One look will warn my Seigneur you would kill him if you could.'

He bowed as Ralf drew rein. 'Welcome to Fernet-le-Forêt my lords. I will have an accounting for your steward after this harvest, or so I hope. It has been a good first year.

Ralf laughed, glancing at the baby kicking in the shade. 'In more ways than one it would seem. I am told that Englishwomen breed like sows.'

Robert's face tightened and when he did not answer, Isabelle crowed with mirth. 'My lord, you have angered him! He believed you likened his wife to swine.'

'Not I, said Ralf sincerely. He did indeed think surly English peasants were of less value than the breeding sow in his bailey, but never willingly offended any man who served him well. 'You have done a great deal of work here since I last rode past.'

'The season has been kind,' answered Robert, pleased. He picked an ear of oats and rubbed it between his hands. 'The grain is heavier than any I grew in Brittany.'

Ralf glanced around, estimating how soon Robert would be able to bear the whole cost of arming a knight from a holding which might prove richer than he had thought. 'It is the same at Reredfelle. Our freshly cleared land grows better crops than ploughlands worked by many households. Anyone can see that such good earth is wasted on the English.'

'We did not slave for tax-gatherers and rent-collectors before you Norman scavengers came,' said Lulla tossing her head. 'We were happy with what we had.'

Ralf could not have been more astonished if his falcon had blasphemed. 'What a shrew I forced you to marry, Robert! And one that understands Norman too.'

'I will not bite if you speak directly to me.' Lulla squeezed a clod of earth as if she meant to throw it.

Isabelle frowned angrily. 'My lord, do not endure such insolence! This woman is a scold who should be in the castle cage.'

Before Ralf could answer, Robert turned on Lulla and drove her away with kicks and blows. He remembered well the cages which hung over most castle walls, where the occupant was a target for filth and insult. When Lulla had gone, spitting like a wildcat, he met Ralf's eyes steadily. 'My lord, you have a fine falcon on your wrist.'

'Indeed you should know' Ralf answered eagerly, relieved that Robert had made it possible for him to ignore Isabelle. She ruled his household well, but somehow there was not much comfort in it. I have a mews built now and any time you want to admire it, you are welcome. My steward always said that you weren't given your name for nothing, and would have made an even better falconer than a sergeant.'

'Isabelle tugged at his sleeve. 'You will never let that bitch go free to boast how she insulted you!'

Ralf grinned and jerked his head at Robert, man to man rather than lord to sergeant. 'Remember, come and give your opinion of my birds next time you visit Reredfelle market.' He wheeled his horse, leaving Isabelle no choice except to follow.

'He is a merciful man,' said Robert furiously to Lulla afterwards. 'I warned you to stay silent and what did you do? Gave any baron but he good cause to hang you from his walls!'

'I don't mind!' screamed Lulla. 'When will you realize that my life is not so sweet that I would hold on to it any cost?'

'You have a child, your life is no longer your own to lose,' answered Robert sternly. Ah, you have a husband too, he thought but did not say.

'I spoke the truth. If you Normans hang people in cages for the truth, so be it. You know as well as I do that one grain out of every two will go in tax next year.'

'Wars cost money.'

'Where is the war? Tell me that! No, I'll tell you! I heard some horsemen talking by our well. The war is in Normandy. Why should we pay because Normans wish to fight?'

Robert shrugged. 'Fernet-le-Forêt is Norman now.'

'And when we show your king our writings and win Ferenthe's freehold for ourselves, will you still pay two in every three grains elsewhere?' Lulla shoved Garin against his chest. 'Perhaps you will, because you have served a lord too long to know how else to live, but Garin won't. I'll see he grows up knowing that Ferenthe is his alone.'

'Then stay alive to tell him. Remember too the Sieur d'Escoville's mercy, and how easily small men are destroyed when they lack a lord to defend them.' Robert turned her so she looked over the forest, spread out on every side. Here and there smoke rose into the air to show where clearings were, but that was all. 'Think sometimes too of the land beyond Ferenthe.'

Lulla twisted in his grip. 'You called it Ferenthe, instead of Fernet-le-Forêt.'

'Aye, so I did. What will Garin call it, do you suppose?'

'Ferenthe,' she answered flatly.

'Perhaps. I pray God that if our hopes be realized in this matter of your writings, he also never forgets that his land is held from a Norman king.

Lulla looked and looked over the dark forest, as if she wanted to close her eyes and die. 'Yet this is the hope men live by,' she said at last. 'The hope that what is rightfully theirs, is theirs to cherish unmolested.'

'Aye, and it is the king's peace which protects that hope,' he answered flatly.

They had to wait two more years for the king to visit Reredfelle, and in all that time no one in Ferenthe, except Athelstan the priest, spoke a single word to them. Two years of drudgery and two more children born; one died at once the other perished of a fever at six months old. Two years of clearing and ploughing ground that never gave again so bountiful a harvest as in that first year's growing. Two years during which Robert built a better hut and mated Cheerful with a bought heifer, two years when the Wealden English became more unforgiving than before, as they were forced to work without wages on bridges and causeways over wet ground, so the Normans could race from one possession to the next.

Lulla became thin and sour during those years, and Robert more like the cured leather than before. Only when his eyes rested on his wife did something in him soften still; he knew this was ludicrous yet could not help himself. As Lulla found excuses for the many unkindnesses of Ferenthe, because this was the place she loved, so he found excuses for her lack of charity to him. Only one thing worried him about this passion of old age, and that was Leofric. He wanted to know, heaven knows why, whether Lulla had ever lain with her brother. And because they were left so completely alone with their crops and beasts, the matter began to obsess him. Lulla knew nothing of this, how could she when silence pressed like wool against her head? Sometimes she, Robert and Garin laughed together, but the moment laughter ended they drowned in silence again. Because he had known nothing else, Garin too was growing up behind closed lips.

Then, one soft green evening, they heard the king was to lie that very night at Reredfelle, before riding on again for Pevensey. They left immediately, after putting Garin to sleep with a calf for company. Christ above, how could they have heard such news so late, when rumour travelled through the forest as if blared by trumpets?

Ralf d'Escoville had extended his castle during each of the years since he settled there. The peasants of Reredfelle cursed his building madness but neither complaints nor runaway serfs stopped him: the baily was extended; a defensive turret placed here, a forge there; a hall added to the keep. Through it all, Ralf remained as merry as a tumbler at a fair, careless of black looks and the whining of his lady, who was breeding for the fourth time in under four years. All he wanted was for everyone to marvel at the good fortune which enabled him to squeeze so many fines and rents out of his lands that his castle was already larger than many he remembered in Normandy.

Now King William himself had come, trailing behind him the records of his kingdom packed on sumpter horses, and more bishops and knights and squires than anyone could count. William often rode out with only half a dozen cronies for company, but this time he was on his way to fight in Normandy. He was also displeased with Ralf d'Escoville, who rejoiced so much in his good fortune that he had begun to skimp on repairing royal bridges. He would be reminded of his duty if his barns and fields were eaten bare. William spent his life reminding barons of their duty, this was the lightest of his punishments, with worse to follow if it wasn't heeded.

Lulla had several times seen Ralf's castle from below, the only break in the monotony of her life being the twice yearly fair at Reredfelle. She had never seen it look so splendid as on that April night when King William stayed within its walls. The timber ramparts were hung with painted cloths and shields, torches flared in the wind and the feasting was so great that savoury smells drifted into the huts by the stream below. During the journey across the wilderness where Edred had once hunted boar and which was now Ralf's hunting park, Lulla had been filled with a kind of angry joy which came from having purpose in her life again. Once she began to climb up to the guarded castle entry, she became alarmed. Through the years of silent brooding she had never considered the possibility that King Aelfreds's writings might not seem important to new Norman rulers; now, suddenly, even to her they appeared insignificant. Dead English kings simply did not matter any more, and when she had taken Aelfred's ancient vellum from its hiding place only the massive untouched seal matched her imaginings. To such self-confident predators as these Normans, the English must be of less account than moles, known for their burrowings in the soil.

Robert felt none of this. Castles and crowds of men brawling around campfires had been his life for so long that what he saw seemed natural, although more disorderly than the sergeant in him liked. His Norman tongue took them through the gate, and the guard answered his questions readily enough. Then he limped to the nearest campfire and carried a scoop of soup back to Lulla, waiting in the shadows. 'We are too early, the king is still feasting. Here, you'll feel better with this inside you.'

Lulla drank, tasting only gall. 'He will not listen to us, later or now.'

'We have come a long way to decide that at the last stride,' said Robert sharply.

'I know he will not,' answered Lulla. 'In our clearing I couldn't have understood how it would be, but now I see what conquest means.' She was ashamed to speak of the terror which had perched on her shoulder like a raven of ill omen ever since she passed Ralf d'Escoville's gate. Run! She thought in panic. Go back to Ferenthe and be content to hold what you have, however abject it may be. But prudence came too late, and withered as quickly as it flowered. Better by far to die with passion, than live as a half-crazed crone: with this resolve her raven took flight and joy returned to her life, because even had she desired it there was no going back. But in the raven's place came Fate, in the form of a man she had never heard of, called Fulk le Sourd.

Fulk was a man of unimpressive size, whose soft smile was said to make brave men shake with fear. William distrusted him but gave him border baronies to rule, where brutality paid. He was in Reredfelle that night only because it was unsafe to leave so evil and powerful a man behind the king's back while he campaigned in Normandy.

With time to spare while the feasting finished, Robert was unable to resist inspecting Ralf d'Escoville's mews. Lulla had never closely considered her husband's name before, since men often bore names for which the reason was long forgotten, but the moment they reached the corner of the bailey where the baron kept his hunting hawks, she saw how expert Robert was in their handling.

She also felt tenderly towards him, as she had not since – well, she could not remember ever feeling so tender towards him before. He had been good to her, and whatever danger there might be, they faced it together. Suddenly, she wanted to know some of the things she had not troubled to ask him before.

'At eleven years old I was bound to the lord of Coutances's falconer,' he answered when she asked why he was called the Falconer. 'Then the Sieur was killed and his castle lost to raiders, so I rode to avenge him with the rest. I wanted very much to return to handling falcons; everyone said I had a knack for the craft and I loved it. They nicknamed me Robert the Falconer because most of the Sieur's men came from the same places in the Cotentin, and so had similar names. But before I could find another lord my brothers died of pestilence, and their holding became mine until raiders came there too.'

Lulla watched his work-knotted fingers smooth feathers and feed raw meat into beaks shaped like sickles, glad that he had this chance to enjoy a devotion she had been too selfish to discover. 'How shall we know when the king is ready to listen to petitions?'

'You will hear the shouts change pitch,' said a soft voice from behind her. 'From gluttony to drunkenness.'

'I expect both would sound the same to me,' answered Lulla lightly, and turned.

'You are not Norman?'

'I'd prefer to say that you aren't English,' she retorted.

'Ah.' Torchlight glinted on eyes hooded like the falcon Robert held. 'But you speak Norman?'

She gave him back stare for stare, even laughing a little. 'Even an English scullion may learn the robbers' tongue, if it suits her.'

There was a smack of bone on bone, a faint snap like a twig breaking as Fulk's fist struck home with all his strength behind it, and Lulla lay in the mud with a look of astonishment on her face. Robert was still gathering wits scattered by Lulla's bravado, part crazed as it seemed to him, when she sprawled at his feet. He dropped on his knees beside her, fear and anger at her folly equally mixed. 'Are you hurt?'

Her face was grey, her voice little more than a gasp. 'I saw the raven fly across the bailey when we came.'

And all at once a most desperate fear took the place of anger as Robert tried to see where she was hurt. He had seen death too often to mistake that look on anyone's face.'

Already Lulla' breath was coming in thick pants and below the neck she lay quite slack. 'Robert?'

He bowed his head. 'I am here.'

'You will go to the king in my place?'

'I will go and demand justice against your murderer.'

'That too. But Ferenthe, you will . . . for me . . .'

'Aye,' he said, and wept. 'For you I would do anything. But tell me quickly, did you ever lie with your brother?'

Her lips curved in wonder. 'All these years . . . and I never knew how that . . . stuck in your throat.'

'Did you?' he shouted, and would have shaken her so great was his desire to know, except she looked as she had on the day he first came to the pool of Ferenthe. So he kissed her instead and understood that he would never know the answer to his question, because she was dead. He stood, and drew his sword, beginning to run from shadow to shadow to see if Fulk le Sourd was still there, whom he had recognized at the first word he spoke to Lulla. Such a commotion to set the hawks flapping great shadows on the wall and when the falconers came running they stood awestruck at a scene straight from the pit of hell, where black spirits tore damned spirits with their talons.

Robert was hauled bodily out of the mews, then shackled and taken before King Williams's marshal, who took precedence over Ralf d'Escoville's steward while the king was present. A woman had been murdered, and it was King William's boast that his law was so terrible that anyone might travel unmolested from one end of his kingdom to another.

Robert's mind had cleared by the time he was thrown on his knees in front of an austere figure in a blue furred robe, partly because he could not yet grasp the reality of Lulla's death. All he could remember was how he had railed at her over Leofric; why had he thought it mattered if she had lain with her brother, when never again she would lie with him.

'You were found with a sword in your hand and a woman dead at your feet, while this castle is under the especial peace of the king's presence.' The marshal said. 'Do you deny it?'

'The woman was my wife, and killed by Fulk le Sourd.' Robert wondered how his voice could sound so cool. 'Christ help me, I fought alongside his following once and could not be mistaken.'

'What were you and your woman doing in the mews which tonight keep the king's own hawks?' Questions beating like swords on a shield gave Robert no time to consider his replies, even supposing he had been in a state of mind for caution. King Aelfred's deed was explained and discovered in Lulla's belt, their purpose in coming to petition the king described. William's marshal and the marshal's following were always sober and worked fast, expecting a fresh brawl at any moment.

As a long-served sergeant, Robert ought to have expected what came next, but neither rough handling nor the heat of fire on his face meant anything to him.

'Stretch out your hand,' they said, and he stretched it out like a child expecting a bone. Instead, they dropped a glowing ember on his palm.

Then, quite deliberately, Robert clenched his fist on it, while the stench of roasting flesh enclosed them all. 'Fulk le Sourd killed her,' he said hoarsely.

The marshal's men stared at him from under their iron nosepieces, thunderstruck. They had never seen a man who did not so much as flinch under the order, which was designed to test his words for truth.

Robert shook off the cinder from where it stuck against his blackened flesh, wiped his face with the back of his other hand. He felt clammily cold, but no pain at all.

The marshal signed. He had believed this bog-oak sergeant from the moment he named Fulk le Sourd as the killer, but ordeals were prescribed and must be endured. 'Guard him well until I order otherwise. Tie him in the mews, since the rest of the bailey is full.'

'Aye, my lord' they were still staring platter-eyed at Robert, who stared at the mud between his feet.

The marshal went to whisper in King William's ear, Fulk le Sourd being too powerful a man for him to confront. Too powerful for William either, perhaps. Yet.

The men detailed to guard Robert tied him to one of the timber perches in the mews so that unless he kept his eyes closed he could not avoid seeing Lulla. She looked like a drying hummock in the mud. The years when she had toiled by his side, the three births in the ox-shed from which only Garin survived; her unforgiving temper and the way laughter sometimes splintered sunlight through her eyes: all had become a mere tidemark in the mud. A falcon directly above where she lay screamed and flapped its wings until great black shadows whirled again in torchlight; her soul is not at rest, thought Robert fearfully.

Daylight came early in such fine April weather, and with it the bustle of the king's departure. Robert hung buckling at the knees from the thongs which secured him to timber, and whatever shock had stood between him and pain the night before, his hand now hurt so much that he looked at Lulla's body and scarcely saw it. Trumpets blared as the sun rose, setting horses neighing, soldiers cursing and hounds baying. The Falconers began to fuss around their charges, avoiding Robert as if he too was dead; tying jesses, pulling on the heavy gauntlets they wore when carrying a falcon on their wrists. Robert licked his lips and somehow stiffened his knees, using an old addition to hunting birds to hold his senses in their place.

'Ho, there!' he called to his guards. 'Does the king ride out today?'

The men shuffled and spat, angered by being left so long guarding carrion in a stinking mews, but a falconer recognized Robert as the man who, the night before, had touched hawks as if he knew what he was about, and answered in their place. 'The king rides for Pevensey, but expects to hunt along the way.'

'Pevensey.'

'He embarks tomorrow for Normandy, to fight the King of France who has invaded the duchy, God rot him. I come from Rouen myself, and that French whoreson is burning his way from one end of the Seine valley to the other.'

'When will the king return?' asked Robert, stupefied. Fulk le Sourd would leave with William and be out of reach before the sun climbed above the trees.

The falconer shrugged. 'Next year perhaps. It's going to be a long campaign.'

Beyond the mews wall, noise rose to a crescendo, and Robert could imagine the scene exactly; mounted men and baggage-horses were trailing out over the hollow-sounding timber bridge, that extra blast of horns meant the king himself had appeared. Then the merry sound of voices and hoof-beats dimmed until only the commotion of lesser departures was left behind. Probably no one remembered he was here, and the guard would leave him tied until his legs ceased to support him. Then he would hang from his wrists until he rotted. Robert would not have minded, except that Garin would even now be waking in their ox-shed, alone beside a calf. He had reminded Lulla once that she had lost the right to throw away her life, now he must remind himself.

He roused to the sound of hoofs as the marshal rode into the mews, furred robe changed for hunting leather. 'Guard him, I said, not crucify him. He is an innocent man, or had you not realized?'

Robert fell on his face the moment his thongs were slashed, before somehow wavering to his feet. 'Fulk le Sourd?'

The marshal slapped gauntlets absently on his thigh. 'Gone with the king. He is too great a quarry for you, my friend. King William has the need of loyal subjects in the Seine valley at present, and Fulk is one of his greatest barons.'

'He killed my wife.'

'He struck an English peasant woman for insolence and was unlucky enough to unjoint her neck, also to find her wedded to a Norman. You say you fought beside Fulk's followers once, so you know how he has burned, raped and tortured through most days of his life. The king was before you with his claim these many years, and if he has patience to wait for a better time, then you must leave justice to him. It is in good hands.'

Robert stared at those slapping leather gauntlets, torn between rage and resignation. He was also exhausted by shock and pain. 'My lord, I loved her.'

The marshal's horse sidled as if iron thighs transmitted instant exasperation. 'Go plough your land, Robert of Fernet-le-Forêt. I told the king that you came to petition him to confirm an ancient grant, and of his grace he was pleased to do so. Call it a token of future justice, if you will. So take your new charter and be thankful.' He tossed a crisp scroll at Robert's feet, wheeled his horse and was gone.

This chance to pacify an aggrieved but loyal subject at Ralf d'Escoville's expense had come most opportunely for William. When Ralf pointed out that the scraps of vellum said to be a grant from King Aelfred were illegible, the king's only comment had been that the conditions on Ralf's own grant which bound him to maintain tracks and bridges in the Weald were clear for everyone to read. Any common sergeant who had been as fortunate in his timing as Robert the Falconer, should, in the marshal's opinion, praise God and the king, and find himself another wife. If his woman had not died at the hand of Fulk le Soured, then he was most unlikely ever to have reached past a household which prospered on the d'Escoville ambitions nor brought his petition anywhere near the king. And if by some miracle he had managed it, then the marshal had handled those pitiful fragments of vellum and knew that in most circumstances King William would not have wasted his clerks' time on anything so unfruitful.

Robert would have liked to bury Lulla under Ferenthe's great oak beside Leofric, her brother, as if by doing so he said: Lie in peace where you belong and think kindly of me sometimes; I know you could not love me. But he was incapable of carrying her there and so was forced to watch while she was buried in the common pit outside the castle wall.

He knelt afterwards beside Lulla's grave, too stunned for grief. He could not even be sure she would not suffer in purgatory, since she had only sometimes believed in Christ. Ah, Fulk le Sourd! If you were here I would brand your face with a flaming branch, unjoint each limb before I killed you! But Fulk wasn't there, and by her death Lulla had won Fernet-le-Forêt for Garin, who would have woken by now to find himself alone.

A foot-trail was still the only direct way from Reredfelle to Ferenthe, across Ralf's hunting park. As Robert set to walk the miles which lay between him and the ridge, sunlight struck the huge leaf canopies above his head which had changed little since Edred's day. A path still seemed alien in such a setting and at its lowest point wound between undrained swamps. Swaying with weariness, Robert saw only the next step of his way, heard nothing beyond the blood buzzing in his ears.

'Robert the Falconer,' said Isabelle d'Escoville. 'Thief.'

She was riding one of Ralf's horses and both breathed through flared nostrils, as if they had galloped a long way in fury.

Robert stared at her blankly, then he sat on a treetrunk while he tried to make sense of the Lady Isabelle barring his path. 'I am no thief, lady.'

'Fernet-le-Forêt is ours.'

'Petition the king if you think so,' he answered carelessly. Ralf was too shrewd a man further to enrage his king over a single manor when he had gained so much already, and might still lose it all. It never crossed Robert's mind that the baron's lady might not worry about her lord's calculations, nor his wishes either.

With no more than a toss of her head to warn him, Isabelle drove her horse straight at the log he sat on. Fortunately the beast wasn't trained in war and did not use its hoofs as a weapon, but only the dense undergrowth saved Robert. He somersaulted backwards and swerved like a stoat, the horse shying and rearing while Isabelle slashed at him with her whip. Before she was able to ride on and over her enemy, she also had to leap the fallen tree on which he had been sitting. By the time she had snatched round to come at him again, Robert had bolted into cover.

He crashed through briars and over rotting branches, panting for breath. Being ridden down was no sport for an exhausted man past his fortieth year, and he must keep to the worst terrain, tearing his hands and clothes, where a horse could not easily follow. And whereas Ralf would never murder him in his own hunting park, the Lady Isabelle when beside herself with rage quite easily might. The devil fly away with judgings, she would think. Next year or the year after, when the king returned to England was a long time away.

Five miles of rough country lay between Reredfelle and Ferenthe, and Robert took most of the day to cover them, missing his way often, saved only by his soldier's sense of direction. The last steep climb up to the ridge almost finished him. His burned hand was on fire, his leg ached, his belly flapped against his bones, but at least the haste and difficulty of his journey gave him no chance to brood. He sighed with relief when eventually he reached the grassy track which ran the length of the ridge, rutted and wider than it had been when Gytha's people flitted from glad to glade. Only when he came to the edge of the trees, did he hesitate. Straight on and he would come to the huts huddled around Ferenthe's pool. If he wanted to reach his own palisaded yard without being seen, he needed to make his way there under cover.

Then he shrugged.

There was really very little choice. Unless the people of Ferenthe grasped that their interest was now identical with his, then he was finished. Lady Isabelle could make up any tale about his death she chose, and when William sent his sheriffs to inquire into it the villagers would say they had seen nothing.

He tore off some young bracken and scrubbed at his face and blooded hands; breathed deeply and stepped out from among the trees. The ploughland was silvered with spring mist, the sky a luminous pale blue. He could see three horses hobbled by the pool, Isabelle and two huntsmen dismounted beside them. One of the huntsmen carried a boar spear and the other a falcon on his wrist, as if the lady hadn't said why she ordered them to follow and support her.

Robert stopped across the width of the pool from where they waited. Several Ferenthe people had gathered close by, understanding only that this was a quarrel between Normans: a welcome spectacle but not for them to meddle in.

'Seize him.' said Isabelle.

The two huntsmen mounted obediently but they looked surprised. Justice was their lord's affair, nor was it usually left to huntsmen pulled hapchance from the forest.

'There are two of them and – what? – a score of you.' said Robert, clearly and in English so the onlookers from Ferenthe would understand. 'Are you going to let them take me? I have done nothing except receive a charter for the manor of Ferenthe from the king. So, while I live, I am your only master under King William. You may not like me. You may envy my son's inheritance, spit on the coins you pay to us in rent, but Robert the Falconer's kindred will live here, as your neighbours, not in a distant castle. Lulla died yesterday in Reredfelle, and I will die today if you let them take me. If that pleases you, then look aside as you did on the night she came begging for help while I lay sick.'

The two huntsmen paused. Neither understood English but they could not mistake the mutter and movement around them. Some men ducked out from a hut between them and Robert, and stood looking pensively at the pool. They were not armed and did not speak.

'Go on, cowards,' Isabelle screamed at the huntsmen. 'Or explain to your lord how I alone took a runaway captive, while you stood by and watched.'

Robert laughed. 'Don't fear that, lads. The Sieur will spit blood if he hears you broke King Williams's peace, when the king himself is scarcely half a day's journey away. Besides, Ralf d'Escoville isn't lord here any more, if he ever rightfully was.' And Christ's suffering bones, he thought in amazement, as for the first time the meaning of this struck home. That's true. No man except me is lord her any more. 'Son of a bitch!' he said loudly. 'Get off my land.'

'This morning I saw the king's own marshal order this man's release,' one of the huntsmen said. 'Before God, lady, I think we should ask the Sieur d'Escoville what he intends to do.'

'You heard what I said, and I swear I will strip flesh from your bones if you stay on my land any longer.' Robert seized an oaken flail lying beside a hut, his fear and delight at speaking such words so great that they tumbled out on top of each other.

Isabelle took no notice, scrambling up anyhow on to her horse and spurring it forward. But the pool edge was now a solid block of expressionless brown faces, which eddied between her and Robert the moment she tried to change direction. A pair of men-at-arms willing to use their swords could have broken through easily; two hesitant huntsmen and a single resolute woman riding a horse too strong for her, could not.

Robert pushed through the crowd to the huntsman with a falcon. 'Let her fly.'

'Are you crazy? There's no prey here for a hunting bird.'

'You're on my land uninvited, so we'll just say I have a fancy to see a trained falcon fly once more in my life. There are usually skylarks above the trees so she'll enjoy her freedom while it lasts, the same as I shall.

'I'll never lure her back in a place like this! The Sieur d'Escoville –'

'Christ's blood, I don't care if the Sieur d'Escoville loses his hawk! Let her fly.'

The falconer looked at the flame in Robert's eyes, and fumbled with the leather jesses.

'Give him some room,' said Robert quietly, and the people of Ferenthe moved back. In all the time he had lived beyond the thickets, he had meant no more to them than bent shoulders and the sound of axe-strokes on the wind; a Norman and a threat. Now, between them, they were running other more dangerous interlopers off their common territory.

The falconer whipped the hood from the bird's head and for a moment it stood posed; red eye, killer's beak, great slashing talons gripping his forearm. Then he swept his arm upwards and the falcon rose, circling in the evening air. Straightened and swept slowly over the pool, ploughland and enclosing trees, perhaps because it was unused to flying when there was no prey in sight, but to Robert this was Lulla bidding him and her heritage farewell. She had sprawled face down in mews mud while black spirits squalled around her; now she was soaring into the blue dusk, a flicker of sunlight on her wings.

'God curse your soul,' said Isabelle. She understood, or thought she understood, how Robert had deliberately humiliated her by forcing the falconer to lose a valuable bird, which would also ensure that Ralf heard what she had tried to do. 'God spit in your eyes and drag out your entrails through your mouth. May this place never prosper and all your sons be cowards.'

Robert laughed. 'Take your curses elsewhere, lady. Fernet-le-Forêt is mine, and that is what matters.'

He could hear Lulla laugh too, the same eagerly joyful laugh which Leofric would have known well but he had only occasionally heard.

Her spirit would rest easily now, since her death had set Ferenthe on a new and freer path, and enabled its people to send the Lady d'Escoville away with their mocking laughter in her ears. Robert watched the horsemen ride away down the path until they were lost in darkness under the trees. Above their heads the evening star glittered among long black storm clouds blowing out of the west: no matter what storms filled the years to come, nothing could change the victory of this day. Nor change the different unrolling of events which victory brought, as King Aelfred's writings had also brought many things, including Leofric's and Lulla's deaths.

Robert turned to walk back to his hut beyond the thicket, praying that he would find Garin safe. He felt like a man whose life is done; ready to sit by the hearth while others sweated over ploughs and tax-gatherers and the whim of barons. Jesu, it was going to be hard, alone. Years must pass before Garin was old enough to hunt and fill his own barn; he would be lucky to stay alive long enough to see it.

'God be with you,' said Ylifa as he passed.

These were the first words she had spoken to Robert the Falconer since he came to Ferenthe, three years before.

... THE WITNESS:

There is no great statue of William the Conqueror in England, which perhaps is not surprising, although Alfred still keeps guard in Winchester, his sword raised against the sky. I was camped in the Hampshire hills just outside the city in May 1940 while, across the Channel, the Germans were motoring almost unopposed through France. Most of the British army was cut off at Dunkirk and I remember thinking we might need another Alfred before we finished. I was pilot, and Cliff Masters the observer, of an old Lysander C for Charlie, which flew one wing down but reliably as a spotter aircraft for artillery. At the end of May, as the news became worse, we were snatched from digging trenches and told to fly to Hawkinge in Kent.

I don't know what I thought or expected.

Lysanders were armed with two machine-guns fixed to the undercarriage, which consequently were nearly useless, and another on an inconvenient swivel above the observer's cockpit, so we weren't going to be much use against the Luftwaffe. But, untried and lumberingly slow, we were on our way to fight.

We flew quite low on that trip from Winchester to Hawkinge, my green South Country edging past the fuselage. It was a beautiful clear day on which to say farewell; a bloody bad kind of day for dodging Messerschmitts. Soon, I saw the Weald coming up ahead. A flecked maze of fields, villages, confusing roads, fragments of forest. No pattern to it but a harmony, perhaps. Dunno, as Cliff would say with one of his shattering crashes of laughter. Dunno nuffin,' mate.

Ashdown, Ashurst, Hartfield; Crowborough Hill, Brightling Beacon, Tisbury Hill, Mayfield, Riffield, Furnace Green. Ferenthe, as Edred called it, who also travelled this same way. As gracefully as a

Lysander could, I put C Charlie into a roll. Once, twice. Each move meticulous, a loving salute to the place where I was born. They were playing cricket on the green and faces stared up at the spark we struck in the sunlit air. As I levelled out I saw an extraordinary sight; a ditched rectangle as sharp-cut as the day Ralf d'Escoville forced us to dig it.

I knew that all you could see from the ground was an unremarkable farmyard, though Granny Paley told in her tales how Fawkners Farm was built inside a palisade the horsemen made. In 1940 little was known about aerial archaeology and so on, as I banked around the church tower it seemed miraculous to see Robert's ditch and bank, the marks of vanished barns, a well and entry gate all clearly etched by the westering sun.

Once upon a time . . .

Listen to me, young John, Granny Paley said. Once upon a time gurt armoured horsemen came across the sea and trampled our people down. A lord crowed on his dunghill at Riffield and a mut-faced sergeant settled right by our hearths. Robert the Savage we called him and for years wouldn't so much as pass the time of day. Wait, I said, you called him Robert the Falconer before and said Fawkners Farm remembered him. Aye, that was his rightful name and in the end we called him by it and chose him as our headman. Because, you see, by then he felt softly for the land as we.

How odd, I thought, as I turned the Lysander east again, that today I should recall Granny's tale of an invader reconciled. All the same, I was damned if Nazis were going to be offered the chance of settling in. Edenham passed swiftly below as I opened the throttle wider. More shadows showed in the grass there, which must be the vanished mills and furnaces of Francis Wyse's making. I glimpsed a figure which might have been my brother Mark, shading his eyes beside a herd of cows, and waggled C Charlie's wings.

All of which brings me neatly back to the time-and-distance problem I mentioned at the beginning, although it's still too early to explain my part in the solution. But I can't wait any longer before introducing Granny Paley, the true chronicler of Furnace Green.

In Christmas 1918, when Granny first began to tell me her tales, she must have been over eighty years old, the only child of a hedger-

and-ditcher named Richard Paley. As the last of countless earlier storytellers on the ridge, I believe now that she recognized my eagerness to listen and set out quite deliberately to spin and spin her silver words before it was too late. Some of what she said I was too young to remember, and some of her tales had lost whatever meaning they might once have held. Others were little more than ancient spells spawned by the forest. The rest ... the rest ... Once upon a time Granny Paley gave me one end of the thread of truth. Now I too, am very old and feel the same compulsion to pass on this gift of the past, a little refined by my modern itch for proof. I wanted to know what fitted where and why, whereas to Granny all the past was one.

Of course her favourite tale was about her own ancestor, Rico Parleybien. How he came to the ridge carrying silver words in his ballad-monger's pack and though he stayed there only two days, nine months later a child of his getting was born to Meg Harlot. Thereafter, in each generation of Parleybiens there was at least one who inherited Rico's gift with words, and with them spun afresh the magic of the past. Most also added some tale of invention, gossip or excitement from their own lifespan on the ridge. The resulting tangle needs a great deal of unravelling and I have spent part of the last forty years trying to do just that, but what Rico's descendants achieved seems to me most wonderful. Even Granny herself, the last of the Parleybiens, was unable to read or write, and few of her ancestors can have been suited by the life of labourer on the soil. As I, too, was unsuited to it. Yet, century after century, despised and wretchedly poor (for, apart from Rico's great-great-granddaughter, Mary, you seldom hear tales of their doings among the rest), they toiled like beasts without ever losing their shining sorcery of words.

4

DUSTY FEET
1450

Late autumn was the time for merrymaking. The harvest had been gathered into rick and barn, fresh-killed meat laid in troughs of salt, hung on rafters or up chimneys, the ploughing begun. So, with time to spare and a few coins to spend, the countryside danced round celebratory fires, drank their new brewings, bargained, boasted and competed at fairs and markets. The last warm spell of the year often held back winter for a while, the sun turning oak leaves into a golden sea which lapped at the scraps of settlement, spume-edged by glittering beech trees.

In the middle of the fifteenth century, four hundred years after Lulla's death helped to preserve Ferenthe as a tiny freeholding among great lordships, such a lovely season came to the Wealden hills. By then, like many other things in England, life on the ridge represented a compromise between Saxon and Norman; the villagers followed the Norman custom of name and surname, many of these borrowed from the conquerors; the village itself was called neither Ferenthe nor Fernet-le-Forêt, but something between the two: Ferneth. The very language was hybrid, and, having taken what it wanted from several different tongues, English was now poised to sweep their bones aside.

A track had been beaten between the chapel and the original settlement around the pool, and near where Robert the Falconer settled a cluster of huts had grown. The land thereabouts was known as Fawkner's Fields, young Harry Fawkner being the sole surviving son of old Tam – the Widow Tiw knew how many generations Tam was removed from Robert and Lulla, his wife. The Widow alone might also remember how Fawkner's Fields were torn out of a rowan thickets by sweat and axe and Cheerful, the ox: although, oddly enough, the tradition of naming at least one Ferneth ox by that name had survived, the present Cheerful being a mighty breeder with many progeny on the surrounding holdings. Of course no one knew how to question the unseen Widow, but any insoluble problem was consigned to her, men and women alike saying, Ah, the Widow Tiw might know! Throwing up their hands and laughing when they said it, meaning that no one could guess the answer. Yet children still danced the Widow's dance around the harvest fires, and threw garlands in the blaze to discover whether their fortune would be good or ill. The men had a fellowship too, about whose rituals no woman was meant to know (although, naturally enough, they did), and once a year they built a mighty fire on Tiw's hill, became very drunk and pranced there until they dropped.

Rico Parleybien had decided as a child that a life spent following a plough was not for him, and at fourteen years old he left his native Suffolk and took to the road. Thereafter he drifted from one end of England to the other, playing a hand-whittled pipe and telling stories. Children loved Rico and to them he told tales of giants and fauns and ogres; when girls wanted their fortunes told he spun their dreams into such a web of delight that for a while they forgot their lives would be spent slaving over pots and crops and crying children. And around tavern hearths at night he told stories of war and trials of skill, in which soft-skinned, rosy lipped women waited for the victor. He could make his audience chill with horror or laugh deep belly-laughs of lust, and though the censorious called him idle every place he visited begged him to return.

Even Rico scarcely remembered that he had been born Richard Stekkar of Woodfastlea, because everywhere he went the children flocked around him, joining hands and begging Rico the easy-tongued for a story. So Rico Parleybien he became.

On this late September morning, Rico was climbing the steep hill which led to Ferneth Ridge. There were other people on the road, all except he bent under burdens because tomorrow was Ferneth fairday. Rico carried only his pipe, a pouch and a cloak, sometimes playing a few notes as if in answer to the birds, and looking around him with the air of a man who enjoys everything he sees. At this time Rico was perhaps thirty years old, although he did not know his age and cared less; his hair was brown, his eyes grey-green, his beard knifed short.

As it happened, Rico had never passed through this part of Andredsweald before, now known more simply as the Weald. When he reached the top of the hill he looked about him and felt his spirit kindle as it always did at the sign of beauty, whether in women or the land. From where he stood the hill fell away sharply, so he looked over a golden blaze of trees and bracken. A Lord's hunting park by the look of it, untouched forest criss-crossed by cleared rides. Straight ahead of him the ridgetop track wandered onwards, although a side turning bore sharp left, towards a timber chapel with a sapling growing out of its sagging roof, some dozen huts clustered by the graveyard wall. Sheep and a few cattle grazed between the ridge edge and the huts, beyond them the purple-brown lines of ploughland. Nearer and standing by itself, was a hut with a wilted bush above the door. Rico wiped his mouth in anticipation, because a bush meant a tavern with fresh-brewed ale, and ale meant idling men who would wet a dust-filled throat in payment for a story.

He was not mistaken. Outside the hut some old men sat on a flat-edged log, their eyes slitted against a westering sun.

'Good day to you all,' said Rico.

They studied him warily, then one of them nodded. 'You came by way of Tonbridge?'

'Aye. The market is a great occasion when the lord's in his castle there. Plenty of folk gathered who are glad of a tale, or to have their fortune told.'

'It's fairday here tomorrow.'

'So I've heard from everyone on the road.'

Silence, while they chewed over what he had told them. A tale-teller, eh? A good ballad-monger was worth more than jugglers or magicians, who also came to fairs, because his wares could be remembered through long winter evenings, then retold in many different forms.

'Would you drink some fresh-brewed with us?' another offered after a pause; he was called Jack By The Wood, from his minute holding scraped out of forest beyond Danesdell. A horn of ale was not much to risk on the chance of a well-told tale.

'Fresh ale is just what I fancy after so much dust,' answered Rico, and he sat on the vacant end of the log, squinting at the sun as solemnly as the oldest there. Experience had taught him that people who lived their lives amid the monotony of similar furrows needed time to become accustomed to a stranger.

After a while they picked up a disjointed conversation.

'There's Brother Benedict,' said Jack By The Wood unnecessarily, because they could all see the black-skirted monk.

'Thinkin' of his stones instead of souls.'

They all snickered. 'And how to keep John the Carver sober.'

'Not at fairtime, he won't. No man could, not even Benedict.'

They laughed again, and drank in unison.

Rico listened, saying nothing. This was part of his gift: he enjoyed listening as much as spinning wonders with his voice, and when he had listened he made people marvel by adding characters they recognized into his tales.

'Pity Brother Benedict thinks too much about his stones to notice what else John the Carver does,' remarked another man, licking ale from his lip.

'Priests don't have a sense like other men, Trotty,' answered Jack, after careful consideration.

Trotty sniffed. 'I wouldn't say Benedict hadn't sense. Too much sometimes if you ask me.' Everyone laughed again, as if Trotty was often in priestly trouble. 'But if God's a Christian man, I wonder sometimes what he makes of Benedict a-worrying over stone. The old chapel's been good enough for dunamany years.'

''Tis falling down.'

'If that's how it is, that's how it is!' answered a man called Tam, who seemed to command respect among his fellows. 'My Harry, he've got his hands full with ploughing without haulin' this nor that for Brother Benedict.'

'Reredfield has a stone church, but I did hear that our tower will be higher than theirs, if it's ever built,' answered Jack a thought which cheered everyone up, the man called Tam turning to Rico as if the preliminaries had gone on long enough. 'I'm Tam Fawkner, and my land is over there.' He jerked his head in the general direction of the chapel.

Rico drained his ale and stood. 'I am Rico Parleybien, the best story-teller you'll ever hear. If you care to come tonight I'll tell you how great King Harry beat the French at Agincourt, though his pale queen wept instead of rejoicing when a messenger brought the news of victory to court.'

'Why should the queen weep over a battle won? King Harry wasn't killed that I ever heard.'

'Wait, and I will tell you. Also how a dragon with a flaming sword – ' Rico broke off, knowing exactly how to leave his listeners agog. 'Well, there's no need to spoil a story. I'll tell about the dragon tonight as well, in return for ale and bread.' He went off rattling the coins in his purse, so they would not think him a beggar.

The fair was to be held on open ground midway between the huts around the chapel and another huddle of dwellings beside a distant pool. This and the area around the pool was common grazing, even though no one now remembered why Ferneth had grown in two parts. At the edge of his new fields Robert the Falconer had left some thicket uncut, partly because he had cleared as much land as he could manage on his own, and partly to keep a screen between himself and the other villagers, so making a truce between them easier. This remnant had long since been cleared, but distrust remained between pool-dwellers and the rest. By the time Rico came to Ferneth the pool had become mired by over-use, so only the poorest day-labourers lived there. As families prospered, they built better homes on open ground near the chapel or followed the example of Danesdell and lived on their own steading. Jack By The Wood's was the smallest of these, then there was Corndown, which Leofric once received as a bridegift, and Edenham Mill beyond that again, the name remembering Hwita's father, Edmer. There the Wyses now milled grain. Some two miles beyond Edenham a community of monks had come looking for seclusion, and founded an abbey which over the centuries became famous. This abbey was called Ockham: The Place Where Oaks Had Been.

Rico knew little of this, although he had heard of Ockham. But the division in Ferneth was clear to see, the fairplace exactly placed between the pool and the chapel. He looked around him briefly, then drove a branch into the earth where he wanted his pitch next day and immediately some children scampered over to demand his trade.

'Why, I tell stories and foretell the future,' he said, and laughed when they began to clamour for tales of goblins and princesses. Children never needed time to become accustomed to a story-monger, so he squatted on his haunches and asked the nearest what kind of story he would choose.

'About the witch who lives on Tiwshill! About the prince who kissed the maiden! About a gallant knight on a white horse!' they all shouted at once.

Rico clapped his hands over his ears. 'Mercy! I yield!'

Which was the cry of a loser at a joust. 'Coward!' A small boy stuck his nose in the air. 'My sister can weave a prince, a witch and – and –'

'A knight on a horse,' prompted Rico, grinning.

'And a knight on a *white* horse, all into one story. She could, easily.'

Rico looked around at bustling preparations for the fair, his eyebrows raised. 'Then bid her come tomorrow and we will have a contest to discover whose tales please best.'

At that the children began yelling and rolling in the dust with excitement, as if tomorrow already held more joys than they could bear. Rico hauled the boy who had spoken from under a kicking pile of his fellows. 'They don't seem to believe your sister will win.'

'She will! Alice doesn't tell her stories to just anyone, but if I ask her then tomorrow perhaps she might. And if she did, she'd win.' The boy was about eight years old, the side of his face disfigured by old bruising.

'Don't believe him! Drogo's a liar and his sister's mazed. You're often beaten for lying, aren't you, Drogo?' the children ran round him screaming.

The child, Drogo, stood stiff as a staff between Rico's hands, then he spat at the nearest taunting face, wriggled free and ran off. The children tumbled after him, belling like hounds and upsetting stalls and penned livestock on their way.

A strange child, Rico mused as he shouldered through the crowd. Anything different interested him, and Drogo was like a weasel caught in the open by an owl: defenceless, defiant and scarcely more than bones for a predator to void. As a small wind rose out of a clear evening sky, dust was beginning to blow across the fairplace and Rico's mind switched from Drogo to his need for a lodging. Men were gathering into knots, talking as if to make up in one night for a year of monosyllables; the women had vanished to tend their hearths.

'Looking for anyone in particular, then.'

'Ah, for you, who else could it be?' Rico bowed like a squire and flourished his cloak in mock gallantry.

The woman gaped; she was comely but not, apparently, swift witted. 'How could you know it was me when we've never met?'

'I've met you at every fair form here to London, and beyond.' Said Rico sadly. Folk were how they were made; it was not good being disappointed afresh each time you met stupidity or spite. 'Are you called Kate or is it Mary?'

Her expression cleared; she understood simple questions. 'Meg.'

'May I come in then, Meg?'

She nodded, bold eyes sliding from his face to his crotch.

Women who accosted strangers outside their hut on fairday eve never had a man by their hearth, only children. Meg was the same, and shoved the children outside the moment Rico entered. She jerked her head. 'You mustn't mind Edwulf, he's too sick to go out.'

Rico glanced at the thin shape coughing in a corner. 'Poor brat. Is he yours, or do you mind him for another?'

She had to think about that. 'Mine' she said finally.

'You're sure?'

You think I'm foolish, don't you? Well, perhaps I am. But I know my own, even though I must sell my milk to live. When I've two or more at the breast, would it be wonderful if I forgot which is which? I don't, but would it matter if I did?'

'I'm sorry.' Said Rico, humbly. 'No, I don't suppose it would.'

'My dugs are all I've got, you see,' she confided, and untied her dress to show him huge breasts with nipples like chewed bark. 'When I'm in milk I can feed three easily, four if I must. And so I live, and the childer mostly, too.

Rico nodded understandingly, the hut was clean and the smell from the pot was good. The sight of those monstrous breasts had stirred him, though his first reaction was disgust; but then he was very easily stirred where women were concerned. Only green and cruelty dismayed him into coldness. He ran his hand up her arm. 'Ah, Meg. Good women are hard to find.'

'I'm not good. Brother Benedict says I shall have to spend a long time in purgatory, no matter how hard he prays for me.'

'I think you're good,' he said, kissing her. 'You give affection with your milk, and everyone lives as best they may.'

She chuckled, nestling her body into his as if he was simply another sucking mouth. Lusty men abounded in Ferneth, but skilled and sensual men were rare: she would look forward to this night's bedding.

All the same, she needed to hide impatience when he took so long fondling her that she began to smell stew burning in the pot. In her experience, the purpose of fondling was to tease feeble men into strength and therefore it was clearly a waste of time with Rico. What Meg could not be expected to know was Rico's weakness: he needed to love the woman he lay with. For a travelling man who needed women often, this made matters unnecessarily difficult.

She kissed well, he thought as he took her to the straw. Though built like a cow, she kissed with tongue and lips and sharp fingernails in his back. He had been fortunate to find a generous and good-natured harlot to lodge with in Ferneth, even though she might be a trifle mazed.

Mazed, the children had yelled at the child Drogo.

'One of your children isn't called Drogo, is he?' he asked.

'Nay, the only Drogo is John the Carver's brat. Meg thought nothing of the question, nor any longer of her burning stew. She had never dreamed of the skills Rico possessed nor would she ever find them again; begging, starving from moment to moment now, for what he could astonishingly give. She needed anyway to breed for milk to see her through the following spring, and since Meg was filled with bountiful affections she instantly decided that if only she could conceive by him, then she would most particularly cherish any child of Rico's.

Drogo bolted into cover by the pool and lay there panting while the hunt swept past. He had been a fool to chance being found near the pool, where if they discovered him the older boys would hold him under the water, but from here his own hearth was sufficiently close that when they tired of searching for him, he could reach it unobserved. He wriggled deeper beneath an overhung bank: soon, Alice would be home and he safe until next time.

He buried his face in poolside earth and thought of his father, John the Carver: he was never safe from him. And this time he had boasted of the stories Alice told! If John heard that, she would suffer ridicule more cruel than any beating.

The children searched desultorily for a while and then went off. Too many opportunities filled the eve of Ferneth fair to waste it hunting Drogo. They could do that any day of the year.

After a while Drogo heard a low whistle and scrambled to his feet, bare toes squelching in poolside mud. 'Alice! I didn't know you were back.'

'I passed the pack on my way. They didn't find you, did they?'

Drogo shook his head. Alice was five years older than he, and took the place of a mother who had died when he was born. They fought fiercely as allies against the outside world; lying and stealing if they thought this would ease the harshness of their lives, their only loyalty resting in each other.

Alice rumpled Drogo's hair, which stuck out like a briar. 'Come then and help me stir the supper. Fast.'

No need to tell Drogo why they needed to be quick. If John came home early, and he easily might on fairday eve, then he must not catch them unprepared.

Already John's latest wife (his fourth) was as slatternly as the rest, pride beaten out of her within two seasons of her marriage. Alice knew that she herself would long ago have been the same, except she needed to fight for Drogo. And he for her: which kept them sane although often badly beaten.

'Alice,' said Drogo in a small voice.

'Aye?'

'There was a ballad-monger on the fairground, bragging of how he told the best stories in the land.'

Alice turned, her thin face flowing. 'Oh, Drogo, do you think I'll be able to listen to him tomorrow? I should like to hear how a true ballad-monger tells his tales.'

'I told him you were better than him.'

'You know I – ' Her voice altered suddenly. 'Drogo, you didn't!'

He nodded.

She wrung her hands. 'Holy Virgin, help me. If our father hears, it means the worst beating of the year.'

'I think he will hear,' said Drogo, weeping. 'The ballad-monger said you must have a contest with him, and word of that will surely spread.'

They stared at each other in dismay. John the Carver worked stone and timber like an angel, but behaved like one of Satan's demons. He liked his women and children cowed, and though he had not so far molested his daughter Alice, neither she nor Drogo could ever please him. Above all, John detested to see any glimmer of his skill reflected in his children: he was a master craftsman, not they. Drogo drew pictures in the dust which Alice preferred to John's carvings in wood or stone, because they danced merrily where her father's more artful faces gave her a feeling of unease, but Drogo must always be sure to sweep the dust smooth before evening. As for Alice, she had long ago learned to keep her mouth shut on her imaginings. Only to Drogo did she whisper about the leaping images in her mind.

'Well,' she said now. 'It's no good thinking about it. He won't hear until tomorrow, I suppose, and by then he'll have drunk too much fresh-brewed to listen.'

Drogo brightened up at that, as she had meant him to. John was a mighty drinker so this was certainly their best chance of escaping punishment until after the fair was over, and the morrow of the fair was bound to be filled with beatings anyway. John was particularly vicious-tempered after a carouse. Better not think of it until then.

John's latest wife met them, whining, at their hut door. Poor woman, her life was even more unenviable than theirs. John never bargained in Ferneth for a wife, since there was no maid foolish or desperate enough to wed him where he was known. Instead, after each one died in childbed or of a broken will – or both – he picked the next from among the women who came to seek a hiring at Reredfield fair. On these occasions he washed his face and hands in the pool, ordered Alice to weave him a new belt of coloured wools, and went off looking the best husband any female could wish for. His black hair shone, his cheeks glowed, massive muscles filled the leather of his breeches. And if men sometimes wondered whether his skills were sufficient to account for all the coins he spent on ale, why, folk will always tattle about something. The truth was that John sometimes went out at night and waylaid travellers on the track which ran from Ferneth to Reredfield, as much for excitement as for gain, although the gain was pleasant. If a woman travelled late, then she had most cause of all to regret her tardiness. Yet whatever Ferneth suspected, and Alice and Drogo were too young to suspect anything worse than casual lust, he was never caught. King's justices did not often ride the country any longer, but if they should come wanting to hang robbers in the Weald, then John the Carver could rely on his neighbourly dumb looks and shut mouths about his doings. A state of affairs which King William, four hundred years before, would not have tolerated for more time than it took to hang the whole village.

Alice looked around their hut, nervously wondering what her father would find fault with tonight. Everything smelt mouldy because the hut leaked, but surely nothing was left undone which John expected her to do. There was meat as well as chopped roots in the pot, including bryony in large enough pieces for John to recognize. Bryony gave a man potency, or so her father said, and nothing enraged him faster than any suspicion that his daily diet of the root had been withheld.

Alice was sixteen years old, the budding curve of hip and breast easily seen beneath the scanty clothes she wore. She had inherited her father's stiff dark hair and dark eyes, but where he glowed with health she was sallow and thin, her bones starkly slanting, wide-lipped mouth distrustfully downturned. A life of poverty and hopelessness taught those who lived it how to keep virtues out of sight and none more so than courage, which only inflamed ill-temper further. Nevertheless, Alice was courageous because she refused to abandon hope.

Sometimes she looked at Hawisa, John's fourth wife, and thought, I won't stay here to die of a kicked belly like my mother, nor of fear like Hawisa. Even a hiring in Reredfield market would be better than staying here. But always wariness stood behind her, saying, Fool.

Hawisa accepted John at market. Lal Baker ran away from Ferneth to seek her fortune and was found dead a day's walk away. England was in turmoil and many years had passed since a king boasted that anyone might travel from end to end of his realm in safety. And how would she feed Drogo if she took him with her, as she must? At least here they ate John's leavings.

He came in humming, without a care in the world. Then stopped humming and sniffed. 'Christ's entrails, what are you cooking? Mud and dung?'

'Good meat. Some of the mutton Brother Benedict paid for your carving in his church,' Alice answered anxiously.

'I didn't ask you.' John thrust a crust into the pot and stuffed it, dripping, in his mouth. 'Holy blood and bones! Do you want to poison me?' He spat his mouthful back in the stew.

'It is good meat,' insisted Alice. 'Good, very good.' She couldn't think of anything else to say.

John slung his tools at her and she knew better than to dodge. If they hit her he might be satisfied; if they missed then he would find worse ways to make sure of punishment. She dodged all the same, instinct too powerful to be denied.

'Bitch!' yelled John at once, and came over. 'You've eaten the meat and thought I wouldn't notice!'

'I told you. It all went in the pot.'

'I saw Alice put if there,' whispered Drogo. 'Every last piece. I wanted one to suck and she wouldn't let me.'

'Liar,' said John, quite pleasantly. 'I'll beat you later. Now, Alice, where's my meat?'

Alice shook her head. If it wasn't meat it would be something else.

He reached for her, a slack smile on his face, and began the beating. He enjoyed beating Alice. Beating Drogo was a duty and beating Hawisa habit; but beating sixteen-year-old Alice was as heady a pleasure as downing fresh-brewed ale.

It was after dark when Rico left Meg and sauntered along the dusty lane which led past the chapel before curving back towards the tavern where he hoped most of the village would be waiting to hear his tales. Although content by habit, tonight Rico felt happiness like something he could hold, his body eased and his mind at rest. For as long as he wanted to stay at Ferneth Meg would welcome him, and tonight he felt he wanted to stay a long time, he always felt like this when he had lain well with a woman; the trouble was, the feeling never lasted.

There was a light in the chapel, flickering through an open door. Curious, always curious, Rico picked his way through piles of loose stones and peered in. The air smelt rotten and the roof sagged so low that the pine-knot torch only lit the floor. He pushed back the door, which squeaked on perished leather hinges and stepped inside.

'Have you come to beg forgiveness for your sins?'

Rico jumped, and turned. 'The begging might fit into a lifetime, but forgiveness would take longer than I have to spare.'

'God keep your soul for not being puffed with pride. Even so, you must repent or burn in hell.'

'I do repent. And then next day I find sin wearing as fair a skin as ever sin could wear.' Rico could see nothing in the darkness beyond the torch.

'They say that though a handsome face counts for much, even witchcraft cannot equal the charm of words timely spoken.'

Rico laughed, taken by surprise. He had never encountered a priest with a sense of humour before. 'I do not find it so.'

'No?'

'Sometimes, perhaps. But women usually prefer deeds to words.'

'I am sure you can oblige with deeds as well,' said the voice drily.

Rico thought of Meg, and smiled.

And the priest standing behind the light shifted suddenly, his body tensed by that smile. God curse my flesh and make it die, he thought wearily, aware that what he really felt was envy, because only a man freshly come for a woman smiled like that. He lifted the torch from its bracket. 'I have to be careful where I put this, the roof is dry at this season and we want to save some of our timbers for the new church.'

Rico glanced at sods bulging through haphazardly placed supports. 'You will have to work fast.'

'We are working as fast as Ferneth can afford, but Ockham Abbey is building a new nave two hundred paces long, and every mason in these parts has gone there to cheat the brothers.'

'Of whom you are one?'

'Brother Benedict, yes. But I dislike revellings in the cloister and begged permission to come here as priest.'

Rico studied the face he could now see chequered red and black by the flame. A beautiful face, no other word described it. Bone and character clearly sculpted for all to see: vital eyes; long, austere mouth. He also held himself as a knight in training would, rather than a priest; a falcon among sparrows in this forest hamlet.

'So how do you like your calling as a village priest?' said Rico at last.

'God forgive me, I do not like it.'

'Ah, now I see why you preferred that I should admit to fresh sin each day. No matter what, honesty keeps in virtue.'

Brother Benedict smiled faintly. 'But confession can be bitter.'

'Why are you talking to me like this?' asked Rico curiously. 'I am not a man who gives any thought to his soul from one year's end to the next.'

He saw the other consider, as if the answer was important. 'Probably because I am lonely. Think nothing of it. We all have our times of weakness, but face the world again on the morrow. Come and see the church I am building, now the moon has risen.'

The moon indeed sailed across clear skies, spilling black shadow from dug holes and scaffolded arches.

'It's big,' said Rico, squinting upwards.

'Not if you have ever seen an abbey such as Ockham.'

'I've seen a dozen abbeys, but they served communities of two hundred souls or more. Here you have – what? – half a dozen farmsteads and twenty huts.'

'Less. Five to fifteen.'

Rico grinned, understanding that this monk laughed at himself. 'Well, then.'

'I build not only to house souls, but to glorify God.'

'How many masons have you hired to help? You say they're all flocking to Ockham.'

'Up to six if the means are given. Usually John the Carver, because he loves the feel of his chisel in wood or stone which is set to last.' Benedict held his torch so Rico could see some capitals ready-carved: a wicked, cross eyed devil grew from the stone and a demon shrieked in silent torment. Four carvings were complete, two more rough chiselled from their surround. All were as fine as anything Rico had seen in the rich churches of his Suffolk childhood, better probably. All had something about them he didn't like, a slyness, a gloating over evil and suffering, which gave a sardonic droop even to an angel's eye. 'They're good,' he said at last. 'But I don't think they would make me weep for either the beauty or the cruelty of this world.'

He heard the monk draw in his breath, as if iron closed on bone. 'Why do you say that?'

'It is how I feel, and I am a man who can weep over many things. I prefer God's good stone to the delight in a torturer's face, however well carved he may be.' The dying glow of the torch might have made him imagine the look of pain on Brother Benedict's face, but in case he had not, Rico hastened to admire what little he could see of dressed stonework and leaping arches. An astonishing amount of work must have been done by Benedict himself, this lordly and disciplined man labouring like a serf each day, pausing only for prayer when his Order ruled he must. Yet as he looked around, Rico thought only what a splendid tale this would make, how a man who must have held a high position renounced the world but then rebuilt it stone by stone to ease the tedium of a wilderness exile.

Rico possessed uncanny skill when he looked into the minds of other men, and understood at once that Benedict built this church for himself and not for God alone.

After Rico left, Benedict went back to work. He was building the first of a pair of buttresses, the space between them part-walled. The week before he had persuaded two master-masons on their way to Ockham to cut stone for a window and two inside arches: Benedict could set a wall but only craftsmen could obtain so exact a line on an arch that the eye never paused in its upward sweep.

Benedict worked as he did all things: without fuss or offering any concession to frailty of the flesh. He glanced at the sky occasionally, calculating time, otherwise he toiled up and down scaffold poles carrying stone until his head reeled. As a child it had been drilled into him that tired or not, a man must keep his back straight and his weakness hidden, and he was too old to change the habit of a lifetime. He liked working at night when no one came to gape, but understood the extra care he must take because he was so tired. Usually he felt closer to God as, under black skies or tremendous spreads of stars, the fevers of fatigue sent his mind spinning after visions.

Tonight, Benedict attached each task with an ardour which came close to fury. He struck out at stone, carried beams single-handed which normally would have burdened two. Passion rode on his trowel and frenzy in the way he ran along his half-finished wall from one buttress to the other. Merciless war was being waged within his spirit, a war between truth and delusion, pride and temptations he had overcome, but no good came of it in the end because stone was the victor. Very late in the night, his senses shuddered as he paused halfway up the ladder with a block of stone on his shoulder. He bit his lip and tried to steady himself; he had a church to build and must not weaken now. No one but he could cajole Lord Scovyll into generosity, the monks of Ockham into sharing a trifle of their wealth with Ferneth; nor did he think many priests could put sufficient fear into the toughened souls of the ridge, so its inhabitants lent their muscle and their oxen when they were needed.

Benedict dropped the stone he was carrying without realizing its weight was gone, began to fumble his way down the ladder a step at a time. If he fell, probably he would break a bone and never build again: and so strong was his will to build that only as his foot touched the ground did consciousness finally slip away.

When he opened his eyes a thin dawn breeze was blowing. Jesu, he must have worked through Lauds and lain like a log through Prime. Never since he took his vows eight years before had he missed any of his daily offices. He wanted to rise at once but, chilled close to death, his body at first refused to answer his command. Above his head the only completed arch cut cleanly across yellow sky, bearing-timbers notched in place, cornices and corbels carved. How strange he mused, to stare at shapes I placed and know they will exist side by side for centuries. May they love each other and live happily together. And he smiled, feeling his strength return.

Two more years of labour, and Ferneth's new church would be sufficiently near completion not to be abandoned when he died. Two? Six, more like. Benedict was a realist and knew that at forty-seven he was already old for the age he lived in, and would not live to see his design completed.

He stood, carefully.

Curse Rico Parleybien, who sinned and laughed and sinned again. Curse the tongue which said John the Carver's skill would not make him weep for the cruelty or beauty of this world. Benedict knelt where one day an altar would be raised, and lifted his face to the dawn. 'Not curses but praise for Rico, O Christ. The sinner who revealed more to me of the kind of man I am.'

Benedict was a son of a great house of Clare, a knight renowned for skill at arms until the day he heard a black friar preach in the ruins of a sacked French town. Smoke and screams everywhere, and in the middle of it this one man screeching like a barn owl. The friar was rough and spoke patois; normally Gilbert de Clare would have ridden past him without a thought. But the campaign had been unusually bloody, his wife and children were recently dead of plague, and so he listened. And as he listened, his life changed. Not because of what the friar said, which was as irrational and badly phrased as most such outpourings, but because Gilbert realized he was sick to the heart of what he did. He was then thirty-eight years old and trained for war since childhood. He was, quite simply, weary of blood, yet possessed nothing except his prowess in arms. As a younger son of a minor line of Clares his lands were few, and situated in a poor part of Lincolnshire. Nor, at a time of pusillanimous rule and royal quarrellings, did he care to serve at court.

All his life Gilbert de Clare never compromised on anything. If he fought, he fought to kill. If he loved, and he had loved his dead wife, he loved passionately and for ever. When he tired of being a knight, he became a monk.

Perfection fascinated him. He hated Ockham Abbey, where he served his novitiate, because it was petty-minded and corrupt. He hated Ferneth because he was a great lord by blood, yet constrained to humility among boors. He did not despise his fellow villagers, as he would not despise a well-muscled ox, but nor could he easily sustain himself with only oxen for company. So he decided to build a church, nourishing his spirit on problems of mass and thrust, bludgeoning his body into submission with heavy labour. God knew, Ferneth needed a new church, when the chapel built by Theobald was more than half dissolved back into earth. A church which nevertheless was conceived because he had failed in his calling. Benedict had seen the understanding on Rico's face: the strolling ballad-monger knew that he existed as much for this his own creation as he did for God.

Quite soon, Benedict rose from his knees and went over to where the first of John the Carver's capitals was in position. 'It is beautiful work,' he said aloud. The figure he looked at was St Peter, the keys of heaven in his belt, one hand raised in blessing, a cock crowing in tangled foliage behind his back. It was indeed exquisite, except that this Peter would betray his lord and never repent, providing the price was right. Benedict had long ago judged John to be a savagely evil man, but held his tongue because of his mastery in wood and stone. No longer; since Rico had reminded him that mastery alone was not enough.

Benedict turned and left the church, walking briskly; he needed some bread inside him before he tackled a brute like John. As he crossed to his hut, a cock crowed in Fawkner's Fields . . . once . . . twice . . . thrice.

It was going to be a fine day for the fair.

When Rico left Benedict he knew he had to hurry. He had promised Ferneth a story of battle and chivalry, and no one would be in a mood for enchantment if sodden with ale before he even began. Then word would spread that Rico Parleybien was a swindler and few would come to listen to him at the fair.

Wat Apps's hut came as close to being a tavern as a place like

Ferneth could support, quite why no one knew. Wat never complained when his living space so filled with people that his brats had to sleep outside, though a more likely reason was his wife's light hand with barley. A horn of her new ale made a man merrier than two of the most other brews. Even so, Rico was startled by the number of men crammed into a wattle hut. There was no room even for a fire, which burned outside the door, sparks streaming into the sky. There were women and children crouched in the shadows, and fresh branches thrown on so liberally that everyone was warm.

'Pick your way through the clutter, Rico,' called Wat Apps. 'Hush your blether the rest of you. He's got stories like other men get fluxes.'

'No need for stories,' called a packman. 'Christ's blood, the whole country is thrown to the wolves and you want tales of Good King Harry and Agincourt! What about Feeble King Harry at Westminster, an' his thieving pack of varmints?'

There was a shout of assent, and Tam Fawkner nudged Rico in the ribs. 'You heard anything about all this coil in Kent.'

'I passed fellows on the road who were sworn to spill the blood of wicked royal councillors if the king didn't do it for them. There was fighting a few days ago, or so the gossip ran.'

'Well, I'm off to pierce a few black hearts alongside of them. Why, the French have burned Rye! It doesn't bear thinking of,' interrupted a shock-headed youth with ardent eyes.

'I'll come with you Harry,' called another voice. 'The French in Sussex! Whatever would the bowmen of Agincourt have said?'

'They'd say they won their victory because o' good bows at their shoulder, and not because the likes of Harry Fawkner skewered a king's councillor,' said old Tam sharply. 'What d'you mean by saying you're off when there's ploughing's still to be done?'

'I can still plough all the rest of my life,' answered Harry, his son, fiercely. 'Tell us the tale of Agincourt, Rico,'

Rico hesitated. Properly told, the ballad of Agincourt roused listeners to tears and frenzy, and this audience was already roused. 'Another night. What do you say to the tale of two knights at a tournament instead?'

But they would not let him change his mind. He had promised them Agincourt and he must tell it. This was a night when they wanted to hear of English valour, especially since several of the strangers sprawled about their fire were pledged to march on London to help call treasonous councillors to account. There had been rumblings of unrest for months. After generations when Englishmen became used to victory against the French, the tide had turned and everywhere the news was bad. Ferneth's isolation meant that the tales of defeat remained unreal until the French landed and burned Rye, less than thirty miles away. Rye was Sussex. The French, the whoreson French, had burned a Sussex town. No one thought how Sussex men had been burning out the French for years, nor remembered that four hundred years ago some of their ancestors had come that way, and conquered all England. Everyone now expected an English king to win abroad and keep the peace at home. When one failed, like their present feeble Henry, they howled for the blood of traitors in high places. Month by month unrest had spread and simmered, and now it reached Ferneth.

'Agincourt! Agincourt!' everyone yelled. 'Tell the tale of how the French were beat, Rico.'

'Well, it was like this,' said Rico, resolving to tell it coldly this one time. 'King Harry and his bowmen, bowmen like you and me, lads, and not many fine knights either . . .'

But whatever his resolve, Rico was incapable of telling a good story badly. Stained leather, tired troops and blaring trumpets leaped to life as he warmed to his task, and in Wat Apps's hut men yelled to greet King Harry and stabbed downward with their thumbs when the slaughter started. Even the French were no faceless enemy but victims weeping with the horror of it all, as also was King Harry's wife, a Frenchwoman wedded to a foe. ' . . . And so at length King Harry found no one left to oppose him, and rode out master of the field. The bowmen unstrung their bows, surrounded by more riches than any could imagine, for the whole chivalry of France lay dead at their feet. Thus did two thousand English vanquish twelve thousand French, because they were valiant men.'

'And now the French burn Rye,' said Harry Fawkner. He jumped to his feet, eyes blazing. Stubble sprouted on a jaw too young for beard, his hair a mass of curls which Ferneth women of all ages found irresistible: he hated the way old crones reached up to rumple it, but was too good-natured to say so.

Everyone yelled at once then, those on their way already to join the uprising and those who had never given rebellion a thought until tonight.

'I'm going straight off tomorrow to join Jack Cade and his company in their a-putting of things right,' added Harry. 'The king will listen if he's told what's going on, and hang the traitors who keep black tidings from him. You watch how things change once he knows Rye's been burnt.'

Rico stood abruptly. 'Jesu! Rebels are hanged, not councillors! The king will have known these many weeks how Rye –'

But no one was listening to him any more. Instead they thrust elbows into their neighbour's ribs and stamped on the earth floor, roaring defiance. Rico looked at them, hands on his hips, eyes sombre; then he tore a long strip of wattle from the wall and thrust it in the fire. Soon it was a streamer of flame, lifted high and crackling between his fingers, and everyone stopped shouting, at once, astonished by such a sight. 'Listen, all of you.' Rico crunched out sparks in his fist. 'You'll hang if you go, I've walked the roads of years and never saw a rebel prosper yet. Cade may say he's going to tell the king what's wrong in his realm, but I tell you the king is not so foolish that he doesn't know what's wrong. All he lacks is the skill to put it right. And so evil men ride high; petty thieves and murderers along the highways, greater thieves and murderers at court. What chance has Cade to lance such a boil as that, with his few hundred followers from the Weald? The king and his barons will slaughter them where they stand.'

'The king won't ride against us,' said Harry confidently. 'We're his, don't you see? Kings lead us to victory like at Agincourt. Well, Rye weren't victory. When we tell him that, he'll line up those barons and slice off their heads.'

'I'm with you,' said Wat Apps, fat childlike face alight. He rubbed his hands. 'Well, we're going to London to see the king, just think of that!'

'Wat Apps, now you listen to me! You don't go traipsing off to London!' howled his wife.

But though most other Ferneth men were looking thoughtful after what Rico said, jolly little Wat Apps remained firm in his resolve. He would go to London and be rewarded by the king for telling him the French had burnt Rye. Rico repeated again and again that rebels ended on a gibbet, and by the time he finished most of his listeners had decided that their own hut was the best place to stay. Only Apps, Harry, and another boy remained adamant in their determination to go.

Tam Fawkner summed it up when he drained the last of his ale. 'Well-a-day, boy. You're no serf to be bound where you don't want to be, but heir to the freehold of Ferneth. The last of us after dunamany years. Go if you must an' come back if you can, but I'll find the ploughing mortal hard alone.' He stumped out.

'Of course I'll come back,' said Harry defiantly.

'When shall we leave?' asked the other boy. He was sharp-faced and quiet, looking as if he might be less of a bull on the loose than Harry.

'We're away at dawn,' offered one of the travellers. 'Come with us if you like. The sooner the better if we're not to miss the fight.

Harry flushed. ''Tis fairday tomorrow, and there's someone I have to see before I go. We'll catch you up, won't we Greg?'

'Someone to see? A maid belike, Curlylocks,' scoffed the traveller.

'All right, so he has to see a maid,' answered the boy, Greg, calmly, while Harry spluttered rage. 'Fine fellows we should look if we went off without so much as God be wi' ye. I don't doubt that England's affairs will wait one more day for us.'

'This folly will kill you unless you have a care,' Rico said in an urgent undervoice to Greg, while the packman and Harry continued to quarrel.

Greg shrugged. 'I'll have a care, but I couldn't let Harry go alone, don't you see. He might think he could really reach the king and get a pike stuck in his belly.'

Rico drew back, relieved. 'I thank you for salving my conscience.'

The boy laughed, he could not be more than seventeen, younger certainly than Harry. 'You'll watch your tongue next time you tell the ballad of Agincourt. But I've long fancied a season out of Ferneth and this is as good a way as any other.'

'It's a fine life, the life of dusty feet,' answered Rico. 'I know I couldn't bear to follow the same furrow every year.'

'Nor I. My kin are millers.' Greg stretched and yawned. 'You get dust on more than your feet, milling.'

After they left Wat Apps's, Harry Fawkner and Greg Wyse walked together as far as the lane outside the chapel, where Ralf d'Escoville had once paced in moonlight as bright as this, plotting how Harry's ancestor, Robert the Falconer, might serve his purposes. There they halted, because Harry was nearly home and Greg must walk two more miles to Edenham Mill.

'We shall have a tale of our own to tell when we get back, won't we, Greg? About London and what kind of a dance king's councillors kick at the end of a hangman's rope' said Harry.

Greg agreed, having learned to take the easiest course with Harry's fancies. Unlike Brother Benedict, Greg did not find thick wits exasperating; as the son of an unusually devious father, he found them restful. He thought about this journey he and Harry would make as he trudged on to Edenham along the track Leofric once followed through the forest, which still jinked capriciously left and right as if through glades in a forest. Even so, Edenham was more quickly reached by way of Corndown and some leisurely corners than by plunging across cleared land where the rougher places were let uncultivated. Ferneth had grown slowly over the previous four hundred years, except for the sheep which were beginning to encroach even on the ploughlands around the village. To the west, the lords d'Escoville (now slurred to the more local sound of Scovyll) had expanded their hunting park across the ravined wilderness right up to the steep edge of Ferenthe Ridge: where Guthlac died, hounds broke into deep-throated belling and youths outdid each other in gaudy dressing.

But here on the track which led east to Edenham Mill, the old sense of spaciousness remained. Unending near-emptiness as far as the horizon, broken by a few wattle, timber and reed huts clustered behind thornbrush stockades; only the Abbey of Ockham sprawled across its clearing, and in the distance drifting smoke occasionally showed where men continued to pick at the forest.

Edenham lay at the bottom of a slope beside its brook, which in summer sometimes had too little water in it to drive the mill wheel, but tonight Greg heard the wheel's clatter as soon as he turned the corner beyond Corndown. Often the frail mill shook to the wheel's vibrations, but when it was still he could not sleep. Then everyone on the ridge had to grind their grain painfully by hand, and the miller's family starved.

There was a rushlight burning on the granary wall, and Greg frowned. His father never burned a light unless there was profit in it. With sheep everywhere, there was less trade for the Wyses nowadays, which was why Greg had other ideas about his future. Meanwhile, the mill leaned closer to the stream each year, its floors rotted and the roof became spotted with green moss. Fawkners, where Harry lived, was snug and watertight, another good reason for Greg Wyse to plan his life carefully. Greg was not envious of Harry, merely determined one day to build the best house in Ferneth for himself. It didn't seem very likely, when each year sheep only made them poorer.

Greg pulled aside the leather doorpiece and immediately foul-smelling shadows seemed to leap at him; an irrational, unexpected fear chilled his skin as he crossed himself. Demons were everywhere and though he did not expect to find them at Edenham tonight, you could never be too careful.

His father turned. 'Get you down to sleep with the rest tonight.'

'You said to tell you when I returned from Apps's.'

Sim Wyse grunted. 'I wanted to know you weren't lying ale-sodden in a ditch. Off wi' you, we start milling before daybreak.'

If Sim's family desired to waste a day cavorting at Ferneth fair, he made sure they made up the time they lost. Even so, Greg was curious to find a visitor at the mill so late, and a spectacularly ill-smelling and secretive visitor at that. He strained his eyes in the dimness but could see little beyond a shape. 'Should I fetch ale for your guest?'

'Begone, I said! Ale indeed, for a chance-met stranger come to beg for gleanings!'

Greg's lips tightened. He did not believe this man was unknown to his father and if he had been, the grudging meanness of refusing him ale caught Greg on the raw. When I have prospered, then even chance-met strangers shall praise my hospitality, he vowed.

After he left the granary he stood for a while on the tiny platform above the mill wheel, there its racing paddles shook teeth and thoughts alike. Greg had been very young when he discovered that his father would do most things for a coin, including joining forces with a vagabond and robbing pilgrims on their way to Ockham Abbey. Like John the Carver on the westbound tracks, Sim Wyse had discovered that the lawless state of the country offered him more chances than legitimate trade.

As Greg stood wondering, his father and the stranger ducked out and walked away briskly beside the brook, talking together.

Cautiously, Greg followed, slipping into shadow. He could just see the stranger towering above Sim; surely only monks or knights were ever as tall as that. Ordinary men met scarcity so often and worked from the time they staggered at their mother's skirts, that not many of them grew straight or tall.

Greg hesitated when he saw his father's chin often on his shoulder, then he retraced his steps to the mill and, once out of sight, sprinted for the track. Greg respected his father's senses too much to attempt following him across moonlit ground if even half an eye watched behind. After Sim bade him farewell, probably the stranger would rejoin the track somewhere beyond the mill, where it became no more than a footway leading to Ockham; already Greg would have wagered a good deal on instinct which told him this straight-spined intruder came from the abbey, either as a monk or traveller.

Greg needed to run nearly a mile before reaching a place where he judged himself to be ahead of the stranger and could plunge back towards the foot-trail which led to Ockham through the forest, there to lie in wait. His breath had scarcely steadied before he heard the squelch of footsteps and breathed the stench of urine this man carried with him like a second pelt. He also hesitated as he came close, as if he sensed another human presence, before continuing on his way, but faster than before. And as he passed Greg saw the tonsure on his skull; he was a monk.

When he had disentangled himself from the briar where he had taken cover, Greg stood staring at the footprints slowly filling with water on the path: prints of bare feet made spatulate by labour. Certainly not those of a cloister-monk, who at Ockham lived like barons; hunting, wenching and wearing the latest fashion in doublet and pointed boots. Then, as he stood there, Greg heard the sound of someone else coming from the direction of the mill and stepped behind a tree. This time it was his sister Nicola who came pelting out of darkness and he snatched her arm as she went past, his hand clapped to her mouth to stop her screech. 'So what are you doing, lovely, following a tonsured monk?'

Immediately he spoke the fright drained out of her, and she giggled under his hand. 'What a toss you gave me! I quite thought one of the Widow Tiw's hounds had jumped out from behind a tree.'

'One very easily might, if you persist in jauntering around the forest in the dark. None of which answers my question.'

She pouted, her face tilted provocatively to the moonlight. 'What is it to you if I can't sleep at night?'

Greg tightened his grip. 'More than a little, if you intend to drowse in a monk's arms instead.'

Nicola did not struggle but leaned softly against him. She never struggled, but usually gained her way. 'Everyone knows the monks of Ockham come like rutting hounds to seek women where they can. Why, our father is mightily proud that his father was none other than an abbot.'

This was true. Sim often boasted that he owed his blood to the lucky chance whereby a monk returning from the hunt came on his mother reaping at the forest edge.

'Our grandsire was a vowed monk who became abbot, this rascal you thought to follow is a mere serving brother.' This was not the objection Greg had meant to make.

'Serving brother you may call him, but he will soon be richer than Lord Scovyll himself!' Nicola twisted free, and stood facing him.

'Some men will say anything if it buys a wench cheaply.'

'I swear it by Christ and the Virgin. Ask my father.'

'I think you must tell me yourself,' said Greg, alarmed of course, whatever plot this was, his father would know of it.

'Why should I?'

Greg sighed; he was very weary, having begun his shovellings on the granary floor at first light. 'Sit down beside me.'

'Why?'

'Because I mean you to tell me everything, and I am too leg-weary for standing while we bicker.'

It took him until the moon set to worm out every detail, occasionally needing to keep her by force from escaping him. Eventually it was not so much his trapping questions which overbore her, as the reflection that she would look a hag at the fair if she stayed wakeful through the whole of the night. Then, proudly, she told him that Brother Edmund planned to steal the abbey treasure.

'I'm hearing you right?' demanded Greg, dumbfounded. 'A serving brother plans to break into Ockham treasure chest? Or does he mean to pillage the altar, and die accursed afterwards?'

'So you see how rich we shall be,' added Nicola, taking no notice of this. She was pleased, really for the chance to share her anticipation. 'Edmund knows he will be pursued, so he plans to walk in the stream from the abbey to the island – you know, by Coneyburrow.' Greg nodded. The brook divided near some woodland which harboured rabbits escaped from the abbey's warren, and purled over stones, thus surrounding a clump of willow on a knoll. 'No one will guess he would dare stay close to the abbey, but of course he must not move until the hunt dies down. Even then, he'll need help to leave. I carry his child and he's promised to wed me once we're safe. Meanwhile, he'll pay for the food we take him, and promises my father many coins for carrying him to Tonbridge among our sacks of flour.'

'When is the robbery planned?'

She shrugged. 'He hasn't told me. Don't you think Edmund must be splendidly clever to have thought of such a thing? Why, I can't even dream how much treasure an abbey holds. Edmund came to the mill one day with Ockham's grain for grinding, and we met by the stream all summer.'

'Then, as soon as he made sure of you, he broached this – this besotted plan for robbery and flight?'

She wrinkled her brow, remembering. 'He always talked of how he wanted to leave Ockham, but only with gold in his belt. I didn't listen until the tax came in. Coin for the king, Edmund said. Left at the abbey while Cade's rebels make the roads unsafe. Once he said he intended to take that, then I knew he could rely on our father's help.

'Let's go back then,' said Greg heavily. 'I must next speak with him.'

He covered the ground back to the mill with the long strides of anger, Nicola hop-hopping behind, begging him to tell what he meant to do. He took no notice, and found Sim snoring on the granary floor.

'Go and sleep, this is between my father and me,' he said curtly to Nicola.

'Nay, it shouldn't be you at all!' She shook Sim impatiently. 'Father, Greg is angry about Edmund.'

Sim sat up and spat dust out of his throat. Can't a man sleep without – son of a bitch! What did you say?'

Greg explained that Nicola had told him about Brother Edmund and exactly what this meant: Sim Wyse must give up any notion of receiving stolen treasure from Ockham Abbey. Otherwise he himself would tell Brother Benedict what was afoot.

When Sim grasped the enormity of his son's betrayal he raged and swore, then pounded after him with his fists. Greg dodged most of the blows and simply repeated his threat to tell. He did not add that he was sworn to go with Harry Fawkner to London and so himself would be away from danger: If Sim knew that, he would promise anything and break his work as soon as Greg had gone.

Grey light was lifting over the trees before Sim gave in, whereupon Nicola burst into tears, the two of them stamping distractedly on the rotten boards. 'Our fortune made in a single night, and you throw it on the midden! Your sister carries a monk's bastard, did you know? And you refuse the offer of a ring on her finger and honey on her bread!'

At this, Nicola howled louder than before.

'Make your fortune by some less foolhardy robbery,' retorted Greg. 'What is one more bastard in the forest, when set against Ockham's hounds tracking the king's tax directly to our door?'

'They wouldn't,' said Sim sulkily. 'You don't know how clever

Edmund is.' He flicked a glance from Greg to Nicola, who immediately resumed blubberings which had begun to diminish for want of breath.

Greg shook his head, thoughts slopping in his mind. He felt sluggish, but knew very well that his father was not reliable either in schemings or on an oath. 'I'll go to Brother Benedict and say you've repented of an evil intent. Only he can enter Ockham and see any monk he chooses without arousing suspicion. We have to stop Edmund before it is too late; once he comes here with stolen coins then you'll be hanged whatever happens.'

At that Sim howled more loudly than Nicola, swearing he wouldn't touch the abbey treasure if only Greg kept their secret secure. 'For as surely as water is wet, Benedict will run tattling to the abbot and then where will we be?'

'Not Benedict. He will cleave your pelt from your bones with his anger and I wish him joy of trying to make you repent, but he would never betray the confessional. Those who are caught stealing from the king or church do not simply hang. As you well know.'

Everyone knew the hideous maimings which awaited certain kinds of criminal, its purpose best served if everyone did know.

Sim laughed, an odd note in his voice. 'Nay, but he might. Because by now the abbey treasury is already robbed.'

'Jesu,' said Greg, with the stillness of despair. 'I wondered why this Edmund reeked worse than a hog in rut. But don't you see? He mixed you and Nicola into his schemings, came here immediately before his robbery because he meant to leave a trail the abbey boarhounds couldn't miss. You believed his lies about hiding close by and wedding Nicola afterwards, but all he intended was to set you up as quarry for the hunt. While he breaks clear.'

Brother Edmund, meanwhile had climbed a low place in the abbey wall, washed the stench off himself in stream water and donned a clean habit he had left hidden. Then he clutched his skirts about his thighs and sprinted to reach the choir before the Matins bell fell silent. Matins it was called, he reflected sourly; Last Trump would be a better name. In such a cold hour of darkness, any sensible man was warming a woman or slept well-soused in ale.

This first mass of the day was ill-attended at Ockham. As a mere serving brother Edmund was forced to go because the Abbot liked hearty singing, and since he maintained that two in the morning was an unseasonable time for a dignitary of the church to rise – a view shared by most of the cloister-monks – the lung-power of the lowly was needed if the chants were to carry as far as the lodgings where Abbot Thomas lay abed.

Normally, Edmund was able to drowse on his knees but tonight he prayed fervently and sang like one exalted, until his fellows nudged each other and whispered that he must have spent the evening among the cellarer's kegs. He also occupied his mind by calculating when the sub-prior might be expected to discover that a substantial proportion of the royal taxes had vanished.

When Edmund stood for the next chant he wondered at first why Brother Domenicus turned to glare at him; bobble-nosed old goat-bladder, what could he know about a man who sang for joy? So Edmund sang louder than ever, and only when the melody faltered on the edge of laughter did he realize that instead of the *Sanctus* he had intoned his calculations aloud: *Unus . . . Duo . . . Quattuor . . . Septem?* In seven hours from now the sub-prior would scamper from chapter house to abbot's lodging, screeching that the Devil had flown away with the king's coins.

The night was still completely black when the brothers hurried from the cold nave into colder cloister. Splendid stonework on every side roused no wonder among men intent on bolting for warm bedstraw: some monasteries reckoned their day started at Matins, but Ockham, in common with many others, allowed serving brothers to rejoin their more privileged fellows for another three hours of sleep.

Edmund slipped behind a pillar until the last figure vanished from sight, then he let himself out through the door which led from the cloister into the infirmarian's herb garden and walked briskly past the carp pond and into the paddock beyond. This was bounded by a rough stone wall which was not too difficult a climb for a man who regularly left the monastery about his own affairs. A scramble and a heave and he was up; hung by his hands a moment before dropping lightly into the abbot's private garden. No lights showed; Abbot Thomas only roused when the chants were thin. If all was well he quickly snored again.

The same stream as drove the water wheel at Edenham flowed at the garden edge, and divided the chapter house from the bakery before plunging through a weir and into a series of fishponds. Access to this stream from the ponds was treacherously difficult; from the abbot's garden it was simplicity itself, although cold in October.

Edmund stripped quickly except for a pouch hung around his neck, grunting aloud as he lowered himself into the water. By the time he had waded to the chapter house wall the level reached his armpits. No matter; after this night he would bargain for a plump wife to warm his blood at nights, and pay priests to seek forgiveness for his soul.

The water flowed fastest close to the chapter house wall, the bed of the stream scoured smooth where it was confined by stone. Edmund held his breath as he floundered in darkness, groping for the hold he knew was there. Smooth, slimed stone everywhere, and the cold so painful it frightened him. Let no one say he had not earned his treasure, if ever his sons' sons whispered of how Edmund the Monkman had made their family fortune.

At last! His fingers closed over a grating set into the wall, and at once he felt leather wedged inside it. He had known it must remain safely there, but had never entirely escaped the fear that somehow it might have slipped through the bars and dropped out of sight in black water. Up to his neck in that same water, it was more difficult than he expected to use a knife to slit through waterlogged leather, then wheedle coins through the bars and into the pouch hung at his neck. God's bones, he might even drown from the weight of so much gold!

The day Edmund had heard that the king's council intended to deposit tax-money at Ockham he had known his chance was come. Left as a foundling babe at the monastery gatehouse, he never knew who his kindred were, except they did not want him; consequently he became prey to dreams, and imagined his mother as a great lady who had lain with a squire of noble blood while her lord was absent. By the time he was a man, Edmund had so woven these imaginings into his being, clothing them with colourful cloth and building fine manors for his kind to live in, that his life at Ockham as a menial became intolerable to him. When one of the monks tired of his braggings and said he was most likely a goose-girl's brat, Edmund put a black fungus in his soup the brother was so weakened by the flux which followed that he died the next winter, which Edmund regarded as a judgement of God.

There would have been no difficulty if Edmund had decided simply to leave the monastery, since many of the monks disregarded their rule whenever it suited them: great Ockham, founded two hundred and fifty years before as a retreat from the world, had long since rotted away from its ideals. The rub was that Edmund felt no desire to leave the abbey as a beggar. He fingered chalices and jewelled croziers whenever the chance arose, but the more he did so the greater his ignorance appeared. Life beyond the cloister was too mysterious for him to be sure he wouldn't be caught or cheated if he attempted to sell anything noticeable. In fact, he was nearly sure he would end on a torturer's slab.

The abbey did of course possess its own treasure in coin, but it was disappointingly small. The monks were always quarrelling about it, the community being divided between those who wanted to spend Ockham's rents and benefactions on their own amusement, and those whose amusement took the form of devotion to expensive architecture and in consequence ran up such enormous debts that rents were pledged for years to come.

No, the risks of pilfering the abbey treasure were not worth while, when all he might find were tally-sticks awaiting payment. It was at this point in Edmund's cogitations that the French burned Rye, sending a tremor of fear through royal tax collectors at every haven along the Sussex coast and infesting the inland tracks with malcontents. Nothing could have been more timely. Most of the tax payments for eastern Sussex were temporarily stored at Ockham and, while the monks were still discussing whether the king would notice if some of these were diverted to satisfy Ockham's more pressing needs, Edmund had slipped past their noses and snatched what he wanted. He was not surprised to find it easy, since he believed himself very clever; in reality, he merely took advantage of the monks' greed. The previous evening, while they all squabbled around iron-slabbed chests in the chapter house, he had concealed himself in the chute where the monks relieved themselves during a long meeting, this drained directly into the stream through an iron grating designed to keep the abbey chests secure: it was the work of a moment to lower himself down and crouch on this grating, freezing and stinking as the wrangling went on long enough for most of the community to need to visit the chute. At long last, acrimony was adjourned to the refectory and Edmund was able to leave his malodorous hiding place. He used a crozier to break open the feeblest-looking of the chests, and stuffed as much coin as he thought he would be able to carry into a leather pouch. This he dripped down the chute, where it came to rest against the grating. Then, with extreme difficulty, he climbed a pillar, snapping several carved fronds on the way. It was this climb which had convinced him he could not carry out any weight of coin that way, and at the end of it he needed to break out through a window filled with precious stained glass. The outside wall was smooth, again as a defence against marauders, but Edmund was both light and tall and took no damage when he hung from the sill and dropped three times his height to reach the ground. By daylight though, the sub-prior, who always was first about his business, would see the shards of shattered glass and raise a might screech.

At first Edmund had regarded the sub-prior's early habits as a serious check to his plans: he needed time to get clear away. Then he remembered Nicola, the wanton from Edenham Mill with whom he lay when he felt so inclined, and knew his problem solved. If the hunt went west, and then wasted most of a day trying to torment non-existent information out of the Wyses of Edenham, Edmund would have a clear run eastward through the forest. Once he reached a busy track, any track, he was nearly safe. His scent would be lost among other travellers, while the coins he carried eased his flight as far away from the Weald as possible. So the moment Edmund picked himself off the grass after his leap from the chapter house, he ran all the way to Edenham, knowing the time was fearfully short if he was to accomplish the rest of his plan successfully. The stink of urine on him would help the hounds along this false trail, and confuse them if later they were set to look elsewhere. Sim Wyse's cupidity was even more convenient, since he wanted to believe any explanation Edmund offered, and grabbed at the damning coins he brought hotfoot from the chapter house. He had hidden more coins too when Sim's back was turned: the monks would soon discover them and so confirm Sim's guilt.

Edmund laughed aloud as he thought again how clever he had been; Sim deserved to be roasted on a slow fire for his greed, and so he would be until he died, because once they found those coins the monks would never believe that the rest, together with the thief, were not hidden close by and as he thought this, several coins slipped through Edmunds's icy fingers and plopped into the stream; no matter, there were more than he could carry in the pouch behind the grating. He wished he could save time by sliding the whole pouch through the bars, but the grating left room only for his fingertips.

Entrails of Christ, the water was cold!

Numbingly, terrifyingly cold. Ten times colder than when he came this way two summers ago, searching for the outlet to the chute. That had been when he had planned to rob the abbey treasure, before he realized how unrewarding this might be. Frowning, shaking his head, keeping his mind on the coins and nothing else, one by one he teased them through the grating and placed them in the pouch at his neck. It would take all his remaining strength to wade back to the abbot's garden before he drowned: anchored by gold in water so shallow that in summer a child might have played in it safely.

The weight of so many coins unbalanced him and he also had to wade against the current. Yet once he succeeded in struggling away from the chapter house wall, the stream became no more than a shallow brook again. Not even the dimness beginning to flap inside his skull could enchant resolution from him once the water level dropped from neck to thigh. So he reached the abbot's garden again, sat naked except for the weight against his chest and held his head until it stopped ringing like a bell. *Unus . . . Duo . . . Tres . . . In manibus tui, Domine.* Then Edmund scrabbled his robe on anyhow, kilted it and stepped back into the stream.

He still had a long way to go, wading in water as far as he could, in a further effort to outwit the hounds. A long way to travel eastward, while the trail he had laid led west to Edenham Mill.

East to the life he deserved, which the saints had pledged him by their help this night. Henceforth he would wear only the finest cloth and eat the richest meats.

The stream went under the outer abbey wall through a conduit; black, terror-stricken wading that, while water thundered past his ears. Then it crossed pasture lit by the moon, but all Ockham slept and no one saw him. And at last it brawled into the forest which stood thickly around the abbey fields, and Edmund became no more than a shadow on silvered water, wading on bleeding feet and purpled icy thighs into the wilderness and away.

Behind him, the abbey bell began to toll for Lauds.

The sub-prior discovered the broken chapter house window immediately after Prime, as Edmund had calculated. He ran for the abbot, and for all his bulk the abbot outpaced him on their return. Both men were close to seizure by the time they reached the chapter house door, and unable immediately to make the abbot's key turn the massive iron lock although they raged at each other to make haste. When the door opened at last, the curses died on their lips.

From the moment the sub-prior burst into his lodging mouthing something about broken windows, Abbot Thomas had known what he would find. He had also been incredulous, since he had personally made sure the chapter house was locked and empty the night before: the king's council would hold the Abbot of Ockham responsible for pilfered tax.

Abbot Thomas stood just inside the door while his eyes darted from a bent crozier on the floor to the snapped hasps on a pair of royal saddle-chests, then on again to damaged stone fronds below a broken window at least twenty-five feet above the floor. Surely no one could climb in that way, nor out again when weighed down by gold?

'Go into Prime,' he said to the sub-prior. 'See who is there and command them to stay until I come. Then bid everyone except my huntsmen join them in the choir. Send them here with boarhounds on the leash.'

When the sub-prior had gone, the abbot trod light-footed across to the ease-chute. Far below, against the glitter of moving water, he could see what might be a leather pouch tangled in the protective grating. 'Hm,' he said aloud, and again when he went to look at the ransacked chest. The thief had taken mostly gold and left copper and silver behind. Even so, there was some gold spilled on the floor and left in the chest. The abbot unlocked the abbey coffer standing against the wall and tossed inside all the gold coins he found. Not even the thief (may his flayed pelt fry before his eyes!) would know how many coins he had left behind, and the abbey might as well benefit from calamity if it could. Abbot Thomas did not consider that he, too, was a thief, only how badly the abbey needed help to build their splendid new nave. The Abbot of Ockham was one of those monks who possessed unbounded enthusiasm for innovative architecture.

The hunt erupted without warning down the slope towards Edenham Mill. The first Sim Wyse knew of it was when unleashed boarhounds hurtled at him out of undergrowth, curved to spring. Huntsmen followed and one, dismounting, called off the dogs while Sim lay where he had tripped, stupid with fright and unable to believe his throat was still whole.

'Get up,' said a cold voice and a man reined in above him, a monk from his tonsure but dressed in green and leather, a feather in his hat.

Sim stood, hands to his throat, surrounded by men and dogs and horses.

'Where is Brother Edmund?' asked the voice, quite gently, although the face it belonged to showed no mercy at all.

Sim shook his head. 'A brother from Ockham, here? Oh no, my masters.'

'The hounds followed him here.'

Sim wrung his hands. 'It is Ferneth fairday and half the world treads the track above this mill, but no one stays except myself. Went off at first light, my women did, and I'm to follow when the milling's finished. That is, begging your leave, masters. Me having nothing else to tell, like.'

'The trail we followed goes no further, my lord,' called a huntsman.

'Well? You hear what Lambert says?' demanded the voice which Sim feared belonged to Abbot Thomas, who was reputed to be as clever and filled with pride as the Devil himself.

Because of Greg, however, Sim was not entirely unprepared for this encounter. 'What does that show, masters?' he whined now. 'If there's no trail beyond and no one here but me, then your hounds must have played you false. They're boarhounds, and tracking boar is different from tracking men.' Which happened to be true, boarhounds being bred for courage rather than sensitive noses.

The abbot turned to his followers. 'Look everywhere, for coins as well as a fugitive.'

And before Sim's horrified eyes, they began a search which razed his home from the ground it stood on. Hooked poles tore off the thatch, axes splintered planks his very millstone was tipped in the stream. Two young huntsmen even trod gleefully on the water wheel, whirling it faster and faster until its paddles broke; the granary and spout floors were dug over, corn trodden into pap. Sim shouted, cursed, begged mercy on his knees, and finally wept, none of which made a tittle's worth of difference to the work of destruction.

When nothing was left of Edenham Mill, yet no coin larger than a copper groat had been found the monks mounted their horses and rode away, shouting, into the forest.

They would have taken Sim with them to hand over to Lord Scovyll, since monks were forbidden to heat irons and shed blood in a torture chamber, but when Abbot Thomas rode over to order him bound, a strange thing happened.

The miller was sitting, dazed by catastrophe, on his own smashed hearthstone, surrounded by air where his mill had been only a short time before. He looked up when the abbot's horse came close and spoke as if to an equal, without rising but very loud and clear. 'My life is finished by your hand. May you be cursed by earth and fire and the Widow Tiw; may your entrails fill with maggots and crows drink from your eyes.'

And as Thomas stared at a man whom disaster had instantly tipped back into heathenism, he felt his vitals cringe. This goat-faced miller could not touch a son of Christ, and yet . . . and yet . . . 'I am Abbot of Ockham,' he said, as if he uttered a charm against more ancient gods than his.

'Aye, an abbot if you say so. As I was a miller. But shall I tell you what I see? Your abbey in ruins like my mill, its stones tumbled in the stream and crows flying through the door.' Joy instead of despair rang in Sim's voice and there was a little shifting light in his eyes, as if his gods were dancing gleefully there. A sight which made even stiffnecked Abbot Thomas cross himself.

A listening huntsman had less complicated senses and simply kicked Sim off his hearthstone for insolence, kicked and kicked again until he tumbled backwards down the bank and into the stream. Thomas watched silently, rebuke stuck in his churchman's throat. He was glad when Sim splashed out of sight into the stream.

When the huntsman would have gone to haul Sim up again and on to his crupper as a captive, Thomas called him back. 'We have wasted enough time here with nothing to show for it. Take the hounds and start casting afresh from the abbey.'

'But the miller?' protested the huntsman. 'I swear he knows something, since the trail we followed ended here.'

'As he said himself, boarhounds do not always scent true.'

The huntsman laughed. 'This trail was strong enough to smell myself. Leave him to me, my lord, and I'll bring word where your treasure has been hid before the Sext bell rings.'

'Let him alone, I said.' Thomas hauled his horse on its haunches and left the man gaping, but waited near the track for the sulky cavalcade of monks and huntsmen to pass him. Several would be scheming how they could slip back and torture the miller and so gain knowledge of the treasure for their own profit. As he rode away from Edenham, the Abbot of Ockham, a cultured man trained at the University of Padua, stared unseeingly where a moorhen swam alone in a misty pond almost lost among the trees: he knew he had left Sim untormented not so much because he realized that the trail they followed must be false, but because he remained sufficiently superstitious to fear bringing black malediction inside the abbey walls.

Thomas snapped his fingers for a bow, and when a huntsman handed one over, he nocked an arrow and shot the moorhen dead.

Greg Wyse had run for Brother Benedict as swiftly as he could, but when he reached the place where the track curled down towards Edenham and heard silence instead of the mill wheel's roar, he realized the night had not been long enough for all he'd had to do.

'I told my father not to stay behind,' he threw over his shoulder to Benedict. 'The chase was certain to come here first.'

Benedict tried to keep up with Greg's impatience but, like most men trained as knights, he had never mastered the trick of walking distances fast. 'The monks of Ockham would not kill. If he is taken, then it will only be as far as the abbey.'

'Whence they will hand him over to the royal justices for torment.'

'He conspired to steal the king's monies, and couldn't have expected less if he was caught.'

Greg had taken his sister and mother hotfoot into hiding near Ferneth chapel, since, once Greg explained it to her, Nicola at least was so angered by Edmund's treachery that she would blab everything she knew to the first man likely to avenge her. He had then searched out Benedict and spun the best tale he could to protect them all, pretending that Sim had been a dupe in Edmund's hands. Greg fancied himself as a liar and was annoyed to discover from Benedict's cool tone that he had wasted his time.

'You came to me because you believed I might protect you from the wrath of Ockham,' Benedict was saying now. 'If you thought I might succeed in anything so unlikely, then you cannot also believe I am a fool.'

But just then Greg saw – nothing. Nothing at all where the mill should be, only grey-white earth. 'Christ's blood!' he shouted in astonishment. 'The mill! Its gone!'

Benedict shook him, hard. 'Do not blaspheme. A mill is not much for a determined man to strip down baulk by baulk.' God knew, he had seen more substantial dwellings torn apart in sacked French towns. 'We will go together and see how much is left.'

Nothing was left, except some splintered timbers and sodden grain oozing underfoot.

'Most of Jack By The Wood's crop was here, waiting to be ground!' shouted Greg; he kept darting from place to place and was incapable of speaking in a normal voice. ''Tis fairday, see? No one wanted to hump flour back home this week.'

Destruction for the pleasure of it, thought Benedict, looking around. Sim Wyse perhaps deserved to lose his home, but trampling good grain into the mud meant hunger for the innocent.

A moan sounded close by, and they both jerked round to see Sim lying half in the stream, near where the water wheel hung in shreds. When they climbed down, his eyes opened, enormous in an earth-coloured face. 'They didn't take me away.'

'No,' said Greg, his voice steadier now. Injuries were commonplace, unlike a mill which disappeared. 'What happened?'

'They came like you said they would. And went because I cussed 'em.' Sim smiled weakly, but with the same joy that had so disconcerted Abbot Thomas.

'I told you it wasn't safe to stay. Can you climb up the bank if I take most of your weight?'

'I didn't expect you back. I thought you'd run for good. Me, I've never been one to run.'

'Nor me' snapped Greg, annoyed. If only he had been able to return in time with Benedict, the mill might be standing now.

'Ah well. Each to his own.' Sim's eyes shifted to the priest and his lips drew back. 'That abbot now, he ran wi' his tail between his thighs.'

'Why?' Benedict decided that Sim's strangeness was probably due to a seizure, brought on by shock perhaps, rather than bruising.

Sim licked his lips. 'He saw it, same's me.'

'Saw what?'

Silence, rasped by breathing and the sound of water pouring over wreckage. 'His place destroyed just like my mill. There was ravens cawking around his head . . . and fallen stones at his feet.' Slime trickled down Sim's chin and his head wagged from side to side. 'Aye, and when the Black One comes for me, 'twill come for – him too.'

Greg gazed at his father in shocked disbelief. 'Those accursed monks have killed him, then say they belong to Christ.'

'I would guess at an accident. Nor is he yet dead,' answered Benedict, kneeling beside Sim. He was unimpressed by ravings but did wonder whether he could give last rites to anyone so clearly in the grasp of demons.

'And the mill? Would you guess that fell down by chance?'

'Don't waste your anger, Greg. You know your father's greed and folly is as much to blame for this as Ockham's fear of the king's wrath. When mixed together fear, greed and folly make a destructive brew.'

'So does revenge,' answered Greg between his teeth. 'How do you think we shall live now, with our livelihood gone and my father lying like chopped timber on the ground?'

Benedict hesitated, wondering how to prevent a son of Christ from squandering his life in a fruitless feud against the abbey of Ockham. He understood brawling squires but knew his judgement of peasants was less certain. 'Answer me this one thing honestly,' he said at last. 'Have you profited from this crime?'

'Nay, how should I?'

'In the name of Christ, so be it,' answered Benedict flatly, recognizing at once that Greg lied.

'You have asked your question, what now of my revenge? Demanded Greg.

Benedict considered, I have to return to Ferneth, where I left important matters unresolved. Cover your father with leaves and bracken to keep him warm, then find someone to help you take him into shelter.' And he stared at Greg as a knight might at a scullion, which is to say as if he saw nothing where Greg stood.

'Christ's blood!' Greg's voice shook. 'Take him to shelter where?'

To Ockham, where else?' answered Benedict, and this time he smiled.

'Ockham! This was their doing!'

'Robbers often suffer in this world and always in the next, it is a certainty they accept. So Sim has little cause for complaint. As for your mill, I would have gone to Ockham tomorrow to demand justice for you, but now I reckon justice will best be served if the monks must care for this their victim in their infirmary until he dies.'

'You would have gone to Ockham for me, but now you will not,' Greg said slowly. 'Why?'

'I would have gone because I believed you injured by this day's evil. But you have profited, haven't you? And those who gain from sin are best left to make of it what they can.'

Benedict walked back alone to Ferneth across pastures brawling with sheep, and no one seeing him would have guessed either his weariness or his anguish. He thought he had failed Greg Wyse, yet when he'd tried to pray for guidance, only a knight's instinct answered. How could he have come all unprepared, from armoured arrogance to cajoling yokels in a wilderness? How believe that mortaring stone and walking where he should have ridden had any meaning, except that he too was squandering a life? And as he thought of waste, Benedict felt his own lusts stir again, as they had when he saw Rico's smile the night before, and immediately he walked faster. After years of abstinence he was still enough of a Clare to grieve for his lack of heirs, when even so wretched a rascal as Sim Wyse died regretted, with a son by his side sworn to avenge him.

Then he breathed deeply, disgusted by self-pity as soon as he recognized it in himself. He had loved and fought his way through most of a lifetime, and was become a poor sort of pilgrim if he could not accept with grace the consequences of freely-taken vows.

John the Carver meanwhile was mightily pleased with himself, a state of mind from which he seldom departed. He enjoyed women, drinking, fighting and carving stone or wood, not always in that order to be sure, and since Benedict had taken the addle-brained notion of building a new church in Ferneth, John's life had been so filled with work he loved, that exaltation seemed a permanent instead of an occasional state of mind. And for him, exaltation meant a sunburst of energy released, so he drank deeper, beat his women more harshly, fought like a madman whenever the chance arose. For all of which there would be ample opportunity on Ferneth fairday. He flexed his muscles sensuously. Many dolts would come to the ridge today who had never heard of John the Carver, who were therefore willing to fight him for groats or pitchers of ale; shins could be broken in kicking bouts and this afternoon a bull was to be baited by dogs. John possessed the destructive lusts of an immensely strong child, and in some ways was very easily pleased.

Left behind in his hut were his wife, son and daughter, all thankful to see him go. Alice scoured the pot, tossed the bedding and swept the mud floor with venom, all to the accompaniment of Hawisa's moans. Alice had lain most of the night too badly bruised after her beating to sleep, and because she only dozed the cruel sounds of John pounding into Hawisa's body had seemed more unbearable than usual. John either wanted Hawisa or he did not, sometimes he left her alone for weeks, other nights he took her several times between dusk and dawn. Alice had turned her face into sweet-smelling bracken as the sounds went on and on; lack of hope came closer with each such night, while courage shrivelled.

'Hawisa is sick.' Whispered Drogo next morning, after John had gone.

Alice slapped fresh mud into a worn place in the floor. 'She's tired, that's all.'

Drogo shook his head. 'She's swallowed a demon.'

This was Ferneth's term for any sickness of uncertain cause, though Alice was in little doubt about the cause of Hawisa's groans. Better by far if she did swallow a demon, rather than be vowed by a priest to live with one. Alice went over to where she lay. 'It's the day of the fair. Come out and forget John for a while.'

Hawisa lifted her head, showing split lips and eyes milky from weeping. 'How could I?'

Alice shuddered. Hawisa had been comely when she came back with John from Reredfield market. 'One day enjoyed is better than naught.'

Hawisa shook her head; a day, a week, what difference did it make when a great bull of a man crushed all that made her life worth living? Yet strangely enough, she also admired John's brutishness and strove to please him. 'I told him there'd be another brat come springtime.'

Alice shrugged. Only she and Drogo survived out of all the children born to John, most of them birthed by women already worn out by harshness. 'Come with us to the fair. I'll wait, and you can put on the gown in your chest.'

Hawisa wavered. When she wed John she had brought with her a cloak, two wooden trenchers and a stool, and a gown inherited from her mother, who had been given it by one of Lady Scovyll's maids. Hawisa treasured these possessions but lost them one by one. The stool my grandfer carved,' she would say, or 'Food tastes sweeter for being eaten off a hornbeam trencher,' until John would curse another's carving or say that she should thank God for food where she found it, so stool and trenchers vanished. The gown alone remained, hidden away and made of cloth so old it had faded from blue to grey.

Hawisa brightened, as she thought of it. 'I should like that. Do you think –'

'Keep a close watch, and if you see John coming, run. Then it should be safe,' advised Drogo, dancing on one leg.

Alice helped Hawisa up while she still hesitated. 'He won't be looking for us today, you may be sure. Enjoy your gown and hide it again before morning.'

Hawisa nodded, her mind scampering to how finely her gown would flutter in the sun, and for a while she forgot her pains.

The pain was bad, though. Hawisa knew John couldn't help the nights he gave her, strong men being made that way, but she wished the pain afterwards was less. Her belly dragged and she found it difficult to keep her balance while Alice helped her to dress, but this was common enough and she scarcely noticed it.

Alice did not notice either, feeling scramble-witted herself, stiff and unfed except for scraps. Still, she had four groats hidden in the roof-thatch and would spend one of them on buying a ribbon for her bosom, another on a pie. Then Harry Fawkner would admire her, and twine his arm about her waist. Alice smiled; Harry had several times shown that ribbon or no, she was the maid for him.

She felt into wet thatch for the coins, hidden in a scrap of cloth. Felt, dug, felt again. 'They've gone!'

'What's gone?' asked Drogo, from where he drew figures in the dust.

'My groats! I had four hidden, saved from when I worked for Wat

Apps.' Alice felt as mazed as folk said she was. Her groats, her own groats treasured for the fair, so Harry would see she wasn't a poolside beggar, were gone.

'Perhaps you didn't search deep enough,' Drogo jumped on the table. 'Let me. I can reach right in.'

'There,' said Hawisa, twirling her skirts in delight. 'How those track women will stare! Bitches. Just because they live by the chapel, 'tis no cause to sneer at us.'

Alice's eyes swivelled to her stepmother. 'Aye, landless pool people. Why shouldn't track folks sneer when John the Carver must needs steal four groats from his daughter?'

Ah, Harry, she thought in despair, will you sneer too, from your snug homestead close by the chapel door?

'John wouldn't steal,' said Hawisa indignantly. 'He has a pouch full of groats. Don't you think that on fairday he might like to see how well my blue gown looks?'

'No,' Drogo answered for them both. 'And he wouldn't call taking Alice's groats stealing, just picking up what he reckoned was his.'

'I think he'd like me to wear a finer dress than the track people,' Hawisa squinted at her bodice. 'Oh, it's torn,' look!'

'The cloth is rotten.' Alice's voice was flat. 'All right, show him, if you want him to rip it off your back. God rot his black soul!'

'God rot whose black soul?' demanded John from the doorway. He had won his first fight and drunk at a draught the pitcher of ale which had been the stake, thereby winning a further wager of a haunch of mutton. Consequently, he had returned in joyous humour to leave it by his hearth.

'Yours,' answered Alice without hesitation, courage fresh-kindled out of fury. 'Where are my four groats?'

'What groats?' inquired John innocently? He looked around in mock search, then stiffened. 'What's that you're wearing, woman?'

Hawisa sidled uncertainly but, incredibly, still clung to her fantasy in which John approved of her wearing a gown which put the track people to shame. ''Tis my gown for fairday, and belonged to Milady Scovyll's own mother once.'

'A murrain on Lady Scovyll and her cloth!' yelled John. 'Have you no pride? We aren't serfs of the Scovylls here!'

He seized her by one arm and before he even touched it, the rotten cloth tore. Then tore again as he threw Hawisa violently on her bracken bed.

'I warned her how it would be,' said Alice dispassionately. 'Where are my groats?'

John took a fistful of coins out of his pouch. 'You mean some part of these?'

He was grinning; there must have been twenty times four groats there.

'Only you know if mine are spent or not, but any four will do,' answered Alice.

John prodded through the coins. 'I don't reckon any are yours. What right have you to keep earnings to yourself?'

'Wat Apps gave me four groats for myself after I helped in his brewing when his wife was sick. They're mine. Give them back.'

John's nostrils drew in sharply. 'Take them, then.'

For a long moment Alice looked at her father as if uncertain of his meaning. His wide lips smiled and there was a sheen of sweat on his forehead. Then, slowly and tiredly she turned to Drogo. 'Go to the fair and I will join you later.'

'Come now,' said Drogo, very low and urgent.

'Later. Sweet Jesu, Drogo, go!'

John tossed the boy one of the groats. 'There, brat. Buy yourself a pie.'

Drogo clutched the coin wordlessly, the first he had ever been given for himself, and scampered off. He swerved when he saw some children dancing around the piper, and then again from the scent of cooking meat. There was only one person he could imagine helping Alice now and that was the priest: a strange, hard man but not afraid to interfere in other folks' affairs.

At first, Alice did not struggle in John's grip, her senses already raped by ale-soaked breath and relentless power. Yet even as instinct told her that this was an assault best endured by apathy, she began to resist with such little success as agility and wiry despair could give. John cursed and swiped her one-handed so she fell to the floor with her head ringing like an anvil.

'Come at me then,' said John, grinning hugely and unbuckling his belt. 'Hawisa, you may say when you think the time has come for me to finish with Alice and begin on you.' He picked up his daughter and threw her on top of his wife, so they both lay retching air. Then he began to beat them with his belt: long methodical strokes which cut and burned, a promise of greater power to come. When Alice tried to lurch out of range, he slammed her against a wall and his mouth came down on hers.

'John the Carver. Beg Christ's mercy on your knees, or know what the black pit is,' said Benedict from the doorway.

John turned sharply. 'Get out of my hut, sir priest.'

'No,' said Benedict. He was standing with one hand lifted as if it rested on a sword, Drogo peering round his skirts. 'I should have come here long ago and did not because your craft helped build a church. Now I serve notice that either you repent of your sins or leave Ferneth, never to return.'

John barked a laugh. He was by no means sober after his draughts of ale. 'Repent of what sins?'

'What sins indeed? I doubted you knew the meaning of repentance, but was bound to offer it. Which leaves us with the other choice. You leave Ferneth for ever.'

'Not at your bidding, nor any other.'

Alice had been watching like a sleepwalker; she knew the priest had no power to make John leave, and her life would be infinitely worse after ineffectual interference with John's desires. 'Sir,' she said; reasonably she hoped, although her heart shook against her ribs. 'If you heard me cry out it was because we joked together. On fairday we are all well drunken with ale.'

Benedict had scarcely noticed Alice before, except as one among many underfed pool folk. Now her voice touched him, cutting calmly through brutishness. If new bread could speak, it would sound like that, he thought irrelevantly. And with the thought he vanquished the last of his pride, which in the past made it difficult for him to tend the souls of churls. 'Take Hawisa and Drogo with you to the fair, and do not return until tomorrow,' he said, without moving from the doorway.

Alice glanced from the monk's still figure to John. 'Sir, he will not let us go.'

'She has cast a spell on me,' said John loudly, and struck her. 'Witchcraft! I did but beat the Devil out of her, and you should thank me for it.' Blood suddenly ran like hot lead in his veins and he rushed at Benedict, shouting. No one, not even a priest, should tell him what to do.

Benedict sidestepped with contemptuous ease and tripped him as he passed; I will always make a better fighting man than priest, he thought wryly. 'The only witchcraft is your own foul lust. Will you go freely and hope for redemption, or do I fight you for it?'

John had leaped back on his feet, now he paused. 'Fight.'

'You fancy your strength, do you not? As priest I tell you to leave this place where your soul is damned by the violence you would do, and seek peace in pilgrimage. This you have refused, but my purpose is the same. So I fight you for it, if that is all you understand. If I win you go this very night, leaving your family behind, and never return.'

'And if I win?'

'Then is my soul damned as well as yours, because God will have turned his face from those I mean to save.' Benedict had never been a man who wasted breath on orders which would be ignored, and knew that John cared only for his own desires. In this life a priest was powerless against him. It remained to be seen whether a knight would do better: an old knight past his fortieth year, tired and out of training.

'I agree,' said John at once, relishing this most unusual of fights. 'Most willingly. At the fair-bouts this afternoon.'

'No. Here and now. I do not care for Ferneth to see their priest brawling in the dust.'

'Do you mean to kill him?' asked Alice, very cool and clear again, while Hawisa and Drogo stared mumchance at the scene.

'I am a priest,' answered Benedict. He would very much have liked to kill John the Carver.

'Then you lose no matter what, if you fight here. Should you win, he will deny his wager and put his knife in your back one night while you are praying.'

'At the fair, then,' Benedict agreed resignedly. The girl was right, of course, and gossip of the fight would add only a little to the tale of a mad priest who began to build a stone church singlehanded.

'Weapons?' said John, grinning. 'What say you to cudgels?'

'Blessed Virgin, no! Sir, choose a weapon you know, a sword or dagger perhaps,' cried Alice.

John laughed aloud, not minding in the least that his daughter preferred the priest to himself as victor. Rather, he took it as a compliment to the terror he inspired. 'He is sworn not to shed blood. Cudgels, eh, sir priest.'

Benedict nodded. 'And your pledge before witnesses to leave Ferneth for ever, alone and leaving your kin unmolested, if I win.' He felt ridiculous, challenging a boor when his last bout had been in a tournament attended by the chivalry of England, but also grimly pleased to be fighting again after eight years of restraint in many things. He did not trust John, though, and stayed until Alice hauled Hawisa to her feet and left with Drogo for the safety of the fair.

Then Benedict went to pray for strength; and cunning too, if he was to win.

The fair at Ferneth that first day of October was a joyful occasion. The sun shone and the wind which often made the ridge a bleak place to live blew softly from the south, stirring the bright colours of best cloaks and draped booths. A whole ox and two sheep roasted on charcoal fires, vats of strong ale were drained almost as fast as they were set on the cradle, beribboned girls peddled hot barley cakes and white bread. Gleemen, beggars, palmers and packmen jostled through the throng or squatted surrounded by their wares; boys wrestled for oranges – seldom seen in Ferneth at other times of the year – or tumbled to catch a squealing greased piglet. Later would come serious contests with bow or cudgel, while the children held their own tournament, riding on each other's backs at a makeshift quintain. And as dusk fell, dancing would begin and the whispered pairings with whores or sweethearts.

'I thought I'd never find you in the throng! I've been searching since the gleemen came.' Harry Fawkner pounced on Alice as soon as she left Hawisa, seated vacantly by a fire.

'I was kept,' answered Alice shortly, and then she smiled. 'You look very fine.'

Harry patted his new jack of scarlet cloth. 'Why not, when I'm squiring the prettiest maid in Ferneth to the fair?'

Alice felt a pang because she had not even a ribbon to wear, her groats still lost to John. 'Oh, Harry, I'm not.'

'You are,' he said stoutly, although he was disappointed she looked so drab. 'I have the most splendid thing to tell you.'

'More splendid than your new jack?' Alice spoke lightly but her heart pounded against her ribs. She loved the pride of walking on handsome Harry Fawkner's arm but dreaded his desire; after life with John the Carver, just walking out with Harry was enough for her, since Alice couldn't imagine any man's body offering joy.'

'Much more splendid; he gazed at her, struck by a sudden doubt. 'At least, I hope you will find it so.'

Alice nodded, words sticking on her tongue.

'I am going to London to tell the king that Rye's been burnt!'

Alice felt relief and the most acute disappointment, all at once. Then her mind fastened on the remaining thing that mattered: at this time of crisis Harry was leaving Ferneth to go roistering off to London. 'To London? Harry – why, would that Drogo and I could come too!'

He laughed and slipped his hand around her wait. 'Would that you could, but it'll be dangerous. The king – ' he frowned, not truly understanding why Rye had been burned. 'I expect they will try to stop us reaching the king, but they won't succeed.'

'Who will?'

'They,' said Harry vaguely. 'Those who profit because French pirates aren't defeated. But I'll be back, and soon. Greg's coming too, and Wat Apps.'

Alice went into a peal of laughter. 'Poor Wat will moan for his good wife's meat broths and his own fresh-brewed from the first night he's on the road.'

'Do his pot-belly good,' said Harry, grinning. 'Now, which would you like first, a hot pie or –'

'Hot pie. Dear harry, I'm starving,' said Alice firmly; in some strange way her mind was refusing to remember the squalor left behind in John the Carver's hut. Never had she been so merry or chattered so heedlessly. Harry was enchanted, and found himself watching each expression of her honey-gold eyes, the promise of her lips. Before, she had always held him away, though pool folk were lucky indeed if a farmsteader considered them worth attention: though Harry would never intend to force an unwilling woman, neither was he sensitive enough to guess how her father's brutality made Alice fear even a grasping hand. Nor did he see the stiffness with which she moved, perceive the unnatural excitement of her manner. Harry thought deeply only about his land, but his good humour was contagious and he knew exactly what he wanted: a strong pretty wife who would not trouble him with ill-humours or ill-health. He understood the reasons why he should not wed Alice and even agreed with them, but only the chill he felt in her had so far stopped him from asking her to go with him to the wood behind Fawkners farmstead. Most Ferneth lovers slipped away there whether they intended to marry or not, to wander handfast and tongue-tied, or brazenly seek a hide in which to lie.

At the fair his doubts vanished as Alice laughed and chattered, snuggled unselfconsciously into the crook of his arm as soft and sweet as honey in the comb.

'Here,' he said after they had eyed most of the booths, let me buy you a bunch of ribbons, lovedy. Which colour pleases you best?'

Alice turned to him, glowing. 'I had groats saved to buy one, but –' she gulped, joy vanishing as memory swept back.

'What have I said?' cried Harry, bewildered. He had thought she would be pleased.

'You said everything which would delight me most,' she answered gently. 'Harry, when will the contests start?'

'Soon, and my ribbon at your breast will warn anyone who jostles you that they have me to reckon with.'

Alice touched his rough curls fleetingly. 'Then I should like a green ribbon if we may find one.'

'We'll find it if we have to turn the fair skinside out.' He immediately believed that he had imagined horror in her look.

They bought green ribbon from a packman, and Harry kissed her as he tied it in a clumsy bow, delighted when her lips parted under his. Virtue was expected in a wife, but awkward if it began too soon. Though Harry loved unwisely, like most village men he was shrewd enough to try out a maid before he wed her, and follow custom by seeking a blessing from the pool as well.

'Harry!' called Rico Parleybien, from where some children sat listening to his tales. 'Wat Apps tells me you haven't seen sense, even after the ale-fumes cleared.'

Harry pushed over, Alice held tightly at his side. 'Did you think I would? I'd like to see the king in his fine castle, and tell him all the bad things happening in Sussex.'

'A pretty maid is a better reason than any I could think of to keep you safely by your hearth.' Rico's eyes were on Alice.

Harry flushed with pleasure as Rico's voice told him the ballad-monger coveted his woman. 'Aye, but there's all the rest of my life to spend by a safe hearth.'

Rico swept off his feathered hat, and bowed to Alice. 'Drogo says you tell fairer tales than I, mistress.'

'I'm sure I don't,' said Alice hastily; but because she had never spoken to anyone except Drogo about her imaginings and this man might understand, she added, 'It's just that sometimes I enjoy . . . seeing things as strange and beautiful instead of how they are.'

'Aye, there's a true teller of tales,' Rico said approvingly. He turned to the children. 'What say you? A tale from Alice or from me?'

Immediately a great clamour arose as each child shouted something different, while Alice privately decided that, for her, tales were the easiest part. It was words dancing to a rhythm she only sometimes heard which she desired to master.

'There, you have your judgement,' added Rico ruefully. 'I am the stranger and you they might hear every day, yet they dispute over which of us to listen to at the fair. You win, fair maid.' His feathered hat again swept the dust. 'The prize is – ' he paused, lips pursed. 'Your fortune told?'

'Oh no,' said Alice paling, while the children shrieked and danced begging to watch a sorcerer's art unroll the future.

Rico's eyes narrowed. He was taken aback by such brusque refusal when most maids swallowed his glib lies whole.

'Why not?' interrupted Harry eagerly. 'Alice, I should like to hear what the years hold for us.'

Alice bit her lip. The years might easily hold nothing for them. Rico saved her from answering by leaping like a spring hare on the booth and twirling three times on shabby boots before crouching to face the children. They stopped clamouring and laughed instead. 'We'll punish her, won't we? A tale instead of a fortune from Alice, Queen of the Wordsmiths.'

'I would like to hear your fortune,' muttered Harry, but the children pushed and pulled Alice to the booth, some turning somersaults at her feet.

And though she protested, Rico saw the shadows vanish from her face, because as soon as she sat beside him, on the booth all she thought of was her story. As I said, a true spinner of tales, he thought exultantly. Rico completely lacked the vice of envy, and rejoiced if he met a kindred spirit: felt compulsion too often himself not to recognize that every other thought was banished the moment Alice began to spin her gossamer threads of illusion. For Rico, the tale came first and he lived each life whose words he spoke; as he listened to Alice he realized that she told a tale only because that was what the children wanted. For herself – well, what did she want? Rico wondered. To conjure up beauty where none had existed before, perhaps. She was a very simple girl who had never left Ferneth in her life, but she painted the few and humdrum words she knew as a monk might gild a manuscript.

'Many years ago there lived a young queen who was said to be the most beautiful woman in the land,' she began. 'Her skin was as white as dandelion down and her eyes shone like water in the sun, but her greatest beauty was her hair. It was neither black nor gold but halfway in between . . . '

Harry hunched his shoulders, bored and annoyed that his wooing had been interrupted. He wished he had never come near Rico Parleybien, who sat Alice beside him on a booth so everyone would call her more mazed than before.

'Harry,' said Greg Wyse, seizing his arm. I've been searching for you everywhere.'

'And I for you,' answered Harry promptly, glad of a chance to forget Alice until she pleased him better. 'The gossips say your mill has burned down.'

'Not burned, torn down. Those accursed monks of Ockham were robbed of their treasure and came looking for it at Edenham. My father's lying as stiff as a fish under a drift of leaves.'

'Dead?'

Greg shook his head. 'He might as well be. Harry, I mean to come with you to London tomorrow, but must put Sim in shelter first. Benedict said to carry him to the infirmary at Ockham since he took his injury at their hands.'

Harry grinned. 'I like Benedict.'

'He's a prying whoreson!' snapped Greg. 'He even tried to tell me it was more our fault than theirs the mill was destroyed, when nothing is left of it but sticks and tramped mud.

Harry thought about this, brow wrinkled. He liked things kept simple and consequently thought simple things, but wasn't easily fooled by people he understood. 'You hid the Ockham treasure before the monks came?'

Greg began to deny it, furious that a thickskull like Harry had glimpsed his secret, then stopped. Harry's mouth would be easiest shut by loyalty. Across the brief silence Alice's voice came to them clearly ' . . . and one morning the queen was on the castle battlements combing her hair, when a great bird flew past. It was ugly and fierce, with a big hooked beak . . .'

'Aye,' said Greg. 'But it wasn't how you think. I know naught about treasure, except the man who stole it laid a false trail to Edenham and hid coins there for the hue and cry to find. So would he gain time to escape while we fried on the monks' gridiron. Last night, after I left you, I saw him and Sim with their heads together and forced Sim to tell me what they plotted. Then I guessed what the whoreson must have done. God's bones, how we searched! High and low, burrowing like rats through corn bins and thatch until we found a tidy fistful of coins. I said we must flee but Sim wouldn't leave the mill, he said it looked like guilt when there was no longer anything to tie us to the robber. Perhaps he was right, because those accursed monks were too close behind for us to go far, all cluttered up with women. So I took away my mother and Nicola, since both would have blabbed under the first beating they received, and bade them stay out of sight . . .' he hesitated.

'Where?' Harry was listening with shining eyes.

'Behind the alter stones of Brother Benedict's new church.'

Harry began to laugh, a great infectious bellow shrilly echoed by the children, because Alice had just told them how the queen refused to give the fierce ugly bird any of her hair to line its nest. So the bird cast a spell on her, croaking that her locks would fall with the leaves, and behold, they did! Until the beautiful queen was completely bald.

'What a sheep's head Alice is making of herself in front of everyone,' said Greg disapprovingly. He dropped his voice. 'Benedict's church must be safe for today, and by tomorrow the monks should have picked up the true thief's scent. Then, as Christ in heaven sees me, I will not rest until they have paid for the injury they have done us.'

'How many coins did the thief leave as bait at Edenham?'

'Eight. Six silver and two gold. All safe hidden now.'

Which probably meant at least double that, thought Harry shrewdly. He clapped Greg on the shoulder. 'Your fortune is made, and no one to share it with if Sim is like to die.'

'My mother and Nicola,' Greg answered, scowling. Not that he minded sharing such luck with them; indeed, he would have thought poorly of himself if, after such propitious beginning, he was not soon able to house them better than ever before, but he could not forget

Benedict's unerring instinct about who had profited from this day's doings and who had not.

'Never mind,' said Harry cheerfully, not understanding the reason for Greg's discontent. 'Ferneth will believe you are ruined by Edenham's destruction, and give alms to keep your kindred snug while you come with me to London.

'. . . after her last lock of hair had fallen out the queen's head was left as smooth and white as an egg. At this fearful sight she screamed and fainted, and when her ladies came running, they were too mazed to speak. As for the king, his grief was so great that he sobbed aloud . . .'

Harry flicked a glance at Alice's absorbed face, annoyed afresh as he remembered Greg's disparaging comment. 'Quick, then. We'll harness one of our oxen to a sled, then you can reach Ockham with Sim tonight. I'll hire a boy to drive the beast back and meet you tomorrow at Ockham's gate.'

They ran together from the fairplace, along the village lane to Fawkner's farmstead. To one side of this lane substantial cottages had been built, reed-thatched and standing foursquare on thick oak beams, which made the hovels around the pool look like hogsties. Some even boasted glass in their windows.

'We're rebuilding again soon,' said Harry over his shoulder. 'Tam fancies an upper floor and says he will do it when I wed.'

'Alice?'

'Aye.' But Harry hesitated as he said it, not quite sure again. He also slowed his pace because the lane was thick with people coming to the fair, these the more prosperous folk who had stock to tend before they enjoyed themselves. And during the past fifty years none had prospered more than the Laffams of Corndown and the Fawkners behind their nearly vanished bank. Previously, Greg had never failed to covet Harry's inheritance each time he entered Fawkner's farmyard. Now he did not, because within a day and a night everything had changed for him he thought instead of the gold and silver coins which Brother Edmund had so prodigally left at Edenham, and the uses he could put them to. God's mercy on a treacherous hog of a thief, who through Greg Wyse's cleverness had made the first step to his fortune easy. 'I mean to buy up wool,' Greg confided to Harry as they harnessed up the ox.

'The monks of Ockham live by buying and storing wool until they alone are in a sufficient way of trade to bargain with the shippers of London and Rye.' And Harry frowned, his grievance abruptly recalled. 'Christ curse all black French souls, who burned Rye and cost us good markets this last year.'

Greg sighed, wondering how many more times Harry would tell him what the whole of Sussex knew. The journey to

London would be mightily tedious if all Jack Cade's followers took their grievances so much to heart. As for Greg, all he wanted was to see London's great Blackwell Hall, where he had heard that the bulk of all England's wool was sold. There he meant to begin learning how to prosper in his chosen trade, with the firm intention of ruining Ockham once he did. 'I expect to stay in London,' he said eventually.

'Stay? Why, when we've seen the king –'

'Oh Christ,' said Greg rudely. 'You won't see the king. If anyone with a grievance could break into his court, don't you think he'd be properly fuddled by all the people there? I'm not tramping to London just to get an arrow through my throat.'

Harry rubbed the ox's muzzle. 'You can't make flour without grinding corn.'

'Aye, and you don't tell kings their councillors are fools without getting yourself hung for insolence. We'll go together and see, eh? Then you come back safe to Alice if that's where your mind lies, and I'll stay awhile to learn my trade.'

Harry shrugged sulkily, his bright day dimmed first by Alice and now by Greg. 'Thieves' coin never did any man good.'

Greg clicked his tongue at the ox. We'll see, he thought, each one of the hidden coins already many times spent in his imagination. It might take a year to learn the things he had to know, then he would come back to Ferneth and begin driving monks grown fat on easy profits out of their trade in wool. He hauled at the traces to guide the ox cast to Edenham and as he did so his interest was caught by the place where he left the new cottages behind. 'Gillap, Cheerful,' he said aloud, giving Tam Fawkner's the time-hallowed call to turn left, little realizing that another Cheerful had laboured just here long ago, pulling rowans out by the root,

Now that is a good site for a house, thought Greg, looking at it through narrowed eyes. Beyond the last cottage but before the common ground which stretched to the pool, a paddock of enclosed turf had been nibbled smooth by Tam Fawkner's sheep.

Greg tossed his fringe out of his eyes and urged the ox forward again. He would stay good friends with Harry, and one day buy that land. Immediately, and by a natural jump in his desires, he decided to return to Edenham by way of Corndown, where Stigo Laffam would certainly have left his youngest daughter to watch his sheep while the rest of his enormous tribe, begotten on more women than Ferneth could remember, enjoyed themselves at the fair. Stigo was a blustering rascal who suspected everyone of almost everything and would never leave his sheep untended even on fairday. The rest of the family were as great rogues as he, except this youngest daughter who lived peaceably among a squabbling and voracious kin, which meant she did all the most disagreeable tasks. Greg Wyse had begun by admiring Emma's sweet temper, but then he discovered that she laughed more in a month than they did at Edenham in a year. She also responded with uncomplicated delight to Greg's early, almost shamefaced interest; after a season of snatched and secret meetings they loved each other rapturously. So Greg, though both ruthless and avidly ambitious, intended to marry Emma, whom Stigo cheerfully said was too useful at Corndown for suitors ever to be encouraged by a dower. Thus did Greg Wyse disprove the belief that only the good can love to their own material disadvantage.

God rot Stigo's sheep, thought Greg suddenly. Why should not Emma come with me to London this very day and only return as my wife?

'Lallay! Lallay, hie my sweetheart to my side,
Lallay, my dove . . .'

sang Greg Wyse as the rightness of this thought came to rest against his heart. And through the years to come, his delight in this moment would remain an undimmed memory; years when he continued to love and be faithful to his wife, built his house at the corner of Ferneth lane and pursued the monks of Ockham with a truculent venom which never once remembered how much he owed to Brother Edmund's villainy.

At the fireplace Alice was coming to the end of her story. ' . . . and that night the king's castle was lit by torches and all the people danced, because the poor packman had succeeded in bringing seeds from the Hair Tree to the queen at the hazard of his life.' She paused, smiling at the rapt faces gathered around her on the grass. Although she had only whispered her tales to Drogo before, she did not feel awkward sitting on a booth for everyone to see. 'Shall I tell you a secret? The poor packman's name was Rico, and the king rewarded him with so many gifts that he had to slip away in the night for fear he would be weighed down with gold and unable to travel the roads as he wished.'

'If Rico went to London the king would pour so much gold into his pack the bottom would drop out!' squealed a voice.

'He'd become a pillar of gold in the king's court!'

'He'd melt and become a golden path to heaven!'

'Surely you have a tongue of gold,' said Rico soberly, as children who had never imagined anything beyond their daily lives hurled extravagance at each other for the sheer joy of hearing it. 'A Hair Tree, for mercy! What made you think of that?'

Alice shook her head; words danced or they did not, and one day she had seen dew on a myriad spiderwebs spun across bracken which made her think them into hair trees. Her absorption chilled abruptly as she remembered how Benedict and John waited to kill each other. No; Benedict would not kill, but offered himself as a sacrifice because he was a priest who once had been a knight, and that was the way he thought. Rico saw the change in her face and shooed the children away. 'No more tales until after dark! Then I will tell the fable of the brave and cowardly knights, but only for those who have kept a groat unspent.' He lifted Alice down from the booth. 'Or shall I take them by the heels and shake them until all their groats fall at your feet, in payment for the Hair Tree tale?'

The children scampered off at once, and Alice laughed. 'You know the best way to clear them from underfoot.'

'I've never yet learned how to charm coins out of folk who have already heard their tale,' said Rico ruefully. 'You were right, though. I would steal away from any king's court in the night, rather than sell my dusty feet for gold.'

'Even in winter?'

'Ah, well now. I have some pleasing places to go in winter, where tales may be traded for ale and a warm hearth.'

But Alice was no longer listening, staring past his shoulder to where Stephen of Osweard of Danesdell was beginning to beat Ferneth's ox-bladder drum. 'The contests! They're beginning!'

'Is your young bull fighting?' Rico looked around, expecting to see Harry somewhere close. Instead, he saw Meg standing by some tumblers, watching him with Alice. 'I have to go,' he said hastily, an easy man who hated quarrelling.

Alice did not answer, forgot he was there as she followed the noisy fairday crowd behind the drum, sunlight turning golden above her head as the air sharpened toward evening. By tradition, the Ferneth fairday bouts were held near the ancient Meeting Oak: there the children could climb into gaunt, half –dead branches, the women stand on its roots for a better view, while the men laid wagers and linked arms to form a tight, unyielding circle. Year-long feuds were settled at the fair and grudges spilled into blood, although most of the combatants fought for honour rather than enmity, the ultimate winner proclaimed cock o'th'roost. But because some quarrels were bitterly felt and long nurtured while they waited for fairday, in these contests any trick was acceptable and serious injury not infrequent; confined together in tiny huts or working on scraps of land, some kind of acceptable end to each year's wranglings was a necessity. The cock o'th'roost fights were more ritualistic and seldom resulted in more than bruises or a cracked head. If he was at his castle of Reredfield, Lord Scovyll presided over these bouts to give them some sanction from the law, but providing no riot followed, he seldom objected to yokels fighting like the boors he knew they were.

Alice thrust her way towards the oak, to find his lordship recently arrived and towering on his horse above chatter about his appearance. Ferenth always gaped at the Scovylls' jewels and velvets, their gaily accoutred horses and bright cloth, partly because they seldom saw them. The rest of the year they heard horns below the ridge and glimpsed flying figures along the cleared rides of Reredfield hunting park, but the Scovylls mostly left Ferneth freeholding alone. In this time of turmoil in England, a baron needed to keep his eyes fixed on what was his, or he lost it.

Today, Lord Scovyll wore hunting leathers, but his sons more than made up for such dull practicality. Their cloaks were of scarlet, blue and yellow velvet, their boots as soft as fleece, the toes curled high and ending in tinkling bells, their fringed reins blowing gaily in the wind. 'No wonder Rye was burnt,' said Harry furiously to Wat Apps. 'They might as well hang bells in their caps as well, and earn a living as jugglers.'

'To think the likes of them may win a place in paradise simply by kneeling to put their hands within the king's,' sighed Wat, who was occasionally perturbed by the thought of an aleless purgatory.

'Keep your tongue between your teeth,' snapped his goodwife, making little slapping motions with her hands, as if she itched to feel his cheek beneath her fingers. 'Though God-a-mercy, you're foolish enough to get yourself hanged a dozen times over once you get to London.'

'Ah, we'll soon be back, with a reward in our pockets for telling the king what's amiss,' Harry searched with his eyes for Alice. She had no right to cavort off into the throng while his back was turned.

Mistress Apps stared at him, unappeased. 'I never heard such foolishness. A reward from the king, indeed! Cock's bones, what next?'

Wat sighed. He had been arguing with his strong-minded wife ever since the night before and yearned for peace again. If Harry had shown the slightest inclination to release him from his oath he would most eagerly have seized it.

But Harry did not, his renewed doubts about Alice only strengthening his desire to achieve some splendid deed before he was forced, irrevocably, to make up his mind. That fratchety, bothersome boy, thought Goody Apps indignantly, he's as bad as a hound that expects a pat for laying a dead squirrel instead of good fame at the huntsman's feet. She was fond of her kind fat Wat, and quite as terrified he would run off with some London wanton as she was convinced that consorting with brawlers led to the noose. Why, God-a-mercy, the king's men would hunt Cade's followers through the hedgerows until every last one of them was caught! She stared at Lord Scovyll, turning an unexpected idea over in her mind, then, without giving her courage time to vanish, she elbowed her way between leather backs until she reached the old lord's side. He was talking to Brother Benedict and for some time did not notice her kneeling by his horse's hoofs.

'Get up, woman.' He said irritably, when eventually he did. 'If I had been riding a war-horse you would have been butcher's offal by now.'

He spoke English with a Norman twang. The Scovylls were one of the few great families who still spoke French amongst themselves, and for a moment Goody Apps did not understand him. Then Benedict jerked his head and she heaved to her feet. 'A boon, sir.'

'Well?'

She licked her lips. She had never spoken to a baron and was mesmerized by his florid face and small scowling eyes.

'What would you ask of Lord Scovyll? As a Clare, Benedict was able to interrupt Scovylls.

'His sign,' she answered boldly. 'We keep ale by the hearth and wish to hang a sign instead of a mere bush outside our door. I crave permission –' her mind was blank; though she had seen it often she could not remember the Scovyll arms.

Benedict studied her more closely, a frown between his eyes. As if he saw into my heart, Goody Apps thought, frightened. She practised many small meannesses she preferred to keep hidden from a priest and wanted to cross herself, but did not dare while he spoke in the strange lords' language to the grim old baron on his horse.

When he had finished the baron nodded and wiped his beard on his sleeve. 'You may have my leave, so long as the sign is painted by someone who knows his trade. I want no monstrosity leering at me the next time I ride past.'

Goody Apps scurried triumphantly away, remembering now that the Scovyll sign was a black bear. God send the old lord stayed loyal to the king. Then, when royal troops came searching for Cade's followers, they would see a new-painted Scovyll bear on Goody App's wall and pass without searching inside for rebels. But no sooner was Mistress Apps away from the baron than she began to worry afresh, in case he should be tempted into treason once his sign was on her wall. A worrier by nature, she was unused to anxieties so catastrophic that she could no longer enjoy them.

Since he left John the Carver, Benedict had spent his time kneeling before Theobald's altar in the sag-sod chapel. He could not have named the feeling which prostrated him in a gloomy burrow he despised instead of on his new stone chancel floor, but probably it was wry self-knowledge. He wanted to pray and would start calculating loads if he was surrounded by his own part-finished handiwork; consequently, he missed discovering the Wyse womenfolk hiding behind his alter. An unspiritual man who worked hard at his obligations, Benedict had prayed with discipline he brought to all his actions, although as soon as the fair drum began to beat he stood at once, feeling comforted. The unnumbered souls who had bared their fears on this same mud floor had reached his aloneness, and for the first time he was pleased that some of the old chapel timbers would be incorporated into his new church, instead of regarding this as a disagreeable economy.

On his way to the fairplace he had seen Meg the Harlot sitting weeping on her step, and paused. Benedict was not embarrassed by harlots. 'How is your child today?'

She shook her head, snuffling. 'A mite easier, but what difference will it make? A black bat will soon seize his soul, I know the signs by now.'

Benedict's tongue was poised to send her scuttling to beg mercy for pagan thoughts, but he stayed silent. Meg would continue to believe in black bats whatever contrition her lips cobbled together, and he was in no mood to waste himself in futile causes. 'Take comfort, mistress. The little one is too young for sin.'

Meg lifted a tear-dabbled face. 'Much you know of it, sir priest. Ten brats I've birthed and only two are left alive. Take comfort you say; how can I, when I loved each one?'

Benedict thought of his own sons, and also his wife. 'We must. We have to, since death and life are one.' Instinct told him that if he urged Meg into prayer now, she would curse Christ while her child lay dying. Instead he touched her, and added 'Often courage is the only defence we have.'

Meg looked after his straight black back, surprised. Courage, she thought; aye, I have need of that. She came draggingly to her feet as the coughing inside began again, called cheerfully and went to hold a syrup to blood-crusted lips. The sooner this child was dead the better, and truth to tell she had wept only for herself. For the look she had seen on Rico's face at the fair, which told her he cared more for a silly maid's fable than Meg's plump breasts, and would be off again tomorrow. For the child of his getting she so foolishly desired, a child which, if it was born, was only too likely also to die coughing in the bedstraw. But perhaps Rico's child would live to face the world as he did, free of burdens and with its imagination leaping from one thing to the next. So Meg harlot dreamed as she sat with a hand to her belly, as if she already felt new life stirring there.

Benedict saw the Scovylls had arrived as he reached the roasting ox. No peasant could dye cloth to such a bright colour and even the Scovyll huntsmen swaggered in green of a sharper hue than Ferneth people wore, while scarlet and light blue flashed where the young lords scattered the crowds with their horses.

'Ah, Gilbert,' said old Lord Scovyll, who despised a knight turned monk and always addressed Benedict by his former name. 'A good day for the fair.'

Benedict glanced at the sky. 'And cold enough by midnight to kill a few elderly drunks tumbled out of sight. I hear there is unrest in Kent.

'Aye, a rogue called Cade has led a rabble to Blackheath, and parleys there for the right to march into the city.'

'A fool as well as a rogue, then. No matter what their grievances the Londoners will never let a rabble of armed peasants into their streets.'

'Why, so think I. Which is my reason for remaining at home with a fever. My cubs would be off tomorrow if I let them.'

'To slaughter peasants or attack the king?'

'Both, my dear Gilbert, both! Would you believe such folly?'

'Easily. Ride with the rebels for easy loot and change sides when London Bridge is shut in their faces, why not?' Then spill a few peasant entrails afterwards in recompense, secure in the knowledge that poor blithering King Henry will forgive them. Or so unblooded youth might think.'

'He probably would, too,' said Scovyll scornfully. They were speaking French, and though neither particularly liked the other, when surrounded by a crowd which could not understand what they said the urge to frankness was instinctive. 'But I don't choose to have my sons hated as butchers by their neighbours, nor disloyal to their king because they crave amusement.'

It was at this point that Goodwife Apps came to beg her favour from the baron and when she had gone a short silence fell between the two men. 'Revolt makes strange bedfellows,' said Scovyll drily at last.

Benedict laughed. As priest at Ferneth, he missed above all the shrewd wits and barbed words of his peers. Roger Scovyll knew as well as he did that a clucking hen like Goody Apps would never risk begging boons from barons without a very good reason. 'At least she sells excellent ale.'

'Then I'll make sure they pay with a draught for using my sign, next time I ride past.'

Providing fat Wat scurries home fast enough once Cade's men scatter, thought Benedict, who heard most whispers flying around Ferneth. 'I am fighting soon,' he said.

'Holy God.' Scovyll stared at him astonished. 'And you a priest, or so they say.'

'And I a priest. There are some things only fighting will achieve.'

The baron chuckled. 'You'll have a grand time explaining yourself to your master, Abbot Thomas of Ockham.'

'On the contrary, he has some explaining to do to me when next I see him.'

'Keep your back to the west,' said Scovyll practically. 'You don't want the House of Clare ill-wished because a churl bested one of its sons in a scuffle.'

They stood in silence after that, watching the village boys mill each other untidily in the dust. Then Rufus Laffam crushed Will Carpenter's ribs in a bout marked by exceptional spite, since Rufus was suspected of raping Will's daughter on Midsummer Eve. Lord Scovyll swore and kicked his horse into a sudden table of bodies which followed this unsatisfactory result, Will being liked and the Laffams much feared for their brawn and temper. Many of the men were belligerently drunk by then, which was why on fairday Ferneth liked having the Scovylls around. A few hard knocks were to be expected, but no one wanted to wake on the morrow to find they faced the hangman's noose for riot.

When that excitement died down, the drum began to beat again and flushed red faces turned as names for the next bout were bawled above the commotion. John the Carver stepped forward at once, and everyone shouted at the same moment when they realized the drummer had made no mistake, and the priest was John's opponent. The circle of linked arms broke as each man turned to his neighbour in disbelief: the priest, the priest was going to fight John the Carver.

Under Lord Scovyll's curses and kicks from his henchmen the circle was formed again, anticipation as thickly spread as honey on a feast-day. Behind the crowd a blazing sunset spread across the heavens, redness reflected from clustered faces in the old oak above. Keep your back to the west, Benedict thought, and smiled. Sound advice from an old warrior who kept his sons from brawling in their homeland, although Benedict himself had fought too often to need advice. He turned to the drummer. 'Proclaim the wager. If I win, then for his soul's sake John the Carver leaves Ferneth, alone this very night. On pilgrimage, never to return.'

'And if he wins?'

'I leave that to him. I doubt I shall be interested.'

Another stir went round when the drummer chanted the wager, and Benedict scanned faces pensively. Perhaps he would not see them or any men again, and so disgrace the House of Clare. Fretting Mistress Apps and drunken Wat; dozens of prosperous, dishonest Laffams. Rico, sitting with the children in the oak: he would make a ballad out of this day's happenings and never know that it had been his words which set Benedict on this path. Tousle-haired Harry Fawkner with his arm round Alice, her eyes burning across to where Benedict stood. He ought to have told her that if he lost, then she must take her chance on the road this very night.

John came at him the moment the drum stopped.

Benedict knew a great deal about combat but almost nothing about brawling inside a circle of yelling peasants. He was quick though and very tough; pain and fatigue affected only his outer rind, a cold intent to win remaining intact within.

John swung his cudgel shrewdly, so Benedict had to duck and jink to avoid it. He carried no weapon himself which felt very strange and made the watchers gape, although it helped his speed. Twice John missed Benedict's head by the thickness of a wheat grain, but against a lithe opponent the cudgel was an ill-chosen weapon in attack, where wild swipes were the usual method. In defence . . . if John had chosen simply to harry his enemy for a while, then matters might have been very different.

John yelled and struck again, stamping dust. Keeping his back to the fierce sunset, Benedict weaved and feinted, occasionally catching a glancing blow on rib or upper arm but so far moving easily. It was becoming difficult to judge distance in such uneven light but the dazzle was squarely in John's eyes, which would not last, already the sun was dulling, and Benedict tiring faster than he liked. He was, after all, old for foolery of this kind. When John struck next, Benedict stepped inside the arc of his arm, moving his body like a sword he lacked and most ardently desired. Head down, arm stretched, braced fingers driving bladelike for John's unguarded belly, all the strength of a trained and wiry body flowing into a sword-master's strike, precise and deadly. In the instant of contact pain flashed up Benedict's arm, a finger broken probably, but his hand sank almost to the wrist in yielding muscle. The shock of such a blow was bloodless but as crippling as if it had been delivered with tempered iron. John spewed breath and his guard wavered; Benedict seized his arm with his good hand and threw him heavily while his senses were still scattered. For a moment a more savage triumph filled him than any on the battlefield; to fight and win again after years when God fastened shackles on his nature, this set him free. He barely stopped himself from stamping John's body into bloodied fragments.

But he was also Benedict of Ferneth, a cold and distant priest, so he picked up John's cudgel and held it to his throat instead. 'I suggest Our Lady of Walsingham for the first stage of your pilgrimage.'

John was still retching, hands to his belly, while all Ferneth stood yelling. They had respected John because he never owed on a debt and was a good craftsman besides: they did not like him and also revelled in the thrill of watching their priest spill a man twice his weight in the dirt. To save John's soul, he said, but these two had fought for hate, which would spice a winter's gossip. So they shouted and thumped Benedict's back in triumph, whose back they never before dreamed of thumping in all the years he'd lived in Ferneth.

'You still fight well, though eight years as a monk have slowed you.' Lord Scovyll said grudgingly when Benedict had struggled free of the crowd.

'I enjoyed it, which means another penance.'

'Ach, monks! Whoever heard of penance on a good man fighting fair? Tell me, why did you risk so much? The brute was strong.'

'But not skilled, also half-drunk and in a rage. Why? Well, that's between him and me.' Benedict examined his crooked finger critically. The pain was bad, from his knuckle to just below his ear. Pain also which he hadn't expected from a labouring heart and lungs. Lord Jesu, don't let my heart burst where everyone can watch.

'Here, let me,' said Scovyll to his fellow of the house of Clare. 'How do you feel?'

'I'll be all right.'

Scovyll dismounted and took his hand by the wrist and finger, pulled them strongly apart, twisting. Breath rattled in Benedict's throat as bone caught and grated. It seemed a long while before the pain eased to a throb and he discovered he was leaning against Scovyll's horse, which stood like the trained beast it was. He wiped clammy sweat from his face. 'Thank you.'

'I've splinted more men than I care to remember in the aftermath of battle.'

Benedict nodded, feeling nauseated and cold. I had forgotten how old I am, he thought, and looked around for John. 'I don't trust him.'

'You beat him, didn't you? He won't stay to be laughed at for losing to a priest.'

'Aye, I suppose so.' He discovered his right hand was strapped to a dagger scabbard which kept the finger straight. 'I'll make sure of it, all the same.'

Scovyll remounted and reined away, then bellowed in English so everyone would understand: 'Watch your back, Gilbert. But if they should ever bring your corpse to Reredfield, I shall know who to hang!'

He went off, slapping his thigh and laughing.

Watch his back or no. Benedict knew he would be good for nothing until he had rested. He could not see John among the faces which swam in and out of his vision, all pale green and blurred as he struggled to bring them into focus. The noise was deafening. The fair always gathered new life after dark and died only in the small hours when the ale ran dry.

Placing each foot carefully, Benedict walked from the oak across the fairground and down the lane until he reached his hut. He would be all right once he had rested.

Harry could not understand why Alice wept when Benedict won his fight, her slight frame shaking with the force of released hysteria until he feared a curse must be laid on her. He hated women's tears and resented being made to look a fool, wanted to beat reason into her or leave until she sobered. He did neither, because she was Alice, after all. Also Lovers' Wood wasn't far, which seemed to him the best cure of all for tears.

Alice did not notice where he was taking her, wanted only to be away from prying eyes, and away also from John's malevolence until he was chased out of Ferneth by the ridicule of losing to a priest. When would he go? Before everyone woke in the morning, surely.

'We'll be quiet here,' said Harry.

She lay beside him on dry leaves, thankful to find peace. In the distance she could hear shouts and drummings racketing to the sky, but dulled; much closer were the intimate sounds of others besides themselves in undergrowth, and the wind in dry autumn leaves. When she opened her eyes again she saw that the fine weather was ending and the clouds blowing across the stars.

'Don't shiver, lovedy. I'll keep you warm.' Harry unlaced his breeches and lay on top of her, clumsily.

'Not tonight. Harry, please.' Alice began to weep again, helplessly, knowing tears were wrong with Harry.

'God's blood!' he shouted angrily, aware that others in the wood would hear them. 'How dare you come here only to shove me away? Did we not become promised to each other today?'

She shook her head; she couldn't remember promising him anything.

As for Harry, it never occurred to him that Alice would not welcome him when, all the time they watched the priest's strange fight, her body had so curved into his that he had scarcely been able to wait for it to finish. He could not be expected to know that while Benedict fought she neither felt nor saw anything else.

She made a fool of him by playing the virtuous maiden, which banished tenderness from his mind. She wanted him no matter what she said, and, God's bones, he wanted her.

In common with most Ferneth boys Harry had sneaked a few times to Meg Harlot's hut, otherwise he knew as much and as little as his rams and oxen. He was crude and fast but Alice expected nothing better. She even slept a little afterwards, worn out by the emotions of the day.

When she woke the sky was dimly grey, wetness dripping off bracken by her nose. Harry woke too and kissed her eagerly, reaching for her again at once.

She squirmed away and stood, her back to a tree. 'Nay, Harry. I have to go.'

Why must you? Everyone will sleep late after the fair. I must set out soon for London with Greg and Wat, so give me another memory to take, lovely.

'I'm tired.' She watched him through narrowed lids.

'And I feel as if I could overcome the king himself!' He flung out his arms and stretched, muscles crackling. He had not guessed how much sweeter Alice would be than Meg Harlot. 'I won't force you,' he added, and learned that he did not want to, any more. 'Alice I don't know how long it will take us to find the king and come home again.

'Take care.'

'You want me to, you really do?'

'Of course,' she said impatiently. She didn't wish Harry ill, but this last night had put him at her mercy, because he enjoyed what they had done and she did not.

All she wanted was for him to go, so she could think.

He stared at her, baffled and hurt. 'Well, I'll be off.'

'Me too.' She slipped away among the trees before he could demand a parting kiss.

The fairplace looked like storm-wrack in the dawn. Chewed bones, charred wood and tattered booths lay alongside snoring bodies; a few stray sheep cropping calmly around the debris. No one stirred as Alice scampered across dew-soaked ground with her toes tingling from the cold. By now, surely, John would be gone. In windy air above the ridge a lone lark sang; black forest, green grass, bronze leaves the frame to everything she saw, ahead of her the pool shimmering secretly beneath chill mist. The earth without John was so beautiful that Alice ran with arms outstretched in a gesture to freedom now beginning.

She ran round the pool edge, hearing more snores from the huts he passed, and burst in through their entry, afraid her new happiness might be lost by finding Drogo or Hawisa with the ague after lying in the open without her care. They were both there and so was John, a knife on the table beside his hand. 'Come in, wanton,' he said. 'We've waited a long time for you.

'Run,' squealed Drogo, and squirmed blue-faced under the hand clamped across his mouth.

'Let him alone! Mother of God, you'll kill him!' Alice clawed at John's fingers.

'And you,' John said softly. 'If I must be a beggar on the roads, then I prefer to leave all tidy before I go.'

He picked up his knife and held it to Drogo's throat.

'Come here or I kill him now. Sit down beside Hawisa.' When she did so, he flung Drogo away from him across the table edge.

Alice sat, stroking Drogo's cheek as he lay on the board, whooping for breath. The change from happiness back to hate and fear had been so quick her mind was blank.

'You can't make us leave Ferneth with you,' Hawisa blinked red-rimmed eyes.

John flicked the knife against her cheek, drawing blood, and laughed. 'It depends what kind of journey you have in mind. Drogo, you first.' Almost lovingly, he scooped the child off the table and set the knife beneath his ear.

'For the love of Mary,' Alice whispered, terror making her choke. Head back, she spat straight in his face. He grunted and grabbed at her, dropping Drogo, his hands this time around her throat, thumbs gouging deep.

Alice's senses spun instantly from such merciless pressure, which eased only while he picked up the knife again: the edge felt oddly hot against her skin. Which didn't matter, since all of her life meant nothing, after all. Then her senses reeled into blackness, and the question of whether she died from John's knife or his thumbs in her throat spun with them into the void.

It seemed a long time later when she opened her eyes and saw

Drogo standing over her, tears trickling into puffed bruising around his neck., 'He's dead. Hawisa hit him with the axe. Alice, what shall we do?' His voice was no more than a croak.

All Alice wanted was never to wake again, but with Drogo's help she fumbled to her feet. She knew no more than he did what they should do. John lay on the floor, looking as terrifying in death as he had in life, sprawled from hearth to doorway. His head was a strange shape and he was quite clearly dead.

'Brother Benedict might help,' whispered Alice; a normal voice seemed unthinkable. But what could Benedict do now, when murderers were accursed and run to earth like foxes?

'We have to get rid of him?' said Drogo fiercely. 'Everyone will believe he has slipped away before the village wakes. 'We'd be safe then.'

'Get rid of him,' echoed Alice blankly.

'Do you think anyone would believe us if we said Hawisa did it?' Drogo jerked his head to where she sat twisting straw between her fingers, and something in his face made Alice wonder. Did even she believe that Hawisa had killed John, or had Drogo - ?

The two of them stood silently side by side, staring at John's body. Stigo Laffam led Ferneth's hue and cry, and if he caught them they would be dragged behind his cart all the way to Lord Scovyll's dungeon, to rot in the dark until they were gibbeted.

'We could bury him under the hearthstone,' Alice said tentatively, after a pause. There was a drying pit beside the hearth; if they could enlarge it sufficiently to take John's body, then perhaps no one would ever discover what had happened.

'In here?' Drogo's croak turned to a squeak.

'We can't take him outside.' Her mind was racing now. 'People will be stirring, although maybe too blurred of mind to notice we're late out. It has to be in here, Drogo. We could put him under the bedstraw and run but once he was found, nowhere would be far enough away to hide.' In a land of few people, sooner or later most fugitives were caught. Except those like Edmund, former serving brother of Ockham, who possessed the effrontery of the Devil and a pouchful of gold which enabled him to swagger with the gentry and live out the remainder of his life most prosperously, in distant Cheshire.

So Alice and Drogo buried John the Carver in a shallow grave beside and under the hearth stone, curling his legs into the drying pit and tramping loose earth flat. All the time they worked, Hawisa watched with indifferent eyes and Drogo did not once speak. And when they finished the hut floor looked as it always looked. After waiting until no one was close, Alice and Drogo crept down to the pool to swash away bloody earth stains in cold water.

Ferneth fair was over for another year, and so Rico Parleybien shouldered his pack and decided to strike south-west for Arundel Castle, where the Fitzalans kept a sprawling, lavish state. A tale-monger like himself always found a winter's welcome among so many courtyards and halls, and the sooner he set out to reach there the better, he too had seen those clouds blowing in on the dark and he did not trust the fine weather to last much longer.

'You keep these bronze pieces I earned yesterday he said to Meg, kissing her heartily. Rico liked to be well remembered after he had gone.

'I hoped you might stay a little longer.' Meg lifted an expressionless face to his.

'I stay nowhere long.'

'You have to, through the winter.'

'Aye, but where I may earn my keep with tales and ballads.' Though Rico spoke gently he knew he would be crazed by spring if he was forced to live a whole winter in Meg's hut.

She had known yesterday that he wouldn't stay, but still hoped for a few more nights in which to conceive his child. A spring pregnancy meant a strong babe and plenty of spare milk to sell, and any infant of Rico's would surely be filled with a grace and joy which might help to ease the harshness of her life. The fact that she herself would have liked his company longer was neither here nor there: men such as Rico took what they wanted and left when they chose.

She did not look up when he went.

As soon as he was outside, Rico let his breath out in relief. God's blood, he had been lucky there! If Meg had pleaded or wept on her knees, then his soft heartedness might have forced him into waiting at least until her sick child died, and then who knew what might happen if winter closed the roads? Rico so much disliked refusing any woman what she asked that he often crept away at night from pouting lips or pleading eyes, though once he left he instantly forgot them. He began to whistle as he crossed the fairplace. As yet the rain held off and the road stretched enticingly before him.

He paused by the pool to drink, kneeling to scoop water thirstily into an ale-dry throat until someone called his name.

He stood up politely. 'A fine bout you fought yesterday, Father.'

'Have you seen John the Carver this morning? Benedict asked.

'I haven't spoken to any man. Ferneth is suffering a sore head, it seems.'

'Strange, I did not expect him tamely just to go.'

Rico studied the priest's expression. He looked unwell and had probably intended to be up earlier than he was. 'You expected a knife in your ribs while you slept?'

'Perhaps. But as it happened I slept until dawn and missed both Matins and Lauds.'

'I've missed them myself, these many years.' Answered Rico blandly.

'Ah, but you can't hear all the abbots thanking God that you aren't one of their monks? About John, though. Alice says no one has seen him since last night, nor has he been home.'

'So he did just tamely go. What will you do with his carvings?'

'Place them in the church. Men may learn from the image of corruption as well as from the good. Unfortunately, building the church will go even slower now, with only my eye to keep the plumbline true.'

'You won't do it,' said Rico bluntly. 'No man could, with only travelling journeymen to help him. A new church needs skilled masons like a war needs knights, or the first onslaught will destroy it.

Benedict looked at the still waters of the pool, and beyond them to where Alice stood in her hut doorway. He had not believed her when she told him John had not been home. Yet if John had been there and gone, where was he now? The child Drogo and Alice both had necks bruised purple, Hawisa gibbered in a corner: a slatternly, foolish woman, but not crazed before today. 'I hear that Alice told a fine tale to delight the children yesterday,' he said abruptly.

Rico nodded. 'She has a gift for words.'

'Where are you bound next?'

'I thought Arundel for the winter. Any great household loves a ballad-monger.'

'If I asked, would you take Alice and Drogo with you?'

'Nay! I journey alone,' said Rico in alarm.

'Then I throw in your face what you said to me just now. You won't do it. No man could. A life needs skilled help too.'

'I manage well enough.'

Benedict hesitated, frowning. His senses warned him there was danger in that hut; the kind of warning which in the past had helped him avoid an ambush, although the traps he faced now were baited by the Devil. Alice had wept for joy and Drogo screeched delight when he defeated John but neither was rejoicing now. They stood blank-eyed, scarcely making sense of anything he said, not working, guarding the entry of their hut as if they dared not leave it.

Possessed. Terrified. Guilt-ridden.

Guilt-ridden? Yes, that fitted what he'd felt.

Jesu Christ.

Benedict turned back to Rico. 'The girl can earn her keep by telling tales and the boy draws clever likenesses. Probably he has inherited a part of his father's skills. I beg you to take them away with you.'

'What if John catches us on the road? There's lawlessness enough at present, and bodies are easily hid.'

'It will not happen. I swear it, but do not ask me how I know. John is still in Ferneth, which is why I want those two away. Hawisa – well, Hawisa is beyond men's aid.

'You said you didn't know where John is,' said Rico feeling trapped.

'I know he is here and will not follow you.' Benedict's tone was definite; John had brought butchery on himself, but if they stayed, neither Alice nor Drogo would ever shake free of hauntings. 'Rico. I have asked, and now begged you to do this. If those two stay in

Ferneth, they are damned. And so I warn you: I can curse as well as bless. Refuse me this and all your splendid words will wither on your lips, your spirit become a nut that lacks a kernel.'

Rico rubbed his mouth as if it felt dry already. Any other curse he might have shrugged away, but he dared not risk malediction on his art. 'All right,' he said sulkily. 'I'm not responsible for them, mind.'

'But you are. Alice is brave and hard-working, you could do well together. Or not, if that seems best.' Benedict went over to where the two stood aimlessly by their hut, talked a few moments and then drove them inside to collect the few belongings they would need. When they reappeared each carried a frieze cloak and a pouch, but neither took any interest in what was happening and Rico eyed them with dismay. He did not deserve to be ill-wished by a long-nosed priest, and without reason too.

Then he shrugged. Easier to do as he was asked and shake off unwanted burdens later. Besides, only yesterday he had thought Alice's wide mouth and dark eyes fetching, been intrigued by a woman whose gift, he suspected, inclined more towards troubadours' verse than tale-telling. Even when he felt at his most obdurate, Rico preferred to please and be pleased if he could.

Benedict watched the three take the road together, Rico stalking resentfully ahead. If he kept that pace up he would be out of Alice and Drogo's sight before they reached Twisbury Hill. But where the path plunged into the trees at the edge of Ferneth clearing, Benedict saw Rico turn, glance skywards to where great clouds were boiling over the horizon, and wait for the others to catch him up.

They may perish of hardship on the road, but this must be the only way their souls might be saved, thought Benedict. Now, I wonder what they did with John?

He had to crouch to enter their hut, and once inside the only light came from the entry. The new cottages near the church were better built, but the poolside huts were all the same: wet in winter, airless in summer, usually with someone very old or young lying in a corner. No wonder evil flourished in such places, when generations and sexes were tumbled together beside their beasts.

Benedict could feel the skin chilling along his spine. Evil was here, very close. Then Hawisa gibbered quietly to herself and the spell was broken. He moved to where John's tools lay stacked against a wall, and when he looked closely saw blood and hair caught between the blade and haft of an axe.

He wiped if carefully and replaced it where he found it. After that, he quickly discovered fresh-stamped earth by the hearth.

He went next to visit Goody Apps and offered to paint her a fine black bear on wood, in return for such services as Hawisa would require to stay alive. She clucked and fluttered out of habit, but in the end agreed. 'I want a Scovyll bear, mind. Not any bear no-one would recognize. The Black Bear at Ferneth, they'll say. And all Sussex know this as a loyal house which serves good ale.'

'Wat has gone to the rebels, then?' Benedict did not suffer fools gracefully.

'Lord a'mercy! Where did you go a-hearing that?'

'He has, hasn't he?'

Her face crumpled. 'Aye, this morning, the poor fool. Ah, tell me, sir, do you think he'll come back safe?'

'Who else has gone?'

'Harry Fawkner and Greg Wyse., Harry were telling how he means to wed Alice from the pool, but mark my words, Tam will thrash such nonsense out of him, perhaps it's as well he's gone for a while, so much on fire for the wench he was. Spent the night in the wood, I wouldn't wonder.' She sniffed. 'Naught but rubbish, pool folk. But because Wat swore he'd go to London if Harry did, he wouldn't change, though if he'd a grain of sense he'd never have listened to Harry's wildness. Just think of it! My Wat who's never been further than Reredfield, buck-eyed at all the London harlots! Sir, do you think I'll ever see him back?'

'If he stays close to Greg Wyse and does what he's told, then he'll be back,' answered Benedict, who trusted clever rogues more than he trusted honest simpletons.

He next went to pray for those whose destiny he had changed since this day's sun had risen, to try and pray for John the Carver's soul, but wasn't left long in peace. Meg's child had died so she came to offer a groat for the burial and finding him in the chapel, she knelt to pray for little Will. Some Ferneth folk muttered behind their hands when they saw their priest on easy terms with a harlot, but Benedict never found it difficult to condone the simpler sins of the flesh. Because I've whored so long myself, he thought ruefully now.

'Burn Will's bedding before you allow the other children back in your hut,' he said as she left. 'The healthiest winter I remember on campaign was when the huts we lived in burned down three months in a row.'

'But cold without a hut.'

'We had women to help us with warmth,' he said, smiling. 'I'll come to watch beside the child tonight, but I have to go to Ockham now.'

On his way he visited Tam Fawkner, who agreed without fuss to spare a man to dig a grave. Certainly Tam, a canny and pious man, was capable of beating even a full-grown son if he announced that he intended to take a pool wench as his wife, nor ever afterwards let contention rest, so perhaps the boy was well quit of an unsuitable love. As for Benedict himself, he was very weary and on the road to Ockham the rhythms of prayers incongruously mixed with war-songs served him in the place of thoughts.

The abbey of Ockham was built on an open hillside surrounded by forest, thus revealing its rich extent all at once to the traveller. On that morrow of Ferneth fairday a gleam of sun shone on grey stone, picking out the detail of courts and walks and walled gardens. Nearest to the forest stood the great gatehouse with its crenellated towers and ribbed façade, the only opening in two miles of wall, although there were more covert exits, as Brother Edmund had discovered. Behind the gatehouse stretched pasture cropped by sheep, then fishponds, weirs and working buildings, all built of the same grey stone and adorned with brightly painted saints in niches. Next came the stables and a pinnacle Brewhouse designed by a monk who had learned his trade on cathedrals; gardens filled with vines, herbs, tethered goats, stone shrines, beehives and succulent fruits. These were divided by swept yards and paved cloisters, where swagged ceilings were gathered into place by the escutcheons of past benefactors. Then there was the chapter house, a fretted prayer in stone; lidded vats, grain pits, barns and wool stores. An infirmary larger than many a king's lodging, and a refectory lit by resplendent glass. The kitchens, where four hearths were each wider than a man could reach and sweating lay brothers ladled broths and stews into emblazoned bowls. The monks of Ockham fasted, complaining dismally, only on the greater feasts of the year.

Next came scores of offices and lodgings. The dorter, almonry and guest hall; a scriptorium filled with precious manuscripts and deeds to Ockham's acres; paddocks for horses and mews for hunting hawks. And dominating all the rest, the buttresses and chiselled windows of the abbey church, with its painted pillars and chequered floors, its shrines and tombs and relics, its golden high alter, carved stalls and bell-chiming tower.

Benedict stood for a moment where the path from Ferneth and Edenham broke through the trees and the abbey was spread, immediately and completely, before his eyes. He did not regret his decision to leave Ockham for the humdrum earthiness of Ferneth, but loved this place for its majesty and power.

He passed the gate without question, although Abbot Thomas kept armed guards on call; any son of Ockham was recognized even though he came only once or twice a year. As a matter of course Benedict went first into the abbey church, feeling as he did so a most unmonkly pang of envy for the many masons perched on scaffolding where a new nave was being built. Even two such craftsmen would make all the difference to his new church in Ferneth.

His prayers finished, he went to the abbot's lodgings and noticed afresh how empty the sprawling buildings seemed. Ferneth teemed with life though sickness cut down many. Cattle and sheep bawled in pens, oxen trudged patiently over the ploughland. In all of great Ockham there were, what? Twenty professed monks?

'Twelve,' the abbot replied in answer to his question, after Benedict had knelt and kissed his ring. 'And eighteen lay brothers.'

'Also farm servants and their families.'

Thomas waved a hand. 'I don't know how many of them, since they stay away from the abbey buildings.'

'It's very few,' said Benedict.

'My son, any number be it small or large may serve God faithfully.'

'I have naught to say against monks serving God,' answered Benedict equably. He quite liked Thomas when he forgot to be pompous, but respected neither his vocation nor his blood, which was good but inferior to Clare.

'As do those of Ockham, in countless ways.'

'As they did not when they pulled down Edenham Mill yesterday.'

'The churls had robbed the abbey.'

Benedict shook his head 'Most unlikely.'

'They knew who the robber was.'

'So do you. Shall I start pulling down your bakehouse?'

Thomas's double chin and powerful hooked nose turned mauve. 'Christ's bones, I'll have you scourged for that!'

'You have the right, and I a soul which requires correction. Which does not alter the justice of what I said. You do know who the robber was, don't you?'

'I do now.' Said Thomas irritably. 'Edmund, a lay brother who was succoured by this abbey as a child. He has vanished and we are searching for him in the forest.'

'If he was clever and ruthless enough to rob the chapter house and lay a false trail for you to follow, then he won't still be in the forest. He'll have used the stream to reach the highway, where his scent is easily lost among many others. Which brings us back to Edenham and Sim Wyse.'

'His son carried him to our infirmary. He is being tended as one of Christ's unfortunates.'

'This monastery's unfortunate,' said Benedict softly. 'A victim of hasty and foolish judgement.'

'He was no innocent. He knew why we had come and hoped to bluster his way out of accusation.'

Benedict went to stand with his back to the chimney, which was freshly carved with hounds and griffons, Thomas's ancestral beasts. 'But you found nothing there to confirm suspicion.'

Thomas shook his head reluctantly. He knew he should refuse to be cross-questioned, but with Benedict he was always more conscious of facing a Clare than one of his monks. 'Only because we did not discover the right place to look. Boarhounds! I owned an Irish wolfhound once, now that was a beast which could scent against the wind.'

'Really?' Benedict was momentarily divert.

'Aye, and die rather than loose its jaws on prey once caught. If I'd handed Sim Wyse to the torturers – '

'But you didn't. Why not? The Church encourages the king's justices to spill blood on its behalf.'

Thomas shifted querulously in his velvet-seated chair. 'It would have taken too long. If the royal taxes were to be recovered then we had no time to lose.'

'And by then you had guessed how finely you'd been duped.'

'Wyse knew something,' repeated Thomas. 'We shall never know what, now he lies like a block of wood. I was tempted to lock up his son when he came knocking at our door, but he's too much of a dolt to understand aught of plots.'

'Greg? Yes, I suppose he could act the dolt. You may have lost a good chance there, my lord abbot. Greg Wyse will bear a grudge against this abbey for the rest of his life.'

Thomas poured wine into a silver goblet and pushed it over. 'Ockham has nothing to fear from a peasant. What's done is done: mercy for the son, misfortune for the father. I shall answer for both eventually. Advise me instead what message I should send the king to tell of his lost tax.'

'Your Grace. The revenues of Rye and the Weald were lost two nights ago whilst in Ockham's care.'

Thomas spluttered into his wine. 'I did not jest. You know more of courts and kings than I. So I asked for counsel.'

'And I gave it. This king is soft and pious and will not hang abbots. Tell him at once, while he has a revolt on his hands. His barons will have left him like unwanted baggage by some wayside altar, very likely your message will go astray. Thus will confusion later confound the issue?'

'I swear I shall hand Edmund to the disembowellers if he's caught! You truly believe we should send at once to the king, though ill-tidings are never well received?'

'Aye, since in these times fortunes may change from day to day.'

Thomas looked depressed. 'In many ways. An inquiry is to be held into discipline at Ockham by the superior of our Order.'

'I must remember to tell him what happened to the Wyses.'

Abbot Thomas sipped his wine. 'I doubt the visitants would be interested.'

Benedict ran his fingers absently over the carved mantle, considering. The day had dulled and the first drops of a rain which would soak him, walking home, were hissing in the hearth; the scents of woodsmoke, painted wall-canvas and fresh rushes mingled agreeably beneath a plastered ceiling. 'Very well,' he said at last. 'I agree to keep Ferneth and Edenham from making complaints against Ockham's monks if the visitants should come asking for them, and in return accept the loan of two masons to help in the building of our new church, their wages and materials to be paid for by the monastery.

Thomas sighed and picked up the flagon. 'You aren't drinking.'

'I suffer from the sin of pride and have not previously connived in felonious bargains over wine.'

'We are of one community, are we not? You wanted masons and I, discretion. What is wrong in that?' Thomas rubbed at the flagon with his sleeve. 'I have often wondered what happens to the goodness God puts in wine when it is left undrunk too long. The virtue vanishes no matter how tightly it is sealed into the cask. Could it be the same with souls, do you suppose? An alarming thought indeed for those whose minds are sealed too tightly against the easements offered by this world.'

Benedict took the cup Thomas offered him, and laughed. 'Why, I can point the way in which you may satisfy your curiosity, I believe. When mortal illness strikes you, direct the good brothers to seal your still-living carcass inside a vat, and see whether your soul flies free on death. Or not, of course.'

'Sacrilege, exclaimed Thomas, deeply shocked. 'The abbots of Ockham lie on silk before the high altar when they die.'

'Then enjoy your silk, my lord abbot, and leave curiosity unslaked.

A fitting epitaph for old Ockham before the visitants come.' Benedict stared out through distorting window glass, wondering about his own epitaph. What would he want it to be? He had accomplished little except discomfort since he became monk and priest. He still fought his enemies with rage and sinew instead of prayer, built a church to save his mind from rotting, continued to judge souls by instinct rather than the grace of God. *Here lieth Gilbert, a son of the House of Clare, knight.* There were worse epitaphs.

Outside, the rain thickened into the first downpour of winter and turned the byways of the Sussex Weald into quagmires. He would be chilled and exhausted long before he reached the priest hut of Ferneth again.

Wetness drummed on the shoulders of Harry Fawkner and Wat Apps too, as they trudged to tell a foolish king that all was not well within his realm, and also on Grey Wyse, who was holding hands with Emma Laffam and dreaming of the night to come, together in stable-straw. Dreaming also of prosperity and revenge, and how to keep blockheaded friends from having their necks stretched.

Several miles beyond Twisbury Hill the rain blew into the faces of Rico, Drogo and Alice. Harsh, unrelenting, cold. Drogo and Alice were past thinking about anything except the effort of keeping going a little longer, and Rico thought only of a hedge-tavern he hoped to find at the next crossing of paths. He had been cursing, singing and yelling at the other two for a long time now, forcing them to put one mired leg before the other. He didn't know why he still bothered. Leave them now and death would be more merciful than trying to stay alive.

Drogo sank to his knees and Alice turned, hauled him up and struggled on again, the child's weight hanging on her arm.

'Here,' said Rico. 'I'll carry him.' Drogo's body was not much more than bones, but in these conditions even bones were a burden.

Alice watched him her mouth softening. 'We'll spin a tale from this, once we have the strength for words again.'

'I always have strength for words,' answered Rico. 'Come, I'll sing a chorus I learned in London which will curl heat into your maiden's ears.'

And so, armed with words and courage, eventually they reached a tavern some hours after dark.

Behind them the rain was already finding John Carver's untenanted hut an easy target for its malice, washing mud from its wattle walls and blowing around the door-covering to lie in pools on the floor. Before many years had passed, the roof would collapse and the walls crumble, dark nettles sprout from the place where their roots were nourished by the body which lay beneath the hearthstone.

. . . THE WITNESS:

I was born at number twenty-six, the Street, Furnace Green, Sussex, England. Great Britain, the World, the Universe, as we used to write in our primers at school, which seems only fitting to me now, when I have come to believe that all of life is one. A belief we would have ridiculed then, when Empire Day was a proud half-holiday after we'd paraded the flag.

Number twenty-six was a two down, two up cottage with a lean-to scullery at the back, and I the sixth and last child of John and Elizabeth Smith. Had I grown up in the cottage where I was born then we should never have had space all to sit down at the same time for meals. Fortunately, when I was seven years old we moved to Edenham. This great event occurred in 1913, after my grandfather died and my grandmother decided there was sufficient room for us to join her there. More accurately, Grandmother had no intention of looking after Edenham's pigs and hens when we could do it for her, and since she was extremely close with money it seemed a splendid idea to have her farmyard work done for nothing. Later, the inconvenience of so many extra people squeezed into a fairly small house became a constant irritant.

I was sad when my grandfather died, but also excited to be going to Edenham to live. On the Saturday we moved, my father hoisted me on top of a cart for the journey, where I sat between a washboard and a cooking pot I had to prevent from falling off. The road between Furnace Green and Edenham was patched and muddy; I remember watching sticky lumps cake on the wheels, twirl half round and then fall off with satisfactory thuds. Every yard of that short journey is clear in my mind, perched high above the hedges as I was. I had never seen any sight so splendid as the ridge viewed from a giant's height on a shining April day, and was so busy looking around that a sharper jolt than the rest threw the pot off on to the ground. Since I was holding it as tightly as I could, I followed into the mud. Everyone shouted at me for dreaming, and I was made to finish the journey on foot.

Edenham was smoky-dark and made uncertain by my grandmother's temper, but I loved it from that very first night, spent in a sagging box-bed shared with my brothers, Mark and David. Later, David and I often pretended this fourposter was one of His Majesty's battle-cruisers or a fuzzy-wuzzy fort, while the stream which ran past Edenham became the Amazon or (in winter) the scene of Scott's trek across Antarctica. But best of all was Edenham's kitchen, where ash glowed in the mighty hearth all year round. That kitchen reached out to me, as it still does today: brick floor, oak dresser, glossy wide-planked stairs. The fireback my mother scoured free from centuries of soot: FW 1553. The same year that tragic, fanatical Mary inherited the throne of England and storm clouds began to roll down on Francis Wyse.

But just look what he left behind.

If immortality should endure only so long as someone is remembered – a point on which I have occasionally been inclined to speculate – then Francis is still alive, his imprint firm on the place he loved, the manner of his death a part of our inheritance. As I grew up at Edenham I thought I would be more than content if in four centuries time I, too, should still be remembered in Furnace Green. Which isn't in the least likely.

After Abbot Thomas destroyed it, the site where Edenham Mill had stood went back to scrub for eighty years, until Francis Wyse came to set up his trade where his ancestors once milled flour and so helped to pioneer the first craft in which England became supreme. *Once upon a time* . . . As I sit tonight beside his hearth the ash glows brightly still, and lights the tiny toiling figures the first master of Edenham cast into his fireback: puddling, pouring, mould-making. When the glow changes shape I seem to see them move, hear the clang of hammers from the meadow by the stream.

5

THE IRON YEARS
1534 – 1589

A girl was lying at the edge of the trees, watching. Beyond her, rough-cropped grass stretched down to a stream on the far bank of which a young man was pacing, running to cut notches on an ash branch, running back to pace again. After a while he paused, looked around, and then stripped off his breeches and jerkin before slithering down the bank and into the stream.

The girl began to shake with laughter.

She could not see what he did next, although she heard him yelp as he entered bitter autumn water, and then a flurry as he lost his footing. The girl wriggled from under the bush where she had been lying, and tiptoed down the slope to stand above where the young man stood waist deep in fast-flowing water, intent on something she couldn't see. 'Good day to you, sir,' she said, loudly, to make sure he heard above the brawl of the stream.

He spun round. Of course. It had to be you, Mistress Mary.'

'What are you doing, naked as a pike in the stream?' She liked looking at his flat back and strong muscles, and looked at them boldly. Francis was the shortest of the four Wyse brothers, and the youngest by several years, but Mary Parlben liked him best, the other three being trap-faced men always quarrelling amongst themselves.

He looked at her measuringly. 'I suppose you mean to stay, no matter what I say?'

'Tell me why you're there and I'll think about it.'

He laughed, and hauled himself up the bank, careless of his nakedness. 'I don't mind telling, but not because I've been held to ransom by a pretty lass.'

He shook himself like a hound, pulled on his breeches and slid his feet into clogs, slung his jerkin over one shoulder. Then he came to where the two banks drew closest together, although the drop down to the stream was very steep. 'Jump and I'll catch you.'

Mary didn't hesitate. She gathered her grey kirtle in one hand and jumped. 'Now tell me what you were doing.'

Francis looked at the face almost level with his own, a proud face for the daughter and granddaughter of harlots, full of determination and good spirits although he knew her life was hard. 'Did you know this place used to be a mill?'

Mary shook her head; humiliatingly, the memory of his naked body was filling her mind. She lived in a hut where men came often to lie in the straw with her mother, slept with her brothers without giving a thought to their difference from herself. But pauper brothers were sold as apprentices at seven years old, and Mary despised the nightcomers who through the years had worn her mother to gaunt and dying bones. She kicked their shins if they came too close and whenever she saw Father Poctor fussing over the village's sins, she remembered that he was among the shamefaced who slipped through the wattle of their back wall instead of using the door, and as she grew older judged men as would a flesher buying carcasses. Except Francis Wyse. For three years now just seeing him had made her breath come short and hard, partly because he treated her with the courtesy of a young man for a maid when the other young village men saw her only as the harlot's daughter, and jeered when she refused to behave as they expected.

But from the moment Mary saw Francis climb the stream bank with his body naked in the sun, infatuation vanished and something very different possessed her in its place 'A mill,' she repeated, as if that was a deep thought indeed, 'Aye, of course. My old uncle Parlben tells fine tales of Edenham Mill, but I never know what to believe when there's naught here, like.'

'Nothing's been milled here since my great-grandfather was young, when the monks came one day and destroyed everything. Now I've a mind to see what I can make of it again. My father has enough sheep and land to leave a living for my brothers, a dower chest squeezed for Meg and May, but precious little will remain for me. He said I could have this patch as my own if I'd a mind to it, and I have.'

Mary stared at the slope above the stream. 'How much?'

'Up to the track on this side and round to that oak there. Two acres perhaps, not much.'

'Oh, but it is! Anything of your own is much!' Mary owned a kirtle but no underclothes, a single pair of winter clogs but shared her mother's cloak. 'What will you do here? Keep swine?'

'Nay,' he said slowly, touched by her eagerness. 'I've a mind to fire iron. I was looking in the stream for where the mill wheel used to turn.'

By now he was looking at her with the same boldness as she had looked at him and Mary dropped her eyes as she used to when she admired him from afar. She scuffled her bare toes in the dust as if she was a child, wishing she could say something he might remember. But she wasn't a child any longer. Sweet Jesu, she was not! Sixteen years old and with Francis Wyse close beside her, womanhood burned in her bones. But when he kissed her she turned her face swiftly away, afraid he might think she was a harlot like her mother.

'Mary,' he said. 'Mary.'

She dabbed a quick inexpert kiss back at him, keeping her eyes closed as if by doing so harlotry might not matter. Ah Jesu, it mattered, as she knew.

'Mary,' he repeated, tongue tied. The curve of her cheek reminded him of petals in the rain. 'Mary.'

She opened her eyes; grey changeful eyes, long lashes shadowing her cheeks. She did not speak or move, nor did she kiss him again. Love, pride and longing all in the looking of her eyes.

His hands tightened on her shoulders. 'Mary, love, will you wed me?'

She choked, then burst out laughing. 'For that, you deserve I should take thee, and then where would 'ee be?'

'Will you?'

'Of course, if thee were to mean it.'

'I do mean it.' She kissed him rapturously then, without answering, frightened in case speaking might change his mind.

Francis Wyse offering to wed her, and all because she caught him naked in a stream! She couldn't believe her luck. But in the instant when Mary offered herself to him with her eyes, Francis had understood the choice before him. He could tumble a harlot's brat and suffer shame and embarrassment ever afterwards, or chance everything on a scandalously unsuitable match, receiving in return a lifetime of devotion and staunch loyalty. Or, of course, he could walk away without doing either, but that choice scarcely occurred to him.

For Francis, such insight into another's mind was rare, since his thoughts were usually filled by forge-iron and furnaces, but just because it was rare, he valued what he saw. From the Wyses' house at the end of Furneth Green's single street he had seen Mary Parlben grow from a dirty brat by her mother's hearth into a maid comely enough to turn any man's head, a maid moreover who had peeped at him in admiration for three years now, and hired herself out as a halfpenny drudge because she refused tread the harlot's path.

More practically, Francis was nineteen years old and needed a woman now he meant to strike out for himself: a wife came cheaper than the journeyman he couldn't afford, and a wife whose impoverished kin was incapable of haggling on her behalf came cheapest of all. Mary was used to working like an ox and since, on that autumn day, Francis lacked even a stick-hovel of his own, he could not expect a bride who would help his enterprise by bringing a wedding-chest with her. Thus did need, desire, shrewd judgement and instinctive compassion change Francis Wyse's purpose from simple seduction to a formal wooing with all the swiftness which characterized the important decisions of his life.

He never regretted his changed mind, although he immediately enjoyed a seduction as well. After that first kiss one thing led rapidly to another, until they lay together in long grass where Francis intended his mill to grow. Both thought this a good omen, a pledge with their bodies to the place where the rest of their lives would be spent, and Mary astonished them both by coming to him like a creature who wanted to blot out her heritage in him, to have and give and have again, until Francis forgot the sensible, commonplace reasons for deciding to wed her and only remembered his desire.

They walked back to Furneth Green together, hand in hand. Neither saw any reason to hide their troth, nor to prevent others from seeing what had happened between them. Their future was now simple to foresee so why seek complication? There would be the two of them, a stream and a patch of ground where they would labour all their days. Children would be born and, given good fortune, some survive to inherit their parents' trade; no wonder that for such straightforward minds a single afternoon had been enough to decide what they wanted from each other, to seize it and start talking about how to dam the stream.

After leaving Francis by the door of Wyse's, a house built of brick and tile as well as timber, with an upstairs floor which had been the marvel of the village when Greg Wyse built it seventy years before, Mary ran to where her mother's hovel leaned against the back of Fawkner's barn. 'I'm to be wed,' she said at once, joyfully. 'Mam, I'm to wed Francis Wyse just as soon as he sees Father Poctor.'

Joan Parlben leaned on a wooden paddle where she was stirring a cauldron of wool. 'You're what?'

Mary tumbled it all out then, sparkling with pride. Why, what a miracle to wed from a harlot's hovel! And Mary had experienced nothing in her life which made her believe in miracles.

Her mother laughed as she finished, laughter which turned to coughing. Joan was between thirty and forty years old, coarsened by toil and as pithless as last week's mushrooms. Not many men visited Rico Parleybien's great-granddaughter any longer, born like most of his descendants without any future to call her own. 'Some folk will spin any tale to help them take what they want. And he did, didn't he? I've eyes in my head, my girl. So there's another brat for the straw, unless you're lucky.'

'Nay.' said Mary proudly. 'He meant what he said. Francis Wyse isn't one of your lying packmen. We're to wed and live at Edenham Mill.'

'Edenham? There's nothing there.'

'There will be. We'll build it and it'll all be ours.'

Joan sucked spittle through gapped teeth, impressed despite herself. If Mary wasn't being fooled, then she'd tripped over better fortune than any girl in Furneth Green. She wouldn't even have to quarrel under one roof with the wives of the other three Wyse sons, chivvied by old Gaffer Wyse from dawn to dusk. Instead, in a single leap she'd be behind four walls of her own. Far enough away, too, for malicious gossip about Wyse marrying the likes of her to be easier ignored. 'You never,' she said, this time offering doubt as defence against unlikely hope.

'I will then.'

'What'll you live on, out there alone? There's John and Mark and Rob Wyse who hold all their father's sheep between them, an' a more tight-fisted lot you never did see. Chop a lamb's tail in half they would, rather than sell a little over weight. That's why Francis was apprenticed to park Forge, 'cause there weren't a living for him here.'

He's out of apprenticeship and has worked two years as a journeyman. Now he means to build a forge of his own.'

Joan nodded slowly. 'Aye, well. He'll be needing a woman then.' She chuckled, coughed again. Eh, old Gaffer Wyse'll be wild young Fancis pitched on you, lass. I hope he stands by his troth to thee then.'

Francis anticipated no difficulty on this score. He wanted Mary, and never changed his mind at another's bidding. He found his father seated by the hearth, old Simeon being over fifty and crippled by rheumatics, and said at once, 'I've paced out the flat place at Edenham and there's room for a forge and finery. A furnace can only go where the abbey lands begin but will have to wait anyway until I've some profits to invest.'

'The abbey will never sell land to a Wyse.'

'Ah, why not? It's old tales how great-grandfather spoiled their wool-buying trade. The fat monks of Ockham will be pleased by any profit I can offer them.'

'What can you offer? A furnace, in the name of God. Whatever next!'

'A gunnery range, perhaps,' answered Francis, grinning.

'Lord Scovyll has one where he tests those damned dangerous mortars of his, which are tied together out of bundled strakes.'

'You may not need to waste your silver on grasping monks,' injected his brother Rob. 'There's talk in Tonbridge market that the king's men will shut up the abbey.'

'Get away with such talk!' Simeon thumped his stick on the floor, another luxury which had made the village gape. There's no cause to close Ockham since Abbot Rainer ruled. In my father's day it were a devil's roost by what he said. Now, though the monks may be fat they're harmless, and where else would poor folk go in hard times?'

'Or us,' Rob agreed, belching. 'Since they give away corn to anyone with a tale to spin. Five bushels Mark got from them last year when it rained late in the spring, and he pretended to be ruined.' And he and his father laughed together at a tale they never wearied of retelling.

'About Edenham. You will give it to me like you said?' Francis used to laugh with them but somehow no longer wanted to, perhaps because he intended to set up as a master whom other men would try to trick.

'Aye.' Simeon sobered at once, profit or the lack of it being a serious business. 'I promised, didn't I? The land and twenty shillings' worth of silver, but 'tis all you'll get. Don't expect a single groat when I'm dowelled into my box.'

'Timber?'

'Take what you need out of Danesdell Wood. Alfred and Jack By the Wood owe me five months' rent.'

'Nothing too well-grown, mind,' said Rob, cautiously.

'I'll need good straight oak for the wheel-shaft and beech for the hammer beam,' answered Francis flatly. 'Smaller stuff will do for charcoal, but once the forge is fired I shall burn four cartloads of cordwood a week.'

'I'll sell it to you.'

Francis's mouth tightened. 'No likely, you won't. I'm no soft monk waiting to be cheated.' He turned to his father. 'Jack and Alfred need Danesdell Wood for their swine, but there's Gregs Wood nearer Edenham. If I clear that for charcoal, it'll make prime land for sheep, after.'

Simeon stroked his chin. 'Aye. So long as you clear it right and don't let the land run to waste. All the stumps out, mind.'

Francis nodded.

'You'd better write that in his deed then,' Rob said angrily. 'Or how do you suppose a manor court will know what's right in a few years' time, if we should dispute over briars and stumps?'

'The lad will do as he says, and it's easier left on his word. Now if it was you, Rob – ' The old man shook his head. 'I'd be worried about writing it even, knowing you'd find a way through any scratchings. Eh, Francis?'

Francis shrugged. He avoided quarrelling if he could, which wasn't easy in the Wyse household, and made a vow there and then to make sure that Edenham Mill was kept as free of brawlings as lay in his power.

'Changeling,' said his father, disappointed. 'I told your mam you had too easy a nature to be mine.'

'You wouldn't be giving Edenham to another man's son, patch in the wilderness though it is,' answered Francis shortly. His mother, Simeon's third wife, had died when he was born and he imagined her as all that Simeon was not: gentle, loving and truthful. 'I pledged myself to Mary Parlben today.'

Simeon regarded him with a dropped jaw. 'The Harlot's brat?'

'Aye.'

'Who weds the likes of them? Take her and be done with it.'

'I'm wedding her just as soon as I've seen Father Poctor, and so I'll thank you to speak of her different.'

'It's easy to know how you spent your day,' observed his brother, and laughed.

Francis's face flushed violently red. He was slow-tempered, but relentless once aroused. 'Keep your tongue between your teeth. Mary not being aught to do with you, like. I'm wedding her and that's all there is to it.'

'Even without Edenham? Asked Rob softly. 'You won't expect us to give good land on such a bedding surely?'

'With or without Edenham. Like my father, I keep my given word whether it be writ or not.'

'You headstrong young fool,' said Simeon angrily. Do you want a wife who'll run over the country like a bitch on heat from the very first day you wed her? Once a harlot, always a harlot.'

'I just said, what I do and she does is naught to do with anyone but us. Give me Edenham and we'll go. Nor is Mary a harlot. Call her that name again and ten of your ewes will be dead next morning. Twenty, the time after.'

Simeon smacked his lips thoughtfully. 'At least she'll know the tricks which keep a man lively through dark wet nights. Nay, lad, don't bristle up at me. 'Tis you who'll be chasing after her, not me. Take Edenham and your wench and tame both of 'em if you can. I'll deed the land to you next manor court.' He chuckled suddenly. 'I'd give a keg to see the Father's face when you ask him to wed you to Joan Parlben's brat.'

The church at the end of Furneth Green's one street was not quite as Brother Benedict had visualized it over eighty years before. The walls were of square dressed stone, the windows solidly set and the steeple a landmark on top of the ridge. But the building had been unfinished when Benedict died through a fall from scaffolding, and it was easy to see precisely when this catastrophe had occurred. The upper courses of the walls were rougher in appearance and only the chancel arch was stone. The rest were timber, and although the trusses were stout enough the men who crafted them had known little about the stresses their construction would have to bear. The tower, too, though it sparkled impressively in the sun, had been bodged together by men best skilled in keeping sheep. Sometimes a year had gone by with little done, but Furneth folk were stubborn and also proud of their new church: in 1510 a finial was fixed to the steeple top and a three-day feast marked the completion of a mighty labour.

Francis Wyse took the church for granted, although his father remembered poaching deer for the feast of dedication. He did not know that Brother Benedict's grave lay where Theobald's altar once had been, just to the right of the new south door, nor that the iron-hard rafters in the porch came from the original sod chapel, shaped by an axe when Aelfred reigned in Wessex. He wouldn't have cared if he had known, his mind being on Father Poctor's extortionate charges for a marriage mass.

'Three shillings!' he repeated, staggered by such an amount. 'How many ploughmen do you wed, if you charge so much?'

'As many as can pay. Guard against sin, the mass-book says. Take a woman and sin no more.' And Poctor laughed, being a sinful man himself.

'Then you can't charge them three shillings, or they'd be dead before they saved enough. Why, Jack By The Wood scarcely sees ten groats from one month's end to the next!'

'Ploughmen pay in other ways. Four weeks' free burning I took out of Jack to pay for his daughter's burial, and now I hear his other brat is sick. It's the hand of God, when I'm short of firing for the winter.'

At these words the same fury seized Francis as when his brother spoke slightingly of Mary. Normally uninterested in the affairs of others, he was occasionally capable of outrage over matters other men considered trifling; once he had broken a forgeman's arm when he surprised him forcing a terrified apprentice to pleasure him. 'You will wed us for a fee of one shilling. Since even that is more than your due, we will agree that Jack also gets free burial for his child if she dies.'

Poctor laughed in his face. 'That I shall not, and if you live in adultery then I send to the bishop to have you arraigned for it.'

Francis rasped a fistful of greasy cloth at the priest's neck. 'Nay, Master Poctor. Take my shilling and say your masses, or regret it. I desire to live according to the law, otherwise I would kneel with Mary to pledge our troth under God's sky and believe we pleased Him very well. He must long ago have sickened of your impiety.'

Poctor's face darkened, partly with rage and partly from the pressure on his throat. 'I'll see you gutted first.'

Francis smiled and released him. 'Don't count on it.'

Three nights later the thatched roof of Father Poctor's new brick-built priest house burned off, and he escaped with only the cloth he slept in. While it still burned he pummelled his way through villagers watching the excitement and ran the length of the street to Wyse's like a man possessed, where he found Simeon seated on a bench outside his door, watching the flames.

'Where is your devil-ridden son?'

Simeon studied him, heavy –lidded in crimson light. 'I've four of 'em for my sins. Which one?'

'Francis,' Poctor spat the word.

'Not here.'

'Where is he? Christ's bones, I mean to smell the smoke on his clothes while it's still fresh!' Poctor was fairly dancing with rage, bare-footed in the mire. 'Then will I lay evidence against him. He'll hang for this.'

Simeon rasped at his beard, maddeningly deliberate. 'Aye? You don't think that Lord Scovell sitting in judgement on his bench might think you'd decided to smell smoke on the lad, no matter what? Francis is a good workman and served his apprenticeship at his lordship's Park Forge. Interested in iron his lordship be, and often a-visiting his forge.

He offered Francis the furnace-master's place there, if he'd stay on.'

'Christ!' shouted Poctor, and tore at his cassock. 'What proof do I need? The heretic had this planned, knowing he could wheedle the old lord.'

'You need to be careful of that robe if all the rest are burned,' observed Simeon kindly.

Poctor's thick creased face filled with venom. 'Furneth Green does not belong to Lord Scovell.'

'He's king's justice in these parts.'

'My church is in Ockham's gift, not his. I can swear your son spoke heresy in my hearing, saying he would sooner kneel under a tree than hear God's holy mass, and if he doesn't hang then I'll see he burns instead! Even Lord Scovell cannot meddle with the church's judgings.'

'Well', said Simeon slowly, tapping his stick on the doorstep, 'I wouldn't argue with this holiness of yours, but if I were you I'd watch my step before I went a-blethering off to Ockham. I hear the king himself has his eye on that.' And he roared with laughter, slapping his thigh and shaking his stick at Poctor's slack-jawed gape. 'Shall I tell you where my Francis is while your roof burns off? With that trollop he fancies, more fool him, getting himself wed by Lord Scovell's private chaplain. You'll have to ask his lordship whether he smelt smoke on the boy's clothes, or not.'

Poctor spat where Simeon's stick had tapped. 'Francis did it. By witchcraft maybe if he was at Riffield, but I know of no light or ember in my house which could have reached and burned away the thatch.'

'Have it your way – Father.' Simeon hesitated derisively on the word. 'I'm only offering a friendly warning, since by my reckoning Francis has the best witness in Sussex to swear he weren't here when your hut took fire.'

'My house! No hut, and better built in brick than yours!'

'And we had a peck of trouble with sparks in the roof afore we trimmed the rafters back,' greed Simeon. 'I remember a couple of fires when I was a lad, but now we've bettered the smoke-hole all seems well, and you'd best do likewise.'

There was a long silence while Poctor clawed at his beard and thought. Then, without another word, he turned and went away.

'You watch out for yourself.' Simeon said to Francis when he returned next day. 'He's rancorous Satan-bait, that Poctor. You should have burned him inside that house of his while you were at it.'

Francis grinned. 'Which might be a more difficult sin to purge than taking the roof off an unworthy priest. We could see the glow from Riffield and stood beside Lord Scovell himself to watch it. I'm safe enough.'

Aye, for now. But Poctor's the kind to swaddle a grudge, and strike when your back is turned. He'd be safer dead.'

'As to that, it's in God's hands. I'm certainly not taking it into mine. I heard Jack By the Wood's lass died last night, though, and intend to show myself to Poctor before we go off to Edenham. I wouldn't like him to think he could charge Jack a month of burning wood for a burial.'

Mary stood silently beside her new husband, still over-awed by the size of Wyse's when all she knew was hovels. Ever since Francis had ducked through the entry of her mother's hut the evening before and demanded whether she was willing to wed him that very night, events had spun past like black water down a race. The moment she nodded acceptance Francis had whirled her away to Riffield, though when they arrived at the castle and saw the sky still dark behind them, Francis began to worry in case his forgeman's trick hadn't worked: glowing charcoal sealed in a twist of clay-puddled hay to delay its burning and thrust into the thatch of Poctor's house. But even as Lord Scovell's chaplain, for whom Francis had once worked a handsome sanctuary screen, agreed to marry them on the morrow, the castle watchman called out that there was a fire in Furneth Green.

Mary stole a look at her husband's face; she had felt so triumphant at marrying, actually marrying a fine man like Francis Wyse, that she had danced and sung with him all the way back across the park, drunk on delight. Believed her life was settled, its pattern a matter for rejoicing; after three years of watching him she had thought Francis's every move familiar, but by this quarrel with Poctor he became a riddle, the future filled with unexpectedly powerful enemies. Mary had been reared to survive no matter what, and survivors kept their thoughts to themselves and grovelled when they must.

'Why did you do it? She asked suddenly.

'I told you why when I gave you the choice not to wed me.'

As if I'd take it! She said scornfully. 'Nothing had changed between you and me.'

He laughed and pulled her hand into warmth between his elbow and ribs. 'Ah, but you never bargained for a quarrel with the church which looks set to last a generation. Nor did you think I was the kind of fellow to lose my temper over matters you think unimportant. But I am, and so last night you could have changed your mind if you wanted. Now it's too late.'

She shrugged. She had never for an instant considered changing her mind. 'But why? She asked again.

'Did I do it? I don't know. I have a demon in me sometimes which will not let me pass villainy in silence. Don't fret, lass, it doesn't happen often.'

They sat that afternoon on the churchyard wall, talking about how they would build their forge, until Father Poctor came past. He scowled when he saw them, covert village sniggers having only strengthened his conviction that Francis had indeed been responsible for his lost roof, but would have stamped past without speaking, except that Francis stood respectfully. 'Bad news, Father.'

'For you!' shouted Poctor furiously. 'Be sure I will send a reckoning of your sins to the bishop. We will see which burns brighter then, your tallow or my roof.'

Mary's senses spun, and in that moment she agreed with Simeon. So long as this priest lived they would never be safe.

'Nay, such was not the bad news I had in mind,' answered Francis easily. 'I wanted to tell you that when my brother Mark was trading with the Ockham clerks this morning, the king's offices arrived to shut up the abbey and turn out the monks. There was great wailing and wringing of hands, but soon the gates will be locked behind the last of them. Ockham has fallen.

Poctor stared, transfixed. 'All the monks turned out?'

'Aye, King Henry's officers said there had been more quarrels between His Majesty and the Pope, and, because of it, with monks and abbeys too. Priests like yourself will no doubt remain secure, providing there's no complaint against them.' He paused deliberately. 'I hear Jack By The Wood's lass died yesterday.'

Poctor might scarcely have heard, he was so dumbfounded. Ockham. The great abbey of Ockham shut up on the whim of a king's officer. It was beyond belief.

But when the news was confirmed by people who had seen monks, servants and lay brothers milling around outside locked abbey gates with no more than a coin and a loaf of bread given to each, Father Poctor decided to wait on events before drawing attention to himself with excessive fees or complaints of heresy against a parishioner. When Jack By The Wood came to beg a burial for his daughter, he was astonished to be charged no more than a single week's kindling as a fee.

After they had seen Poctor, Francis and Mary set out for Edenham, he with an axe over one shoulder and forge tools strapped to his back, she driving the young ox which was Simeon's bride-gift to them – and the cause of a furious quarrel with his brothers, who thought Francis had been given enough.

'There have been whispers in Tonbridge market these past few months that the abbey might be shut up,' observed Francis. 'Poctor will look to his interests for a while, and leave us to ours.'

'He'll never forgive the grudge he owes you,' said Mary, watching the sun glow on the ox's plump flanks. Their ox. Imagine, an ox of their own, when before yesterday she had scarcely owned anything in her life! 'Oh, Francis, why did you have to provoke him so!' she exclaimed. 'Think how happy we would be if only all was well behind us!'

'All's well in front of us,' answered Francis, and began to whistle in breathy puffs. 'Sing, sweeting. It's hard to whistle while my nose nearly touches my knees under a load of tools and pots!'

So she sang, and he whistled, and Poctor was left behind them.

After they reached Edenham they worked from dawn to dusk

under a bright October sun. The air was soft and the trees glowed against blue sky. Winter might have been months away instead of gathering power just beyond the horizon. Occasionally someone hailed them from the track, once a charcoal-burner begged some cloth to bandage a gashed thumb, otherwise they saw no one and thought only of their own affairs. By the time five days had passed, a split-log hut thatched with heather stood on the site of the old mill, with a lean-to for the ox and a hearth dug into the shelter of a bank. Until they could bake some chimney-bricks it would be too dangerous to cook inside so small a space. The weather still held fair, so next they began to stack dead wood for winter fuel, drive pegs where Francis planned his forge-hearth and hammers, his casting pits, fineries and, one day, a furnace of his own.

'Iron.' He said one day, nearly two weeks after they had wed and while they sprawled in fern at midday, drinking water and swallowing cold gruel. There was not time to hunt while the good weather lasted, scarcely time to cook as winter began at last to whine through the trees. 'It's the most beautiful thing you ever saw, when earth turns red and changes into metal. We'll level a moulding floor and bring in sand, then you shall see how iron from the furnace races to fill the smallest tendril drawn there. And almost at once you can pick it up, a miracle set in sand. I never tire of watching it, and nor will you.'

Mary rolled over, smiling. She was tired, since Francis was a fierce taskmaster of himself and her, but never so happy in her life before. Everything smelt of dew and earth and cut timber, and all they built was theirs; he was hers, and she loved him. Loved his strong, square body and impatient eagerness, by day for iron and at night for her. Her very bones melted in the night. 'How long before I see it, do you think?'

'This time next year, I swear it. A furnace – well, a furnace of the kind I want will take a while to build.'

'Next year! How shall we live with nothing earned?'

'By hammering other men's makings. But an ironworks isn't like brewing ale or weaving cloth; once fired, a furnace should burn for months while the ironmaster snatches what rest he can. I need ore-pits, hammers, charcoal, enough iron for anvils and heads before I sell a single piece of my own. A dammed pool, a sluice and race. A water wheel –'

'Stop!' Mary clapped her hands over her ears. 'I shall be a crone before I see a drop of iron poured.'

He knelt and kissed her. 'Nay, sweeting. You'll never be a crone, but like iron fresh-tapped forever.' And for all the haste which gripped him, after that they lay together on fern and little yellow flowers, spinning out the kind of lingering pleasure they had not known before. Step by step like a welcoming, I love you how I did not love before.

Those two weeks before winter came, alone in the place where Edenham Forge would grow, sealed Mary and Francis together in ways neither had expected. And at the end of that time the clouds rolled in, rain roared on their heather roof, and they woke during one night to hear the beat of many feet on the track to Ockham.

'Whatever's happening?' whispered Mary. She felt Francis roll away from her side and grabbed at him. 'Have a care! It might be – 'She did not know what it might be, but pictured a cloven-footed horde with eyes of flame.

'Wait where you are,' he answered, low voiced.

Mary did nothing of the sort, scrambling up the moment he ducked past the cloth they had hung in the doorway. The night was dark and wet, storm clouds scudding over-head, but there were lanterns bobbing on the track and the sounds of more people than normally travelled that way in a year. Mary clenched her teeth on a scream as she saw the shape of animals walking as if they were men, and jesting together among little glints of light.

'It's all right,' said Francis, reappearing out of the darkness. 'Here's Mark, he'll tell us what's happening.'

Mary gasped and went into a peal of laughter. 'Eh, but I never thought to see the sharpest fleece-trader in Furneth Green frolicking under his own ram's horns!'

Mark Wyse brushed past her; an irritable man who thought well of his consequence. Tonight, Mary could just see that he was wearing skins stitched into a cape and, pushed back on his shoulders, a mask made from the skull of a ram. He also stank, the skull never having been cured. Then Francis used flint and tinder, blew on the reed twist they floated in grease to give a glimmer of light. 'There's most of the village up there,' he said to his brother.

'Aye, even Gaffer Wylkin is hopping one-legged behind.'

'You're going to Ockham?'

'How did the word fly out?'

'It didn't, or not here. I guessed, which wasn't hard when only the abbey lies this way. Nor is everyone prancing as rams and mules simply to gather firewood in the forest. All that puzzles me is what Ockham means to you.'

'A livelihood,' answered Mark sulkily. 'God's death, Francis. How will I trade for wool if Ockham is no more?'

'The same way our grandfather traded wool in the teeth of Ockham, and prospered from his enterprise.'

'It isn't so easy now! The market is for half-made cloth and the great merchants have our trade engrossed.'

'So you've let Ockham undertake the risk,' observed Francis drily. 'No wonder the Wyses are less prosperous than they were.'

'I tell you, the cloth trade is become so great that a man with only a few bales to sell is underbid!'

'Then you stay as a shepherd and be satisfied.'

'Never! We go to restore the monks into their place. There were ten bales of my wool seized in Ockham's barn, and the monks due to pay me on All Saints Eve.'

'Ask the king's clerks for what is due.'

'And they will say, "Aye, perhaps, come back next year when we've discovered what is what" I want payment now, not after I've starved two years waiting for it.'

Francis rubbed the stubble on his face. 'What do the other Furneth folk want?'

Mark glanced at Mary, standing silently at Francis's shoulder, and laughed. 'Well, Joan the Harlot wants the monks back in their dorter, when the only trade remaining to her is monks who lack a better choice.'

'Ah,' said Francis quietly, and put his arm across Mary's shoulders. 'Now that's been said, brother, remember if you should need help after this night's work, I do not owe debts of kinship to those who mock my wife.'

'I shan't need help. The king can't know his officers have stolen

Ockham for themselves. He'll reward us when we seize it back again.'

'King Harry will rebuke his own servants if he chooses, not reward those who try to take his authority into their own hands.' Francis knew nothing about kings and very little about why King Henry's clerks had ejected the monks from Ockham, but he had worked since childhood at Park Forge, where he found Lord Scovell a just lord only of those who obeyed his will.

'Aye, but the whole of Furneth Green is with us, said Mark carelessly; the very idea of rebellion was unreal if everyone was in it together. 'Father Poctor comes for piety, I for wool, Gaffer Wylkin for his place in the infirmary straw, Joan Parlben for her harlotry. Each of the rest for something different. And if the king should decide to string up a whole village by the neck, how could his judges tell who we are when Ockham will be stormed by bulls and goats and rams?' Mark snapped the skull over his head so that all they could see were horns and rotting jaws.

'My mother goes with the rest?' Mary spoke for the first time.

'Aye, mayhap there'll be trinkets on the altar she might fancy, now she's mostly too sick even for bedding monks.' Mark vanished into darkness, leaving only stench behind.

Francis pinched out the wick. 'I ought to have stuffed those ram's horns down his throat.'

'No – no – Quarrels inside a family are the worst of all.' Mary disliked all the Wyses except Francis, not one of them was worth a feud. 'They must be crazed to think they can take back an abbey once the king has seized it for himself.'

Francis laughed. 'There speaks a voice of sense. Sweeting, when men run in a pack they forget all else until the reckoning comes.'

'But Mam has gone with them. I can't – '

'Only caperings will happen tonight. They'll take or not take the abbey, and then go home. Afterwards is what matters, when King Harry hears the tale of what's been done.'

'She'd turn back if I reach her before they enter the abbey.'

Francis shook her, in exasperation more than anger. 'There isn't any need. I tell you, nothing much will happen and they have been clever enough to wear masks. But don't you see? Poctor is with them. After this night's work, he'll be the one in danger while we'll be clear, with a hold on him to keep us safe for life.'

'Aye,' said Mary after a pause. 'I see that. It's more than luck for us.'

The beat of feet had long faded while Mary still lay tensely in their bracken bed, picturing the people of Furneth Green trudging towards Ockham, clowning sometimes when a familiar face peered from beneath feathers or daubed cloth. Their hands would be grasping sickles and their minds be blinkered by the grievances of monks, who would promise God's grace, forgiveness, anything, if only they were put back in their place again. As soon as she heard Francis's breath deepen into sleep again, very cautiously Mary came to her feet. His leather cape hung on the wall, which when she put it on reached nearly to her knees. She scooped a handful of ashes from the hearth to smear her face, and when she reached the woods, broke into a run. The path beside the brook, where Greg Wyse had once forced his sister to reveal her part in a tale of villainy, was trapped with soft places after a night of rain, but Mary was used to the woods and not often forced to drop her pace. By now, her mother and the rest must be close to the gates of Ockham, she hated to defy Francis but Joan was too sick to walk to Ockham in the wet. She might fall in a ditch to die or, such was the way she had attracted ill fortune all her life, be the one villager caught by king's clerks impotent to stop stronger law-breakers than she. Mary did not love her mother, but had pitied and stood by her for too long to change the habit now.

The path came out of the forest close to the wall which enclosed the abbey buildings, and Mary groped her way along its rough surfaces until she came to a place where it was possible to climb over. Brother Edmund had come this way eighty-four years before, on a very different mission. Once she had scrabbled to the top she could see dark abbey buildings bulked against darker night, and the bobbing specks of lanterns racing from the gatehouse towards the abbey church itself.

She was too late.

Bitterly disappointed, she stared at those lights, thinking that now she would never be back at Edenham before Francis woke. Then she swung her legs over the wall and jumped blindly, hit something and rolled in soaking grass. The wind immediately felt much colder and sent shivering chills through her body. She picked herself up and ran, hands outstretched, in the direction of the lights, and as she ran more were kindled, glowing through stained glass and spilling out of open doors.

Mary paused, then turned aside across some kind of garden, flattened herself beside an open door. Shouts and strange braying noises came from inside. Once, the clash of metal and a scream. She was very much frightened by the strangeness of it all, by the curse which might rest on intruders into such a place and the anger Francis must feel when he woke and found her gone. The first anger of their married life, which might not easily be outgrown.

She did not know what she expected when she looked through that arched door and into the abbey church, but what she saw transfixed her. A piled magnificence of stone soared into a dimness so vast she could never have imagined such a sight. Furneth Green's church was the largest building she had ever been inside, but here huge embroidered hangings stirred in cold draughts and walls upward between rows of lancets, the pillars carved and flowering like forests of faery stone until they vanished into darkness. Mary stared and stared. Surely it was worth any risk to see so magical a place. Her heart beat loudly and she forgot Francis's anger, wished only that he could have seen this with her.

Furious voices, mixed with a braying sound, broke into her wonder, echoing strongly away to her right. She hesitated, wanting to flee, had to force herself to move away from the relative safety of her door to hide behind the nearest pillar. She couldn't see any more from there, and slipped slowly and reluctantly towards the heart of the church, flattening herself against a wall as the light grew brighter and shouts burst into cheers. A few steps more and the most extraordinary scene yet burst on her eyes: a great gold altar glowing between two cressets, to one side of it a tall monk sitting on a throne while a farmyard of animals capered around him. The braying noise came from those Furneth villagers who were imitating the beasts whose masks and skulls they wore, the cheers from others who had thrust a rebel monk into the abbot's chair. No one seemed to have been killed, although two men in livery were holding their heads in the aisle, and another was cursing steadily while he bound up a bleeding arm in a tapestry cloth. Sacrilege, thought Mary fearfully, her eyes on the crucified Christ below the great east window.

Then, even through all the uproar, she heard a familiar cough. A sound she would have recognized in Hell itself, having shared a hut with it all her life.

'Let's get her out of this Noah's Ark and leave while we can,' said Francis softly behind her back.

Mary jumped. 'How did you get here?'

'The same way as you, I expect. This time do what I tell you, and wait here.'

Mary waited, torn between annoyance and relief. He wasn't angry although he might be later, but behaved as if she could do nothing for herself. Still, he had come when he found her missing, and care which grew out of love was not to be despised.

The noise in Ockham abbey church was fading as its majesty gradually mastered rowdy triumph. A few people had knelt in awe when they first entered, now the rest looked uneasily into mysterious shadows or up towards the soaring, hidden roof. Somewhere out of sight the returned monks began to chant, a soft sweet sound as if the stones spoke their own responses. Mary felt her knees weaken, her spine shiver under the spell and splendour of this place.

Joan was still coughing as Francis returned with her through a line of pillars, his arm supporting most of her weight.

'Back the way you came,' he whispered.

Mary nodded, dragging her mother's other arm across her own shoulders. She had been right to come. When the rest slipped away home Joan would have been left behind, an easy scapegoat coughing on the altar steps.

To their left lay an empty transept, the open side door beyond. Dormitory, cloisters, storehouses, day-stairs: a monastery held a thousand hiding places and, in the dark, also a thousand traps for the ignorant. Joan was scarcely conscious and coughing, coughing; if anyone challenged them, lacking masks they would be easily recognized. But no one came. The wet dark night slowly gave way to a wet dark morning, and once across the wall, all they had to do was trudge head down through the mire two long and uphill miles to Edenham. Eventually Francis had to carry Joan on his back, and he was stumbling with exhaustion long before they reached the shelter of their hut again.

'If you hadn't come I should never have reached home with her.' Mary felt she had been ungrateful in not thanking him for coming and, above all, for not once reproaching her.

'Of course I would come,' he answered, surprised. 'It was worth it anyway to see the abbey as it should be seen, with monks singing a thanksgiving in the choir.'

'You too?' she cried and then promptly felt ashamed because she had assumed he would only see beauty in water wheels and iron.

He gave a gasp of laughter, but lacked breath to reply.

The restored monks of Ockham were left undisturbed for a month, chanting their offices and inscribing a list of lost possessions which they intended to present to the king as justification for their action against his over-zealous and light-fingered servants. The village of Furneth Green hummed with self-congratulation. Father Poctor, who had never felt so powerful as when he pranced in a bull-mask before his people, freely forgave any sins committed on the night they repossessed the abbey, and a few unscrupulous households dug hiding places for the scraps of plate or cloth purloined during their visit to the abbey.

At the end of the month a file of leather-jerkined men drew rein outside Ockham gate house, demanding entry in the name of Henry, by the Grace of God King of this Realm of England. By then it was winter and the tracks of Sussex were shin-deep wallows of mud, but the news spread fast. This was no huddle of clerks whom men might delude themselves were acting beyond their authority, but King Harry's policy which said that monasteries were no more. Why this should be no one in Furneth understood, nor, really, did they ever find out. There was a quarrel with the Pope, men said. Well, anyway, monks were idle everyone knew that. And monasteries were rich and the king short of funds, said others, and laughed. In Furneth Green they did not laugh, but waited in terror for retribution. A riot against officious clerks would surely have been overlooked, a challenge to King Harry's policies, never. But at least the kind would not be able to prove whence had come the mummers' figures who broke into the abbey to force the monks back into their place. So the villagers held their breath and waited, wondering how much proof really mattered to a king.

'Do you think we should hide in the woods for a while?' asked Mary anxiously, two days after the monks were turned out the second time. 'Edenham is the nearest settlement to the abbey, the king's men might easily come here first.'

Francis licked rich gravy off his fingers. 'I never ate so well at Wyse's sweeting, as I do here.'

Mary flushed with pleasure. Before she wed she had seldom done more than throw scraps in a pot, but while she drudged for ha'pence had watched enviously how substantial folk baked and stewed and brewed. 'I was never wed to a poacher before,' she answered after a pause.

He laughed. 'Why should we starve while the abbey deer grow stringy with age around us? Tell me, do you want us to hide?'

Mary considered, while draughts wailed between the timbers of their hut. 'I think we should stay.'

Francis leaned across to kiss her. 'Why, so say I. The guilty run away, and tomorrow I've the shafting for our water wheel to mount.'

'I thought I heard something,' she said nervously, head tilted to listen. She was certain she had heard something.

Francis opened the door which he had hung only the day before in place of a cloth. Outside stood a boy, hair plastered wetly across his face. 'Not King Harry this time! Come in out of the rain, lad.'

The boy came in hesitantly and stood dripping on the earth floor. He wore a brown cloth tunic, lewdly chopped short around blue thighs and belted by a knotted rope: a parody of a monk's garb although he was too young for vows.

'Come by the fire,' said Mary, ladling broth. 'Are you lost in the dark?'

'Not lost, but turned out to wander.' He spoke slowly as an idiot might, yet lacked any look of doltishness.

'From Ockham?' asked Francis.

He nodded, his eyes on the broth.

'Eat up, and answer questions later,' said Mary briskly.

The boy needed no further urging, gulping soup and tearing bread so that it was clear he must have been wandering some time before he summoned the courage to approach a lighted hut.

'Tell us what happened at the abbey,' said Francis when he finished. 'What is your name?'

'Richard. Richard Mercer. 'I am . . . I was . . . ' His young face hardened. 'I am a novice of the Order. There are other abbeys where I may go, so I intend to travel to one of them as quickly as I may.

'Not this way. There's no other monastery in these parts.

'To Canterbury then. Even this king dare not touch Holy Saint Thomas's shrine.'

Francis shrugged. Who knew what a king might or might not do? 'Tell us what happened.'

'The king's men came, followed by a snot-nosed steward. They called on the keeper of our gate to open in King Henry's name, and when he did they drove us out in the middle of a chant. All the doors were locked: church, kitchens, refectory, all. Then were the monks asked to accept what was done as right and take preferment elsewhere, as priests of parishes.

'In the circumstances, not an ungenerous offer, perhaps. How many accepted?'

'All of them,' answered the boy bitterly. 'So then the soldiers unlocked the refectory and they began to feast together, the monks bawling out how pleased they were to be freed from our Order's vows. Only when they were well drunken did the steward speak again. The king, he said, offered full pardon to all the monks of Ockham except the ring leaders of the riot, and even they could receive mercy. Providing they told who helped them to storm the abbey, disguised as goats and bulls.'

Mary's throat knotted in alarm. 'What did they answer?'

'They gave names, having minds like cow-pats. Priest Poctor, Mark Wyse, Henry Baker and Thomas Laffam, were the ringleaders they said, and led poor monks astray. His Grace of England will reward you with fat livings, replied the steward, and he laughed. So I told him to his face that I would walk barefooted to any monastery which would take me, rather than accept reward for betrayal. Walk bare-arsed as well then, they said, and cut off my habit at the buttocks.' He looked at Mary, tears glittering in bright blue eyes. 'I am sorry to disgust you, mistress.'

'How could you, when you alone refused to sell others into vengeance?' said Mary warmly. 'Francis, I could stitch the cloth which hung in our door so it would make Richard a kind of tunic. If you will spare it.'

'Aye, but he'd do better wearing my spare breeches.' He grinned. 'For all they'll hang like mill-sails on you.'

'I can't wear breeches,' said Richard stiffly. 'I'm grateful of course, but sworn as a novice.

'Don't be a fool, we aren't living in a fine stone abbey here. You'll die of the chills if you try to winter bare-shanked in a hut. Take what you're offered with Christ's own grace.'

The boy bit his lip. 'You're very good, but I wasn't asking to stay.'

'Nor was I offering you food and straw for life. Walk to Canterbury if you wish, but not bare-legged in winter. A wasted life will merely cheat the church of a servant who might serve it well.'

Richard considered this, then nodded; his awkwardness in speech came from a novitiate which forbade chatter, Mary decided. She grasped Francis's arm.' 'What will happen to your brother and the rest?' shouldn't we run to warn them, now we know the monks have blabbed their names?'

'It must be too late. How long since you left Ockham, lad?'

'I walked out of last night's feasting.'

Francis nodded. 'Then the king's men will have taken them by now.'

'But they didn't come past here. We haven't seen any strangers all day, and no one can use the track without us seeing.'

'I think they'd go through the forest,' offered Richard, scrabbling into the breeches Francis threw to him. 'The first we knew of their approach was hammering at the gate. They catch suspects easier if no one has warning of their coming.'

This proved to be the case. Francis did in fact struggle down the water-filled track to warn the Laffams of Corndown first, theirs being the nearest settlement to Edenham, but the king's men had been and gone, taking Thomas Laffam with them. When Francis reached Furneth it was to hear similar tales of armed men appearing out of the trees, of royal writs read and men seized under the noses of helpless, terrified families, Mark Wyse and Father Poctor among them.

'I can't grieve for either of them,' said Francis when he returned, soaked and weary in grey daylight. 'I owe my father enough to try and save his son if I could, but all my brothers tormented me as a child and would have cheated me as a man. We also breathe easier with Poctor in a dungeon. He won't be pestering his bishop to burn me for heresy for a while, since I never understood King Harry to be a forgiving kind of man.'

Mary laughed, relieved. Joan Parlben had been left in peace, only the men named by the monks having been taken by the soldiers. 'God bless King Harry, then.'

'Aye, though the ruin of Ockham will hit poor folk hard when the next spoiled harvest comes.'

Richard Mercier stayed with them from day to day, and then, as an unusually harsh winter set in, from week to week. The boy was useful and though they could not afford to pay him for his labour, they ate well. Francis poached game and rabbits, ranged through the monastery woods most nights gleaning what he could. He would have been hanged if caught and Mary never slept when he was out, but the risks weren't great. That first winter after Ockham was shut up, the king's clerks ate and drank their way through the abbey stores while compiling a selective list of loot for their master's perusal: how could he ever know what his servants consumed or pocketed? Nor, as they piled carved choir-stalls on a roaring refectory fire, did warmed and well-fed clerks feel like patrolling the abbey demesne.

'You're useful to me,' said Francis bluntly whenever Richard protested that he must not stay to be a burden. 'There's food in plenty, and another pair of hands means I'm well up on the work I have to finish before the spring. Tomorrow we'll strap the trip to take a hammer.'

'I have a better idea how it might be done,' Richard answered eagerly. 'If we fit a spur chock as well, why shouldn't it drive a second, smaller hammer too?'

After that there was no more talk of Richard leaving. It was true that with so much heavy work to be done another pair of hands was invaluable, but above all Richard dedicated himself to anything he did. Francis had to teach him everything when he came, but this was not the first idea he had contributed to their work. He was also unobtrusive, obliging, and passionately fond of nature, pausing often to muse on all he observed without ever skimping on a task. Mary and Francis had lived all their lives in a village surrounded by forest, but only after Richard came did either reflect on what they saw, and then not as a consequence of anything he said. Indeed, he often whistled rather than spoke a greeting, observed silences as if he was still a novice, vanished after supper so they might be private in their hut. Rather it was that his delight became infectious, and Richard's thoughts could be read like weather in the sky. He did not think it odd to study a pattern in the ice, and if he rubbed mud between finger and thumb then any watcher must perceive that what he saw was not a lump of dirt, but the miracle whereby God made all things grow.

He even ate with such relish that every dish seemed the rarest imaginable, and because he loved all of creation, he was deeply happy in everything he did.

'You won't make a good monk,' Francis observed one night, when the snow was piled so deep outside that their hut was warmer than it had been for weeks, all the chinks being frozen solid.

Richard looked up from some timber gearing he was polishing. 'A contented monk is what I hope for.'

Francis pulled down his mouth in mock condemnation. 'How can you be? A monk must do penance, and since for you even fasting is a joy, how can you find anything of which to deprive yourself for Christ?'

'I can't,' answered Richard, smiling. 'Like Mary, whatever love I give I am only increased by what I receive in return.'

Francis had been teasing him, but now was taken aback. 'How dare you suggest that Mary has less love from me than she offers?' There was a time when – aye, I looked for a comely ox. But I found a wife.'

Richard laughed. 'My win, I think. Let Mary tell you what I meant, but I'm glad you weren't ashamed to acknowledge love.' He got up and went out into the frosty night.

'What did he mean?' Francis asked at once.

'I think . . . I think he must have noticed something you have not. Which is strange in a novice, really. I shall birth our child in the summer.'

Francis rubbed his hands with pleasure and kissed her at once, satisfaction even in the feel of him. 'Sweeting, you ought to take care. My mother died in childbirth.'

'Well, mine did not,' retorted Mary, somewhat nettled. 'It was only after birth that Joan's children sickened.'

'Because they lived in a pest-hole and scavenged scraps. You will eat well, I promise. Even if I must poach from Lord Scovell himself, though I daresay Ockham will be easier to raid for some time yet.'

'I must remember to thank Richard. I would have been displeased by talk of poaching and pest-holes only, if he hadn't first forced – '

'You know I love you, and need no force to say it. It's just that I'm handier with axe and bellows than – than – '

'You're floundering deeper in the mire.' Mary's eyes were dancing. 'Than wasting breath on a wench who is already far too vain, I expect you meant to say.'

'I expect I did. Ah Mary, lovedy, I also meant what else I said. Take care, for truly I would not know how to live without you.

Mary's pains came on her as Francis was preparing for the first burn of his own iron. He did not yet have the furnace he craved, with a force-draught produced by water-driven bellows, but had to rely instead on methods which Brac of the hill people would not have found too unfamiliar. 'It isn't that I don't mean to have one of the new furnaces,' he said again and again to Mary. 'I will, and soon. But I have to bake bricks and dig a great deal of clay, spend months of work to build it even after I have both. The trouble is we need iron now, so I can make my forgeman's tools and because we'd never last another winter without wares to sell.'

So he piled sticks and ore in what looked like a huge bee-swarm on the ground, each spadeful of ore chosen or rejected after careful consideration. This first burn must be right, both as an omen for the future and because from it would come the massive hammer-head for his forge, the tongs and rakes, ladles and hand-hammers he had to have before opening Edenham for trade. After ten months of punishing work, though they still lived in a leaking hut, the water wheel was made and hung, the timber gearing cut and the mill pond dug, two hearths build and some precious charcoal made and stored under cover. Another month and, God willing, the wheel would cease to chatter idly and Edenham resound again to harnessed power.

When he had built his bloomery heap to his liking, carefully Francis struck a spark and blew until it glowed. 'You do it, lovedy.'

Mary knelt clumsily, thinking, I must not spoil this for him. She had been pretending for most of the day that her pains had not begun; now they were spacing closer together and she must tell him as soon as his fire was lit. 'Pray for us Richard.'

'In the name of Christ,' he said at once. 'Lord, we beg thy blessing on this mill of Edenham and the craft which will be done here. We also entreat your mercy for the men labouring at its fires down the years to come.'

Mary spilled glowing tinder on a wick woven out of grass. Flame flared briefly, died, burned steadily as the three of them blew on it. Like a glowing serpent, the fire crawled down the wick and disappeared into the brushwood, ore and charcoal pile.

Francis sighed with relief. 'Down at Park Forge, the ironmaster used to make us take the whole stack apart if the wick failed. Lay a second wick without driving out the devil who cursed the first, and though the fire may burn the iron will shatter when you try to work it. Or so he said.'

Still on her knees beside the stack, Mary let out a little moan, clenched her teeth on the next pain and saw the grass spin under her eyes when it came. 'I'm sorry' she kept saying as Francis carried her to their hut. I'm so sorry. I'm sure it won't come for a long time yet. Send for my mother, please. Then go back to your iron.'

He knelt beside her. 'Richard has run to fetch her.'

Mary held his hand, horned life a hoof from heavy labour ever since childhood. 'Leave me.'

'When Joan comes.'

But when Joan came, a long time later because the journey along the track from Furneth Green was difficult for her, Francis refused to allow her inside the hut. Dimly, Mary heard quarrelling voices but could make no sense of them.

Her pains were very bad by then. She had worked beside Francis through all of her pregnancy, giving little thought to the child beyond pleasure that she had proved so quickly fruitful. Ever since Mary could remember her mother had birthed children without fuss, there was nothing to it. Sometimes babes were even born in the furrow where their mothers worked. Usually it was the hazards of life rather than the birthing itself which killed nearly half these babes before they were out of swaddling clothes, but with a good husband who would poach if necessary to keep his family fed, Mary hoped her children would grow up straight and healthy. All anyone could do was hope, after all.

But, surprisingly quickly, this birthing began to outlast her strength. She crouched for a while, believing this would speed matters, and shouted at Francis to leave her alone when he came to see how she fared. Soon, she could crouch no longer, and lay while sweat poured off her heaving body.

'My mother!' she gasped next time Francis's face swam against the roof. 'For the love of God, where is she? She knows how to bring out children swiftly.'

'She is too sick to tend you. Richard has gone for Goodwife By The Wood instead. Courage, lovely. She will be here soon.'

'She cannot . . . be too sick . . . to come. I heard her.'

But he closed his lips and shook his head. Then the next pain wiped everything else from her senses. When Goodwife By The Wood arrived at last, Mary had begun to scream; she bit off her screams, but couldn't help wailing instead, tossing on dry bracken bedding.

'For the love of God,' she heard Francis say. 'The child refuses to be born. Ask what you will, and I'll pay somehow if only you can bring it out.'

Goody By The Wood earned food or groats by saying spells over difficult birthings, but her tricks were instinctive. All she knew was when to soothe and how to hold, the twist which could ease an infant into daylight. She surveyed Mary now, hands on her hips. 'She'll birth this one by herself or not at all.'

'She can't! Get down and use your skills, woman,' said Francis between his teeth.

'I haven't any skill for this.' She groped between Mary's writhing thighs. 'A boy, caught fast astraddle. Such can never be birthed while the woman stays alive to grip it tight. Afterwards, if I rip her quickly, perhaps the child might live.'

At their feet Mary thrashed and moaned, stared up at Francis with dulled eyes. 'Joan.'

Goody By The Wood cackled. 'Aye, Joan the Harlot has birthed more children than any in Furneth Green. Let her try to turn the brat if she dares. Me, I know when botched fumblings are likely to go astray, and end in the fumbler being called a witch.'

'Joan has a pox, leprosy perhaps by the look of her. She might birth the child, but –' Francis felt half demented by indecision. When Joan had reeled into the clearing, Mary's mother or no, he had recoiled instinctively from letting her handle either Mary or their child. The woman was dying and stank of the sores gnawing flesh from her bones, yet she had come a mile and a half in the heat of the day to tend her daughter, and he'd had to tie her like a mad dog to keep her away from Mary's side. Which was worse though, to let Mary die in agony now, or allow Joan to try and help this useless hag and wait for the first sore to break on Mary's body afterwards? A risk made even more unacceptable by his private conviction that Joan was too far gone to remember such skills as she might once have possessed.

'I can't let her near!' Francis scrubbed at his face with trembling hands. 'For Christ's sake do what you can.'

The old woman pulled out a knife, of the kind used for gutting rabbits. 'If I have your word on it, master. So start digging the grave and when the death rattle starts I'll cut your son out for you.'

Francis seized her arm and hauled her anyhow out of the door. 'Dig your own grave, if that's all your thought! Richard. Fetch me water and drive this hag away.' He turned back into the hut and knelt again beside Mary. She grabbed instantly at his hand, wringing it until the bones crackled. Her labouring body had temporarily shaken off exhaustion, but could not endure much more of this.

Richard stumbled into the hut, slopping water from a leather bucket, took one look at the tangled hair, wild eyes and bloodied anguish which was nearly all that remained of Mary, and bolted out again.

Francis plunged his face into the cold brook water, forcing calm out of the shock of it, scrubbed his hands first in water and then goose-grease as shepherds did before a night's lambing.

'Jesus help me,' he said clearly. Jesus remember, too, how long it was since as a boy he had helped at lambing time. Nor were men welcome at birthings in Furneth. They brought ill luck and were a clutter underfoot, banished to the Black Bear as soon as women's pains began. But he was alone at Edenham save for a poxed harlot, a ghoul and a squeamish boy; by the time he sent for some other woman with a rudiment of skill, it might be too late.

Women couldn't be so different from ewes foundering with a rump-end lamb, surely.

'Lie still if you can, sweeting,' he said, wishing Richard was there to hold her. Careful, very careful now. Arm thrust in, hand groping for the hold and turn he had to make.

But she couldn't stay still; heard nothing, knew nothing now. So think of lambs and too hastily tapped iron, both brought to ruin by clumsy haste. Sense how to slide his fingers past the scrawny feel of unborn bones to the delicate touch he needed, which somehow would lift and then move an infant who was caught in a womb like a closing trap.

And so, as the moon rose above the forest edge, Mary was delivered of her son at last. By then she had lapsed into a drained white stillness which was not far from death. Deliberately, Francis bound the cord and cut it, wrapped the child and left it to yell in a corner; it sounded lusty, and he daren't let Mary sleep yet.

'What is it?' she whispered when he lifted her. 'Does it live? Is it all right?'

'Aye, a fine lad. I wonder you haven't complained already about him yelling. Our peace is quite cut up. Eat, dearling.'

Obediently, she made a show of eating, was forced by him to drink both broth and ale, and when the child quieted he laid it against her cheek. She turned her head as she heard the beat of a different heart, and smiling, drowsed at last.

It was night when Mary woke and put her hand to her flat belly. Almost immediately the bundle beside her stirred too, and she felt a hungry mouth nuzzling in search of milk. She fumbled to bare her breast, lay blissful in the dark as she and her son settled together where they belonged. Surely there could be no feeling in the world to compare with the tug of a firstborn at the breast. 'Francis?' she said softly.

Bracken crackled. 'How are you, wife?'

'Well, is not our son beautiful?'

She felt him grunt in amusement. 'You haven't seen him yet.'

But she was asleep again, the day she had endured no more than a dream in her mind.

Francis did not forget so easily, although his charcoal bloomery had continued to burn without his attention, which he considered a good omen for Edenham Forge. He made Mary sit through the hot days of summer, polishing paddles for the water wheel, the first time in her life when she felt herself to be idle. She even dozed occasionally and woke feeling alarmed, so strange a feeling was it to sleep in daylight. The colour returned to her face as one sunny day followed another, and Richard ceased quite so obviously to avoid her.

'What is the matter with him?' she asked Francis one day, while watching him rake ash from his charcoal heap. 'Even in a monastery he must have seen women with babes at the breast.'

'You think so? Ockham was kept more strictly after Abbot Rainer.' Francis squatted on his haunches. Tomorrow I shall open the stack and discover whether we have fired good iron, or not.'

'Then what comes next? But you haven't answered what I said, or didn't you mean to?'

'Then I work the pig iron into the tools and wares I need; and no, I didn't mean to.'

Mary threw the daisy chain she was making at him, so it lodged over one ear. 'Wretch, Why not?'

'I think the quicker that particular birthing is forgotten, the better.'

She stood in one lithe movement and came over to link her hands around his shoulders. 'Richard saw how I was, I suppose. He must have. Well, if he really means to be a monk, a different experience won't have harmed him. But, Francis – it was you, wasn't it?'

'What was me?'

'I thought Goody By The Wood, but now I remember . . . things. You birthed Nicholas and saved us both.'

He turned, within her hands. 'Saved myself as well. You don't mind?'

'I don't wish to face God's judgement yet,' she answered dryly.

He hesitated, his eyes on baby Nicholas sleeping in the shade. There are some mutterings in Furneth.'

'Let them mutter! Does Nick look ill-omened?'

He shook his head, although not immune to apprehensive dread himself. All men who worked in iron were superstitious, kept countless customs to ensure their work was good. 'Poctor is back,' he said at last.

'No! What of the others?'

'Set loose after a flogging. As a cleric Poctor escaped with a fine, paid by his bishop. He has brought an oath back with him which every grown male must swear, which says the king is now head of the Church.'

Mary laughed. 'King Harry must possess a fine sense of humour to give Poctor such a task!' She kissed Francis passionately, as she never had when new-wed, for fear he would think her a harlot. 'I am well again, and now your iron is cooked there is no more excuse for you to leave me alone at nights.'

'You must be churched first. By Poctor.'

Mary wrinkled her nose. In her mother's hut the rituals which demanded that after childbirth a woman must be purified before sleeping with a man again, had been a matter for derision. 'Well, I suppose he will not dare refuse to carry out his duties for a while. Francis, I'm all right. It won't happen again. Nick took his own way into the world but next time I shall birth like any woman would. You can't sleep apart from me for the rest of your life.'

'Not if I'm to keep my senses,' he agreed. Yet there remained that odd reluctance, as if he knew they had struck a mine of bad ore, from which no good would come.

And as if to prove that this feeling was a no iron-forger's fancy, their first great quarrel flared next day, as he raked the iron pig from the opened remnants of his fire.

'Bid farewell to forest solitude,' he said, fingering it. 'This is good metal and from now until the end of our lives, Edenham will never be silent again.'

'I shall grow so used to it that silence will seem strange. Francis, I have just fed Nicholas, will you keep an eye to him while you hammer? I mustn't delay any longer going to see my mother, when you said she was too sick to tend me.'

'No,' he said harshly. 'I forbid you, Mary. You are not to visit her again.

She stared at him, dumbstruck. 'Of course I must! Francis, you knew what my mother was when you wed me. You can't prevent me from tending her when she's sick. I ought to have gone days ago.'

He struck cooled iron irritably, the clang of it high and clear. 'She is poxed. I will not have you or my son go the same way.'

Mary paled, the pox a name for all manner of foul infections. 'She is sick and worn out. In the name of the God you pray to, you can't refuse to let me show her mercy now. No matter what her ailment.'

'I can. I do, though I fry in Hell for it. I mean what I say, Mary, and shall enforce my will.'

'How?' She demanded angrily.

'You spoke of the God I pray to. What of the oath you swore to obey me all your life?'

'Francis, please. I have to go.' She met his eyes squarely. 'Though I fry in Hell for it.'

'You mistake me. That is my burden for forcing you to obey me. If you should go despite my wish, then shall I take Nicholas to a wet nurse that same day, and not tell you where he is.'

'You wouldn't dare. Children die with wet nurses because no one watches over them.'

'Children die from poxed mothers, or live to scream for mercy.' He locked his hands together in a gesture of determination. No trace now of the passionate lover or the eager craftsman Mary knew. 'So forget your conscience and lay any sin on mine. You will not see your mother alive again.'

Mary was never quite able to accept this. Although she did not go to see Joan because she knew Francis meant what he said, her will held against his while she used wiles, arguments and threats to wear down his resolution. Though reluctantly churched by Poctor she refused to lie with her husband, annoyed to discover that she found this quite as hard as he. Nothing made any difference. Francis did not force her and pretended infuriating deafness when she railed at him; he hammered iron until she wondered he did not drop from exhaustion, and slept outside their hut although the season had turned wet and cold.

After four weeks Mary had to face the fact that either she gave way, or such bitterness would enter their marriage that no matter what happened, they would never be happy together again. Then she wondered whether they would be happy anyway, because Francis's brother Robert came before she could bring herself to speak, and asked whether she knew that her mother had died the day before. 'Though folk say it could have been two or even three days ago,' he added spitefully. 'The stink in her hut being so bad that even her brats had run off.'

Mary scarcely heard, beyond the bald fact of Joan's death. Too late, too late. Nothing she did now would ease her mother's end, alone in a reeking hovel.

Long afterwards Francis came where she sat on a tree-trunk near the brook. He did not speak but stood quietly in moonlight where she could see him.

'How does frying in hellfire feel?' she asked.

'It lives very easily up to its repute.'

Impulsively she put out her hand. 'I don't know who was right.'

He held her fingers tightly. 'Neither. Both. We shall both suffer for it, I don't doubt'

But after that it seemed as if their lode held good ore after all. Mary bore eight more children without great difficulty and only three of them subsequently died, leaving six altogether to grow into adulthood: Nicolas, James, May, Sally, Bess and Edward, this last named in honour of King Harry's son.

Edenham Forge prospered under Francis's industry, his knack with iron, and enthusiasm for the new ideas which were overtaking the Wealden craft. For two thousand years men had used much the same methods without feeling any need to change: layering charcoal and ore together, then using goatskin bellows to produce sufficient draught to fuse earth into small amounts of impure but toughened iron. Now this was not enough. Iron was needed in quantity and men were prepared to pay good prices for it, especially the royal armourers if the quality was sufficiently good for weaponry. At first any change only seemed to make the metal more brittle, until men like Francis Wyse who loved and lived their craft set out to improve this situation if they could. For some years, Edenham lagged behind larger ironworks whose masters possessed the capital to experiment, like the one set up with London money among the abandoned buildings of Ockham. Lord Scovell, too, at Park Forge, spent large sums in discovering how to smelt metal of the quality needed.

In those early years, although he scrimped every coin he could, Francis produced only low-grade bloomery iron. But he bought new blast-furnace iron from others, learned how to work it and never stopped planning for the day when he possessed a furnace of his own. This time came ten years after Edenham's water wheel first tripped a hammer in his forge. By then two more ponds were dammed below the mill, a leat and sluice dug, bricks baked, clay puddled, staging built for feeding the furnaces from above during the several weeks of their burn.

'Two furnaces,' Francis said then. 'That's what we need, and to fire them at different times, since after each firing the bricks have to be raked down.'

'You've waited ten years for one,' said Mary. 'How about sparing a few coins for a pair of new breeches before you build a second?'

He laughed, hands on his hips, head thrown back. He was as excited as a boy, far more so indeed than Nicholas, who never became excited over anything, while the other children who had been born by then tumbled unheeding in the dust. 'Breeches can wait so long as we've leather for a patch. Although I shall build you a fine house very soon, I swear.' He yelled at a workman plastering clay and ran to swing himself up on tied-branch scaffolding, his hands shaping what he wanted before he had climbed a dozen steps.

As much as ten loads of charcoal were needed to fire some furnaces, and Francis had built himself a large one: at twenty-five feet high nearly the tallest in the Weald. Charcoal alone was an enormous expense at three shillings the load, and once Edenham's furnace was fired a continuous supply must be ready at hand, and burned ore too; then there would be wages for woodcutters and charcoal-burners, for ox-drovers, forgemen, colliers, firers and smiths. At first Mary had been alarmed by the idea of Edenham turned into a camp for swarms of men, all shouting and quarrelling amongst themselves, their huts clinging like mould to the edges of the clearing. But Francis would never be happy until he was a master with his own furnace, and ultimately she became infected by his excitement. Just hammering metal did become a little dull. Nor could she avoid a secret pride when amongst their workmen were the sons of men for whom she had slaved at a ha'penny a day: Davey Laffam was a forgeman, one of the Bywoods carted charcoal, even Mark and Robert Wyse contracted to haul timber and made everyone uncomfortable by a continuous hail of criticism. The truth was, when Francis began hiring extra labour half the men of Furneth Green came begging for work. Sheep needed only a shepherd and a boy, where two dozen men and women had ploughed and reaped and gleaned before. In consequence, most of the people inhabiting the ridge were, for the first time ever, poorer than they had been a hundred years before.

The furnace was a disappointment at first. Mary expected it to shake and glow with heat, instead it leisurely puffed smoke while a great many men ran about trying to keep it fed. 'You wait until it's tapped,' promised Francis. 'I remember the first tap I saw at Park Forge, I thought Hell itself had opened at my feet.' And as he said it his eyes shifted, for neither he nor Mary ever quite forgot the sin he took on his soul when Joan Parlben died.

'I wish Richard would come to see us again,' said Mary hastily.

'He'll be a parson somewhere by now, providing his conscience isn't too tender.'

'I'm sure it would be, somehow,' said Mary musingly. 'I can't see Richard serving God with less than his whole heart, can you? And for him that always meant becoming a monk.'

In Furneth Green people understood the changes following Ockham's fall even less than they had understood why King Harry turned out the monks, but upheavals had come thick and fast. When Richard Mercer eventually set out for Canterbury he discovered that all monasteries, including Holy Thomas's shrine, were seized by the king, his only remaining chance of a religious life that of studying for the parish priesthood. After much soul-searching this he decided to do, only to be offered the oath which Poctor had brought to Furneth Green, in which he must swear that the king was head of the church, the pope a mere bishop of Rome. He came back for a while to Edenham then, very troubled in his mind, but eventually wandered off again. Since then, eight years before, they had heard nothing. The child-king, Edward, became head of the Church when his father died, and unless Richard could accept this royal supremacy into his faith, then he was wandering footloose still.

Francis tapped the first iron from his furnace five days after it was lit. Mary found herself leaping from foot to foot with excitement as figures scurried about the furnace, the clatter of a second water wheel which drove its bellows echoing her impatience. 'It's only iron like you've seen in the forge a hundred times,' said Nicholas, standing very straight and cool beside her

'It's the first tap out of a furnace your father has dreamed of building ever since he was apprenticed at Park Forge,' snapped Mary. She loved her eldest son, but found his east-wind temperament difficult to grasp.

Nicholas sniffed. He felt excited too, but did not believe in showing weakness.

At that moment the iron was tapped from the furnace with an incandescent burst which lit eager faces, air, grass and trees. A boom like nothing Mary had ever heard; a brilliantly glowing and curving hiss, and there in the trough dug out for it lay a scarlet glow, fading while she watched to crimson, purple and into darkness again. Only the furnace top still reflected fire against a windy night-time sky, touching light on upturned excited faces and fists thumping backs in triumph.

'Well, were you disappointed?' demanded Francis out of the dark, and he hugged her, lifting her feet off the ground.

'Nay, never! I never guessed it would be like – like struck lightning on a tree.' Mary kissed him enthusiastically. 'How long, must we wait before we see it again?'

'Three days, a week perhaps. An ironmaster whistles into the wind and fingers his furnace saying "No, not now." Eh, Nick? Soon the two of us will argue over which moment is the best. Perhaps this time I should have waited until tomorrow, but it's a balance, see? Between running off the most iron you can, yet not leaving it too long.'

'What happens if you do? asked Nicholas.

'One of two things. The furnace clinkers so the burn must be finished too soon, or the iron runs wild. Into pigs mixed with slag perhaps, or bursting the furnace open. I remember one splitting without warning at Park Forge, and two men died.'

'For heaven's sake, tap it off twice as often as you must,' said Mary, alarmed.

'We couldn't do that.' Nicholas kicked his toe in dust. 'Father said it cost half a load of charcoal each time you tap.'

Francis laughed and set Mary on her feet again. 'There speaks the man who will force Edenham to prosper.'

'Promise me, Francis,' said Mary fiercely. 'You won't take chances just to save a few scraps of charcoal.'

'Nay, it's a bad ironmaster who risks a wild tap, and I shall always be ironmaster first and profit-monger second.' He hurried off again.

Nine months exactly after that celebratory night, bonny bouncing

Bess was born, a joyful child from the first day she lay in her crib. She never ailed nor did her bones break when she fell out of trees; she wasn't beautiful, being freckled and red-haired – Mary said ruefully that a more suspicious man than Francis might have doubted his fatherhood – but possessed the happy knack of drawing the best out of anyone she met. She thought the world a splendid, exciting, kindly place, and so to her it was, as if a conspiracy existed to keep her innocence untouched.

Father Poctor baptized her, and though he scowled when Francis paid his fee, afterwards both parents agreed with awe that even he had very nearly clucked at Bess, smiling sunny-faced in his arms. Poctor died soon after, and it was as if an old sore closed. Always his animosity had followed everything they did; he demanded double fees for churchings and burials, daring Francis to complain, exacted every oath that the twists and turns of royal policy demanded of King Harry's subjects during those difficult years, though only those suspected of disloyalty normally had to take them. Fortunately, though a stubborn man, Francis had little interest in King Harry's policies or wives, and was temperamentally inclined towards the new teachings. Like Mary, he judged matters from what he knew himself, and because he detested Poctor he considered that the king was most likely right to quarrel with well-fattened priests. It also stood to reason that in any dispute English King Harry must be right and a foreign pope wrong.

So he swore what he was asked, though his rage at being made to kneel under Poctor's spite sometimes glowed as molten as his iron, and remained sufficiently absorbed in his own affairs that it was no great burden to keep out of Furneth Green, where Poctor yelled across the street if he saw him, that heretic and Antichrist was come.

Now Poctor was dead, and soon afterwards King Harry too. Oddly enough, though Poctor's death was an unqualified relief, it was the king's which made the most immediate impact. For as long as anyone could remember, Henry Tudor had been a force on the horizon of their lives; incomprehensible, dangerous, but reassuring all the same. They had even seen him once. Not long after Ockham was shut up (and, incidentally, not long after he had beheaded Lord Scovell's brother, who in his cups had called his monarch 'a brute beast') His Majesty invited himself to Riffield Castle where for a week his court drank, ate and danced their way through the Scovell rents, thus echoing Norman William's way with the founder of their line. And while he stayed there, one day he rode to view his new property of Ockham. Mary, Francis and Nicholas stood by the track above Edenham as he passed seeing only a great bulk under a wet red cape, head turning constantly, missing nothing. He nodded graciously to loyal subjects as he passed, but what Mary and Francis remembered afterwards was a sense of size and power. Nicholas, most strangely for so young a child, was different. He remembered calculation, which he admired. 'Didn't you see Lord Scovell?' he demanded afterwards. 'He was humbled, you could see it from how he rode.'

Mary stared at her son, astonished. All her life the Scovells had been infinitely great and distant, symbols around which the honour of the Weald gathered. 'What a foolish thing to say, when the king himself visits Riffield Castle.'

Nicholas shrugged. One of his more irritating characteristics was that he seldom argued. He was merely right, and made sure that everyone realized it.

Francis said nothing, but thought about what his son had said. Of course Nicholas had seen the obvious. He himself would have felt humbled into dust if he had been forced to welcome to his hearth any man, king or no, who had killed his brother. And he did not love his brothers, whilst the Scovells were said to be a tight-knit kin.

Francis sighed, and looked to where Nick was meticulously shaping sand to take molten iron, finicking work at which he was extremely good. One would have supposed that holding one's firstborn while he was still in the womb would have set some special bond between them, but the reverse was true. Of all his children, Francis tried hardest with Nicholas and understood him least.

Once Poctor was safely buried, Mary was delighted by her new freedom to visit Furneth Green whenever she wished. She was constantly busy at bustling Edenham, but had missed the relaxation of market day, the chance to stand on doorsteps to share in the gossip of her birthplace. Above all she'd missed the half-guilty pleasures of flaunting her fine marriage. Although she still found it more comfortable to walk barefoot she always put on shoes before she reached the village, flipped her kerchief straight and walked with conscious pride, so everyone could see how virtuous and well-fed she was. This pleasure never palled. She knew everyone in Furneth Green believed Francis had wedded scum; well, she had shown them to be mistaken. 'Good day to you, Goodwife Wyse, and is your second furnace built?' Mother Laffam would say as if she didn't remember Mary sweeping her stable floor. 'Tell me, Mary, what do you give dear Bess to keep her so healthy while I have buried all seven of my children?' That was arrogant Dady Brown, born Fawkner, who had known nothing but ill fortune since she married a brute of a husband, recently and happily dead, leaving her the last descendant of Norman Robert. Just think of a Fawkner coming to Joan Parlben's daughter for advice! And the Laffams of Corndown too, envying the twenty-eight men Francis now employed! Mary hugged her joy like a miser after every market day, although she did try – but not very hard – to stop herself from rejoicing too openly in her fortune.

Perhaps the walk to Furneth every Tuesday was the best time of all, with Bess hoppity-skippity by her side, other figures joining the track from field path and farm so the two of them could giggle together after a glance to see whether their neighbours looked sour or merry. Beddings and betrothals, quarrels and bargainings, all flourished from one market day to the next, with the six days between for speculation to flourish.

'There's John Ellis with his beard close-trimmed again,' shrilled Bess. I do believe he still has hopes of Widow Brown!'

'Hush,' hissed Mary, for the child only repeated what she herself had said the previous week.

'He's wearing fresh linen too, and he's gen'rally very *fusty*.' Bess poked her freckled nose in the air and danced so her stiff skirts swirled. Her mother insisted on clean linen and washed faces for market day.

Mary laughed, unable to resist the temptation posed by a lively daughter as amused as she by the other folks' affairs. All the Parlbens were nosy, gathering and telling tales for the joy of it. 'An orange from the pedlar if you're right, Miss Cleversticks. Though I'm sure I shouldn't encourage you to make fun of your elders.'

'I don't need 'couragement,' Bess trotted a few paces to keep up. 'But how will we know if I earned the norange?'

Mary considered. 'You see that basket of eggs Master Ellis carries? If he goes first to sell them, you have lost.'

'Course he'd go first to market when he's eggs to sell!'

'Wait and see,' answered Mary, smiling.

Bess darted off, unable to wait, and screamed delightedly when Farmer Ellis turned right for Fawkners instead of left to the market. 'A norange! I earned a norange!'

Ellis shook his fist at the pair of them, aware of a joke he did not share. He didn't answer Mary's greeting and plunged off down the street to Fawkners: its ditch and palisade vanished now except that barn, byres and house were spaced around three sides out of four so the shape remained, its purpose long forgotten.

'He's nawful bad-tempered,' said Bess, wide-eyed.

'So would you be if little girls poked fun at you,' answered Mary guiltily; at heart she, too, was an urchin enjoying such pleasures as the world threw at her feet.

'How did you *know* he'd go to Fawkners first?'

'A lifetime spent detesting women like Widow Brown,' said Mary ruefully. 'And don't you dare tell anyone I said that.'

'I won't,' said Bess obligingly. 'She is horrid, isn't she?'

'Aye, and likely to take her wash-paddle to any man courting her, who sold eggs or anything else before coming to greet her. Now you stay here and don't move while I go up to see your grandfather.'

Old Simeon was dying and in no state for a little maid to see, in fact he became agitated when anyone came close. Only Mary was different; perhaps because she was a harlot's daughter and presumed to be used to foulness.

He even seemed cheered by her visits although he prayed each day that he might die.

''Twon't be long now,' he said the moment Mary entered. 'Eh, but you look comely, lass.'

'Not so long ago you'd have called my looks wanton,' retorted Mary. Breath gagged in her throat from the stench of his room, sores and bones all that was left of Simeon Wyse.

He chortled feebly. 'I told Francis he was a fool to wed thee, but I were wrong, weren't I, lass?'

Mary sat on fouled bed-covering. 'Aye, you were.'

There was a long silence, while Simeon seemed to sleep and she wondered how to avoid puking.

'You're better than that sour wife of Mark's, nor the psalm-gabbler Robert wed.' His eyes flicked open.

'Can't you think of a better compliment than that?' enquired Mary, honey-sweet.

'You're too vain already, so I'll leave 'ee to think 'em up for yourself.' A hand like a hook clutched her sleeve. 'Watch out for the new priest. 'Tis said he has some tale of how two of his new flock were spawned by the Devil. Meaning you and Francis.'

'Poctor made mischief, to prevent his grudge from dying with him? Mary's heart plummeted.

'Or some pest-ridden bishop can't let the matters rest. While King Harry reigned and Francis took his oaths, a priest like Poctor could only drip poison to anyone who'd listen. Now there'll be more changes coming, and nobbut a boy on the throne.'

'It's all so long ago,' said Mary, wringing her hands. 'Nearly seventeen years since Francis fired Poctor's roof.'

Simeon sank back, eyes closed. 'Hate festers with the years and priests crack their brains with thinking, having naught else to do. Now this new fellow's here. Looks like a slug they say, and trails slime with his tongue. So watch how you tread, and make Francis do whatever he's told.'

'You may be sure I shall. Why, if I hadn't begged him to pay the double fees Poctor asked, he'd have been taken up for something years ago.'

'Good lass. But there's an iron streak in Francis if he's pushed too hard.'

'An iron man through and through,' said Mary, smiling. 'Who also softens in the fires I light for him. Don't worry, I never believed in causing trouble through pig-headed pride.'

By the time she left, Simeon seemed calmer, as if he had endured this last week only to warn her of approaching danger. Mary knew she wouldn't see him alive again and felt no regret; only a rack-master could wish more life for Simeon Wyse.

Furneth market was held on well-trodden ground near Wyse's, a much smaller space than the fairplace of a hundred years before. This was partly because sheep were folded on every scrap of ground, and partly because as the roads became safer, more people travelled to larger gatherings at Riffield or Tonbridge. Even so, Furneth weekly market bustled as never before, now a growing population found work in the new iron industry instead of being driven away by sheep. Mary drifted pleasurably in the throng, making up her mind how to spend her pence to best advantage. Cheese was one of the treats she liked to bring home from market; especially when she remembered yearning as a child for Goody Bellwasher's mouth-watering confections, made from milk stolen from Wyses' nursing ewes.

'Noise nowadays is money, so I say,' the old woman observed as Mary hovered over the choice of creamy cheeses pounded with herbs. 'I get worried if them hammers stop for more than a breath.'

'It's all very well for you listening to them here, but another matter altogether when hammers shake the ground you lie on,' retorted Mary.

'Nay, each clang is bread in a belly. We hear your man's furnace blow clear from Edenham, and Ockham furnace too.'

'We're building a second,' said Mary proudly.

'And flatting another floor for casting slabs,' piped up Bess. 'I digged sand out of the brook with Nick.'

'Aye, sweetling.' Goody Bellwasher popped some cheese into Bess's ready paw. 'My Susan's boy, Jem, he works for Master Wyse and tell us what's a –doing at Edenham.'

Bess clapped her hands. 'Jem? He made me a doll out of furnace clay. She had knees and a belly and – and *everything*!'

That's Jem all over, he never did know when to stop,' said the woman, chuckling. 'I hope Master Wyse weren't displeased, for he's clever is Jem, and wishful to be hired for better work than plastering furnaces. Did you hear what they're calling Furneth Green?'

Mary shook her head, wondering how to stop such a flood of talk without seeming too lofty towards former equals.

'Furnace Green! Now what do you think of that, eh?'

'I like it,' said Bess positively.

Mary nodded, pride glowing like tinder in forced draught. How splendid that the very name of their birth-place should be changed by what her generation did. Park Forge; Edenham; Ockham. Another furnace she had seen glowing away to the south called Brookside; a new forge opening soon by the track to Riffield. Surely it was fitting that the very name of Furneth Green should change. Yet I'm glad it isn't too much changed, she also thought. This is where I was born before so many hammerings began; a place of more than iron and fire.

Bess vanished while Mary was packing eggs into moss and she sighed, knowing exactly where the minx had gone. Bess was drawn to water as if born a duckling, and while this was turned to good account at Edenham where she was given such tasks as digging sand from the brook, Mary reluctantly beat her when she ran off to paddle in Furneth's foetid pool.

But punishment was no deterrent, and Mary usually kept a close eye on Bess once the attractions of market palled. Still, on such a radiant day you couldn't really blame the child for wanting to slither bare-toed through mud before the hot walk home. How easy always to find excuses for Bess.

The pool still held water through the longest drought, nearly seven hundred years after Edred used the little people's skills to seal it. Otherwise he would not have recognized the place where he and Roda laboured to re-establish Ferenthe. With the coming of the sheep, the village's cattle had become concentrated in the common area around the pool; close by were folds for oxen and enclosures for messy butcherings, while fowl picked in and out of brushwood hovels where, as in Alice's day, the poorest folk still lived. This part of the village was an evil-smelling swamp in winter and fly-ridden in summer, although the inhabitants continued to rely on the pool for their drinking water.

When Tinker Brown married Fawkner's daughter he had ended the old custom of allowing anyone to use Brother Theobald's well in Fawkner's farmyard, showing a crumbling vellum which he said proved that whoever owned Fawkners was lord of the manor of Ferenthe, now Furneth Green. This was bad enough, but the Browns made themselves hated when they hired a clerk to read their deed, because he made out that rent was owed him by most other people living on the ridge.

'To Dady Brown's ancestors perhaps,' scoffed Fatlips Laffam in the Black Bear. 'Her being born a Fawkner, but that weasel Brown was born little better than an outlaw in the forest.'

The uncomfortable fact remained that when Tinker Brown married Dady Fawkner, he became possessed of a clerk-attested deed which called him lord of the manor of Ferenthe. Everyone was glad when he died, but disconcerted afresh when Widow Brown began demanding rents for herself. No wonder John Ellis thinks her a widow worth courting, thought Mary. Thank heaven we're our own masters out at Edenham. A priest looking for trouble was bad enough, without also suffering rogues who called themselves lords of the manor.

She found Bess frolicking thigh-deep in the pool with half a dozen other brats, her skirts hauled high. Which hadn't prevented them from becoming extremely wet.

'The boys here are so much more fun than Nick, who always pulls his mouth down so, and says junketings waste time,' explained Bess, unabashed when Mary spanked her soundly.

'Nick must be – . ' Mary counted on her fingers. 'Fifteen summers old, I suppose. Of course his time is taken up by working for his father. James, too. Try Sally or May instead.'

'They always blab about dirt!' said Bess scornfully.

'It's what I complain of, too.' Mary shook her, hard. 'Bess, I shan't tell you again. Paddle in our brook if you must, but not in this kennel of a pool, nor play with children who as like as not are sickening for some flux.'

'They're Jem Bellwashwer's kin, and I like him better than anyone else. It would be base not to greet them, even if you beat me for it afterwards.' Bess spoke in a small stiff voice, but Mary knew argument was at an end. Like Francis, Bess was unyielding once her mind was set.

'Greet them courteously then, but keep away from the pool,' she temporized.

Bess's grubby hand slipped into hers. 'Our brook's mud is much nicer mud, anyway. Ooh, look! There's the new priest! Do you know, he's *married*.'

'Married? No. Not a priest. He couldn't be.' 'He is, and has four horrid children. He couldn't have even horrid ones, could he, unless he was wed?'

Mary swallowed, remembering Poctor's visits to her mother. Vaguely, she remembered a half-brother, long ago apprenticed to a travelling wool-comber, whom Joan had believed to be his son.

A distant double boom drifted on the wind from the direction of Riffield, and everyone stopped mid-word to listen. In the hush you could hear skylarks calling above the ridge, before everyone began talking again.

'That wasn't a forge-noise.' Bess had known which noise meant what since before she could talk.

Mary picked up her market basket. 'Home we go, and then down with you to the brook to wash. There's gossip here today about how Lord Scovell has hired a gunsmith for Park Forge and begun to cast cannon. He has set aside a field where his smiths may fire the guns they make to see if they throw true, and half Riffield goes to watch. Will Carpenter says it's a tremendous sight. If the gun doesn't burst, it throws a ball from Riffield to Park Forge Wood.'

'Shall we cast cannon? Will we, do you think? Surely Father won't go on making dull slabs when he could be making guns?'

Mary did not think so either, in fact when word that Lord Scovell was expanding his ironworks drifted to Edenham she had seen a gleam in Francis's eyes which only some new notion about iron could light.

'Nick would like it,' Bess was saying buoyantly. Although she railed at him for being fusty, it was always Nick and not the easy-going James she thought of first. 'Cannon! Well, that would be something! Can I light what makes it go bang?'

'No,' said Mary instantly, and loud enough for everyone within hearing turned to grin. One of them was the new priest, only he wasn't grinning.

He had a fleshy face and pursed pink lips, a clay-dab nose below the short-sighted frown between his eyes. 'And whom may you be, mistress?' he demanded, as if his cloth gave an instant right to pry.

Mary curtsied, determined not to cause offence. 'Mary Wyse, of Edenham Mill. And this is my daughter Bess.

'Is she instructed in her catechism?'

'Aye, sir.'

'What age are you, child?'

'I'm not 'xactly sure,' said Bess cautiously. 'I'm younger than Sally, May, James and Nick.'

'Are they instructed?'

'Yes.' Bess answered without hesitation.

'I did not see any of you in church last Sunday.'

'We walked to Ockham,' interposed Mary. Francis frequently had business with the ironmasters there, and combined bargainings with worship whenever word came that a hedge-priest was officiating in the chapel which alone remained roofed out of all Ockham's massive buildings.'

'Your duty is to attend your parish church! How else am I to know whether your soul is endangered by neglect?'

'Perhaps that is between our souls and God,' snapped Mary, forgetting her resolve not to antagonize this cawking crow.

The priest's eyes narrowed. 'Nay, mistress. I have power under a new Parliament act to make sure that everyone here is zealous in their faith. Do you deny the Bishop of Rome?'

'The pope?, Yes, of course.' Mary was relieved to discover the wind still blew the same way as before. You never knew with Parliament acts and kings, and if mattered had changed then she might find it hard to persuade Francis not to eat not only his previous oaths, but convictions firmly held against this dratted pope.

'Wyse. Which Wyse are you? Not wife to Francis Wyse?'

Mary curtsied, and pinched Bess's ear, who also curtsied very elegantly, keeping her eyes demurely lowered. Praise be, the child was quick. 'Aye, sir. And he the first in this parish to swear each oath the law required. Francis is a devout and godly man, mightily hot for the new teachings.'

Behind her, someone tittered. Everybody knew that Francis Wyse's thoughts were hottest of all for Mary and good iron.

The priest hesitated, eyes flickering to the faces gathered to listen to an exchange which promised good gossip during the week to come. 'I shall expect to see your words proven in his daily life. This parish has grown slack after years of rule by a priest infected by old errors. Wicked and heathenish, the bishop called Furneth; filled with people who opposed even King Henry's will.' His voice dropped as if the words alone risked hellfire. 'You tried to keep devil-monks at Ockham when the king in his piety shut it up! Christ have mercy on you, but before mercy cometh retribution. So am I called here, as a rod for your backs.' His head hunched forward as if to spit, until everyone looked at the dust rather than meet his gaze.

'He's dangerous,' said Mary soberly that night to Francis as they dipped stew from the pot.' 'Preece is his name, and he comes from somewhere distant in Kent. So no one knows any kin of his who might help us by offering soft words. There's only a wife and children as like to slugs as he.'

Francis frowned and jerked his head at the children, avidly listening. 'You promised my father we would walk carefully, nor have we cause to do otherwise. Let Parson Preece look to his concerns and we to ours. Cannon, for instance. What say you, Nick?'

'Jem Bellwasher has the touch to become a good mould-maker,' answered Nicholas judiciously.

'Jem? He's still learning his trade as a plasterer. I thought to hire men from Buxted, where they've made cannon for some years.'

'And pay blood for them, because of the name alone. Anyway, Buxted still casts how it did those years ago you spoke of, and where's the sense in that? At Riffield now, so Harry Bywood told me, they use a double hearth and moulds layered with dung as well as clay. If you know the mix and have the skill, then you may cast more detail than anyone has before.'

'Francis crumbled bread thoughtfully. 'I thought I'd dig pits and hang the moulds breech down, d'you see. We'd need a block and tackle, have to pack the pit with straw to hold the mould in place, but that way the iron would flow easier into each part. Then would we mould trunnions and ornaments separately, make a whole which equals the finest ever cast. Finer, one day.'

Mary laughed. 'I ought to have known. You've been planning for cannon this past six months or more.'

'Earth would be better than straw for packing.' As usual, Nicholas ignored anything not exactly to the point.

Francis laid his blackened forgeman's hands on the plank table as if the feel of timber helped to keep his temper checked, and answered Mary first. 'More than six months, sweeting. You know I always had a fancy to pour the best iron in the Weald, and cannon demand the best. Why should Buxted brag when Furneth Green has a taller furnace and purer ore?'

'Furnace Green they begin to call it now,' piped up Bess.

'Well, that at least is a change Buxted can't so easily make.' They all laughed except Nicholas, and Francis's mind roamed back to what the boy had said. Probably he was right. Again. God send him a touch of grace and humour with which to temper insufferable rightness. 'Earth would most likely be best, Nick, though the chill of it might cause the mould to crack as the melt pours in. Good cannon casting depends more on the mould than aught else, providing the iron is right.'

'And Edenham iron is best!' Bess bounced on her bench, and even Nick's face softened at such flying golden spirits.

'Aye, Edenham iron is best,' agreed Francis, smiling, and the very next day set Nicholas and James to digging their first cannon-pit.

It was difficult, unpleasant work. Because Francis planned to tap the furnace directly into a cannon-mould hung vertically in this pit, they had to dig close to the stream whose water must provide the power to drive the furnace bellows. The summer was dry and hot so both boys became caked with dust but even so, water seeped through the pit sides and oak struts had to be driven into place to prevent the walls from collapsing. Francis was too busy to help by day, but spent most of a night mending an old water wheel so it could provide a geared shaft for winding up dug earth to the surface, from where Sally, May and Bess shovelled it into osier baskets strapped on their backs. Sally and May hated such filthy work, being just old enough to shake out their skirts and rub brook water on their cheeks whenever a stranger came to the mill, leaving Bess to stagger under loads so heavy that she lost as much earth as she carried.

James worked steadily, a solid boy who saw and thought of little beyond whatever task he took in hand; Nicholas laboured passionately, hating the squalid hole in which he was imprisoned but tearing the earth bare-handed if necessary so he would be finished quicker. Several evenings later when the pit was nearly finished, he went to find Jem Bellwasher, who lived in a lean-to hut among the forgemen. Jem was probably of a similar age to Nicholas, but apart from a lean, tight face, he looked much younger. All the Bellwasher brood had to fight for nourishment from the day they were born, caught fevers easily, and coughed out their lungs into sodden bracken beds. The few who lived looked like Jem: scrawny, undersized and light-footed in a hostile world.

Nicholas found him cross-legged beside a fire, alone while his elders roistered with some woman. Stray women often slipped out of the woods at night, since forgemen were renowned both for lust and their free spending.

'Two more days should finish the pit,' said Nicholas, sitting beside him on the ground.

'T'master were talking of digging a new pond and setting up more furnaces downalong.'

'He's always talking of what next.' Nicholas approved of his father's ambition, in fact he loved and admired Francis deeply and was often distressed because they could not work easily together. He was also ashamed of these feelings and hid them carefully from sight.

'Young Bess,' said Jem abruptly. 'She's such a lass for loads, you should keep an eye on her. While the other two be squalling and complaining she is bent under an ox's burden.'

'Someone's got to tip each basket as the wheel winds it up. If Sal and May are so concerned to keep their aprons clean, then it has to be Bess.'

'So, swing up the baskets slower if it's the only way to spare her.'

Nicholas regarded him with amazement. 'Are you suggesting I work slower than I could, just to save Bess some work?'

'What difference would it make? A day longer digging a pit. But she's naught but a bitty maid staggering on her feet before the sun is high.'

'No wonder the Bellwashers are dirt-poor if all they can think of is how to work slower,' said Nicholas contemptuously.

'No wonder the Wyses are likely to grow muck-rich if all they think on is how to forge iron wi'blood.'

The fire's core crumbled and a drift of gold sparks flew upwards, while Nicholas first disbelieved the evidence of his ears and then remembered he'd come to ask Jem a favour. 'I don't want to quarrel.'

'Nay, you came to a purpose or I'd be out on my ear already. What can I do for thee?'

Nicholas took a firm grip on his temper; Jem was only a hireling who could be dismissed at his father's whim. 'I have ten groats and two pennies saved. If I gave them to you, would you go to Buxted and learn how to make cannon-moulds?'

'T'master missed two groats last week and another not long before.'

'Anyone can lose a groat. Will you go if I give you enough to live on for a while?'

'They'll be wary who they hire at Buxted.'

'That's why you need my groats,' said Nicholas impatiently. 'Christ's blood Jem! If you hang around a place like Buxted, then sooner or later they'll toss scraps at you! Ask you to yoke up oxen or strip bark for a day, like they would any beggar. But unless you've a coin in your pocket you'd soon have to move on. You're sharp and know how to mix clays for plastering, if you kept your eyes open you'd soon learn the craftsmen's tricks which make good cannon-moulds. One ironmaster keeps secrets from another, but you –'

'They wouldn't be watching a half-fledged gowk, eh?' Jem stared at him out of unreadable green eyes, flecked golden from the fire.

'You certainly don't look like the best plasterer we have,' agreed Nicholas candidly. All furnace-plasterers were small, since they had to squeeze through tapping holes and flues; must be nimble, too, when often they worked on hot stones and inside part-cooled furnaces. But Jem also had an instinct for which mix was right and whether a wall could be repaired or must be torn down. Consequently Francis, who respected skill wherever it was found, had already taught him more than most plaster-boys ever learned.

'Look,' said Jem, very low and fierce. 'You be making a lambskull out of I. I came here two year ago and like you said, most ironmasters would have tossed me a few scraps of work and then made sure a Bellwasher went elsewhere. Any Bellwasher be a waster, all Furneth Green knows that. But t'master fed me, and when he saw I did one thing well he offered me another, but harder, see? Taught me what I know, takes time to teach me more. Now you say, run off with groats you stole from him. Come back if you learn how to make cannon-moulds. What if I can't learn? What if t'master don't fancy stealing another man's craft? How could I come back one day and say to Master Wyse, "Aye, sorry I ran off with groats o'yourn, but here I am again so will you give me my work back, please?" '

'They're my groats.'

'But I don't know, do I? I wouldn't do it anyways 'cepting you told t'master first.'

Nicholas swore under his breath. Unscrupulous himself he had not expected Jem to object to a scheme which, if it worked would give him a valuable skill. Nor could Nicholas guess whether Francis, an ambitious and in some ways a hard man, would approve or not of sending a hireling to spy on a fellow ironmaster. 'I'd go myself, except I haven't your way with mixes, and cannon-moulds are made or marred by the mix.'

'Nor you don't look like a beggar-boy. They wouldn't throw you scraps but kick you out the moment you showed your neb.'

'So you see why it has to be you.'

Jem shook his head.

'What if I dig twice as hard tomorrow, make Bess work faster, carry even heavier loads than today?' As soon as Nicholas spoke, his words echoed inside his skull. Of course he would never carry out such a threat, he only hated being beaten.

Jem scrambled to his feet. 'I'll go tell t'master myself, then.'

'Tell what, in Christ's name?'

'None of this is in Christ's name, but come and listen if you like.'

'I wouldn't – Jesu, I didn't mean it. I love Bess.'

'Aye, there isn't one who sees her as doesn't. But I don't trust you under temptation, see? So I'll just put it out of your reach, and make sure the maid is watched over as she should be.' He ran off through scrub towards the jumble of sheds which had grown up around forge and furnace, so sure-footed across rough ground that Nicholas couldn't quite catch him, although much longer-legged.

'Tell me what you're going to say, curse you!' Nicholas shouted.

Jem threw a derisive look over his shoulder. 'You're coming to listen, aren't you?'

And in that moment he heard Nicholas rattle air like an unleashed hound, saw the moonlit flash of murder in his eyes. Then the instinctive fear of all creatures which must fight for life overtook him and, head down, he ran as fast as he could towards the forge.

The brook barred his path, its water low in summer heat. He hesitated, feinted left when he heard Nicholas coming fast behind him, then bolted along its edge. Stronger and longer of limb, Nicholas would catch him if he tried to scramble down those undercut banks. Away to his right the stream widened into the upper mill pool, muddily stagnant and even more of a barrier. Beyond it was the water wheel, motionless against dark sky, since the sluice was shut to save precious water. As Jem dodged between the tussocks which edged the pool, Nicholas was pounding almost into reach behind him and only seconds remained in which to gather himself for a leap he knew was insanely dangerous. The wheel hung on a thick oak shaft and, like everything of Francis Wyse's making, was exactly finished for its purposes. The slightest pressure would make it turn. Which meant he had to hit the shaft-end squarely and hold on, or his weight would swing the wheel and he with it, then he would be lucky if he escaped with only a mashed foot.

He leaped, hands and feet spread wide, toes curled for the instant shift of balance he would certainly have to make. No one could hit a bull's eye in the dark.

He underestimated how far he had to jump, and the timber paddles struck numbingly at his knees and fingers only. Jem knew his weight was wrong, felt the clack of the wheel as it began to move, wondered wildly whether he should drop into the sluice and chance the paddles crushing his head. Then the wheel jarred and stopped as if a timber was thrust between its spokes, his body thrown inward while his toes scrabbled thankfully for grip.

'You little fool,' said Francis Wyse between his teeth. 'You deserve to be butcher's meat. Quick. Crawl though the paddle before I have to let go.'

Jem wriggled through the oak struts and stood feeling remarkably foolish on the platform built beside the wheel.

Francis straightened, wincing, a hand to his back. 'Lucky for you I was marking the sluice level when I saw you come, what in heaven's name made you try anything so brainless?' He must have seen Jem gather himself to leap for the wheel, and flung from sluice to platform just in time to use his strength as a brake on the wheel. No wonder he was holding his back; and but for that torn muscle he would certainly have thrashed Jem where he stood.

'It was a dare.' In the cold aftermath of his flight, Jem was already convinced he must have imagined the look on Nick's face in moonlight, felt more kinds of dolt than Francis called him. 'I am truly sorry, master,' he added wretchedly.

'It was my fault,' Nicholas must have crossed the brook below the sluice. 'I began to chase him through the trees.'

'You chased him through the trees?' said Francis incredulously. In other circumstances he would have laughed at the idea of staid Nicholas, an ironmaster already in the making, playing tig with a hireling in the dark. He didn't believe it for an instant, which meant –
He grunted at the flash of pain across his back; he had acted instinctively to save Jem from certain maiming, but for the next week at least would be hard pressed to work iron as he must. 'Why?' he added.

Jem and Nicholas exchanged ware glances; neither spoke.

'I mean to know,' said Francis. 'Since I am the loser from what you did, I have the right to understand its cause.'

'It was a private quarrel,' said Nicholas sulkily.

'About what?'

'Bess.'

Jem felt shivering start in the pit of his belly. Such an accusation would finish him at Edenham, where he had become the first of his kindred to lean a skill and eat well every day.

'Is this true? Francis's voice was expressionless. Though Bess was still a child, he understood well as any man the tug of the heart she would exercise effortlessly all her life.

'Aye,' said Jem. He could not deny the softness Bess brought into his life, on this the only occasion he would have the chance to acknowledge it.

'Leave us, Nick.' When Nicholas had gone, he added kindly enough: 'You'll have to go, you know.'

Jem shrugged, staring at planks between his toes.

Francis watched him, frowning. Jem had come to Edenham like a rat breaking into a fowl-run, for what he could devour. Yet the boy possessed instinctive skills and repaid fair dealing with fierce loyalty. Francis had had high hopes of him, but was under no illusion. Folk like the Bellwashers grabbed what they could the instant an opportunity arose, because no one had ever given them anything. If Jem felt desire already for Bess, then he could never again be trusted in arm's reach of her. 'Do you want to tell me anything more? If there's another side to the tale I should give as much weight to your words as to Nick's.'

'It don't matter,' Jem said listlessly. 'She's a maid to turn any man's head. Like you say, master, I'm best away.'

Francis counted out some coins. 'Try for work with Jack Fletcher at Park Forge, I'll speak to him for you.'

'I'm sorry you got hurt.' Jem wasn't really listening, although he heard. ''Tis a poor return for your kindness, master. And I've a favour to beg if you'd listen. Bess. Them baskets from the cannon-pit are too heavy for her when May and Sally do naught to help. I'd be grateful if you'd look to it.'

'I hadn't seen.' Francis gripped the boy's shoulder, all sinew and bone under unfleshed skin. 'Jem, if you can't find work, then come back and I'll see you're placed somewhere. But are you sure Nick hasn't –' He broke off. Has not wronged you he meant to say.

'It's best I go.'

'Aye, perhaps. It wasn't what I asked.'

Jem grinned suddenly. 'I don't know, master. Mayhap we both saw what wasn't there, but one thing's sure. We'd quarrel again if I stayed.'

Francis walked back to his hearth in a thoughtful frame of mind. Strange to find a Bellwasher with as much pride and a deal more worth than either of his sons. He smiled grimly to himself. If the boy found work at an ironworks ahead of Edenham in its craft, then one day Nick might regret a pointless quarrel.

When he reached their lean to hut only a tallow-dip glowed in the dark, although Francis would have wagered a month's profit that Nicholas lay as wakeful as he did. If the choice lay between a torn conscience or a torn back, then he preferred the back. He shifted cautiously and swore under his breath. Part-skilled though he was, Nick would have to shape iron in his father's place for some while to come, which was one way of halving Bess's task of carrying earth from the cannon-pit.

No matter how hard Francis Wyse, his family and hirelings worked, on a Sunday everyone walked to church. Parson Preece had made so powerful an impression on Mary that from the day she met him no one was exempted except by sickness, nor was Francis allowed to combine trade with worship at Ockham's chapel. Wet and drought, furnace firing, or no, when the bell began to toll across Furneth's fields, the Edenham contingent was ruthlessly counted up the track. Francis and Mary walked at the back to make sure no one disappeared on the way, although Sundays were mostly a pleasure after six days of toil. True, the service was long and dull as Parson Preece honked like a gander through his nose, but once her flock was safely delivered Mary relaxed. A new Parliament act required every soul to attend church, but it was the Church's duty and not hers to uplift them in worship. For some, especially those born into a Protestant and nationalist land, this was straightforward enough; for their elders often not straightforward at all, but, like Mary, no one wanted any trouble. So they did what they were told, kept most of their thoughts to themselves and enjoyed a good gossip in the church afterwards. What business was it of Parson Preece what anyone really believed, or whether they still occasionally put out offering to Widow Tiw? Who knew what they thought, about Tiw or pope or devils carousing among the trees; whether the likes of Goody Bellwasher or Frifwith By The Wood thought at all?

Least of all do I know what I think, reflected Mary, studying carved stone as she did every week to pass the time. I like that curved arch there, and the sense of others on their knees beside me; I like to feel there might be something beyond iron and stewpots in my life. I also like to have Francis beside me instead of labouring at his furnaces, and to see Christ on His cross: his face is kinder than either Poctor or Preece pretend. I do not like listening to a parson prate about justice, when he would hang us if he could. Nor do I like this particular carved stone boss I stare at every week. Much as Rico had long ago, Mary recognized corruption even when carved in stone. Just above the Wyses' pew, John the Carver had depicted Adam shut out of paradise and under his chisel the tree of evil rioted unchecked over pitiful lost souls. Mary's eyes wandered, stopped, came back again to a limewashed space above the altar.

She nudged Francis in the ribs. 'The crucifix has gone.'

'And the pictures on the wall. I can just see through the pillars,' hissed Bess, red gold head appearing from the other side of Francis.

Mary felt shocked. Those pictures were the only story-book Furneth children saw; even Joan, a negligent church-goer, had made up fables about the angels, knights and castles, the twin-headed monsters and demons painted along the chancel wall. Joan had said that when she was a child an old white-haired man called Drogo had one day wandered into the village, who told everyone he was born by the pool and that after he left it he earned his bread as a colourman painting cloths to hang in rich men's castles. Then he painted this splendid decoration for their church before he died. Now his work was gone, a blank wall in its place.

'Preece mixed up limewash and ordered Will Apps to slop it over everywhere,' confided Mistress Laffam to Mary after the service. 'Poor old Will was blubbering by the time he finished, a-saying he remembered them pictures being done.'

'My mother remembered too.'

Mistress Laffam sighed. 'Tis a shame to have a down on pleasuring, though I hear t'parson plans to make Harlot Bywood stand at the church door next week. And that I wouldn't mind.'

Mary flushed, ever sensitive to any reference to harlotry, but the women in earshot were clearly pleased that a sinner who led their men astray should be condemned.

Francis was always serious and quiet during church. Even after all her years of marriage Mary was unsure whether this was due to piety, prudence over the matter of priests, or mere boredom once he was separated from his furnaces. After the service he usually exchanged few words with his brothers, who quarrelled even more savagely among themselves after their father died, so becoming poorer once their inheritance was used mainly to spite each other. Consequently, the relations between Edenham and the other Wyses remained cool. Nor did Francis join roisterers like the Laffams behind the church-yard wall, where Will Apps hid a keg of ale before the service; indeed he took more care to move through the thong in the opposite direction to Parson Preece than he did to greet his friends, so on the whole Mary was inclined to plump for prudence on such occasions as she considered his behaviour.

But on this late spring Sunday in 1553, he happened to be talking cannon-founding to Jack Fletcher, master of Park Forge, and since both men were excited by their trade, he forgot to look often enough over his shoulder.

'I see, Master Wyse, that you are again setting the Lord's work at naught,' said Preece behind his back.

Francis turned and bowed. 'Why, how so?'

'I see the Devil's footprints in holy ground! Do not deny it!'

'If you will tell me plainly what angers you, then mayhap I could try to put matters right.'

Preece spread his hands, the only soft hands in Furneth. 'There's no mayhap to it, I say. You stole timber from God's church, and ravaged the land it stood upon.'

Francis's eyes narrowed. He had aged with the years of hot and heavy work, and anyway was not far short of forty, a time when most men began to twist and wither. But he had shoulders on him like a bull, possessed the eagerness of a much younger man. He was also no dissembler. 'The trees Jack Carpenter felled for my new house were fairly bought from Widow Brown. Lovers Wood has belonged to Fawkners since before any man now living can remember. As for ravaging the land, it's been a wet winter and a wetter spring. When the ground dries I will set men to clearing stumps and filling in ruts.'

'The tree felled yesterday was not in Lovers Wood. A name which is temptation in itself, let me say. Only those hardened in sin still call it so.'

Jack Fletcher guffawed. 'You'll have hard work to change it, parson.'

'Let us walk together and see what has been done,' said Francis quietly. 'If timber has been wrongly felled, I am happy to pay what is right in restitution.'

'Aye, let us go and see how you wriggle out of sin.' Preece stalked off so fast that Mary, hastening to see what the fuss was, saw only the two men going off side by side.

'Francis and Parson Preece?' she said blankly to Jack Fletcher. 'What ill chance brought them together when Francis has spent the last five years bowing to him from a distance?'

'Preece is as stiff-legged as a hound spoiling for a fight,' answered Fletcher soberly. 'If you take my advice you'll follow after to help keep Francis's temper leashed. I wouldn't let any snivelling preacher speak to me as yon porker did.'

Mary needed no second telling but hastened between the gravestones where flattened grass showed the way they had gone, saw Francis again as soon as she rounded the tower wall, already bulging slightly from the botched work which had followed Benedict's death. The two men were standing where Lovers Wood adjoined the church-yard, Preece fairly gobbling with rage as he pointed to muddied ruts and a tumbled length of wall.

'I don't deny the ruts are from timber-hauling, but that wall has been leaning so long as I remember,' Mary heard Francis say. He looked quite calm, so she began to hope this new quarrel would soon be over with no harm done.

'It is not leaning but thrown down,' snapped Preece.

'If any wall leans long enough, it will fall.'

'If the Devil moves his creatures to lay violent hands on God's church, then will those hands wither and the sinner die.'

As Mary came close she saw how stiffly Francis stood, his fingers twisting behind his back, and slipped her arm through his. Then she smiled at Preece. 'Sir, we have a good mason at Edenham. Francis will send him to repair your wall. Truly we are sorry if in dragging out our timber, the oxen may have tumbled it.'

Preece turned his glare on her. 'Get you hence, daughter of harlots and woman of uncleanness.'

Mary gasped; after eighteen wedded years when her life had lacked any suggestion of scandal, no one mentioned her ancestry any longer. Nor had they ever done so in her husband's hearing. She felt Francis move and was too late to stop him from lifting Preece off the ground as if he weighed no more than a shock of corn. Then he held him against the crumbled wall. 'If you weren't a parson I'd take your blood for that. Admit your error or as God lives, I'll scrape your nose on stone until you do.

Mary tugged at the bar-tight muscle of his arms. 'Francis, no! What does spite matter? I beg you to come away.'

'If he recants. That's the right word isn't it, for priests found doing wrong?'

Preece flapped in his hands like a landed fish. 'I'll see you damned first.'

'Aye' Watch for your blood on stone then. Francis turned him without letting a toe touch the ground and laid Preece's unremarkable nose against broken stone.

Mary slapped Francis's face, hard. 'Will you listen? The insult was spoken to me, on the Sabbath, in God's own enclosure. I forgive him, so what right have you to take my Christian duty from me? Leave him and come home.'

He stared at her for a long time while apprehensive heartbeats thumped in her ears, then a smile dawned in his eyes. 'Mary, you little devil.'

'Which makes me kin to you,' she pointed out, much relieved.

Francis dropped Preece in a huddle at the foot of the wall, and absently wiped his hands. 'Tell me quickly then. What made you believe the oak was yours? It was clearly outside the wall.'

Preece leapt to his feet like a striking snake, a single dot of blood on his nose. 'Will Apps told me. He remembered the church being finished and said all the trees in that grove were bought for roof timber, but the one closest to the wall was left, in case when it was felled the wall came too. Ask him yourself, or walk through the grass just there. You'll find the stumps of the rest.'

'I ordered timber from Jack Carpenter and dealt with Widow Brown for what he marked. No one told us that one tree outside the wall belonged to the church. God in heaven, who remembers now which timbers were intended for the steeple?'

'Will Apps remembered.'

Francis's shoulders slumped. It was bitter to discover that he might be in the wrong after all, when he had only just drawn back from punishing outrage. 'If it is due, I will make restitution,' he said stiffly at last.

Preece drew himself up. 'God does not have dealings with the powers of darkness, He defeats them.'

And, as Francis said ruefully to Mary that evening 'Damn me if the swine didn't have the last word after all!'

She hugged her knees where they sat round the hearth. 'Do you remember how all this futile quarrelling began?'

'He said I had felled – '

'Nay, lovely. Long before that. Why did Preece set out to stir up trouble for us from the first day he came? We can't be so very much more wicked than other folk hereabouts, for all that I'm a harlot's daughter.'

Francis exclaimed aloud and left his bench to sit beside her. 'Swear never to say that again.'

'I swear,' said Mary, smiling. 'But after most of a lifetime wed to you, I don't care any more. I meant that even the taint of harlotry couldn't make us sinful enough for spite.'

Francis reflected, holding her tightly against his thigh. 'I remember. It began with Jack By The Wood's daughter's funeral fee. How petty can men be.'

'Even you had forgotten,' Mary pointed out. 'Certainly no one else remembers. Instead, if Preece should ever make someone in authority listen, we have our ill repute with two priests to explain away, which stretches back eighteen years. How could we explain it except by admitting sin?'

'All men are sinful.'

'But today you attacked a priest, which is a less common sin than most.'

He stood and pulled her up beside him. 'I was grossly provoked and will beg my own forgiveness from a Christ of mercy. Come, sweeting. Since we must pay twice for it, let's go again to admire the new oak timbering of our house.'

They walked with his arm about her waist; as if we were still new-wed, thought Mary, pleased. Who wouldn't be pleased when after eighteen years of marriage her husband still desired her? Her belly and breasts might sag a little, her skin, too, had darkened with the years of toil, but she was neither stringy nor greying yet, and as lusty for him as he for her. She smiled dreamily and ran her free hand down the curve of her thigh, a movement Francis must have seen because he slid his hands there too, and kissed her. 'I like that smile on your face, lass. The smile of a maid dreaming of her bridal night.'

Mary laughed. 'I was, or near enough.'

When they walked on again it was to cross the brook, where a new house was building at last, although for the moment they continued to live in the tumbledown hovel built in those first days after they came to Edenham. All their children had been born in its draughts although some were conceived where the fancy took them, and all who survived slept together on bracken in one corner. Every step of their way to present prosperity had been discussed and planned round its plain plank trestle: the cannon-pits and boring tracks, fineries and furnaces. Now the years of hardship were over, and perhaps some of the excitement too, as they began to reap the fruits of long endeavour. Francis had bought the meadow which lay just below Edenham and dug deeper casting pits for new and larger cannon there, built tracks on which the cast barrels were mounted to have their bore drilled smooth, a larger finery and furnaces which dwarfed those of his earlier years. There were more water wheels and a freshly-constructed dam which flooded nearly two acres of his new pasture field. Even so, water remained a problem, particularly now so much depended on it. The brook often nearly dried in summer, or froze in a hard winter. The only answer was to dig more and bigger holding-ponds, and ditches to drain as wide an area as possible into their stream, which changed the face of Edenham. When Mary had first watched Francis pacing the slope called Edenham it had been just turf and furze; then slag, cinders and tumbled furnace stone gradually turned greenness into squalor, while the growing number of workers gnawed like leprosy at the forest edge.

But when Francis bought the land below the clearing and built his larger dam there, it immediately became apparent how much more pleasant was the unfouled grass around its banks, and he decided not to wait any longer before building a proper house with an upper floor and separate rooms. They planned a simple construction of oak beams and weatherboard sawn in Jack Carpenter's pit, all resting on fresh-baked brick, but Mary never ceased to be astonished by its size. Francis had been reared at Wyse's and saw nothing remarkable in a brick hearth or upstairs rooms, but Mary accepted hovels as the natural place for her to live and awed by so much space. She rejoiced in it all the same. Few days went by without her stepping through the timber doorway into the place where her parlour would be, or knocking bricks together in her hand to make sure each one rang true.

Bess loved it too and often escaped from mill drudgery to watch Jack and Will Carpenter who, between them, did most of the work of laying bricks, nailing weatherboard and pegging tiles. If timbers had to be raised, then the whole workforce of Edenham left furnace and forge to help.

Bess was there again when Mary and Francis went inside, on her knees beneath the chimney.

'Jack Carpenter showed me how, so I told him I would lay the hearth bricks myself,' she said, sitting back on her heels.

'And what did he answer.'

She chuckled. 'He grouched he'd have to reset them after, when you complained about botched work. But I'll make sure it isn't; I've got all summer to make sure each brick is right.'

'You sound like your father with his furnaces,' observed Mary. Privately, she considered Francis was too easy with Bess, who might skimp her other tasks in order to waste time on a hearth the Carpenters could lay far better, but Francis had always softened to his youngest daughter's charm.

Bess pushed red-gold hair out of her eyes and immediately transferred mortar from her hands to her face. 'I suppose bricks are the same as furnaces, and neither of us likes to be beaten.'

'I was beaten by Parson Preece today.' Francis rubbed discontentedly at grievance.

Bess scrambled to her feet. 'It wasn't you! Jack Carpenter said he never knew that tree belonged to the church, either, and the wall was already fallen.'

'What does it matter?' said Mary irritably. 'It's done and we must pay twice, to keep Preece off our backs.'

'Why should father pay?' demanded Bess passionately. 'The fault was Jack's if fault there was. And what is a single tree after all, when the forest is full of them?'

'Men will quarrel over one twig out of a bundle if it suits them, and pride always causes more trouble than it's worth.'

Involuntarily, Francis exchanged glances with his daughter, and then looked away. Mary was bred from folk who survived by staying as nearly out of view as possible, and could never see that peace would be too dearly purchased on such terms.

'Look, I want to show you something,' Bess said after a pause, and ran her hand over the squared beam which took the weight above the hearth. 'This is from the oak Preece says is his, and when Jack trimmed it, see what he found.'

Seasoned timber was used for the main structure of a house, but the Carpenters swore that green wood over a hearth was best, a belief which owed less to calculation than to an inherited tradition which said a hearth was sacred. And if tempted by the incense smell of sap, then friendly rather than cantankerous spirits were more likely to adopt this new hearth of Edenham as their own. Both Francis and Mary went over to peer at the timber under Bess's fingers, but by then it was close to dusk. 'I can't see anything,' said Mary.

'Feel.' Bess pressed her mother's fingers against something sharp. 'Jack heard his adze strike metal. He says its an arrowhead, which was held tight by the oak's bark a long time ago, but as the heartwood dries, see, you can ease it out to look. It's nice, don't you think, to have an arrowhead above our hearth shaped from other men's iron so long ago?'

'Aye,' said Francis slowly, touching it. 'Forged in a heap of charcoal without forced draught, very likely. Now that must have been tedious labour.'

Bess laughed delightedly. 'Here I am, dreaming of knights and dragons, and all you can say is that the metal was forged by an unskilful smith!'

'Nay, skilful enough I daresay, but confined to grub in cinders.' Carefully, he slid it back into the beam. 'We'll put some goose-grease in the crack to keep it safe.' Like Bess, he was pleased by the idea of this arrowhead above his hearth.

'Don't you dare laugh at your father,' said Mary sharply. 'And mind you keep your hands off bricks when there's other work to be done! Jack Carpenter could lay a hearth within a morning.'

'It wouldn't be the same, don't you see? The hearth is the life of a house. I should like to look at ours when I'm old and think: Those bricks were set in love.'

Mary was silent. She would never have thought such a thing for herself, but very easily believed that a hearth rightly set could bring good fortune. And we need some fortune, she thought, panic-stricken again as Preece's malignant stare leaped at her out of the dark.

'Shall I tell you what I'll do? said Francis. 'I'll cast a fireback to match your hearth which will tell the story of the mill. You can help me design it, Bess.'

Bess clapped her hands and dabbed a kiss at his beard. 'We'll put on the brook, and cannon and the forge and – oh, so many things! Parson Preece dancing with rage in the churchyard. Truly, he danced, didn't he?'

They all laughed together then, Mary reflecting wryly that Bess knew as well as she did how to turn Francis away from resentment. Perhaps harlot blood counted for something after all, and Joan's descendants, be they virtuous enough to wear white robes, would know in the cradle how to please all manner of men.

Nicholas on the other hand was growing into a precise and contentious manhood; careful in all things although undermuscled for the heavier work of the forge. He knew his trade though, and struck harder bargains than Francis. He had recently thought up a scheme whereby he would travel to sell cannon direct to the new royal dockyard at Chatham where, it was rumoured, the young king's chief minister, the Duke of Northumberland, intended to build a fleet large enough to make England respected wherever it sailed. Rumours flew all the time about a great many things, and, at the moment, most especially about how harshly and greedily Northumberland ruled in the boy-king's name: none of it made much difference in isolated Furneth, provided men paid their tax and trimmed their beliefs to the new Protestant wind. And if he indeed meant to build great galleons only thirty miles from Edenham ironworks, then Nicholas believed he could double their profit by selling direct.

Nicholas came out of the old mill-hovel as Francis, Mary and Bess returned in the dark. 'A stranger has come, who begs shelter for the night.'

'I hope you made him welcome,' Mary immediately began to worry about how much stew remained in the pot. Travellers often came down from the track to beg and it would be unchristian to refuse them, but their shelter was so crowded, and vagrants so often diseased, that secretly she hoped that once they moved into their new house, such people would feel too overawed by its magnificence to do more than ask for bread outside the door.

Nicholas looked annoyed, instantly seeing criticism where none was intended. 'Of course, but after talking with him I'm not sure I did right. He says he is a monk, turned out when monasteries were closed and still unreconciled.'

'At least he's honest, if he says so much to a stranger.' Francis quickened his steps.

'He'll make more trouble for us if word spreads we've taken in a malcontent.'

'We're not arguing doctrine, but offering a night's lodging to a stranger.' There was finality in Francis's voice, and Nicholas flushed.

'I wasn't suggesting – But as you'll discover, he's such good company it's difficult not to enjoy disputing even dangerous matters with him.'

Both Francis and Mary had the same though: if Nicholas found a man good company then he must be dazzling indeed. Mary ducked under the entry and stopped dead. 'Richard!'

Richard Mercer, the novice from Ockham whom they had taken in as a boy, had grown into a lean and graceful man, yet everything else about him was so unchanged that recognition was instant. The same sense of delight and an outflowing interest which lifted self out of any reckoning, and same bright childlike eyes, high thinker's forehead and sensitive mouth.

He embraced Mary heartily, while they pelted him with questions. Yes, he had become a monk, taking his final vows only days before the remote monastery in Lancashire where he found refuge was closed by the king. No, he had not accepted a parish priesthood now monks were banished from England, since only God could judge such matters through His vicar on earth the pope. No, he had not starved, there were plenty of true folk who held to the old beliefs; the Duke of Northumberland being a cruel and thoroughgoing heretic who lacked the support to make repression as efficient as he would like.

'Don't say such things,' said Mary hastily, but laughing too because of the droll way Richard said them. 'We don't want the duke's hangmen coming here.'

'Oh, he's much too busy trying to save his skin,' answered Richard cheerfully. 'Haven't you heard? The king is ill and likely to die soon. When he does, the great duke will lead the scamper for cover.'

News, reliable news less than a week out of date, was a rarity in the Weald, but Richard had walked the forty miles from London to Edenham in only three days, staying each night in a house where the owner valued clerkly talk. Now he sprawled in their hovel as easily as he had sat under gilded ceilings, since God blessed both and there was nothing for him to feel uneasy about.

'Why did you come?' asked Francis, much later, when the children slept. 'Not that we aren't pleased to see you, but after so long we had almost given up hope of ever hearing how you did.'

'For two reasons, I suppose. As you may know the superior of our Order resides in Italy; I studied there for a while, and last year was summoned to attend him. He said that once King Edward is dead the English heretics will be finished and monasteries reopened. Therefore he instructed me to discover how much remained of Ockham, and whether our community could establish itself there again.'

'You'll find walls and unroofed arches, and only a single chapel preserved for us heretics to use.'

'Anything cast down can be rebuilt.'

'There are ironworks in the abbey pasture, since the fishpond proved a useful water store and all that chiselled stone is handy for furnace work. You remember the Laffams of Corndown? Their new farmhouse has handsome mullioned windows and a splendid mantle of carved oak beasts, taken from the abbot's lodgings. Tracks, ditching, farmhouses, troughs: there's scarce anyone hereabouts who hasn't used Ockham stone and lead.'

'We can cut and cast anew. It is what our forebears did after all. Once restored to order, the land will yield revenues to support a community.'

Francis hesitated. 'Did you see as you came that we are building a house and new ironworks downstream from here?'

'It was nearly dark,' answered Richard, smiling. 'Are you trying to tell me that you too have used Ockham stone? If so, it's between you and God and no affair of mine. I am concerned for the future, and the triumph of true faith.'

'Nay, I never used abbey stone.' And Francis grinned, thinking of their early feasting on poached Ockham game. 'Since I happen to own an outcrop suitable for furnaces just across the brook and brick-earth close by. But the pasture I'm using was abbey land which I bought from the king's clerks, and others on the fringes of Ockham have done the same. I would yield up what has become rightfully mine if ever your monastery should be re-established'

Richard reflected. 'The king has no right to sell God's land.'

'He sold nevertheless and I bought fairly, according to the law of this realm.'

'A false law, since the monks were turned out by force.' Richard laughed suddenly and struck Francis lightly on the shoulder. 'All the same, Christ's true servants would never allow strips of pasture to trip up repentant souls in search of forgiveness. I'm sure you needn't fear unjust loss.'

Francis rubbed sinewy hands on his breeches. 'But what if I'm not a soul in search of the Bishop; of Rome's forgiveness, but an unrepentant heretic still?'

'You couldn't be! King Henry and his son's minsters may have forced or persuaded men into accepting sin, but once there is no profit in it all true souls will return to their faith. Forgive me, I did not mean to put it so crudely. Most men had only a choice of wrongs if they wanted to live in peace.'

'We are all bound to try and choose the right in matters of importance, and I tell you plainly, Richard, I doubt I shall ever again be able to accept priestly posturings between God and my beliefs.'

'Your new heresy hasn't freed you from authority. I will not call heretic preachers priests, but you must obey them all the same.'

Nicholas leaned forward. 'Not so, sir monk. There is a parson here in Furneth and he is given authority under the law, yes. But so far as I am concerned, God speaks directly to my conscience rather than through him.'

Francis and Mary stared at their son, astonished. Nicholas always expressed himself forcefully on matters of craft and trade, but in religion conformed to whatever was required as they did, without remarking on it. Yet he had reached instantly to the nub of the matter, which Francis felt but fumbled to frame in words.

Richard being used to scholarly argument, saw nothing odd in this. 'What if your conscience has become warped by greed or hate? Would you not then require a priest to call you out of sin?'

'Since I should by then be well set in that sin, I doubt he could do it,' answered Nicholas grimly. 'Only God's power may untwist a conscience, surely.'

Mary rushed in then, afraid of another quarrel. 'Richard, you said you had two reasons for coming here. One was to find out how Ockham stood, so what was the other?'

Richard linked his hands behind his head; he was tonsured but not extravagantly so, the mark of a monk almost hidden by crisp dark hair. Though capable of being a martyr, Richard Mercer was not looking for martyrdom yet. 'I felt I owed you a warning.'

'A warning.'

'I'm not speaking mere tales by the hearth, you know. The king will die soon and his sister, Mary, inherit the throne of England, who is sworn to restore the true Church in its rightful place. Penalties will be suffered by those who fail to repent of heresy in time, and I did not want you or your household to be among the sufferers.'

'Why should we be? We've only obeyed the king's bidding, as loyal subjects should.'

'I suppose I feared to hear what I have heard tonight.' Richard's face was in shadow as the rushlight guttered. 'Once, long ago, you took me in and saved my life, I believe I sought to repay a debt by coming here tonight.'

Mary stared at him in alarm. 'No one could blame us for obeying King Harry and his son.'

'That isn't what he means,' cut in Nicholas. 'Can't you see? There will be different laws to obey now, sent by the Bishop of Rome, who under this new queen will try to take England back into bondage again.'

'Oh,' said Mary, relieved. 'If that is all. We've always been obedient here, Richard. You needn't have felt anxious for us, although we're mightily pleased you came to visit us at last.'

Richard smiled, but turned his head to look at Francis. 'I am glad to hear it, on all counts, Mistress Wyse.'

'At least there is one cause for rejoicing,' observed Nicholas into the silence which followed. 'Preece will bolt for cover with the rest, since no one has been fiercer for the Protestant faith than he. If this new queen should indeed bring back the Roman Church, Preece is a marked man with a wife and pack of brats to explain away.'

In Mary's eyes this aspect of the matter changed the new queen from ogre to benefactor in an instant. Preece gone meant Furneth cleared of menace; given luck, this time for ever. Even so, she lay away for a while, aware of uneasiness she could not name. Laws had a slippery feel to them when they were always changing, she reflected. Ah well, Furneth was well tucked away in its forest; changes would come slowly and offer everyone time to shrug and conform – and guard their thoughts as they had always done.

Francis lay awake much longer. The trouble was, he found it difficult to hammer some kinds of thought accurately on the anvil of his mind. Except in the matter of Preece he felt comfortable with his life and seldom needed to consider problems unrelated to his family or ironworks. He knew, however, that this contentment would vanish if beliefs which now made him comfortable were thrown into the furnace again. Even if Preece disappeared in the process, the cost would be too high. Most men had enemies and until today he had simply avoided Preece and could do so again. Belief was different. You might deny it, turn your back perhaps, but you knew it was still there. He sighed and pulled worn deerskin closer about his shoulders; why couldn't men stop meddling with him, now he felt satisfied with matters as they were?

Nicholas listened until his father's breathing lengthened into snores, then shook Richard lightly.

'I'm not sleeping,' the monk said softly. 'What is it?

'Can you read?'

Nicholas felt the other's surprise, and realized he had stayed awake in case anyone wanted to mumble contrition. 'Yes,' he answered after a moment. 'I was a scholar in Italy.'

'Would you teach me before you go?'

'I am your father's guest and maybe not a welcome one after this evening. 'I can't eat for weeks at his expense without explanation.'

'I should learn quickly.'

'No matter how diligent you are, reading can't be mastered in a day. Nor should I want to teach a doubting soul how to quarry arguments out of writings he cannot comprehend.'

Nicholas's breath caught unexpectedly on amusement. 'I'm a trader, not a priest. What if I swear never to open a book of religion, not even the Bible chained in Furneth church?'

He heard the other chuckle too. 'I should want notice of that bargain. Tell your father what you intend and, if he agrees, then will I teach you letters and figuring. As a trader and friend, you understand. I am instructed to remain near Ockham, so Edenham is as good a place as any for me to stay.'

'I'm seventeen years old, said Nicholas sulkily.

'I can't teach the master of Edenham's son a greater skill than he himself possesses, without telling him first.'

'I need to learn. I want to! I'll never prosper as a master while all my reckonings must be kept on tallies!'

But Richard didn't answer, leaving Nicholas feeling very ill-used. I promised nothing, he thought. I suggested a bargain, but he didn't accept it. If I want to make it my business to quarry arguments against monks and monasteries, I shall. And understand the books they come from. He stretched yearningly in straw; books were wickedly expensive but had he possessed coins of his own, Nicholas wouldn't have grudged even silver shillings for books of worth, if only he could read. Lonely and ungregarious by nature, he longed for a companionship which he sensed was far better suited to his needs than the boisterous simplicities of Edenham.

Somewhat to Nicholas's surprise, Francis raised no objection when his son disclosed his desire to write and figure. Nicholas himself would have disliked any son of his to acquire the power over him which such a new skill implied, whereas it never occurred to Francis that he might be intimidated by anyone else's accomplishments. He was simply glad for Nicholas to learn something which might serve him well.

So when Richard returned from his explorations around Ockham, he and Nicholas pored over pothooks copies into clay, reckoned bars of iron and set figures into order. They had to work by rushlight while everyone else tripped over what they did: Ned was too young to learn writing and James said frankly that scratchings were not for him, but May and Sally mooned over Richard's handsome looks and were constantly in the way, although they learned nothing. Eventually, Nicholas threatened to tell Mary about their secret meetings with the Laffam boys unless they left him alone. Only Bess sat doggedly listening, and then demanded clay of her own to mark.

'Why not? Many a man would be grateful for a wife able to figure,' said Francis, and straightway pounded the clay she needed, thereby precipitating a quarrel with Mary, who felt that he had detected some lack in her. Nicholas soon became accustomed to Bess silently sharing the gift of words with him; it was Richard, the celibate monk who found her presence hard to endure. Young though she was, Bess's sunny humour, quick mind and vivid colouring were disturbing, when seated every night at his elbow.

As matters turned out, Richard's departure was put off from week to week, rather as it had been when he first came to Edenham as a boy. Nicholas had a high enough opinion of his own abilities to expect to read and write within days, and was disconcerted to discover that a whole summer was scarcely sufficient for him to learn, but fortunately, Richard himself received no instruction to leave the vicinity of Ockham while its affairs continued to wait on the king's life.

Then there was the weather. A wet winter and spring were followed by a sodden summer; the crops rotted, sickness spread, and the roads almost vanished. Sussex clay had always made Furneth tracks impassable during protracted bad seasons, now to a long period of wetness was added much heavier traffic than ever before. All over the Weald, furnaces and forges were producing cannon, each one of which required dozens of loads of ore and clay and charcoal before it could be finished; then afterwards it must be hauled to the coast for sale. Somehow the ox-sleds got through even if the teams drawing them must be doubled as the weather worsened, and then doubled again; heaving, straining, floundering, criss-crossing fields to forest in search of unmired ways and then leaving those ruined too. A load of ore could take a day to travel the mile to Edenham from the lode discovered behind Fawkners, a cannon six months to reach the Thames. All of which multiplied their cost. Still, the quantity of ships now being built meant that Wealdon guns were much in demand, and as Francis Wyse said, if the king's armourers didn't worry about price, then why should he?

Richard had no scruples about helping at the Wyse ironworks since his Order was sworn to labour with their hands, and though he prayed when he guessed it was Sext or Terce, he made up for lost time by his skill on the moulding floor. Strangely enough, the men liked having him around. They knew he was a monk but no word of his presence leaked out elsewhere, and if anyone in Furneth heard of a new worker at Edenham than it was scarcely cause for wonder. Men were sucked into the ironworkings from far and wide as sheep nibbled away at their livelihood; French and Flemings were common too, fleeing turmoil at home and offering skills the ironmasters eagerly snapped up. The Weald had long been isolated from the rest of England by forest, now the babel of tongues broadened its dialect almost into a separate language, while ancient beliefs became interwoven with the superstitions of iron-making. Though London was only forty miles away, it might have been over the edge of the world.

But Richard Mercer had worked at Edenham before and few words slipped past him uncomprehended. Even more important, he understood what men did not say and soon became familiar with tongue-tied pleas for help, mumbled confessions, fears framed in ways which stretched back to Tiw and the green spirits of the forest.

'It's strange,' he said one day to Francis. 'I never before dreamed I could be anything except a monk, and hardship only made me more determined. Now I see that most priests scarcely touch the lives in their care, and have a hankering to see if I could manage differently.'

'You could. You are. But what about your vows?'

'As always, they are in God's hands. When the Church and its monasteries are re-established, then we shall see how matters stand. The priesthood of Furneth for instance, used to be in Ockham's gift.

Once this Preece is run off, the abbot may feel there's work here which a vowed monk could manage best, and the abbey wouldn't be far.' He smiled, head thrown back in a gesture Francis remembered. 'Like an ironmaster with his furnaces. I should find it hard to survive completely removed from my chosen place.'

'It would be a great day for Furneth if you took up the living here. I can't remember a time when our priest was not an enemy or a scoundrel, or both.'

Richard flicked a look at him. Francis Wyse was that rarity, a completely straightforward man. A trifle dull because of it perhaps, not imaginative, and well buried in his ores and clays, but he lacked the dross which self-interest and conceit added to most other men. Certainly he ran his ironworks autocratically, with a passion for good work, outbursts of anger and shaming silences. But then ironworks could not survive on forbearance; men were maimed and iron crumbled once slackness crept in.

Richard cleared his throat. 'Have you ever considered what I said that first night I came? I too could be your enemy if you persisted in contumacious sin.'

'Ah, but I don't understand words like that,' Francis said blandly. 'Then if you found yourself unable to explain them to a dullard, why, we'd rub along all right, I reckon.'

Well, thought Richard later. That will certainly be something I have to consider alongside this new desire to become a parish priest, once Ockham is refounded. Because, of course, he's right. I could never accept that the Christ I serve would wish me to yield up a friend to be burned for heresy. Though pope, superior and abbot all ordered me to do it, I could not. No. Never. I could not. And as if in premonition of unthinkable disobedience, he tasted vomit on his tongue.

The rain continued through June and July, the occasional bright day offering hope, only to be doused by the next squall out of the west. Food would be dear and scarce in the coming winter, and more infants die than usual.

In the middle of dreary wetness, the Wyses moved into their new house. It wasn't completely ready because the Carpenter brothers had been held up by the weather, but the roof was watertight, the walls plastered, the staircase in place. Even though glass was lacking from the windows it seemed absurd to huddle in a mud-floored hut any longer when a splendid house stood nearby. Only Bess did not applaud Francis's decision. Her hearth was still unfinished and she feared ill-omens if they moved in while the bricks remained askew.

'Any hearth will be many times better than the pit we use here,' said Mary, who kept wondering what it would be like to sleep alone with Francis.

'It's no good asking Jack Carpenter if he'll finish it for you now,' said Francis ruefully. 'As it is, he'll take weeks to forgive us for forcing him to botch floorboards in a hurry.'

'Once we move in, the hearth will never again be cold for me to finish it properly, and a house *needs* a good hearth, don't you see?' Bess answered stubbornly.

'I'm sorry, Bess, but we move across at the end of the week. Nicholas needs some dryness to cure the cough he has on him, and May will sicken all winter unless her belly settles before the cold weather comes,' Francis spoke kindly, but definitely. They were all weak-bellied as stored grain mouldered in the damp, gathered greenery remained sappy, the year's fruitings unripe.

'Would you like me to come and help tonight?' asked Richard, reflecting that really he ought to admonish Bess for what was clearly a belief in pagan hearth-gods.

She brightened at once. 'Would you? You slap up mixes nearly as well as Jem Bellwasher, who worked here a long time ago, I'm sure you'd be just as good with bricks.'

'I doubt it, since you can't hide bad brickwork, but I don't mind trying so long as it's light enough.'

'Oh, it must stop raining by this evening.' Bess said confidently.

But it didn't, and when she and Richard walked over to the new house after supper, the brook was roaring between its banks in a way Bess had never seen before. 'Look at that! Just think, the water is usually ten feet or more below the bank edge.

Now it was scarcely below the edge at all, and they watched fascinated as the brown torrent frothed past, taking the rubbish of the forest with it. While they waited, a small sapling on the bank began to waver, its roots appearing like witch's fingers out of crumbling earth. An instant after falling, it had gone, hurled clean over the open sluice and out of sight.

Bess shivered. 'I'm glad we didn't build the house too close to the brook. We might easily have done, except Nick said he liked looking over the forest, and that rise is the best place to do it.'

Not for the first time, Richard reflected that there were unexpected facets to Nicholas, but he soon forgot him as Bess lifted her skirts and scampered for the house through thickening rain. They arrived together in the doorway, laughing and shaking wet out of their hair, Bess teasing him about catching cold in his tonsure.

The house seemed dim and secret beneath the curtain of rain. Bess and Richard went from room to room like children set loose, breathing the smells of fresh timber and new plaster, pointing to marks which said where doors or partitions would go, scrambling precariously up the unguarded stair to call to each other through gaps in the floorboards.

'Just think,' said Bess dreamily. 'There's a press where I can hang up my Sunday gown, with room for ten more beside it, whoever do you think would have ten gowns at one time?'

'Ah, but once you live here, you'll need to puff up your importance by changing gowns each day, until I daresay ten will be too few. The master needs to sell a great many cannon if he's to keep pace with the comforts of Mistress Bess.'

She laughed, and ran down the stairs ahead of him. 'Come then and help finish the hearth before ill fortune settles there. Our omens will have to be exactly right if we're ever to become so grand.'

Richard hesitated again over admonishing her on the subject of dangerous belief, and again thought better of it. This one evening was a holiday and he never remembered feeling so light-hearted.

'It's a little out of straight,' he admitted when Bess led him over to the hearth. 'But I like your design. And what a splendid fireback your father made!'

'It is lovely, isn't it?' Her finger traced the delicate pattern, where a stylized brook ran between leafed borders and in the centre was recorded Edenham's story: from hovel, forge, finery and furnace to finished cannon. Tiny figures wheeled barrows and hammered on anvils, drove oxen and constructed sluices. Struck proudly across the top was the master's mark of a bracken frond crossed with a forgeman's hammer as borne by all Edenham ware, together with initials and date: FW 1553.

'I wonder what Edenham will have grown to be by the time your sons look at this,' said Richard slowly. 'I remember the little there was here when I first came as a boy, and marvel at what your father has wrought out of a single lifetime, but Nick will build strongly too. The master loves good iron above everything and spares no effort to turn out fine goods; Nick cares for profit first.'

'Well, he'd better hope this new queen you keep telling us about will go on building ships,' said Bess practically. 'Now, what can we do to finish the hearth?'

Richard squatted on his heels beside her. 'Only Bess, the very first time she laid brick to brick, would be so ambitious. The trouble is, your pattern's difficult to finish against the kerb. Perhaps if we made if half a brick wider you would have –' he measured with outstretched thumb and forefinger. 'Yes. You would have extra space to finish the crosswise grain of brick. Change the kerb into brick-on-edge and it won't alter the part you've finished.'

'Wouldn't it look strange?'

'I can't see another way out without changing the checker you have started, which would be a pity. After all, a higher kerb will keep ash in the hearth. So far you've only laid the bricks on sand?'

Bess nodded. 'I didn't dare mortar the bits I'd finished when I knew there was something wrong. We must, though, before we leave tonight. Will you pull it apart while I close my eyes? I couldn't bear to watch.'

'I'll only have to move the front. Hands over your eyes then, Mistress.' Obediently she covered her eyes while Richard began swiftly stacking bricks: Bess had laid the rear section as truly as any mason would, but then had become dissatisfied with plainness and attempted a diagonal finish which needed more than patience and a true eye if it was to square off against a kerb.

'Open now,' said Richard when he had the last brick stacked. 'Look, if we damp the sand, we can measure the design we want.' They knelt, intent, pressing in bricks and taking them out again, arguing, laughing, insulting each other's notions. 'Yes!' shouted Bess at last. 'Look, the last row fits as it should! Brick-on-edge, what a fool I was not to see that was the answer!' she threw her arms round Richard's neck and kissed him joyfully.

And Richard Mercer, fifteen years a faithful monk, kissed her back. Freckled nose, bright eyes and vivid delight filled all his senses, never had he expected such strength in his own reactions. Monks lied if they said they never imagined a woman in their arms, but in a monastery it was possible to withstand the yearning if withstanding was what you truly desired. Alone with a fresh and joyous maid was a different matter, especially after she'd danced for months through most of his days and dreams.

'Bess. Oh, Bess, dearling mine.' Soon, even her name was gone and they were lying with her spine curved against his hands, her eyes like summer reflections in the brook. Then he began the night-fire kissing he couldn't possibly have imagined, his hands on the strings of her kirtle and fumbling soft breasts which were whiter than curd in the dusk.

Bess was eager and also young enough to know only as a little or as much as she saw around Edenham, at once matter-of-fact defenceless, because what she'd understood before seemed as ordinary as the rustlings in her parents' bedstraw.

When it finished, she lay under him looking like a child who had been battered in the millrace. 'Oh, Christ,' said Richard, even while his body shouted its delight. 'Oh Bess, I am ashamed.'

She moved slightly and he leaped off her as if haste could deny what had happened. But though he would have helped her up she lay still again, her hands moving across the hearth, an odd smile on her face. 'Surely there's naught to be ashamed of, when it was the hearth which bade us to offer it life.'

He stared at her numbly. 'Bess, no. It wasn't like that at all. I wanted you, don't you understand? Though as a vowed monk and guest in your father's home, I can't believe there is a penance which will fit my sin.'

'But it wasn't sin, don't you see? The hearth put its spell on us and took what it wanted! And if it could be thought a sin, why, your scruples were mastered by the little folk themselves,' she added mischievously. 'Either way, there's no shame.'

No shame? How could there be none, when remorse burned as if the marrow of his bones was turned into molten iron? Richard began to shiver as a different abyss opened at his feet: instinct telling him that because Bess was so young, and held beliefs he ought to have condemned, she accepted what had happened almost without remark and certainly as a secret to be kept. Life given to her hearth-gods might be ill-omened by chatter, she would think, if he stayed silent too, then he would be able to leave Edenham with a friendship he valued still unbroken. And the priest in Richard Mercer shuddered more fiercely than before: how utterly he had been defeated, when never had he expected that particular lust to trap him.

What if there should be a child? As they left the house this thought hurtled at him out of the darkness, bringing further terror. By now, the rest of the family must be wondering what had kept them. Secretly, incoherently, his decision to stay silent was already nearly formed.

Lost in wretchedness, he lurched into Bess when she stopped, saying. 'Look! There's something amiss.'

Lamps were bobbing along the edge of the brook, their light smeared over racing water. A raw dark booming shook the earth and as Richard's thoughts steadied, he saw that the millrace seemed to have changed shape.

He pushed past Bess and started running; before he reached the bank he could see water pouring over the top of the dam, the timber stakes and clay from which it was constructed already shredding in the flood. 'What happened?' he had to yell to make himself heard. 'Where's the master?'

'A tree came down the brook and blocked the sluice. When I tried to clear un, ''twas thick enough to jam against the wheel,' Will Bywood shouted back. 'T'master be down there.'

He jerked his head and Richard saw with horror that Francis was standing waist-deep in the white water of the race, chopping methodically at the jammed trunk. So long as it remained caught, the flow of water was sufficiently reduced for a man to be able to brace himself against it, but once it was cut . . .

'We've a rope round 'un and orders to pull like the devil when the tree shifts,' yelled Will, and Richard saw rope thrown over an oak support and men with poles waiting to lever tree roots clear the moment the trunk was cut. Instantly his mind cleared: although he would indignantly have denied it, in some ways he was no less superstitious than Bess. Instead of Francis Wyse's life, his own would be forfeit in payment for a sin he could scarcely live with for a single night. He thrust Bess at one of the men, shouting for him to hold her, grabbed a mallet and clawed his way down the steep race bank. Once down, he was completely surrounded by white water, scouring, driving, hammering at his body, the race a narrow cut through which the mill pool usually discharged just sufficient water to drive a pair of wheels. Because of the rain, for months the sluice gates had been raised to let through a greater flow than usual, the cut so constructed that rubbish could be easily cleared. This time, however, a young ash perhaps forty feet tall had washed out somewhere deep in the forest, and its roots were almost closing the sluice, its branches wedged against the paired water wheels, which shook to the force of the remaining water since they were now prevented from rotating. Where Francis and Richard stood in the sluice bed, water was piled twenty feet high behind their backs by dam and sluice, the ash trunk nearly splintered through by Francis's axe strokes but still holding. Soon, very soon, the dam, both water wheels and all the oak shafting to the forge, would be swept away as pent-up water broke though, the two men tangled in the roaring mass.

There was no chance of speaking in such an enormous din, and until Francis came within a fraction of cutting the ash trunk through, Richard knew he could only wait. Saw the master's head shaken in anger that he had come, but also the grin of thanks. More water, a solid spout of it this time, came through the sluice as the ash began to shudder under the axe, making both men stagger. Now. Surely. Now. Francis paused, struck twice more, paused again. Untied the rope from his chest and, while Richard anchored him as best he could, floundered down the race to attach it to the branches of the ash. They would have to pull those clear before they dislodged the cut stump from the sluice, or the rush of water would destroy the immobilized wheels.

Yet the last few axe strokes which cut the ash in two would almost certainly jerk the stump clear before they were ready, and bring all that mighty head of water down on men still standing in the race. Richard grabbed Francis's arm, bellowing above the clamour of water 'I'll do it!'

Francis shook his head violently and gestured for more rope from above. Lamplight, rain, black water everywhere; half-drowned men, their minds battered by noise and fear and haste. Richard held his mallet as if his hands were plaited to it, thrust Francis aside so violently that he nearly lost his footing. 'A mallet's better than an axe!'

Francis hesitated, nodded. As the nearly severed ash pinched and buckled, it trapped his blunted blade. Nor could they squabble like children when the next instant might see them dead, a large part of Edenham swept away. Besides, the life of whoever remained below would depend on instant timing and quick thinking by the man in charge above, a task for which no one was better suited than the Master of Edenham. With his own hands Francis tied a double thickness under Richard's arms, refusing to hurry as he tested each knot for weakness. Then he touched him once on the shoulder and signalled to the men above to pull him clear, scrambled, twisted, heaved himself up that perpendicular bank.

For a moment Richard stood, quite alone and savouring his atonement. He felt at peace, but also wryly amused to realize that part of his contentment came from a newly-slaked body which knew nothing of remorse. Then he braced his shoulders and drove the mallet at the treetrunk: once, twice, three times. As shredded timber continued to resist him, gouts of water slapped through the sluice in time to his strokes. Then everything happened faster than thought, faster even than instinct. As he struck again the ash cracked, and all he saw was blackness changing shape as solid water struck him.

He was flung against something, pain like an anvil in his chest and ear the only sensation left, then even that was gone and he knew nothing more.

He regained consciousness lying on the floor of the forge, the sound of turning wheels a steady rolling and gulping which did not stop. Outside, men were calling urgently to each other, but the boom of water had subsided into a rain-swollen roar. Richard groaned and opened his eyes. Bess sat on the floor beside him, all bright sympathy for his hurts and admiration for his courage; Richard stared back at her through a blur of splintered consciousness, aware only of rage and bitter disillusion. His atonement for sin had not been accepted.

★★★

Richard wanted to leave Edenham as soon as he had regained sufficient strength to stagger, and fortunately the excuse to do so without offence soon presented itself. Word spread that the king had died three weeks before and, after some tense doings, his sister Mary was proclaimed queen. Richard's duty now must be to report the state of Ockham but, since he intended never to return to Sussex, his conscience insisted he must wait until he knew whether Bess was with child. Yet he could scarcely bear to look at her any longer, self-disgust making what had happened seem as ugly as a witches' sabbath; even while sweet memory insisted it had not been like that at all.

That rain-filled dusk on the hearth of Edenham would be the only time in his life that Richard Mercer would lie with a woman, and though he did not know it yet, his penance was to be an unfailing memory for the many pleasures he had gained.

None of which was made easier to bear when the Wyses believed he had offered his life in the millrace in repayment for succour long ago, and Francis said frankly that without him he would most likely have died. 'Since,' as he observed, 'I doubt you would have known the curses which make men scamper quite so swiftly. We had the branches out of the wheel a breath before the water hit, and you fished from the flood a thickness of bark before you would have hit the paddles.'

How I wish you hadn't, thought Richard. He hardly spoke, and the Wyses thought it was because of the headaches he suffered after his battering, and were even kinder in consequence. His first step to recovery came when they moved into their new house, leaving him alone in the old hovel. They were puzzled when he refused to accompany them; only Bess smiled a secret smile of her own, which drove him to further madness.

But once they had gone, it was better.

Richard was trained in solitude and gradually his summer of brawling life at Edenham set in his mind, like the painted canvases he had seen in Padua; to be meditated on at a distance. And as he meditated, the easy offer of his life began to seem presumptuous, a wasteful gesture of despair. All the same, it was October before he summoned courage to speak alone to Bess. He found her gathering mushrooms when he returned one day from viewing a stranded load of charcoal in Gregs Wood; she greeted him with unaffected delight and came dancing to him through trees already touched by the oncoming winter. 'Richard! I never seem to see you nowadays. Father says you are hankering for the monastery again.' She wrinkled her nose and laughed, the quiet stones of a monastery quite extraordinary to her.

'It is what I'm vowed to, after all,' he said defensively.

'Well, I find it very odd! It isn't as if you couldn't earn a good living competing with other men. You must have learned nearly enough by now to set up as an ironmaster on your own.'

'I haven't managed to haul the master's load of charcoal out of the mire in Gregs Wood, so I still have a deal to learn,' he answered drily. 'Bess, I don't know how to say this, but I must. Are you all right? I mean –' he floundered, though this scene had been rehearsed through many wakeful nights.

She was puzzled, since, as always, she felt as healthy as a buck in spring. 'Is your head still hurting? I'll make a brew which should ease it, if only you'd let me try.'

'My head is perfectly all right, and you must know what I mean. You never said anything, did you, to Mistress Wyse about – about us in the new millhouse?'

'Oh no.' Her face cleared. 'That was between us and the hearth, wasn't it? You mustn't worry so dreadfully, Richard. The house has such a happy feel to it now, and I'm sure some of it comes from what we offered.'

For a moment he couldn't think how to reply although he had guessed fairly accurately how Bess would regard the matter. 'Bess, I have to go away. I ought to have gone long ago, and unless I leave soon I shall be caught here by the winter. I suppose I couldn't leave at all if – you aren't carrying a child, are you?'

She went into a peal of laughter. 'Of course I'm not!'

A great load slid off his mind. 'You're sure?'

Of course I'm sure. She said scornfully. 'You never waited all this time to ask me that?'

And, unexpectedly, he began to laugh too.

Because she thought of what they had done as an offering to the house, she'd never even considered that she might breed from him. It was as simple as that. And so in the end he was able to kiss her farewell; not on the cheek as he intended, but on the mouth. She was as sweet as the forest itself and after a moment he began to tremble in the same way he remembered from before. This time he stepped back and dropped his hands. 'God be with you, Bess.'

'And with you,' she answered fiercely. 'Come back sometime. I think I might be waiting for you.'

'No. You mustn't. I shan't be back.' He looked at her as if he committed more than bright eyes and soft lips to memory, then went slowly on through the forest until he reached Edenham. There he bade farewell to Francis and Mary, and left within the hour for London.

Mary loved her new house, and was constantly underfoot while the Carpenter brothers finished it. She polished and repolished the oak dresser which was so large it had been dovetailed together where it was to stand, scoured pots which previously she had left blackened, burnished the studs on the door with ash and handfuls of grass. She never tired of marvelling that the floor would not become muddy in winter, that the chimney did not smoke and Francis's wrought fireback reflected more heat than she had ever known. She was generous in praising Bess's design in hearth-bricks, nor did she disagree when the girl smiled softly and repeated that a truly laid hearth brought contentment to the whole. For the new millhouse seemed well-omened indeed. Their bellies settled in the dry and Nicholas's cough vanished; and though the farmers moaned the wet weather suited Francis, because so much water drove his mill wheels day and night. Even Preece scuttled about his business as unobtrusively as possible while the new government prepared to return the English Church to Rome, which would not countenance married priests. Then, just after Christmas, he disappeared altogether and it was like having an abscess lanced, the relief was so great.

Above all, Mary loved the room she and Francis shared alone. Will Carpenter made them a box-bed to fill with straw and she often tiptoed up to look at it, or to gaze out of the lattice window. Never before had she seen right over the trees encircling Edenham and though she did not precisely forget that it was Nicholas who had insisted on this site for their house, she often remarked on how fortunate it was they should have staked out their walls in so exactly right a place.

The memory of nights in the big box-bed away from listening ears often made her blush next day; sometimes she wished she and Francis could have had such delights when they were younger, but mostly she was just glad to have them now. Alone, with time and space for skill, Francis could still make her swell with want: sometimes gathering her as softly as summer wind whispering through the forest, at other times as quick as water down the sluice: after these nights she would sing while she stirred her pots, and vow it would be a long time yet before her blood chilled with age.

The first crack in their contentment came more than a year after they moved into their new house. James came pelting down the track one morning, shouting before his words could be understood, and, since he seldom became excited over anything, everyone stood in mid-task and tried to make sense of his bellowing. Francis cursed them back to work at once, since the furnace was ready to tap. James, too, stopped shouting when he realized what everyone was at, seized a puddler and prepared to help.

No matter how long Francis worked in iron, and it was more than thirty years since he had been apprenticed, he still loved the anticipation and drama of a pour. The furnace would have been stoked and fuelled and tended without a break, perhaps for weeks, until the moment came when he knew in his guts the metal was ripe to draw. Quite how he knew he couldn't explain, the time varying with the grade of ore and quality of fuel, also the strength of draught. But he would become restless, start eyeing smoke and laying his hand against the furnace side; would study cinder rakings and peer from scaffolding into the belly of the furnace. Then he would know.

All the men at Edenham sensed the moment when his decision was taken; his head would nod, beard jut at the sky, hands clasp behind his back. They then ran for rakes and mallets, iron spikes and plugs and puddlers. The great bar which disengaged shafting to the water wheel would be thrown back to stop the draught, and Francis himself – always – ran the iron. It was dangerous work and many furnacemen were maimed by spat metal, but never once had there been an injury from a tap at Edenham. From carelessness at forge or finery, yes; and slashed hands or broken bones during heavy work elsewhere. But never from a tap, because there an ironmaster's skill could control the risk so long as he never once allowed his vigilance to slip.

James watched the white-hot metal arch into cannon-moulds packed upright in their pit. Smoke boiled upward and the smell of scorched dung tore at his throat, moulds being made from a mix of clay and dung and hay. Blackened figures stirred and scurried, tramped in drilled unison as they heaved at block and tackle during the short time in which a pour was a success or failure. Then the furnace would be sealed again, the moulds dug out and split, cold iron chipped free from dross before the cannon could be trimmed, drilled, mounted and scoured. But it was the pour which drew the whole of Edenham together, which stopped men's hearts and filled them with triumph as moulds were filled, or red molten threads raced into each frond of an intricate design.

As the last of the smoke cleared and a breeze cut through searing heat, Francis straightened from re-sealing the tapping hole. 'What is it, James?'

James scratched his head for a moment after the excitement of the pour, to gather his thoughts again. 'Preece. You'll never believe it, but he's back. As a fully-fledged Catholic priest this time, a rosary hung at his belt.'

The muscles of Francis's face tightened. 'Mistress Preece?'

'Turned off with her brats to beg, or so they say. We thought he'd bolted into hiding, but all he did was grovel to have his heresy forgiven.'

'Poor woman,' said Francis quietly, and went back to work.

It was left to Mary to say what everyone knew was true; that the Devil was loose in Ferneth, and not a man of God.

Mark Wyse came to see his brother next day and the two men talked long and earnestly by the dam, although they had never been closer than civility demanded. Afterwards Mark drank ale in their parlour and complimented Mary on her brewing, when before he had always been so consumed by jealousy for their fortune that he rarely came except to demand money for trumped-up damage in Gregs Wood.

Mary burst into tears when he left, and clung to Francis where he sat by the hearth. 'You must tell me! What warning did he bring?'

'No warning. A caution, perhaps, that I should offer the full form of words for whatever Preece demands.'

She looked at him, her face a breath from his. 'Or else?'

He kissed her, and stood. 'I shouldn't be sitting by the hearth at mid-morning of a Friday. Aye, or take the consequences, I suppose.'

'The full form of words,' said Mary slowly. 'What does he mean? We have always followed the law in religion; I know you dislike the pope being brought back, but we go each week to mass. What more can Preece demand?'

'He may want to puff off his own pride a little and humble mine. We shall have to wait and see.' He went out.

But if Preece is the kind of priest who changes faiths like a tanner turning leather, who leaves his wife and children to beg so long as his skin is saved, is there any limit to the evil he might do? thought Mary fearfully.

The evening meal at Edenham was usually a boisterous meal, with one or other of the Laffam boys nearly always visiting because Davey Laffam was courting Sal, Walter mooning after May, and the twins,

Matt and Bart, half-crazed over Bess. The Laffam twins saw nothing odd about courting the same maid; as Matt pointed out, though only one of them could actually wed her there was no reason why this should matter. They had never grudged each other a share in anything, so marriage oughtn't to prevent them sharing Bess. But on the evening after Mark Wyse came, the Laffams found attention difficult to secure; Mistress Wyse scarcely touched her food and even little Ned snapped that he was thinking when Bart tried to interest him in a saddle horse he was buying, normally a subject guaranteed to trigger interest. Only James looked as placid as usual, and Francis talked easily about a new law which would compel parishes to repair their roads.

'I wouldn't care to be chosen as an overseer, with the task of making my neighbours break stones for nothing,' observed Davey, grinning. He was the largest of the Laffams and possessed fists like rock.

'Nor I, but there is no denying that trade will be at a standstill soon unless something is done about our tracks and highways. Men are sensible if they're dealt with fairly, and most will see where their interest lies.

Davey looked unconvinced; others might crick their backs over stone without being paid for it, but not the Laffams. 'Perhaps.'

Francis laughed. 'Though I should not seek the task of road constable, you may be sure that if I was chosen, your brawn wouldn't win you exemption.'

'Where is Nicholas? Interrupted Mary in a high, unnatural voice.

'He went to the Black Bear and said he would be late back.' James discovered a hunk of meat left in the pot and speared it on his knifepoint with a grunt of satisfaction.

He's gone to Furneth? How could he be such a fool! He knew it was safest if we all stayed quietly here.'

The Laffams stared at her in astonishment. Though all her sons towered over her, Mistress Laffam still beat them if they spewed on her floor or behaved in other ways of which she disapproved; but she would never have dreamed of questioning their right to drink or wench wherever they wished, providing they slept off the after-effects in the barn.

'Nick's all right,' said James easily. 'He wanted to find out how the land lay before we must go to church on Sunday. He'll keep out of Preece's way, never fear.'

Francis flicked a warning glance at their visitors. 'There's no reason why Nick shouldn't go wherever he pleased. He's a grown man with an eye to his own affairs.'

'I'm not keeping out of piggly Preece's way,' announced Ned. He was eight years old, angelically fair and seldom out of trouble. 'I've worked it all out, and the best thing would be if me and Rory Bywood disguised ourselves as vagabonds. Then we could lay in wait for him one dark night and scare him away. Gibber at him until he does, and howl like jack o'lanterns.'

The Laffam boys broke into hoots of laughter and would have entered into what they saw as a splendid lark, had not Francis curtly ordered Ned from the table for insolence towards his betters. Then he turned to James and began talking about the delivery of cannon.

Mary muttered some apology and fled outside, biting her lips on tears. It was spring and a thin rim of moon swung low over budding trees. A new moon lying on its back, moreover, which everyone knew kept the water in and the season fine.

Francis came out behind her. 'Sweeting, you must not let Preece upset you, when all he has done is return as our priest.'

Mary buried her face in his jerkin. 'I know. I will face him on Sunday as if we had nothing to fear, I promise. But Christ be my witness, I am afraid.'

He held her tightly, and put a finger under her chin to tip her face on his. 'You mustn't be. I do not like priests puffed up in their tyranny, nor a foreign pope ruling over us again, but I have not said so and nor do I intend to. I'm an ironmaster, not a meddler in matters which belong between each soul and God.'

Mary signed with relief. She had never quite understood how far Francis was and was not open to persuasion, but if he said he would keep his mouth shut and conform, then he would. 'Preece is spiteful enough to indict you for a single word out of place.'

'I swear that any quarrel will not be of my making.'

Mary considered this doubtfully. 'What if it's of his?'

'I'll avoid it if I can. The church has more important quarry than me to pursue.'

'But not easier,' said Nicholas, appearing out of the dark. 'Sir, Furnace Green is in uproar. Preece has come back more zealous than the Bishop of Rome himself.'

'The pope,' said Francis mildly. 'It is again his title in England. As for Father Preece's zeal, I suppose he needs to work at outliving the years he spent as a Protestant parson.'

'In the Black Bear they say he has already threatened half the village with the bishop's court for thieving Ockham property, and the other half with heresy or adultery. None of those wed by the new rites since King Harry broke with Rome are truly bound he says, and live in a state of sin.'

'We were wed before.'

'I thought you must have been which is some relief. Preece takes a fee to re-wed the rest, he might find some excuse to refuse you if he could.'

'But –'Mary stopped. 'Nick he wed them by the new rites himself, which now he says wasn't a true binding.'

Nicholas gave an angry crack of laughter. 'Aye. But who would dare remind him of that, when the penalty for unforgiven heresy is burning at the stake?'

There was a sudden dreadful silence, filled by wind sighing through bare branches.

'So it has always been,' said Francis after a moment. 'I never heard of anyone being burned for it, even so.'

'You will now. A carter and a shoemaker have been taken up for heresy in Mayfield, and the talk is that they will burn there while their families watch. This queen means to have conformity of belief and will do whatever is needful to get it. So Preece has all the authority and power he desires.' Nicholas looked directly at his father. 'Sir, my Uncle Robert Wyse, God rot his bones, was telling in the Black Bear how you once set fire to the priest-house roof. He recounted it as naught but a boyhood prank, but only malice could have made him recall such a damaging tale when it would do nothing but harm.'

'Rob!' exclaimed Mary! 'Why should he – ' She broke off, realizing just how much an unscrupulous man nearly ruined by bad weather, ailing sheep and poor markets might hope to gain from the ruin of a prosperous brother. 'May the spirits draw his black brain out through his nostrils! But could he really profit in such a way?'

'I expect the Church decides who will receive a reward for bearing witness against heresy. It is true, then?' Nicholas's voice was cold, as his inheritance too was reckoned in the balance.

Francis had been standing quite still, his eyes on the pale night sky. 'If they don't care about proof, yes. I was at Riffield Castle with your mother when Father Poctor's roof burned off those many years ago. He held me to blame, but neither the king's officers nor the bishop would listen to what he said. Since Lord Scovell himself could bear witness that I wasn't there.'

'The old lord is dead and here is Preece – what, twenty years later? – who needn't worry about proof. Especially if your brother Robert is willing to swear you did it, and I expect he knows one way or another.' Unexpectedly, Nicholas gave a ghost of a laugh. 'I often wondered where the feud between you and Furnace Green's priests began, but never guessed at anything so exciting. I wouldn't have thought it of you, sir.'

'It seemed fitting at the time, when Father Poctor behaved more like a usurer than a priest.'

'Francis, for God's sake mind what you say.' cried Mary, her fingers dug like hooks into his arm.

'Whatever else I may have to fear, I don't fear Nick.' answered Francis, smiling at his son.

'You never feared Rob before!'

Quite gently, but using such strength as was needed Francis pulled her hand from his arm and forced her round to face him. 'Mistress, you are distraught. I would trust Nick with my life and may have to very soon, as he would me with his. He has a right not to be told lies when he asks me why we are all in peril because of something I did twenty years ago. James won't ask and the other children are too heedless or too young to care, but I may be forced to leave a good deal for Nick to do if things go badly for me.'

He believes they will go badly, thought Mary dully. She wrung her hands on the turmoil of her thoughts and scarcely heard the men still talking.

'You ought to hide in the forest.' Nicholas's tone was warmer, although he did not comment on what Francis had said.

'Become an outlaw after a lifetime of crafting iron? Nay, it's too late for me to turn vagabond now. And for what? This is royal policy and not something which might be forgotten if I dropped out of sight for a summer. Once I went I could never come back, and Preece perhaps still be unsatisfied as he watched all of you enjoying as much prosperity as before.' He did not mention his brother, but Robert Wyse would certainly be unsatisfied over the matter of reward if Edenham remained in Francis's gift. 'If he decides to move against me, Preece won't accuse me of burning the priest-house but of heresy. He could just as easily decide to accuse you, and find you easier game.

'Why?' demanded Nicholas, annoyed.

Francis laughed and clapped him on the shoulder. 'I'm an old and cunning fox. They couldn't prove anything against me twenty years ago, and they won't find it any easier now.'

With that, they had to be satisfied. Francis refused to discuss the affair any further and forbade his family to do so either, saying that the less said the safer for everyone. This was undoubtedly true, as rumour galloped down the track from Furnace Green to Edenham: Preece had brought bishop's officers to his house; there would be bonds of recantation issued and penance for sin imposed; blood and bones, have you heard? No less than sixty-two pounds and four silver shillings are to be demanded as recompense for the trespass of Furneth folk on Ockham!

Sunday dawned warm and clear, the first true day of spring at last, and everyone from Edenham walked to mass together. Birds were nesting, buds splitting, creatures scuttling, which made it seem doubly hard that for once no one was able to rejoice in the passing of winter. Even the young children of their workers knew the master was in danger: from a foreign pope, men said, but the name meant little and so they pictured an alien tyrant hiding a tail inside his breeches.

When Francis and Mary walked up the slope to join the rest there was a great shuffling of feet and muttering, the atmosphere quite different from the many previous times they had walked peacefully to church together. Francis paused at the track edge and ran a keen eye over the waiting faces: there must be more than a hundred of them when the families of the thirty-one men he employed were reckoned in. 'What are you thinking of, taking weapons to church? Dickon, Wat, I'm not blind. Take those hammers back to the forge at once. The rest of you leave behind whatever you have hidden, unless you want me to strip you off to look while the women watch.'

''Tis no joke, Master,' said Wat Oxley bluntly, who was chief hammerman at the forge. 'We don't aim to use them, see? Just let parson know he daren't take 'ee from under our nebs.'

'Aye, I daresay. But any man with a weapon in his hand fights quicker than if he had to run and fetch it. You'll have heard what happened when Furneth thought to change King Harry's mind by force and put back Ockham's abbot: the ringleaders were clapped in a dungeon and lucky to come out alive. Kings and queens never overlook revolt, no more than would a master worth his salt. Like me. I told you to leave behind any weapon you have concealed and I meant it. The man who walks armed to mass will never work at Edenham again.'

Wat's eyes shifted to the men around him, and for an instant it looked as if they would hold firm. Then someone threw an iron bar in the ditch, and one by one the rest followed his example. They knew the master would do exactly as he had said, whether one or thirty defied him, even if it meant earning his bread single-handed for a while.

'You should have pretended not to see,' whispered Mary, as they all trooped sulkily down the track. 'You may need a few iron bars in the churchyard before Preece can be made to change his mind.'

'It would make revenge easier for him. As matters are he has only his own spite, a couple of bishop's clerks and perhaps a constable to help him. But if there was an armed affray in our churchyard then would Lord Scovell have to come with his following to exact punishment.' Francis drew her hand beneath his arm and the rest of the walk was completed in silence.

Furnace Green's single street was almost empty, its new and newly-building cottages gleaming in the sun. The church gleamed too, its stone sufficiently recent to reflect light from a myriad cloven surfaces, although part of the roof was still thatched: the upheavals of the past few years had interrupted coin-gatherings to pay for tiles.

Inside, the church was packed, since Brother Benedict had not anticipated an iron industry which, alone, would employ double the number of men as had lived in the parish during his lifetime. Preece stood by the door, ostentatiously counting his flock as they entered, two officials carrying staffs at his back. He scowled as Francis entered, and the whole congregation craned to see what both men would do.

Francis bowed and crossed himself, led the way to the Edenham benches at the back of the church; Preece returned to his counting, and everyone settled back in their places with a sigh.

The mass which followed was ordinary enough. Since Queen Mary ascended the throne nearly two years before a variety of hedge-priests had made the old forms familiar again. Mary had been pleased when the crucifix was replaced above the altar and old Drogo's wall-pictures scrubbed clear of limewash; if Preece's pope would only content himself with bringing back familiarity then she for one would welcome it. Mary did not expect to be fussed by religion and could never understand why other people felt differently; all she wanted was to be left alone in between Sundays, and for Francis not to be at the mercy of vengeful priests who changed their minds overnight about what their people should believe. It didn't seem much to ask, she thought, and studied Rob Wyse through spread fingers while she knelt. God rot him, anway.

Mary didn't know what kind of disaster she had expected, by the normality of a Sunday in Furnace Green – only the older people still called it Furneth – lulled her into not expecting it any more. She was taken unaware when the congregation stood to leave for their customary gossip in the churchyard, and Preece stopped them with a gesture. He held a scroll in his hand and read swiftly in a kind of nasal chant: Lord God, son of the Virgin without sin, Lord God, have mercy. Whereas divers persons of this parish must answer for their sins . . .' He added something in Latin but all anyone understood was the names at the end: James Smyth, Thomas Laffam, Walter the Sawyer, Francis Wyse, Frifwith Bellwasher. He rolled up his paper and walked out.

There was an instant of silence before a babble of talk burst out, everyone asking what it all meant. No one knew. Furnace Green hadn't understood clearly what their rulers wanted from them for a long time now, but this time the menace of not understanding moved close enough to touch. The two bishop's men stood in the doorway, unarmed except for the white staffs they held. One tapped Francis on his shoulder as he came out and jerked his head. 'Wait there.'

'God Almighty, Francis,' bellowed old Thomas Laffam when he too was stopped. 'A fine state of affairs this is, when a brace of turnkeys can bid a man wait on their pleasure without so much as by your leave.'

'I don't suppose that lawfully they can, but I'd prefer to be clear of this without forcing them to reach for a warrant. I expect you would too.' Francis went to stand where he was told.

Mary struggled against Nicholas's hand suddenly clamped on her arm. 'Let me go! Do you think I would let Francis stand alone as if I didn't care?'

Nicholas tightened his grip, his other hand grasping Bess. 'This is the way he wants it. Let Preece make all the moves and not offer the shred of an excuse for a formal charge. But look at the company he makes the Master of Edenham keep! Rogues every one of them. Don't worry, madam, our people will prevent him from being take up by two trumpery knaves, I promise.'

Preece came out from the church, a tall stout man with a double chin and formidable self-importance. He thrust his hands into his sleeves and rocked on his toes in front of Widow Bellwasher first. 'Woman, have you sinned.'

She rubbed her nose thoughtfully. 'If you say so, Father.'

'Not I, but God. You are well known for giving short measure, for living on false charity and for wantonness.'

There was a distinct snigger among the listening crowd. Though Widow Bellwasher had been wanton in her day she would find it hard to satisfy her inclinations now. She was, however, very full of excuses for a lifetime passed in casual sloth interspersed by petty thievery, and no one felt any particular sympathy for her now.

Nor was Father Preece hard on her, in fact he was magnanimous. As he was to Thomas Laffam, a cantankerous old scoundrel widely regarded as a horse-coper and now condemned for profiteering out of Ockham stone. A few whines from Widow Bellwashser and a bellow or two from Thomas got both of them off with no more than admonitions to live virtuously and come to confession the following week. James Smyth, already branded for bridle-robbery, and Walter the Sawyer who went berserk when drunk, fared no worse. Both took their cue from Thomas and mumbled a few shamefaced words which the optimistic might have called contrition, and were let off with trifling penances.

Which left Francis, standing a little apart and watching as if none of this had anything do with him. All around him the villagers pressed close, dressed in their Sunday best and trampling turf where Benedict lay buried; excited, afraid, uncertain what would happen next. A few were disappointed when this most unusual day seemed to be turning into anticlimax. Most sensed that so far they had seen only shadow-play designed for official eyes, since Master Wyse's name would be inscribed among the rascals of the parish, any charge against him made to seem more telling because of mercy to the rest. But when Preece turned to Francis at last, it was with a civil request to step into the priest-house to discuss an adjustment of rent for land bought improperly off Ockham.

Francis hesitated, having expected accusations. 'I bought my pasture field fairly from the royal stewards charged to execute Ockham's affairs.'

'Perhaps that was then the law, but now it reads differently. We need to adjust monies between us as a consequence of this change,' answered Preece reasonably.

'I own that land freehold and have a quittance to prove it. No law can reverse affairs long settled in the past.'

'It can when the Church was grossly defrauded.' Snapped Preece.

'I doubt the Parliament House has agreed that men should be deprived of anything justly bought.'

'The Parliament House! What is that to the matter? Her Majesty has granted back the Holy Church's possessions.'

Francis did not answer, but as clearly as if he had spoken his smile said that on her own, the queen could not do it. Furnace Green might be isolated, but even there men knew that English kings and queens could no longer rule unsupported by Parliament law.

With an effort, Preece grabbed at his vanishing temper. 'Come to my house, Master Wyse, so I may show you my instructions on the matter of church lands.

'Nay, papers are not good to me since I cannot read them. I will take your word on your instructions and if the law is truly changed, then one day Lord Scovell will require my presence in his court. There I think we will adjust our differences easily enough.'

'The Church is no longer in the hands of meddling magistrates! It runs its own affairs.' Preece rounded on his two officers. 'Bring him to my house.'

Francis did not move, even when the men tried to hustle him away. Instead he braced his legs and stood, as awkward as fresh-poured pig iron to shift.

At first there was some laughter as the pushing and heaving began, then an angry silence spread.

'Leave him,' said Nicholas abruptly. He dropped Mary's arm and stepped forward. 'He told you he wouldn't move without a warrant, so run and get one sworn or else go eat your dinner.'

One by one the Edenham men stepped forward to join him, unarmed perhaps, but thick-muscled as all forgemen were, closing in on the two beadles holding Francis. And all the while spring sunshine flooded over Furnace Green, a soft wind blew down the village street and high in the blue sky a lark began to sing.

'I shall laugh on the day you burn. Preece's voice was low and shaking, but few in the churchyard did not hear. He turned on his heel and stalked away, cassock flapping, and after a moment his two men followed.

Preece rode for Riffield that same evening. He heard ale-blurred laughter in the Black Bear as he passed and ground his teeth in rage, well knowing that the drinkers would be savouring each detail of a day when, between them, they had prevented the Church from exacting righteous restitution. It was bitter indeed to need mere magistrates to enforce God-given power; still, property was property and nobles as interested as the Church in preserving it, which was why Preece had judged it best to accuse the heretic Wyse of sharp-dealing first, and leave graver charges over doctrine until he was safe in gaol.

Riffield Castle had changed a great deal since Ralf d'Escoville's day five centuries before. First it had grown in size until his tiny palisaded hill scarcely existed any more, then it was fortified in stone during the long years of medieval uproar until, during the past half-century of domestic peace, the outer walls were quarried for blocks to build the kind of quarters Tudor noblemen considered best suited to their comfort. Two fine galleries stood where the guardhouse once had been: plaster ceilings and glazed windows took the place of loopholed walls and bitter draughts.

Preece was left a long time in the great hallway, resentfully staring at carved Scovell coats of arms; even the red-jerkined server who came at last to lead him to his lordship's presence wore the black bear badge on his shoulder. Nobles no longer overturned the English state with their quarrels, but only because they preferred to preserve their great possessions in peace; they retained ample means to do so if they chose.

Gervase, seventeenth baron and fourth earl Scovell, received Father Preece standing with his back to the huge hearth recently added to his drawing room. Gervase would have preferred to be sitting on his still more recent terrace which overlooked the deer park, but if he received Preece there then common civility would compel him to offer refreshment and a seat. In front of his own hearth he could stand, and damn any thought of hospitality to an intrusive priest.

'You asked to see me? He said at once, since he did not believe in wasting time over disagreeable duties.

'Yes, my lord, I need your help over a troublesome matter in Furnace Green.' Preece was too intent on his purposes to notice brusqueness.

'I am not lord of the manor of Furnace Green.'

'Aye, I know it, more's the pity. But I ask for your help as Lieutenant of this county of Sussex, and its chief magistrate.

'Oh? What is this matter?'

'A man called Wyse, my lord. A noted heretic and thief of monastic lands, who resisted my reasonings after mass.'

'These are matters for the Church. See to it if you wish.'

'I tried my lord. He refused to accompany me to my house, where I would have seized and taken him to the bishop's court. Then his men broiled in the churchyard so as to carry him safely off. My two officers were powerless.'

'I repeat it is a matter for the Church.'

'Not once there was a breach of the peace,' said Preece annoyed.

'How many were hurt?'

Preece hesitated. 'I don't know.'

'Then I suggest you find out and bring any complainant to swear his case before me. As for heresy or monastic lands, they are outside my jurisdiction.

'I think not, my lord,' said Preece softly. 'I have here a copy of a letter written by Her majesty's own secretary to my bishop, in which he says that you, as Lieutenant of Sussex, are required to use all the power you possess to aid the restoration of true religion. He further writes that your lordship has received instructions from the Privy Council in this sense.'

There was a long silence while Gervase snapped a lock on his temper and considered how best to extricate himself from a distasteful situation. 'I have no authority in matters of heresy,' he repeated at last.

'No my lord, but the Privy Council has charged you with the duty of seizing those whom the Church requires to answer for their souls. On pain of royal displeasure.'

Gervase jerked a chain which hung by the mantel somewhere beyond the door a bell clanged. 'I regret that you will have to ride home in the dark.'

'But – but – ' Preece choked. 'My lord, I asked for help which Her Majesty has charged you to provide! I need your men to arrest this man, Wyse. Once he is taken, that is the end of your responsibility. The Church will try and condemn him.'

'I am committed to other duties in Her Majesty's interest for the next few days and then I must return to London. While I am there I will consult with the Privy Council over the matter of magistrates and the Church, since I should not like to exceed my powers. I fear it may be some weeks before I return to Sussex with the answer,' he added blandly.

'You mean you refuse to act as Her Majesty has already instructed you to act! My lord, I ask again for your following to come with me to Furnace Green now.'

'You forget yourself, Father. My following does my bidding, and no other.'

'But this should *be* your bidding!' Preece's face was dark with fury. 'I shouldn't wish to inform my bishop that there are heretics in Riffield as well as Furnace Green.'

Lord Scovell nodded to the man who had come running when he rang the bell. 'Show him out.'

Only when Preece had been led out, still mouthing threats, did Gervase turn and spit in cooling ash. Then he went out on the terrace and stared over the black ridges of his park. Preece deserved to be flogged for insolence and in a better regulated age Gervase would have ordered it done without a scruple, but he was under no illusion that as matters stood in Westminster Palace, he had taken a considerable risk in refusing help to an importunate priest. He did not regret it, although not particularly scrupulous in his dealings. If a seventeenth baron Scovell could not throw out anyone who displeased him, whether a priest or no, then matters had come to a dangerous pass.

'What is troubling you, my lord?' His lady was ten years older than he and horse-faced, but had been an heiress worth marrying both for her acres and shrewd sense.

He turned. 'I think I am unwell.'

'Indeed? Her eyes flickered to the redness of rage still mottling his cheeks. 'I am sorry to hear it.'

'Ah well, necessity might have struck at a worse time of year. Riffield hawking is always best.'

'Do you expect to be fevered long?'

He smiled sourly. 'God, it might be years, I suppose. Tell the steward I am unable to see anyone, do you understand?'

'Yes, my lord. Two royal messengers came last week, and one the week before.'

'I can't attend to official matters in my present state of health. God's blood, that canting priest ordered me to help him burn a man he chooses to call heretic.'

'Who?'

Gervase considered, this aspect of the matter not of particular concern to him. 'He is called Wyse, of Furnace Green. God's teeth and bones, it must be Francis Wyse, the ironmaster. The rest of the family are spineless dolts who have lost the substance their father left them: I doubt they have two principles to rub together between the pack of them.'

'It is easy to see you still covet Furnace Green, when you know it as well as your own estates,' she observed.

'Of course I covet it! And Francis Wyse was once apprenticed at my father's works in the park, I remember him as a lad.' He stared at Ferenthe Ridge bulked against the evening sky. Scovell lands stretched southwards nearly to the sea, yet from his own terrace he looked out on yokels' freeholds. 'I shall not get it now. Her Majesty had agreed to hold an inquiry into lordship of Furnace Green and was disposed to find in favour of my claim, since all the documents are corrupt. She will issue different instructions once she hears I am not so zealous as she would like in matters of persecution.

'Why are you not, my lord?' You hang enough sheep stealers each year.'

He shook his head in exasperation. Women were all the same, even the shrewdest of them. Unable to follow logically from one thought to the next. 'Scovells have never yet run yapping to the bidding of a priest, nor have I helped burn any man. Least of all will I help when that man is a neighbour and the bidding comes from an Italian pope and the King of Spain.'

'On the orders of English Queen Mary, surely.'

He shrugged. England might be temporarily lumbered with a woman ruler, but he could not imagine a female ruling for herself. Anyway, he found it preferable to blame foreigners for the many ills by which this reign was plagued. 'Come to bed, and tomorrow we will spread the word that I am sick. A pity, really. We shall weary of our own company through the summer visitings.'

'My lord?' She said much later, into the stuffing of their mattress.

He grunted sleepily.

'Can you do anything to help this Francis Wyse?'

God's blood, woman! I have refused to arrest him at great disadvantage to myself.'

She ignored that, seeing clearly that he had refused Preece chiefly because his presumption offended Scovell consequence. 'The priest will find others to act in your place.'

Gervase turned his back on her, rustling exasperation in the dark. 'If the bishop sends constables of his own to take a man for heresy, then I can't stop him.'

'You command three hundred servants,' she answered.

'Embroil my name in rebellion, and for a mere ironmaster! Do you hanker for my neck on the headsman's block?'

'Of course not,' she said placidly. 'But if you had a mind to it, there must be more subtle ways than rebellion to protect a neighbour you believe innocent of crime.'

'What ways, pray? And he will be found guilty of heresy, not crime. No, no, I risk sufficient displeasure by keeping out of the matter. Do you know, Her Majesty threatened to take his lieutenancy away from Ralph Howard when he disagreed in council with her policy? Good God, the Howards, bigots to a man! She wouldn't dare, of course, but it shows the need for care.'

I suppose so, she thought as his breathing slid into snore again. And yet . . . when Gervase has so much power, surely the fires of persecution could be kept out of Sussex, and without rebellion. An earl seventeen generations entrenched among his peers could not easily be dispossessed from office nor from his acres, whereas who in authority will care if peasants or forgemen burn?

Francis Wyse was of much the same opinion, although it was difficult not to believe the worse was over. Rollo the Frenchman's youngest son was a stable boy at Riffield Castle and he reported that Preece had arrived and departed within the hour without the help he wanted, nor did anyone have difficulty in interpreting the reasons for Lord Scovell's fever. Quite how all eastern Sussex, from magistrates to vagabonds, understood that poachers remained in the same danger as before while sinners had nothing to fear from their justices of the peace, no one could have said? Nevertheless, this understanding spread faster than a man could walk from one alehouse to the next.

Francis always thought most clearly while hammering iron. Throughout his life he had taken his trickiest problems to the anvil, and there beaten them into a shape he understood. Since the Master of Edenham rarely had time or need to work with tongs and hammer in these later years of his prosperity, everyone knew that when he did, he was best left alone.

Nicholas set aside this tradition on the Thursday following the scuffle in Furnace Green churchyard, although he paused at the forge entry, conscious that this moment was the end of many things; of a long apprenticeship to a master he respected, and to the time in his life when he did as he was told. Then he walked over and threw up the beam which connected the water wheel's power to bellows and hammer. 'I want to talk to you.'

Francis tossed the iron he had been working back on dulling charcoal. 'You just wasted half a morning's work, so it needs to be important.

'It is, since you refuse to discuss Preece at the supper table, and with Mother and Bess so upset I wouldn't say you were wrong. But this is ridiculous and you know it.'

Francis wiped sweat from his face and chest with his shirt and put it on. 'You go too quickly for me, Nick.'

'I don't think so. It is absurd for you to remain at Edenham as if nothing had happened. Madness to talk of trifles when next week you may be arguing for your life. Did you know I keep a man watching the track so that if the constables come, you'll have time to run for the forest?'

'I'd be a poor master if I did not know when a man is missing.'

'But if you went now, or better still if you had gone three days ago, you wold be so far ahead of the hunt they'd never find you.' Nicholas touched the anvil. 'You don't have to be an outlaw. You could earn your bread anywhere iron is worked.'

'Thank you,' said Francis drily.

'Then why not go before it is too late? I know you've been thinking of it, hammering here alone. Later you could send for mother, and I would account to you for our trade here.'

'I am sure you would. Aye, I won't deny I've been thinking of it, but my mind hasn't changed. I'm glad you came here today because I want you to remember what I say. Perhaps one day you may understand my meaning better.' He smiled faintly. 'I'm not sure I understand it myself, except I know this is the only way for me. If I thought Preece would haul me before a magistrate and charge me with firing the priest-house roof, I might run. If lawyers were sharpening their quills to strip me of fields I bought fairly, then I should also run – to hire their like in my defence. Can you understand me so far? Running is something a man does if there is choice; this way or that. To wrangle over laws, or not. Did he commit a felony or not? Francis hesitated, thinking how much clearer it had seemed inside his head, then went on more slowly. 'This isn't like that at all. This is a man, a priest as it happens, although as likely a scoundrel as ever walked the Weald. A man who for his own reasons, wants to tell me what I should or should not believe.'

'So do many men, and whether they are scoundrels makes no difference.' Said Nicholas impatiently. 'I should be surprised if every man jack in Her Majesty's own Privy Council isn't at least half a rogue.'

'Aye, so should I, but there is a difference.' He laughed. 'I'm something of a rogue myself, yet punish the man who disobeys me at Edenham. But I do not prevent anyone from speaking his mind, nor make them obey me for the pleasure of being a tyrant. They obey because an iron-works is dangerous and unprofitable place when it lacks a master. Well –' He rubbed his nose, wanting Nicholas to understand, but groping now himself. 'It seems to me there isn't much difference between Edenham and England.'

'Which has little to do with why you do not choose to go, while there's still time.'

Francis sighed. 'I'm better with iron than words. Nick – I have conformed to everything the law requires and would swear oaths on it if I was asked, no matter what my own beliefs. Because I also believe the land needs a master. I will not be driven from my home by greed and malice disguised as holiness. I will not surrender my own judgement of what is right. I will not run, even to save my life, if the consequence is that my kin and neighbours are nearer to being muzzled donkeys trotting to an oppressor's bidding.'

'Whether you go or stay will make no difference to anyone but you – and us. Furnace Green would seethe with rumour and outrage for a week, then get on with the business of living.'

Francis shook his head. Of course that would happen, no question. Men must eat. But other things would also happen which Nick must discover for himself: as the Good Book said, men did not live for their bellies alone. Especially Englishmen, or so the master of Edenham believed.

'You've been around furnaces a long time,' Nicholas said softly into the silence. 'Aren't you afraid?'

The muscles of Francis's mouth tightened. 'Aye, of course. I'd be a fool if I weren't afraid of burning, but mayhap it won't come to that.' He kicked the oak shaft loose from where Nicholas had notched it, and any further argument was drowned in clamour from the forge.

Three days later Jake Brown, Nicholas's watcher of the day, pelted back down the track, shouting that Preece was coming with a straggle of armed men at his back. 'How many?' demanded Nicholas?

'Ten . . . twelve. I dunno.' The man was wild with excitement and had not waited to see more than staves and swords.

Nicholas swore aloud, then turned as Francis emerged from the cannon-shed. 'Preece is bringing constables to do his bidding. For God's sake, change your mind! It still isn't too late.'

He saw the colour drain from his father's face, and, thinking that at this last moment he had seen the hopelessness of his folly, Nicholas began to hustle him towards the walkway across the dam. Even after twenty years of iron-smelting at Edenham, on the far side of the brook the great forest was close enough to reach in the few minutes which remained. Then Francis seemed to shake himself, dragged free from

Nicholas's grip and ran towards New Mill House.

One by one, at furnace, forge and moulding shed, men's heads began to lift, hammers to slow their beat. In the middle of it all, Nicholas stood chewing his lips and thinking that his father's obstinacy came so close to derangement, he almost deserved to die. Then he would be Master of Edenham. Let his uncle try to take it if he could. He gulped air muzzily. All his life he had thought bad things and hated himself for thinking them, but never had there been a worse time for remembering how much he stood to gain from his father's death.

When Preece and his followers filed across the rough ground between the track and Edenham they saw a knot of men gathering between millhouse and forge, most of them holding the kind of weapons which are easily found around an ironworks. Preece had chosen his time well, because during a working day half Edenham's hirelings were away: carting charcoal or cannon, burning ore, or, like James, measuring up for an order.

'Aha! Cried Preece, lifting an arm so he looked like moulting rook. 'You would resist the Queen's Majesty, would you?'

Nicholas cleared his throat nervously and stepped forward. 'By what right do you come here with armed men?'

'By the right possessed by the Holy Church to correct heresy in this realm of England. I hold a bishop's writ against one Francis Wyse to answer for his sin; resist it at your peril.'

'It is no sin – '

But an anonymous voice beat down Nicholas's half-heartedness with a roar of fury. 'God damn ye, parson Preece, for a split-arsed knave! What d'ye mean by trying to take the master from beneath our nebs?'

Preece's face darkened. 'You'll find what I mean when the court pronounces his heresy. Let us through, or come with him to Lewes gaol.' The men he had brought fanned out as he spoke, two of them steadying arquebus muzzles on stakes they carried.

There was a stir, then the Edenham men stilled again. 'If 'tis a fight ye want, ye've got one,' shouted a different voice. 'The queen's law wouldn't take an honest man from beside his own hearth, and so say we all?'

Preece's eyes bulged and he could be seen to be shaking under his cassock, but with rage not fear. He flapped a paper in the wind. 'Her Majesty's own signature authorized constables to come to Furnace Green today.' He went to stand beside the arquebusiers, daring anyone to move, while two constables began pushing their way through the throng.

Nicholas stood frozen, staring at gaping muzzles and a paper with the queen's own signature on it, and when he did not move the men stood still as well, so the constables dodged unmoving shapes as they might trees in the forest.

'You have my name on a warrant?' said Francis quietly. He was standing on the millhouse doorstep, the door shut behind him.

'You are Francis Wyse?'

'Aye, as Father Preece will swear, I daresay.'

'Then your name is on the warrant,' agreed the constable, and took his arm to lead him back through the men, all of them shifting and muttering now.

'Master, don't go with un!' cried Wat Oxley. 'They've no right to take thee!'

'Aye, but they have, when they bring my name on a warrant,' answered Francis, smiling.

But more voices began to call. They wanted to do something, clutched mallets or chisels tighter as if the threat of doing something would be enough. They were also settled men bred up in a peaceful land, and needed to be led if they were to leap the chasm of rebellion.

Nicholas turned to face his father as he passed: blood beat thickly in his ears and he knew that if he spoke the right words then the Edenham men would forget about loaded arquebuses and the consequences of riot, so long as Preece died with them. He managed a quick thin smile. 'I warned you, sir.'

'Aye, and I would have stopped them if you had not.' Francis hesitated and the constables did not hustle him, although Preece screeched something from up the bank. 'Nick, never blame yourself for this. I know that today you thought first about Edenham and not of me, but so would any man once he had tried and failed to prise a fool loose from his folly. So hold Edenham while you have breath, and be damned to my brother Robert.' And he smiled, flexing his shoulders and looking about him at furnace, forges and fining sheds, at a cannon part-freed from its mould and firebacks packed in bracken ready for delivery.

Then he climbed the bank and walked out of sight surrounded by constables. And when the track stretched silent and deserted between the trees again, Nicholas stumbled behind a shed and vomited in the dust.

Bess was afterwards to say that if ever she saw death still breathing, then it was where her mother sat beside the hearth. Mary's cheeks sagged off the bone, pulling her nose and mouth out of shape; her eyes were dull, her hands clutched into fists so that eventually Bess tore them open for fear they would set hard. When Francis had come running into the house on the morning he was taken, it had been to hold Mary like a drowning man, to kiss her again and again while both swayed wordlessly in each other's arms. At first she was so taken by surprise she scarcely responded, and by the time she realized what was happening he had ordered Bess to keep her mother indoors no matter what, and in a voice which allowed no disobedience. Then he left them and went outside.

If Bess hadn't seen him with her own eyes through the window glass, she would never have believed that the calm man who met the constables on his doorstep was the same frantic figure she had gaped at, locked bone to bone in her mother's arms. But in a strange way the contrast steadied her, made it seem less obscene that she, too, was able to hide some of her grief in order to grasp the everyday necessities of living in a house of ghosts.

Nicholas left Edenham immediately after his father was taken, to walk to Lewes where the charges would be heard. James mooned around underfoot until Bess thrust him out of doors, but once there he could only undertake the simpler tasks of ironmaking, since supervising the furnaces required skills he did not possess. Ned vanished into the forest and came back with a fever from lying in the wet; Sally and May wept for two days and then lackadaisically trailed around doing as they were told, which was some kind of help, Bess supposed, though she grew weary of thinking for a household.

Nicholas returned three weeks later, half falling through the door with exhaustion. 'The trial is set for a month hence.'

'Where?' cried Bess. 'Another month? Why, if it's so long they must have doubts, surely.'

'No, I don't think they have any doubts at all. There are others held with him from all over Sussex, and the whisper is that tyrants rule easiest through fear. So, no matter what contrition or recantation they may offer, all will burn. Then in the future the rest of us will obey.'

'Burn.' The word formed like sand on dry lips; until then Bess had only visualized black dungeons or death by fever.

'Yes, burn,' said Nicholas savagely, beating his fist on oak. 'Christ, I warned him! He should have run when Preece and our lickpenny uncle first put their accursed heads together!'

No one answered. It was too late for what could or should have been done and only Nicholas had a reasonably true idea of exactly why the Master of Edenham lay in Lewes gaol. It was the consequences of what had happened which mattered now. 'It's Sunday tomorrow,' ventured Bess, after Nicholas had scoured his trencher clean.

'I'm not –' Nicholas's voice trailed away as he realized that failure to go to mass merely gave Preece the chance to prove more heresy at Edenham. 'If my father burns I swear that Preece will not outlive him by a week,' he said in a shaking voice.

'We've been walking to Riffield for mass this past three weeks,' added Bess, as if Nicholas had not spoken.

James wiped his mouth. 'By God, Nick! If Bess hadn't thought how we could walk to mass at Riffield, I would have broken Preece's neck by his own altar.'

'But Riffield is seven miles away instead of less than one, how can we walk there once the winter comes?' May wailed. As she had told herself each Sunday since her father was taken, she loved him very much but couldn't be expected to walk fourteen miles to church for ever. Sunday afternoon was the time when Furnace Green maids met their swains to wander the lanes together; she didn't want to be too footsore to enjoy her one time of pleasuring in the week.

'We go to Riffield,' said Nicholas flatly, his hand twitching as if he couldn't wait to hit the first mouth daring to complain. He slept the sleep of utter exhaustion that night, but woke resolved to force himself on Lord Scovell after mass. When everyone gossiped about how the Scovells had refused to go to court since it was ruled by a Spanish king and foreign pope, surely Nicholas could entreat his interest for a neighbour?

Lord Scovell looked both tranquil and extremely fit for a man who had for weeks turned royal messengers away with excuses of ill health. Nicholas stared at him with calculating eyes throughout the Latin mass in unfamiliar Riffield church: he could dimly remember Latin in Furnace Green as a child, but belonged to a generation bred up on English in their churches, and this foreignness only served further to inflame his rage.

As soon as the service was over, he shouldered his way through the chattering crowd and stood in the gateway until the Scovells left. 'My lord,' he said, and bowed. 'I am Nicholas Wyse of Furnace Green, attending this church because our priest plots my father's death. I ask that you will listen to what I say, and use your power to prevent foul injustice being done.'

Gervase Scovell was at first taken aback, and then infuriated by being accosted in this way. Especially on dangerous matters and when the man did not live on Scovell lands. 'Out of my way,' he shouted. 'Steward, clear him out of my path.'

Nicholas knelt swiftly. 'My lord, I only beg for the justice you uphold throughout this county of Sussex. My father is innocent of any crime, and yet is likely to burn.'

'The Church's affairs are naught to do with me,' snapped Gervase.

'I believe you could intervene if you wished,' answered Nicholas steadily.

'I tell you no!' Gervase nodded to his steward, who sent Nicholas sprawling with his white-tipped staff and then saw that the Scovell household, who filled half Riffield church, trampled him out of reach. By the time he came to his feet again, Lord Scovell had gone.

'He is afraid,' said Bess, holding Nicholas's hand tightly. 'He doesn't like what is happening but will not lift a hand to stop it.'

'Christ's blood, he is the queen's lieutenant in the county!'

She shrugged, Bess accepted facts and people how they were. 'As the queen's bishops, I suppose. We ought to be getting home.'

They tramped head down into drizzle, though it was July. This season was like the past three, both wet and cold, and the price of bread would again be starvation-high. The path from Riffield to Furnace Green had opened out since Robert the Falconer's time, but heavy traffic from Park Forge had turned it into a quagmire and the climb to Ferenthe Ridge was as steep as ever. Mud spattered their bodies and faces, the trees outlined on the ridge as sombre as their mood. Each day discouragement came closer to despair.

No one spoke when they reached Edenham again at last. James and Ned went out together, muttering about trapping rabbits, although Ned was still coughing; May and Sally vanished without explanation and Nicholas sat moodily whittling sticks, steam rising from his clothes. Bess knelt beside her mother, who had been too weak to walk fourteen miles and did not seem to have moved in all the time they had gone. 'You must eat. See, I have made a broth from the lamb Mistress Laffam brought us.'

Mary nodded and drank noisily from the bowl, although normally a fastidious feeder since she feared that rough manners would make folk remember that she was bred in a harlot's hove. They were all acquiring bad habits, Bess reflected drearily: wasting time in useless tasks, quarrelling over trifles, the furnaces left to chill and crack. 'We can't go on like this,' she said abruptly. 'It isn't helping Father, and we forfeit the sympathy of our hirelings if we condemn them to starve through idleness. Prices will be so high this winter, they'll need every coin they can earn. If our uncle claimed Edenham tomorrow and promised the men full wages if they worked for him, why, I believe some would be tempted. And the devil take your right of ownership afterwards. The rest would follow once their children began to sicken'

Nicholas looked up. 'So you think I should just forget –'

'I think there's nothing you can do until the trial, and perhaps previous little then. You are Master of Edenham now, and must earn bread for us all.'

As easy as that, thought Nicholas fiercely. God, even Bess is little better than a sow who has overlaid a weanling, he threw the stick he had been whittling in the hearth and walked out. Master of Edenham, aye, and so he was. He looked around him; his eyes were moist and edged with red but as he looked, the piles of ore and charcoal, the pits of moulding clay and half-finished wares stacked in corners transformed themselves into his possessions. Gold coins of profit and cannon for killing England's enemies. His hands clenched as, insensibly, his conscience began to ease: he had done what he could and would do more if it was possible, but cannon sold to arm England's ships were the best revenge he could hope for now.

The furnaces of Edenham were lit again next day, the forges began to clang and roar, James brusquely told to drive his ox-teams harder than before.

Eight men were tried for heresy at Lewes in September 1556, and the bishops' court found all of them unrepentant in their sin. Three, including Francis Wyse, swore that they had regularly attended mass but in each case their local priest confirmed that this was mere dissembling, prompted by Satan as cover for the blackest of wickedness. Father Preece added that the heretic Wyse had long attempted to lead Furnace Green astray. Though he, Preece, had on many occasions wrestled with the Devil in his soul, he continued to defy church laws on usury in his trade, had cheated his brothers out of part of their inheritance – to which Robert Wyse bore witness – and illegally seized land from the monks after Ockham Abbey was shut up. He even wept real tears, begging the court's forgiveness for failing in his duty towards contumacious souls.

'You mustn't reproach yourself, Father,' said one of the bishops, looking down his nose and wanting only to have a distasteful business concluded.

The other prelate on the bench, who possessed a more legalistic mind, turned to the prisoner. 'Have you anything to add, though your own priest finds no extenuating conduct?'

'Nay, I've said what I can.' Francis was shaking with fever contracted in wet Lewes gaol but otherwise seemed composed. 'I've never cheated any man knowingly and the usury laws are not well suited to trade. The clearing where my ironworks stand was given me by my father and never had aught to do with my brother Robert. Nor will you find anyone except my covetous kin who says different. For the rest – ' He looked Preece in the eyes and grinned. 'You appointed a scoundrel as our priest, my lord bishop, and sit in judgement over bloody laws. I do believe that neither he nor they will long endure.'

I do believe; deliberately, Francis had used the language of church oaths, and after a moment of shock the court howled him down.

The Sussex martyrs were burned on a wet morning in a cobbled square near the gaol. Against all Nicholas's expostulations Mary had tried to walk the twenty-five miles from Edenham, but mercifully collapsed by the way and was left semi-conscious in an alehouse while Bess, Nicholas and James went on. Ned, Sally and May were kept by the Laffams, Ned tied in a barn to prevent him from running after them.

When the time came for burning, Francis Wyse's three children stood on the fringes of an angry, lewdly fascinated and turbulent crowd holding each other as if they watched a two-headed monster at a fair. While the procession wound leisurely through the narrow streets, its holy banners blowing in gusts of rain, they still could not believe what was about to happen. The heretics were dressed in penitential cloth, the monks around them shivering in the gale. 'Eh, they'll have a task to make faggots burn in this weather.' Observed a man in a butcher's smock standing next to James.

'You think they might have to wait?' demanded Nicholas, his teeth chattering so badly the words fell out like splintered bone. Any reprieve gave time for the unimaginable not to happen.

The butcher snorted. 'Not them. They'll stoke a charring fire all night if necessary, and they poor devils still be alive at the end of it.'

'Christ!' said James. 'Christ above, no!' Tears poured down his face without any of them noticing.

The butcher spat. 'One of them yours?'

All three stared back, their bulging eyes and unstrung muscles the only answer.

'Aye, I can see how it is. Listen, then. I've seen it in the wet like this before. The only way you can help is to pile on the fuel. There's dry timber stored in the furniture-maker's yard yonder, and if you get the flame high enough it seems to suck the breath out of them. They don't know much about it, like.'

He did not see James's fist coming, sprawled backwards into the crowd from the force of it, under trampling, eager feet.

'He came to gloat. My God, he's seen this happen in the wet and came again.' James screamed, but no one looked at him because at that moment the procession of monks and priests, condemned heretics and tindermen, soldiers and banner-carriers had reached the square where the stakes awaited them.

After three months in goal, Francis Wyse had come close to longing for this day. He would stand upright in sweet air again and everyone must die sometime, after all. He was past the prime of life and told himself that a quick end was not so terrible compared to the indignities of old age.

He walked alertly in the procession through the streets of Lewes, scarcely noticing the crowds or guards or chanting monks. Only when he glimpsed Bess's white gaping face did his mood shatter, the faggot pile leap at him and a thirst to live burst into his senses. He wanted to work iron again, to love his family and cram Preece's foul lies down his gut. Beyond the crowd he could see craftsmen walking briskly about their business, men who despised mobs and their bloody pastimes. All the pride and hope, all the activity of a working life would never be his again.

He fought savagely as they hauled him to a stake piled about with faggots; He did not want to be abased by a futile struggle but could not help himself. It took three brawny guards to secure him, his mind only clearing again as the last chain was fastened. His body was twisted like a pine-knot around the stake; they had not cared how he was secured so long as it was done. The man tied next to him was praying aloud, eyes closed, apparently noticing nothing. Lucky fellow, thought Francis;   He himself believed in God but since faith had so little do with bringing him to the stake, it didn't help him now. All the things most dear to him, for which perhaps he died, were two days' journeying away. Suddenly he was very much afraid of dying, was possessed by such a great love for life that hope in the hereafter vanished. Mary; God send she had remained at Edenham today. He wanted to wipe his sweating face and could not, heard the crackle of fire and tried to think of iron flowing molten in his furnace. I did not run, he thought; at least I am sure I wasn't wrong in that. He clenched his teeth as the heat began to bite, smoke all he could now see; but soon, as grip on his will began to slacken he howled like a wolf in the forest. The heat pulled at the skin of his face, was agony on bare feet and hands: the kind of dull furnace which would shame an ironmaster, lacking life for its task. He clamped teeth through skin to bone, and briefly swallowed his screams again.

The crowd began to still.

A few of the more squeamish scuttled away and the devout fell on their knees, but scarcely to pray when screaming victims prevented any plea, except that the flames might kill soon. The rest stood staring, the smell now frightful. Smoke, grey sweating faces, rain beating out of the sky. Hear us, whatever power there be, and put a stop to such suffering, we beg. Even the monks ceased chanting, as if nothing remained which was not shamed by torment.

Nicholas broke first, pummelling at James, at everyone standing in his way, and bellowing for them to fetch dry wood. He ran, legs flailing clumsily, to claw at a pile of carpenters' planks, and then staggered with them towards the smoke, other men ran, the guards beginning to strike out, tumbling over, retreating in the press. Too late to think of rescue for the pitiful beings flaying at the stake – Ah, God, why didn't we riot before instead of after this cavalry of suffering? Above all, how could this ultimate horror be, that the last succour of a son for his father should be to heap more firewood on the blaze?'

Dozens of men were now hurling thatch, kindling, hacked-up carts and sawn timber on the fires, half crazed by insensate fury. The smoke hesitated, thickened then a flame shot up between green faggots to grasp greedily at dryness. At last . . . at last, the grey clouds driving over-head reflected crimson like a stain of blood, and ashes blew on the wind.

Nicholas, James and Bess left Lewes the same day and walked through the night as if rest no longer existed. Nor could they have rested without being pitched screaming from their dreams.

They found Mary by the alehouse hearth where they had left her, and as dawn broke they sprawled like exhausted hounds at her feet to twitch and squeal in something which was far short of sleep.

'He died,' said Nicholas in answer to whatever question Mary asked, and that was all any of them ever said to her about that day in Lewes.

The rest of the way back to Furnace Green they travelled slowly, because Mary was weak and the others soon became so, unable to sleep or keep food down without puking. Only when Twisbury Hill loomed through the murk at last, with its furze thickets and the ridge beyond, did Bess lift her eyes from the mud between her feet. 'If I was blind I should be able to tell home by its smell.'

'Charcoal, bracken, good iron, sheep and oak,' agreed Nicholas absently.

'Wind across open ground.' Bess shook out her tangled hair so it whipped and caught across her cheeks.

'Preece's blood' shouted James, flailing great thick arms so they all fell silent again.

The stock-pens around the old muddied pool came into sight next, and the ancient dead oak which folk said would bring the village ill luck when it fell. Then the church tower; when James saw that he muttered an oath and shook his fist. The street usually quiet in mid-afternoon, was full of people standing as if they had waited a long time for the Wyses to return.

'It doesn't look as if our neighbours will be too anxious to swear their evidence when Preece is found dead one night,' said Nicholas, exchanging glances with his brother.

'Well?' demanded Mark Wyse, when they reached his doorstep.

'Well?' Nicholas said insolently.

'He's dead?'

'You helped to kill him, so you should know.'

'Nay, not I,' said Mark, alarmed. 'I said nothing against him, nor ever would.'

'You said nothing for him, though Preece's chief witness was another brother.

'No one asked me.' And he began cursing both Robert and Preece. 'I swear on Christ's holy bones I had naught to do with it. 'You know he's run.'

'Who's run?'

'Preece. He piled his traps on Sol Brown's donkey and left the day after he returned here from the trial. Suspicioned it wouldn't be long before he'd be found stiff in a ditch if he stayed, I suppose. The priest-house is stripped, but yestere'en his wife and children came back in. They needing a roof for the winter, like, and all the Weald buzzing with what's happened.'

Mary began to laugh. After having been sealed in silence since Francis was taken, she began to stamp and shout and yell with laughter under the shocked gaze of Furnace Green.

Bess slapped her face, hard. 'Tell us the joke.'

'Don't you see? In the end, Preece was the one to run. He was the one who saw nothing worth dying for, and this time he won't be back. Like Francis. He won't be back either, will he?' she began to weep great gulping sobs.

'Thank God,' Bess said. 'She'd have gone crazed without some tears. We'd best get on to Edenham now.'

'She can bide with us for the night if you like.' Said Mark. 'Robert isn't here.'

'She wouldn't.' Bess stared at him scornfully. It was small credit to Mark that he found the ruin of his brother less attractive then he'd expected.

'Where is Robert?' Nicholas's voice, very low and deadly.

Mark hesitated. 'At Edenham. He claims it as his now.'

James and Nicholas exchanged glances again, this time pleased and darkly smiling, then Nicholas said, quite matter-of-fact. 'Well, who's with us then? We'll pick up the Laffams on our way.' He set off fast down the track towards Edenham, James following.

The gathering in the street watched dumbfounded, not having been in Lewes, where men had hesitated too long to have an easy conscience afterwards. The first to call out was one of the Bywood boys. 'I'll join you against any man who scavenges on the bones of another!' and that began a rush. Mostly of young men anxious to enjoy a brawl but also including those of their elders who, with bitter menaces, had already had a great deal to do with running Preece out of Furnace Green: Jack Fletcher, Master of Park Forge mourning a friend; the Carpenter brothers, grudging as always but remembering Francis Wyse as a fellow craftsman who understood good work; Rollo the Frenchman, himself hounded by Catholics out of his village in western France; also men like Curly Apps, the keeper of the Black Bear, who hated anything to happen without being in the thick of it. They picked up half a dozen Laffams on the way and ran the last stretch of track and slope, bursting into Edenham kitchen like water through a sluice.

Robert Wyse had his feet on Bess's hearth and looked very warm and pleased with himself, three men armed with cudgels and sickles sitting by his side.

Nicholas was first through the door, but James flung his slighter brother aside and had hauled Robert of his bench before his hirelings could do more than dribble gravy down their chins in astonishment. Then he threw him into the fire.

Everyone in the room heard his spine snap on one of Francis Wyse's massive andirons and a tremendous smell of scorching filled the air as, squealing, he thrashed like a butchered pit on hot ash. Hands on hips, James watched in grim satisfaction for quite a long time before, all anyhow, he hauled him out and dumped him on the brick floor. His head rolled and his eyes filled with blood while his lower body lay quite still; within minutes he was dead.

Nicholas moved stiffly from where James had flung him against the oak dresser. A rib hurt and he breathed carefully. 'Hold the three men who came here with him.'

The three looked stupefied as well they might, not one of them having had time to reach for a weapon.

Jack Smith, Henry Baker, John Parlben,' said Nicholas flatly, and, with a strength no one would have supposed he possessed, he grasped each by the hair and banged their faces hard on the table. 'You came as thieves and trespassers into my home, for which you deserve to hang. What say you?'

Christ's blood,' grunted Parlben, some kind of cousin to Mary but whom Nicholas knew only by his repute as a teller of tales. 'I'm a shepherd paid by Master Robert. I did what I was told. Edenham's mine now, he says. Sleep you there and help guard it, and so I did.'

Does Edenham belong to Robert Wyse? Think carefully before you answer.'

Simultaneously, the three men's eyes turned towards the body on the floor. 'Nay, I reckon not, said Parlben.

'Was it ever his? You know many tales and should understand the rights of who owns what.'

''Twas always Francis Wyse's that I remember, but he's dead. What would you have done when his brother says a court upheld his claim? I've a wife and six children eating off what I earn from Master Robert.'

'Francis Wyse is indeed dead,' said Nicholas distinctly. 'He died possessed of Edenham, so I am master now. Dispute it with me if you dare. So what tale will you three tell of what happened here tonight?'

The men stared at him, blood on their teeth and noses, at a loss over how to answer. It was all too quick for them.

'Shall I tell you what you'll say? Robert Wyse fell in the fire, frothing from a fit. He was such an ugly sight afterwards for his kin to see that in the absence of a priest from Furnace Green we took it on ourselves to bury him in the churchyard. Jack Fletcher has authority to swear a coroner's inquest, haven't you Jack?' He smiled unpleasantly. 'I myself will give a fine grave-slab wrought from Edenham iron in memory of my kinsman.'

'Aye, that was the way of it,' agreed Jack Fletcher. With his plumed cap and pewter-buttoned jerkin, he looked out of place in such wild doings. 'I'm church warden, too, and there being no priest I could put my mark to an entry in the register. If we can find a clerk to write it.'

'I can write.' said Nicholas.

'You can? Well now, fancy!' He scratched his head, surprised. Priests and clerks wrote, ironmaster had more important things to do. 'That's fixed up tight, then.'

'Aye,' said Parlben quickly. 'That'll be how it was. Master Robert took a fit like folks often thought he might, him being a high-stomached man.' Baker and Smith muttered assent and immediately nearly everyone in the room looked at Robert Wyse's body in pity rather than anger, as if that was what had really happened.

A grave was dug and Robert thrown into it that same night; Jack Fletcher hesitating over the register and saying he disremembered the date exactly. They finally decided on the 26th September, since this was the day Francis had died in Lewes. If anyone asked then James and Nicholas could easily prove that they were in Lewes too. Probably no one ever would. Lord Scovell heard most things which happened in the neighbourhood eventually, but, though he had not helped Francis he understood the Weald well enough to know when to leave well alone. And once everyone had agreed on a story, Parlben and his fellows would keep to it as closely as the rest of Furnace Green.

A strange winter and spring followed. Edenham ironworks prospered once Nicholas settled himself as master, and though bread prices rose to famine heights the demand for iron also remained high, so Wealdsmen were able to congratulate themselves on steady employment and high wages. Furnace Green was only one of the many villages boasting rebuilt, oak-framed cottages, Edenham sharing its repute with several other works in the region. Nicholas was determined to change this, though. Unlike his father he was not a particularly skilled craftsman, and regarded time spent hammering or in furnace work as wasted, although he understood the techniques more than well enough to make sure Wat Oxley kept the men working hard. What he did know very thoroughly was how not to be cheated by distant merchants, how to place his wares to best advantage and account for every groat of profit. He travelled to Deptford and Chatham to talk to ship's gunners and purveyors; into Kent, where great houses were building which needed decorative iron, and even once to London; but when he learned the man he dealt with intended to resell Edenham cannon to Spain, he revoked his agreement within the day.

Writing and figures became part of the work of Edenham, the kitchen dresser filling with papers, prices and sketches of iron. James was contemptuous of such clerk's doings and enjoyed oversetting his brother's methods, but he was seldom at home. His part of the enterprise was transport, a grinding task which kept several ox-teams busy for nine months in the year. During the other three, the Weald was cut off from the rest of England by mud, so James slept by the hearth and quarrelled with his brother.

This was the strange part about that time. In some ways the Wyses were welded together by horrific memory, engrossed with each other as if what they had seen sealed a pact with the Devil against the world. Yet they also came close to hating each other, because, together, there was no way to forget. If cruel images faded briefly, then knowing, bitter eyes reminded them of their forgetfulness. If they should sleep soundly at night, then the nightmares of others woke them; if one of them laughed, the sound mocked an ever-open grave.

When spring came round at last Bess began to spend most of her time in the forest, idly exploring, trapping rabbits for the pot, collecting firewood or mushrooms. The solitude helped, and she reckoned she had carried her mother's tasks long enough. Mary was physically hale again and would be better working. Bess grieved quite as deeply as the rest and was as thoroughly shocked, but saw no point in deliberately remembering her father's death. Nicholas became angry as she was more and more often missing when work cried out to be done: he didn't believe in anyone having time to waste, most especially women, whom idleness made haughty and inclined to answer back. But Bess's only response was to vanish for days rather than mornings at a time, and by the end of the summer she was again much as she had always been.

One blustering August afternoon she was dawdling along the track which led to Ockham crooning to herself and lazily scanning the hedgerow for herbs, when she saw a man seated on the bank. He looked up as she approached and smiled crookedly. 'Hullo Bess. I saw you coming and lay in wait for you.'

'Richard!' she shouted and rushed to hug him. 'What are you doing here? Where did you come from? Are you going to stay?'

'Whoa!' he said laughingly, but made no move to stand, so she was left feeling foolish with her arms reaching into air. 'Which shall I answer first?'

'Monks!' she cried scornfully. 'Must you be disciplined in your answerings too?'

He hesitated. 'Well – perhaps. Bess, do you mind me here?'

'Mind! Why should I?'

He fingered the black cloth of his habit. 'When I heard what had happened to the master I thought I could never pray as a priest again.'

'But, Richard, it wasn't you!   Did you think we would believe you the kind of ghoul who rejoiced when others burned?' She seized his arm and shook it, as if only through contact could he become again the Richard Mercer she knew so well.

He stood abruptly and moved out of reach. 'I didn't want to come back. I thought you wouldn't be able to bear me near you.'

'You didn't want to come because of my father, or because of me?' she said levelly. Until his confusion reminded her, she had forgotten how they had lain together on the hearth; to her that evening belonged to another life, an offering which had nothing to do with passion. But now he had reminded her of it, she knew immediately how much she would like to lie with him again, and this time for herself.

'Both,' he said at once, with the devastating candour of one trained to scrupulous confession. 'The memory of what I did to you, and through you to your father whose guest I was, has punished me down the years. Because of it I thought I owed a duty to come back if that would help.'

'But you didn't want to?'

'No.'

Bess stared at him, bitterly disappointed, and then, being naturally optimistic, immediately cheered up again. He wanted her badly, she could tell. His face had changed with the years and at first gaze he'd seemed remote, withdrawn, shunning even the touch of her hand. But then his eyes rested on her, and feeling leaped like lightening across grey sky. His brows arched, lips parted, breath shortened, and Bess watched it happen complacently. Richard had always been a completely open man.

'You have come back all the same,' she said mildly, after a pause.

'My bishop offered me the living here in place of Father Preece, who is lately dead.' His voice was expressionless. 'Bess, I only heard how the master was condemned two days before he was to die. I was like a madman, but in the time I failed to reach anyone of importance.'

'I don't suppose it would have made any difference if you had, the church being well set on its course of blood.'

'No. Afterwards – afterwards it seemed monstrous for me to come, when the time for help was past. Really, I think mere cowardice kept me away, when I knew that priest and devil must have become one to you.'

Bess's lips curved. 'Not you, Richard. You could never figure as a devil at Edenham.'

Unexpectedly, tears glittered in his eyes. 'You have a knack of redeeming the harshest loss. But you see, not all bishops believe that burning is the best way to save souls. I, too –'

'My father didn't burn to save his soul. He burned because Preece hated him, and his brother envied his property.'

Richard looked unexpectedly disconcerted. 'The Church would never serve private spite.'

'It could and did. Which is why we manage best without a priest nowadays.'

'Yes, I heard. But don't you see how terrible that is, Bess? The bishop called me to him two weeks ago, and said Christ was embattled by dark spirits here – '

'Some people do go up the hill again,' agreed Bess helpfully. 'But

Richard, - you don't really imagine anything would have been better if my father had been truly condemned for heresy, do you? It seems worse to me.'

'I see how badly you need a priest here again.' He tried not to sound shocked, but he was. 'The bishop asked me if I would accept the living.'

'Richard! You mean it? We can have you as priest and let the world go hang itself?'

'I certainly didn't mean that,' he answered drily. 'I would come to bring you back to Christ. The bishop knew I'd lived awhile at Edenham which perhaps fitted me for the task, but he didn't command me into the living. He told me to come and discover whether I and you could bear it if I stayed.'

She gazed at him, half-smiling, until he flushed and looked away. 'If you can bear us, then we shall most gladly suffer you.'

Richard found it hard to believe her, and only the long disciplines of his calling enabled him to face Mary. When he did, his dread immediately seemed absurd. She was standing by the hearth, her face flushed by heat so that for a moment she looked younger than last time he had seen her, but when she turned to the click of the latch he saw how immeasurably old she had become.

'Richard!' She said, and opened her arms to him as Bess had done. Until that moment he hadn't believed it possible, and held her as tightly as any prodigal son returned.

Nicholas was more guarded, but it didn't seem to matter. That worldly and enlightened man, the bishop was certainly right: this was his place and these his people from now on. Only a priest who had once worked under Francis Wyse might again reach souls set adrift by evil; only a man who loved this place atone for a lost life with his own.

'What about your monastery?' demanded Nicholas, a sneer at the back of his voice? 'I thought you'd want to tear our furnace field from us to support a pack of droning monks.'

'The queen has found monasteries more difficult to restore than she expected. The Parliament House passed such laws on faith as cost them nothing, but reckoned their new lands were worth more than a pope in Rome.' Richard's voice was cool, he knew he would need the patience of a martyr to survive here. Parliamentary greeds had angered him, now they weren't his concern any more.

Nicholas shrugged. 'Oh – the queen. What says her Spanish husband?'

'Philip? He left England months ago and is unlikely to return. He wants a son and Her Majesty is too sick to breed. He also finds England very little to his liking, when he already rules half the world.' He grinned. 'The Londoners pelted his Spanish followers with filth and jeered whenever he rode abroad.'

So this Philip was already gone when – ' Mary's voice shook, then shaped the words defiantly, 'when Francis burned. You mean an *English queen* sat on her throne and ordered such things?'

'She doesn't enjoy it, I promise you. It's said she divides her time between prayers and sickness.'

'You didn't answer,' broke in Nicholas harshly. 'She could have stopped it and did not?'

'Yes.' Said Richard steadily. 'She is a faithful daughter of the Church, and saves her subjects' souls from Hell by persecuting heresy. My bishop says that though some prelates urge her on, Her Majesty is hottest of all for burnings.'

'Oh bother the queen!' Bess broke in impatiently. 'Richard, where have you been all this time? You seem mighty well-informed about the affairs of the kingdom.'

He laughed. 'In London, at Blackfriars, which is restored by the queen's own gift. Though her subjects are laggardly in such matters, she is not. Londoners are desperate gossips, I promise you. So we heard most things, even through a monastery wall.'

Nicholas kicked a log in the hearth. 'If the queen gives back her church lands, it only means that we have to pay higher tax, so where's the piety in that? She's sick, you say. How sick?'

'Try to have a little pity for others, Nick. She is sick to her soul, because she believed that men turned heretic for gain. Instead she discovered that many preferred to burn rather than give up something they held dear. She dies a little with each one, I believe, and will not last another year.'

At this Mary, Nicholas and Ned all exclaimed, looked at each other and laughed aloud, which shocked Richard more than anything which had been said that day. Bess alone was thoughtfully, trying to imagine what it must be like after three years spent saving souls, to understand that all you had done was turn your fellow creatures into ash.

'When Queen Mary is dead, what then?' demanded Ned. All last winter he had looked close to death and wasn't much better now, a bright flush coughed into his face. He was also the wrong age to withstand hauntings.

'Her sister Elizabeth will inherit.' There's no one else.'

'Christ's blood, another woman!'

Richard nodded.

'You don't like her,' said Nicholas shrewdly.

'I've never clapped eyes on the lady Elizabeth. The queen doesn't flaunt her successor through the streets of London, you may be sure. No, I doubt if I should like her.'

'Why not?' They all spoke at once. It was exciting to glimpse events before they happened, when usually the only tidings they received were demands for tax and obedience.

'I doubt whether she's a true daughter of the church,' said Richard reluctantly. 'Men whisper that she'll prefer to rule as her father King Henry did, ordering all things for herself. So will everything be turned upside down again.'

'Good,' said Nicholas. 'God bless the Lady Elizabeth, then. She will have my oath against popes and Spanish burnings.'

Nothing would ever convince Nicholas, and many others like him, that pope and King Philip counselled caution on burnings, reflected Richard moodily.

Mary's thoughts were more personal. 'Richard, what will happen to you if all is changed again? Will Furnace Green lose the one priest who might comfort us?'

'I don't know,' said Richard unhappily. 'You, above all, ought to understand that there are some things a man can't dissemble and remain himself.'

Queen Mary died the following November, and throughout England the bells rang in rejoicing. On village greens and hilltops great fires were lit which proclaimed a very different message from those of her reign, although at Furnace Green all remained quiet and dark. There was some drunken revelling at the Black Bear, but when Gaffer Hawkins went stumbling over to the church to ring its single bell, Father Mercer thrust him out again.

'Unchristian, he said we was.' said the Gaffer mournfully into his home-brewed. 'But I say 'tis powerful weary being Christian all the time, when Riffield be enjoying theirselves.'

With this sentiment the other occupants of the Black Bear heartily agreed; on the other hand, Father Mercer had the knack of making the most unrepentant sinner desire forgiveness. 'There's Twisbury,' said Jack Carpenter cautiously. 'I haven't been there in a while though my Grandfer used to say they had powerful fine gatherings up there in times gone by. A big blaze, like, wi' dancings and prancings. Riffield would see we had a better revel than they if we lit a fire up there.'

A roar of approval greeted this suggestion, since few people had dared 'go up-hilly' as it was called, since Father Mercer arrived the year before. So, disregarding the November night, everyone in the Black Bear who was sober enough to stir, tumbled out of doors and capered along the ridge path. Thus had worshippers of Tiw and Mother Earth come fifteen centuries before, except they would never have dared to approach holy ground when drunk. Men leaped out giggling at each other from the undergrowth and punched noses in mock fury; several pitched snoring out of sight and were lucky if they woke none the worse in the morning. The rest reeled up the wooded slope beyond the path, bellowing bawdy songs. Once they reached the open space at the summit, the problem was to collect enough dry wood to shame Riffield with their blaze, but they solved it by piling dead bracken and branches around the base of a dead but still standing beech, which sprawled branches over much of the inner stockade space. They were beginning to fall silent now, as their blood chilled and eeriness laid hold on them. The old dug banks, half hidden under centuries of leaves, remained trippingly unexpected in the dark; the sigh of wind in the trees and

427

whiff of ancient sanctity quite enough to recall Parlben tale-tellings of dark mystery in the past. Since Francis Wyse had died, somehow the forest with its witches and demons had crept closer to the ridge, nor had Father Mercer yet managed to do more than tidy superstition out of sight.

Jack Carpenter lit the fire and it caught at once, which made everyone shout about good omens; by then they were tired and at first no one joined him when he began to dance. Few thought him odd, though. In the light of day, if anyone had said that glum Jack Carpenter would caper around a bonfire, there would have been guffaws of disbelief. Among the flame-thrown shadows on Twisbury Hill it simply seemed discourteous to trespass in such a place without attempting to express a form of thanks. Then the dead beech began to burn, intermittently at first but eventually with flaring power. Crimson faces stared upward where the flames dyed black night clouds, and all the trees on the hill were reddened too. Then, one by one and slowly to begin with, those men still on their feet began to dance alongside Jack, sweat pouring off their faces from the heat and their minds spinning, spinning as they danced. Spinning the centuries away, Christ and the priest away, until into the void came spirits no one had ever quite forgotten.

They did not stop dancing until they dropped exhausted in the bracken. It was the last great celebration on Tiw's Hill. The last but one, that is, the last being nearly thirty years later, but by then the mood was different and the god different too, although almost equally pagan.

Richard stood outside his tiny hut and watched the flames leap on Twisbury Hill. A year's work lost in a single night of carousings at a heathen shrine, he thought sourly. Sometimes it was hard not to despair when so much of Furnace Green remained outside his grasp.

'You should go and join them.' Bess's mischievous voice reached to him out of darkness.

He jumped. 'You'd be the terror of Lord Scovell's park-keepers if you turned poacher, whereas I trip on my nose each time I'm called out in the dark.'

She laughed and linked her arm in his. 'It's only practice. Aren't you going to ask me in to sup?'

He hesitated. 'If you wish.'

'Why else do you think I came on a chill November evening? You needn't worry about long-nosed neighbours tonight, since half the village is drunken and the other half carousing on Tiw's Hill.'

'Your mother,' said Richard abruptly. 'What a block-head I am not to realize I ought to visit her tonight. How is she?'

Bess chuckled. 'Best without a priest. When we heard of Queen Mary's death I tapped a cask of our strongest home-brewed, and everyone except me is as drunk as a tinker's harlot. Which I reckoned was better than tears or the horrors.'

As Mary Tudor sickened, Richard's judgement had proved correct: few of her ministers possessed her stomach for persecution, and in the south-east Francis Wyse was one of the last to burn.

Bess looked around curiously when Richard lit a rush-light inside his hut. The priest-house was occupied by Preece's family, and to avoid turning them out Richard had built a wattle shelter against the church wall, which would, he said, be not much more uncomfortable than a monk's cell. And while he built it, no one helped. There were disadvantages in not having a priest but Furnace Green had begun to feel safer left alone, feared any change would be for the worse.

That was a year ago: now, though somewhat awed by Father Mercer's formidable virtues, everyone agreed that on the whole their lives were comforted by having Christ and the Church back in their places again. Except on a thick-headed morrow after dancing on Tiw's Hill, of course.

'Your hut isn't very comfortable,' said Bess frankly.

'It would have been more watertight if I'd trained as a Cistercian, who labour with their hands from dawn to dusk,' agreed Richard.

'You should lift your bedding off the ground, and build a proper chimney. I'll ask Nick to send up some bricks.

'I manage quite well, but thank you. There's nothing like a monk's cell for hardening a man.'

'But it's foolish to freeze for no reason! You'll become like one of those old church women, talking to yourself and reeking of stale incense, then what good will you be?'

Richard laughed. 'None, I daresay.'

'Well then. Build your own dwelling if you must, but make it better by forcing the street people to help you. It'll be more useful penance to lay on them than most. Meanwhile, I'll – '

'No.' he said as her fingers brushed lightly, sensuously across his face. 'Bess, I let you come in here because what needed saying couldn't be said churlishly in wind and rain, nor shall we ever have a better chance than tonight to be away from prying eyes. You must forget we lay once together, turn to your own life and leave mine to God.'

'You haven't forgotten,' she said with satisfaction.

'No, nor ever shall. Which is harder to bear than you could imagine. But I am armoured now against the traps you lay for me, being here for a purpose I don't intend to botch.'

'Oh!' Her face cleared. 'Everyone knows that priests are like other men.'

'So very much like other men that the last one here killed your father out of the evil in his heart. No, Bess. God knows I am sinful, but unless I can show Furnace Green some of the grace Christ offers to his servants, then after what happened most of the souls here must be lost.'

'Don't you like me? She asked, like a child refusing to understand what it is told.

'He smiled. 'Indeed, sweeting. I like you very much.'

'You mayn't believe me but there hasn't been anyone else, even though Matt Laffam wooed me very hotly.'

He bent and kissed her gently on the forehead, his hands gripped behind his back. Immediately she stepped back a pace, at once bewildered and furious. 'You great block-head! You – stupid ox! Lie alone on wet bracken in a leaking hovel if you wish, and see if I or anyone else here cares!'

She would even have scratched him, had he not caught her wrists. Since she was as wiry as plaited hide and he a scholar, the task of holding her was harder than he expected. Then, all at once she went slack in his grasp. 'You don't know how I have yearned for you these past months.'

'I was afraid I knew. I hoped you would come to understand that I am sworn elsewhere.'

'Preece was married and unmarried, both. 'Tis said that with a new queen all will change again. I wouldn't mind – I would *try* not to mind – you being a priest, so long as I could share the rest of you.'

'But I shan't change, no matter what a new queen says. I cannot, don't you understand? God knows I make mistakes, but none so great as that. The faith I confess and the vows I took were to one holy church under Christ's pope. They are part of me and you are not.'

She wrenched her wrists from his grasp and left without a word.

Within a year rumour was proved true and, under a new queen, England returned to the Protestant Church. Yet again, oaths were required from churchmen and officials to help bind them to time-serving change, the only difference being that this time popular sentiment was mostly in accord with the lawmakers. After five years of rule so unpopular that many people continued to cling to the notion that foreigners must have controlled the crown, oaths to a native pope-free church were regarded with general approval.

'You'll have to swear,' said Nicholas to Richard when he brought this latest news from one of his journeys to the Medway.

Richard smiled. 'You're an annoying fellow sometimes, Nick. Order your hirelings how you wish and leave me to decide what oaths I'll swear.'

'You haven't any choice.'

'Everyone, always, has a choice.'

'Not if you want to stay as our priest, and you swore to us you would.'

'Let's wait and see how matters turn out,' answered Richard peaceably. 'Unless you propose to run me out of the parish on a sheep-hurdle after tomorrow's mass.'

Nicholas frowned. Always unapproachable, since his father's death he had grown a kind of darkness around him. 'I shouldn't want to, you know that.'

Richard flipped a coin, the debased and clipped currency which reminded everyone how low England's fortunes had sunk. 'I hear that six wet seasons have brought the Browns of Fawkners to disaster. Before, they've sold acres here and there, but now the lordship of the manor as well, or so it's said. To you.'

'Furnace Green is full of blabbermouths.'

'It's true? I fear Lord Scovell won't be very pleased. His kin have been trying for generations to get their hands on the Furnace Green freehold.'

Nicholas allowed himself a small sour smile. 'And now they can wait a few more generations. I wonder how it happened that Scovells own lands for miles around, yet this one ridge in sight of their castle walls has stayed separate freehold? The charter I bought from the Browns was so old I was forced to bribe royal clerks to seal a new one before it crumbled into dust.'

Nicholas had learned the meaning of loneliness. He, beyond all the rest of the family, could not put the squalid agony of his father's death behind him. Mary had never learned more than the fact of Francis's death – often Nicholas longed to shout every last detail at her, just to share his pain; James's grief had seemed satisfied when he killed Robert, and Bess – Bess had some magic of her own for putting the past behind her. Nicholas alone still relived, almost from day to day, the scorching heat of a pyre which he himself had helped to stoke. No one liked him except for the employment he provided, and whereas Edenham used to be a cheerful place to work, now it was known for sober drudgery. Though Nicholas possessed a caustic wit, it was better suited to Richard's intellect than to more boisterous humours; Mary and his sisters thought him dull, James resented his intelligence. He had tried to attract several girls who caught his fancy, but while their kin were anxious for such a profitable connection, the girls found him frightening and Nicholas was too proud to persist with an unwilling woman.

'Well,' said Richard after pause. 'As lord of the manor, you will have to answer for my oath-taking, I suppose. And it is only true justice after all, if you should be the man to send the priest of Furnace Green to Lewes gaol.'

Nicholas paled. 'No one in London believes that Queen Elizabeth is like her sister. She wants England quit of foreigners and prosperous, not torn by factions in religion.'

'God's grace on that, but I still can't swear her oaths.'

'What is an oath? Say the words and mutter what else you will under your breath. The form satisfies the law.'

'A cheat and man of straw? No.'

'A man of straw,' repeated Nicholas, slowly. 'Well, why not, since you're so scrupulous? Richard Paille, the invisible man. Paille is French for Straw,' he added kindly. 'The merchant I dealt with at Chatham used the term for a Dunkirker who vanished instead of paying what he owed.'

'I know the French for straw,' said Richard patiently. 'What has it to do with me?'

'Don't you see? If you refuse the oaths, then the best that could happen is that you would be turned out of your living, to wander the roads as a hedge-priest. What good is that to anyone, when we've become used to you here? But change your name and live quietly in your hut after you refuse to swear, and who will know or care?'

'The bishop, I imagine.'

'Well, perhaps,' conceded Nicholas, to whom bishops were mere income-gatherers and wine-swillers. 'But why should he worry? He will have done his duty by turning you out. He could even collect your stipend for himself, and smile if anyone remembered that Furnace Green was without a priest.'

'Not all bishops are rogues.'

'Are they not? Well, you know best, I daresay. But suppose you were that bishop, my lily white monk. What would you do if you knew that Richard Mercer, papist, was turned out, but an insubstantial fellow called Paille still laboured to save the black souls inhabiting Ferenthe Ridge, and laboured better than any new man you could appoint? You don't feel bound to incite us to rebellion for your pope, do you? Or boast aloud about how you haven't sworn Her Majesty's oaths?'

'I can see that Furnace Green will become even more prosperous now it has a juggling knave as its lord of the manor,' observed Richard. 'No, I would not stir up commotions, no matter what. We've all had enough of those. If you think the people here want me to stay so much that they would keep their mouths shut for years about their unsworn priest, then I would be ungracious indeed if I didn't at least think about their wishes. Meanwhile, we must wait and see what happens.'

'Good,' said Nicholas, enormously relieved. He loved Richard with all the possessive jealousy of an otherwise friendless man. 'It would be mightily inconvenient to be without a priest again, especially when I mean to wed at Michaelmas.'

'My dear Nicholas! I can't tell you how pleased I am. Who is the girl?' The old, familiar pang when he thought of Bess, that vital creature who continued to haunt his dreams, no matter how he exhausted himself with penances.

'The daughter of a Chatham master-gunner. A good connection, since her kin fill most of the ordnance yard.'

Richard looked down at his hands. 'You aren't wedding an ordnance yard, Nick.'

'Aye, but that I am! My God, Richard, what kind of a fool d'you think I am! The wench is fifteen and apt for training, otherwise she wouldn't be worth the risk. A pert town-reared maid would turn a forest clearing upside down unless she was young enough to mould, no matter who her kin were, another surly quarrelsome woman at Edenham would be more than I could bear. I want to be comfortable as well as rich.'

'Poor child,'

Nicholas flushed angrily. 'You know nothing about it. A woman is happiest when she cossets her husband's needs.'

'And you!' Are you happiest as a tyrant over your household?'

Though Nicholas immediately stamped out in a fury, Richard's words continued to echo mockingly in his head. He knew Edenham was no longer a happy place, although he tried to make it so by hard work and restraint. Aye, restraint. How dare Richard call him tyrant, when he bit his tongue a dozen times each week over Bess's fecklessness or his mother's carping about the past? Sally and May had each wed their Laffam oafs and were already breeding litters to add to the sprawling tribe at Corndown, while sadness had bit deep the previous winter when Ned died of a fever. Nicholas swore aloud as he tramped the familiar mud-drowned track to Edenham: God's blood, surely he deserved some consideration for his long hours of toil! No one even remembered it had been he who chose the site on which the millhouse stood; they laughed at his figurings and failed to realize how Edenham's trade had grown, scarcely seemed to care that the long cannon he was casting could throw a ball twice the distance of those made in Francis's day.

The beamed kitchen looked snug enough when he reached it at last, his clothes sodden and boots sucking wetly at his feet. Mary was stirring the iron pot simmering on the hearth, the table was scrubbed to a pale straw yellow, the walls freshly limewashed, it took him a moment to realize that tonight it really was snug, the atmosphere reminded him of childhood evenings in their old hovel, or when they had gathered around this same board with his father at its head, to argue and banter their way through each day's events.

Bess lifted a flowing face from where she sat beside a stranger on the settle. 'Nick, look, Jem's come back. I knew he would, didn't you?'

'Jem?' Nicholas looked at the fox-faced fellow who stood to greet him. 'Who the devil are you?'

'It's Jem Bellwasher.' Bess dragged him forward by the arm. 'Surely you remember Jem? The best furnace-plasterer we ever had, or so you said, but just see how splendid he's become!' She fingered the thick cloth of his jerkin admiringly.

'I remember. Aye, everyone working in iron is prospering.' Nicholas heard the grudging note in his voice and added hastily, 'though it's clear you're more than a hireling these days, eh?'

'Oh, Nick! How could you sound like – like the Scovells rebuking an erring dairymaid, when Jem came all the way from Robertsbridge to greet us!' exclaimed Bess disgustedly.

But Jem Bellwasher was not in the least put out by patronage, and merely remarked that though he might be mistaken for a groom, the Scovells would be startled by a dairymaid such as he.

Bess went into a peal of laughter over this, which irritated Nicholas even more than the sign of her hanging brazenly on a yokel's arm. 'For God's sake, Bess, mind your manners! Pull off my boots and dip some stew, I swear I'm famished.'

'I'll pull them off,' said Jem, and straddled Nick's out-thrust leg so he could brace his other foot against his rump. Since Nicholas was mired to the knees, he felt some satisfaction when filth inevitably became smeared over cloth which was quite as rich as his own. But when he had done, Bess flew out for water and Mary tore some cloth into strips, then they wiped Jem clean with so much clucking and laughter that Nicholas felt more left out than before. After all, he had travelled all the way from Chatham, but no one offered him water to wash in until after Jem was coddled and brushed.

'I have a small furnace and smithy of my own down towards Robertsbridge,' Jem explained, while Nicholas ate in churlish silence. 'I worked two years at Buxted, but left to take a better hiring deep in the forest and never worked so much like a slave in my life. Because of it we poured the kind of iron which makes a man ashamed of his calling.'

Nicholas nodded, interested in spite of himself. 'A careless burn makes the metal too brittle for working.'

'Or overfull of dross. The wares used to be sent directly to London for sale in the hope that fools there wouldn't know what rubbish they'd bought until too late. It worked for a while but in the end some hucksters came seeking trouble. They'd been flogged by the City magistrates for selling false goods, so you couldn't blame them. After that I swore I'd never work for a master again. I'd prosper on my own or tramp the roads as a tinker. It's been hard going since but now I reckon I'm on my way, especially if the new queen re-arms her ships as I've heard she intends.'

'You cast cannon?' demanded Nicholas incredulously. Cannon-founding was the summit of an ironmans's craft, and he had visualized

Jem Bellwasher's forge as a huddle of shacks producing pots and horseshoes.

'I learned from two good masters, here and at Buxted.' Jem looked around him, frowning. 'I never saw this house, though. 'Tis very grand. We'll have to see what we can manage like it, won't we, Bess-love?'

Mary smiled maliciously at Nicholas's stupefaction. 'You should have seen them, Nick. When Jem came through the door yesterday evening, Bess knew who he was at once, and they've been holding hands ever since. If I didn't understand different I'd have said she'd been waiting for him all these years. But there, I reckon he's been waiting for her, and since she isn't wed it comes to much the same.'

'You mean you came in here as bold as a vagabond and in your first breath asked Bess to wed you, like any trollop taken in a hedge?' Nicholas flushed with rage.

'Well now,' Jem said musingly, 'I disremember whether I asked the lass, now I think on it. But like Mistress Wyse says, she weren't wed, which was what I came here to discover.' He grinned, narrow face and dark impudent eyes tilted against the wall. 'The rest didn't seem to need a question. But I suppose it needs asking: Bess-love, will you wed me?'

She laughed and kissed him heartily, as unconcerned with Nicholas's fury as with her mother's complacent pleasure. 'Tomorrow if you wish! Except we'd need to find a hedge-priest for the ceremony, ours being finicky over dates and masses. Jem, how could you have been so long away and I never came looking for you?'

'I saw you once. At Lewes.'

'That day . . . you came the day my father burned?'

He nodded.

'Why?'

Jem glanced at Nicholas and away. 'He saved my life once and was a good master besides. I owed him my sorrow in his death.'

'Saved your life?' said Mary, puzzled. 'I can't remember – '

'He wouldn't have spoken of it, I daresay. Leastways, he spared me crushed feet in the water wheel when I was running from an enemy, and Bellwashers starve when they can't work.'

Nicholas sat, graven, remembering for the first time in years how he and Jem had long ago quarrelled over Bess. And all at once he wanted again to kill him, rather than allow the Master of Edenham's sister to wed one of the vermin bred around Furnace Green's pool.

Mary glanced from her son's set face to Jem's black impishness. Though he had prospered he still possessed the brash swagger she remembered in a bare-legged brat scampering up furnace flues, and instinct told her that, both then and now, Nicholas was his enemy. Yet Jem was simply enjoying thumbing his nose at a man even London merchants respected. 'Bess where have your wits gone?' she said hurriedly. 'There's ale and stew ready to take up to the night furnacemen, and be sure you look in at Cheerful on the way back, to see if she's started birthing.'

'There's still a Cheerful at Edenham?' exclaimed Jem.

'Oh, it'd be ill-omened to let that habit die. Nick, if she births tonight shall we call the little'un Cheerful too? It's time we named the next generation.'

Nicholas shrugged. 'No doubt you'll do what you want. Jem, you're not a furnace boy now, you know. Drink your ale and leave Bess to her chores.'

Jem weighted the cauldron in his hand. ''Tis heavy for a lass and I'm not proud. I expect I'll remember the way to your furnaces well enough.'

'Yes, you go with her on a dark wet night, and don't forget the ox-shed on your way back, neither.' Mary smiled at them and shook her head. 'I wish I were your age again, that I do.'

The door slammed in Nicholas's face while he was still expostulating, the two of them singing as they scampered away like children.

He whirled round to where Mary stood by the hearth, a look of almost comical longing on her face. 'Look what you've done! God's blood, you practically threw them into the straw together and on the very next night after she set eyes on the wastrel!'

'Aye, I did. It's what Bess needs,' answered Mary with satisfaction. 'I'm delighted to see the lass herself again, I'd lend them my bed for the night if I didn't think they'd prefer the ox-shed. Nick, surely you've seen how it is with Bess? She's been spilling over a man since I disremember when, but after Francis died the only one she fancied was a priest. There may have been a reason for such foolishness but Richard was never man enough for her, though I love him like a son. She'd have been like a bitch on heat, with him on his knees when he should have been between her legs. Yet you know Bess. Once she'd decided on her fancy, the lusty lads who could have given her what she needs seemed oafs beside a scholar like Richard. Jem's just right. He may look no more than a slice of sinew, but I'll wager he's got furnace-fires stoked where it matters.' And she smacked her lips so crudely that Nicholas could not prevent his own desires from stirring. Voluptuous, strong-limbed, eager Bess coming to her man like a tawny goddess out of the forest; unwillingly, the memory swept over him of fifteen-year-old Amy Pertwee lisping her consent to his offer of marriage. He would be bold indeed to imagine that she possessed well-stoked fires, or indeed anything much beyond a desire to please. Well, that was what he wanted. That, and a son to inherit Edenham, which he meant to see renowned as the best ironworks in the Weald, its cannon the undoing of England's foes.

It was warm in the ox-shed, redolent with the earth-smell of great beasts resting. Cheerful watched the man and the girl in the straw beside her, a gentle creature stirring uneasily as the new life inside her struggled to be born. Neither ox nor humans troubled each other, being content to mind their own business and share comfort in the doing of it.

'You're as good-tasting as the forest,' said Jem.

'What else am I like?' Bess kissed him, warm temptress in the dark,

'Like? Ah, well, let's see.' His lips wandered from the trembling muscles of her belly until they reached nipples as tight and round as crab-apples in a hedge. 'Like Bess, I'd say.'

She reached for him; her through him and him through her. Spice-hot, furnace-hot, their bodies flowing together like nothing they had words for, like nothing they need have words for.

Nearly thirty years passed, and on a fine autumn morning Mary lay on her box-bed thinking how extraordinary it was that she should be old. She'd never imagined it could come to this – that she would live and live until in the end there would be nothing left except dreams about the past. From where she lay she could see the forest glowing in the sun, and it seemed only yesterday when she lay under a bush and watched Francis paddle naked in Edenham brook. Her fingers twitched on the quilt, feeling again his thick muscled body, fancying his sweetness with her own; surely in all the earth there was nothing so splendid as two people who loved each other truly through a lifetime.

As Bess would agree. Mary had travelled only twice to see her after she wed Jem, the Weald not being a place for easy journeyings, but Bess came each year to visit and Mary was well pleased by her happiness. Jem wasn't puffed-up by success they laughed often and Bess had the look of a woman loved to contentment. They'd been fortunate, too, since Bess bred only three children and all were healthy. A woman who did not breed too easily could be thankful indeed, especially when Bess and Jem were the kind who would tumble together in the straw until the night they died.

Mary's thoughts shifted abruptly: how she envied them.

Francis; I loved you. I can't remember whether I ever told you how much. How old was I when I began following where you went, admiring the set of your back and dark stiff hair? I loved your kindness too, when most men think only severity makes others respect them. Jem is the same, and doesn't need to prove his worth by posturing. What a fool Nick is for all his cleverness, not to understand how lucky Bess has been to find a man she can love with all her heart, pool-brat though he be.

Francis, I wondered often why you wed me, when I was worse than pool-spawn, after all. But I doubt whether you reckoned you'd made a mistake. I used to laugh up my sleeve to see the gossips so discomfited, when I became a sober matron. That's how it is in old age; you only remember the sunny days. It helps a little while I lie here half-dead and wishing the end would come.

Mary still occasionally tortured herself into her clothes and dragged over to the seat Nick had built for her by the window. It was worth any pain to see the life of furnace and forge again, to watch the tawny teams of oxen swaying down the track, bearing Edenham cannon away to the queen's ships. The good queen, as Furnace Green invariably called Elizabeth. Mary often saw Francis down there amid the bustle, and chuckled to herself when Nicholas decided the shed where he was born wasn't good enough even to use as a charcoal store.

Other things changed too: the land governed again in ways men understood, and last year the Spanish fleet beaten in a victory as great as Agincourt. Edenham cannon had been in the forefront of that triumph – and perhaps James too. He had eventually wearied of his brother's hectoring and also of dragging cannon through boundless Wealden mud. Ox teams grew from six to sixteen beasts or even more, drovers becoming little more than muddied flesh alternately soaked and sticky. At the end of a particularly backbreaking journey, James looked at the great ships fitting out along the Thames and decided he would try his fortune as a sailor, just one of many men made restless by tales of English daring on the oceans of the world. He sent a message back with Edenham's drovers that he had gone off with Francis Drake, and was never heard of again, although Mary still hoped she would wake one morning and see him coming down the track. As she told Mistress Laffam, James was well suited to a seafaring life: strong, courageous and uncomplaining.

As for Sally and May, they'd bred more Laffams than Mary could keep track of, she wondered sometimes whether even they knew which of the brats at Corndown were theirs, so like they were to hound pups quarrelling in the dust.

And then there was Nicholas. His steps were often on the stairs at night; a restless insomniac. His wife seemed afraid of him and grudging in affection, although submissive to all he asked of her. *Dull, eh, Francis?* Mary said aloud. *Aye, I think so too.*

Last night when she heard him wandering around the house, she had called him to her room.

He stood in the door, his shadow thrown by moonlight on her quilt. 'Are you in pain?'

'Of course. Are you?' she answered, and heard him draw in breath as hurt man will when trying not to cry out. 'No, why should I be?'

'Then why do you walk at night?'

'Why shouldn't I.'

Mary turned her head on the bolster; no need to halt through more phrases, she couldn't talk to Nick any longer. The house itself breathed silence. Nick's pale wife scuttling about her tasks, never stopping and seldom talking, although Mary would have enjoyed a gossip. She and Nicholas had no children, two were born but both were poor puling things who died within the month.

So, after Nick there would be no more Wyses at Edenham.

Mark left a son who bred only daughters and Robert's children fled the parish after he was killed. One day Mary had discovered Richard looking at Robert's grave-slab, just beyond the church tower.

'It's strange that Robert Wyse should have such a fine iron slab, he said.

'He was the eldest of Simeon Wyse's sons, so it seemed fitting.' Mary had replied.

'Made by Nick's own hand, too.'

'How do you know?'

'I worked at Edenham or had you forgotten? I know Nick's style. As I should recognize your hearthback as Francis Wyse's making, whether he put his mark on it or not. What I don't recall is Robert ever being well thought of in your household.'

'Oh, well,' said Mary vaguely, hoping he would forget the matter, but of course he didn't. Richard Paille, as he was called by then, was always somewhat over-persevering for anyone's comfort. He must have looked in the register for the exact date of Robert's death because Nicholas only cast the year on his slab, and discovered it was the same as Francis's in Lewes, a coincidence too great for him to swallow.

Next time he came to Edenham he asked Nicholas, straight out, whether he wanted to beg absolution for the murder of Robert Wyse.

'No,' Nicholas answered coolly. 'It was James, if you must know, and he's safe away at sea. But if he hadn't been the stronger it would have been me, and I'd still have wished damnation on a blackguards's soul. You can put your absolution on the dungheap where Robert's Preece's bones should be.'

It was almost the only time in years that Mary had felt completely in charity with her son.

Of course, Richard knew that on the ridge he had been given a pack of brawling ruffians to bring back to God, and he stood no insolence from them. He was dispossessed from his living soon after Elizabeth came to the throne, but continued to live in the village under his new name (which everyone thought an odd one to choose), and though the authorities must have known, they never appointed a Protestant vicar in his place. A newcomer came only after Richard died, bringing a wife and child with him; a soft man and fond of ale, who never understood why the village laughed when he engaged Jane Preece as his servant, the youngest of Devil-Preece's brats.

Affectionately, Mary cast her thoughts back to Richard: he had died just after news came that the Spanish fleet was beaten, more than a year ago now. As soon as the victory was proclaimed, bonfires burned everywhere in rejoicing: Mary had counted six from her window. One was on Twisbury Hill, and though Richard was sick before, she believed that when he saw it he thought all his work had been in vain. And so he died. Alone where she sat, Mary spoke as if he sat beside her, as he so often had: *We're black folk in the forest, Richard. Even after so many years you could never quite accept us how we are. I expect some of the men did dance that night on Twisbury, but what of it if they did? After deliverance from great peril you can never be too careful who you thank. I'd like to have been up there myself; by all accounts the revels surpassed any held on the ridge for years. Nine months afterwards there were a great many anxious looks and prying into cribs.*

But, as Mary knew, the god on Twisbury Hill that night wasn't Tiw but the great god Pride; because England was at last on her way in the world, with Wealden cannon firing from the prow.

In the end, perhaps Richards Mercer's most telling memorial was a generation of village children able to write and read from the Bible chained in the church, but as Mary could have told him, this only made them more argumentative than before.

Much later on that autumn morning of 1589, Mary crept one last time from her bed to the windowseat, the journey almost unendurable.

Brilliant colour and tiny white clouds tumbling in from the west rewarded her great effort. Though it was November the trees were radiantly yellow, bronze and orange; oak and beech clung tenaciously to their leaves. The pastures of her youth were changing back to arable as sheep became less profitable, and in the distance she could just see some oxen ploughing. Up to the brazen forest edge they went, to pause awhile before setting off into the sun again with the dark earth flowing at their heels. Over everything lay the stillness of after-harvest, the chill stillness of winter-soon-to-come.

Much closer, in the mill, this tranquillity suddenly vanished. There was a great deal of rushing about and dark smoke rising, they must be about to tap a furnace.

When Nicholas came in for his dinner he found his mother huddled on the windowseat still, smiling a little and with one hand resting on the sill, as if she reached for something as she died. Or for someone.

. . . THE WITNESS:

Almost four centuries after Mary died, I am lying in the same box-bed. On a spring mattress instead of straw, I'm glad to say, but how much else has changed? I feel nearly as decrepit as she, and as lonely in old age. The room is the same, the seat Nicholas made still dowelled to the wall beneath the window; I hear the same creaks as Edenham's timbers adjust to yet another season. Brac's arrow remains hidden above the hearth where Bess and Richard lay together, and Robert Wyse was murdered.

I get up, painfully as she did, and look out of the window. It is autumn again. The brook gleams in the sun even though Francis's leats and ponds are only depressions in the ground, and on its far side are fields where sheep and horses graze; beyond their hedges the shining woods begin. Beyond and beyond again are wooded ridges, all hunched and misty in the distance. Nowadays you need to dodge the traffic on the road above Edenham, and Furnace Green is partly a commuter village; there are worries about deforestation and tree farming. Those misty ridges hum with modern life. But from my window I see none of these. To tell the truth, I can't see much any more, but the wind blows clear and soft, bringing with it scents like sunlight.

Forty years ago I flew a Lysander above those hills, on my way to war. My part in it was slight, but we too won a great victory which saved a heritage. I wonder, did James Wyse ever return to help drive the Spanish Armada up the Channel to destruction? Or are his bones lying as scraps and elements half a world away?

If so, he was the first of many from Furnace Green who ventured to new worlds and paid for their daring with their lives. For, as Mary knew, when that last great celebration took place on Tiw's hill in 1588,

England was reaching for a new and different life. Richard Mercer taught faith, uprightness and charity; he also taught Furnace Green's children to read. Queen Elizabeth brought unity to a troubled country; she also left enormous debts and a Parliament set up in its own esteem. More upheavals followed and civil war came next, grown out of obstinacy and a yearning for conscience and justice as part of all men's birthright, a war which again divided the nation and unleashed more changes. Such great changes this time that they shifted habits of thought and destroyed the great House of Scovell.

As Mary died, all this lay just around the corner. Nor, in Sussex, would the return of peace see the tide of violence begin to ebb. The iron industry had started to decline while Nicholas still remained master of Edenham; drowned in mud and technically laggard as small Wealden streams proved incapable of powering every more ambitious processes. After the Civil War ended, it collapsed. In the uncertainties which followed, the smuggling gangs took over and made murder a way of life. The Laffams of Corndown, rogues to a man, were only one of several families who shaped this new power into a tyranny.

Certainly Sussex grew rich on the smugglers' profits, then poor again in the age of Captain Swing.

Nowhere, really. If Furnace Green is nowhere, our ancestors small people who did not matter, why had Francis refused to run? Why should Edred, whom even his Wessex contemporaries considered little better than a savage, be content to offer his life for a pool of forest water?

Here I pause, only now beginning to realize the inexhaustible extent and rich diversity uncovered in a single forest parish. Some virtues and many qualities; an array of defects too. How far the mix might already be considered distinctively English is hard to say, although it is easy to be tempted into some preliminary, highly tendentious judgements. One thing is certain: everyone, everywhere, inherits as prodigal a past as us, and is conditioned by it, reacts with prejudice or instinctive understanding for reasons they only sometimes grasp.

Once upon a time . . . There's still so much to tell, so much I haven't told. The time-and-distance problem for instance, some more explanation is needed there . . . but it's still too soon. All I will say is, there was a time when friends from the past kept me sane, took turns to sit at my bedside and spin their tales: the tales Granny Paley knew and did not know, told and did not tell. Which might not be sanity as others would define it.

Now I am old and other matters begin to dim, my friends return again.

I welcome them all.

Listen, and I'll continue.

The End